THE PSALMS OF HEROD

by Esther M. Friesner

Borealis is an imprint of White Wolf Publishing.
White Wolf Publishing is a division of White Wolf Incorporated.

The Psalms of Herod is
a product of White Wolf Publishing.

All rights reserved.
Copyright ©1995 by Esther M. Friesner.
This book may not be reproduced, in whole or in part, without the
written permission of the publisher, except for the purpose of reviews.
For information address: White Wolf Publishing, 780 Park North
Boulevard, Suite 100, Clarkston, GA 30021.

Disclaimer: The characters and events described in this book are
fictional. Any resemblance between the characters and any person,
living or dead, is purely coincidental.

The mention of or reference to any companies or products in these
pages is not a challenge to the trademarks or copyrights concerned.

Because of the mature themes presented within, reader discretion is
advised.

White Wolf is committed to reducing waste in publishing. For this
reason, we do not permit our covers to be "stripped" for returns, but
instead require that the whole book be returned, allowing us to resell it.

Cover Photograph by: Pam Cunningham
Cover Design by: Michelle Prahler

Printed in Canada

Chapter One

I will sing a new song unto the Lord,
For His is the kingdom of plenty.
There is no grieving there,
Nor any parting of ways.
The shadow of all sorrow is banished.
The children do exalt Him.
They shall be called the blessed,
The chosen of God.
I will sing a song of praise unto the Lord
And of thanksgiving,
For He has taken the children unto Him
And His mercies are past question.

The baby was still crying on the hill when Becca came back from the milo fields. She could hear it, just as she'd heard it for the past two days whenever she went to work and came home again. Though no one at home spoke of it in front of the children, she had overheard some of the women remarking in whispers that this child was lasting far longer than anyone expected. It was a sign, Thalie said. A sign of what, no one dared to guess.

The wailing was thinner now, but still constant, unrelenting. The child's cry followed Becca down the path, past the dead apple trees, haunting her all the way home.

The child: Lynn's child. A baby girl, the rumors had said days ago, and there had been so many girls born in the neighboring steads this season. Rumors were true, they had to be, or what was it doing on the hill? Lynn, the best herbwife in all the Grange, who could save a life easy as breathing.

This was one life she wouldn't be able to save.

Becca hurried her pace, tried to outrun the sound without looking as if she were running. If one of the other women saw her, she'd be in for a scolding and a lecture, and if one of the men saw her—

She slowed, forced herself into a walk and began to sing a hymn of the Lord King: "Stable Town." She sang it loud, and the trick worked until her path met the main road. Then she remembered "Stable Town" was Lynn's favorite song. She always used to sing it when she came riding around her circuit.

Becca froze in the roadway. She could still hear the baby's cry, even so far from the hillside. She heard it, and she heard Lynn singing "Stable Town" too. The autumn air was thick with ghosts, the hard, stubborn ghosts of the living. Becca's memories stole Lynn's skin and came riding up the road to Wiserways Stead.

When you were a little one, you had to keep your ears pricked for that song. The minute you heard a woman's voice singing "Stable Town," you had to run for home and tell the housebound women that Miss Lynn was coming. It was always Lynn. She never stopped making her routine calls, never got a junior herbwife to sub for her, not even when her belly got so big it was a wonder she could walk, let alone mount the ancient plowhorse her stead's alph had allotted her.

Standing there in the road, the noontime sun enfolding her shoulders with its weak warmth but leaving her heart cold, Becca felt the memories take possession of her, body and soul. Time melted back, weeks and months falling away, until Becca was back at her mother's side in front of the house as Lynn reined in her mount and hailed the women awaiting her.

"Zacharias spoils me," Lynn said as Becca's mother helped her down from the animal's bony back. "I keep telling him and telling him walking's good for a woman who's fruitful, but he won't listen."

"He should," Hattie said, smiling. "If he won't heed the Grange senior herbwife in birthing lore, who *will* he listen to?"

Lynn laughed and followed Hattie indoors. Becca, tagging after into the big house seeing-room, loved that pretty, lightsome sound. No woman in all the Grange had such a freeheart laugh as Lynn.

"Zach listens to himself, the Grange, the Coop, God, and the Lord King, in that order." Lynn settled herself into one of the ladderback chairs beside the hearth.

Hattie gave a small, scandalized gasp and sat down

suddenly in her own chair, as if Lynn's words had knocked the legs out from under her. She clamped her hands to her mouth and her fearful eyes darted all around the seeing-room, marking all the young faces for signs of having overheard. Becca was quick to turn her back, pretending to be busy arranging the welcome plate for their honored guest.

Lynn only laughed again. "Don't fret, Hattie." Laboriously, she bent over to open the traveling satchel that lay on the floor beside her. "I was only playing the fool. The children don't take everything we say so serious. I haven't *tainted* any of 'em. Besides, you've got a short memory. Think back to when we were young...you'll find you used to say plenty of things like that—about God and the Lord King and all—and never thought boo about it."

Hattie folded her hands in her lap and sat straighter in the rigid chair opposite Lynn's. "I made confession of all transgressions and they were stripped from me when Paul took me for his bride." Becca heard the clipped, self-righteous tone her mother used whenever she tried to whip the older girls into line with words alone. It didn't have much effect on them except to provoke a few carefully shielded snickers.

Lynn was no exception. Becca caught a hint of the herbwife's smothered laughter and had to bite her lip to keep from joining in.

"Hattie! You get any stiffer and they'll plant you for a boundary stick. We're all women here, and little ones. Slack yourself some. Now, who've I got to see here? Anyone ailing? Any your girls coming into changes?"

Becca brought over the welcome plate and stood beside the senior herbwife's chair while Lynn said the proper thanksgiving and ate. Even when Becca's mother told her to pull up the little pedestal table, set down the plate, and go find a way to be useful, she stayed, pretending not to hear.

"Let the girl be, Hattie," Lynn said. When she grinned, dimples showed. She took another bite of barley cake. "Could be this is the next Grange senior herbwife standing here. I heard as how her vigil was touched by prodigy."

"Heard?" The angry color flared in Hattie's face, rose some to Becca's cheeks as shame. "Heard how?"

Lynn was taken offstride. "How? How like always. Men talk, too."

"Vigils are women's business." Hattie was grim. "What happened to Becca happens to more than she. It's the hunger and the cold of vigil night gives some girls visions."

"I heard it was more than—" Lynn silenced. She could read more in a person's body than most, being who she was. She knew when it was time to ask no more questions. Becca said a small thanksgiving for that. The herbwife went on, as if what she'd said of rumors and prodigies had never been. "Becca's got a love for the art, and the brains to learn it. Could be she'll be the one to unlock the old lore of bearing boys or girls to choice."

"Lord King grant it," Hattie mumbled, and the women and children waiting to be summoned for the herbwife's inspection repeated her pious saying, Becca with them all.

Lynn did not.

That was the time Lynn told Hattie she was fruitful again, and gave the startled woman advice on caring for herself so she might bear a healthy baby, even at her age.

Becca walked the herbwife out of the big house after

the last patient was tended. She held the horse steady
while one of the stripling boys linked his hands to give
Lynn a stirrup-mount.

From her perch on the plowhorse's back, Lynn gazed
down at Becca. "So, little girl, think you'll have a brother
or a sister?"

Becca frowned. "It's bad luck to talk of that."

"You sound just like your ma. Hattie is your ma, isn't
she? You don't look much like any of the others, 'less Paul
had one who died...All right, no fortune-tempting. Here's
something safe to answer: You really want to be an
herbwife when you're grown, or did you just hang 'round
my shoulders to get out of honest work?"

"I do want to be one! And I did my chores before—"

Lynn raised one hand. "Peace, little girl. No harm
meant. I never mean harm, you know; it's just my way to
speak straight. Like your ma did, once 'pon a time. I guess
home ways still cling to me, marriage or no. I hail from
what's got to be the smallest, most pitiful excuse for a
stead in this whole blessed Grange. Only reason they left
us be was 'cause of the claywork our men turned out.
Always cheaper to barter between steads than between
stead and Grange, Grange and Grange, and trying to trade
for stuff from the Coop? Hoo!"

"Is that where you learned herbwifing?" Becca asked
shyly. She was still holding the horse's bridle, as if afraid
that, once released, Lynn would gallop away and leave
her with a hundred questions burning her tongue. "You
learn it in a little bitty stead like yours? Who taught you?"

Lynn pointed to her eyes, cool gray like the rainclouds.
"Best teachers anyone can have. But if you're really
interested, and your pa says it's all right, I can start
lessoning you on my rounds."

E s t h e r   M.   F r i e s n e r

Becca couldn't hide her joy. She clenched the bridle so tightly that she jerked it down. The old horse only snorted and yanked up on it lazily. "Oh! Would you? I—I do some fine needlework. I could make you some piece goods for—"

She stopped herself. Speaking of clothing for the unborn was bad luck too.

"We'll talk pay another time." Lynn took the reins from Becca's hands. "No formal lessoning 'til after *this*." She patted her belly. "You can start teaching yourself, though. I wasn't much older than you when I began, and I was all the teacher I had. I still recollect your ma, getting the last of her things packed up before Paul came to fetch her, telling me to stop wasting my time piddling with potions and such, else no man'd have me."

Becca stared. "My ma hailed from your stead?" It was the first she'd ever compassed the thought of Hattie coming from anywhere before Wiserways. It was as if the strict, spare woman had sprung up out of the stead earth like a twig. "You and she was sibs?"

"Sisters," Lynn corrected her. "Same ma and pa both, only years between. Like you and this new seedling. Your ma's a good woman, but don't give mind to her predictions. She was wrong about me, for one. By the time I was marriage-fit, I'd brought seven new lives into the world, and that's more than a lot of older herbwives in Verity. The man who took me for his bride got more than just another helpmeet, and Zach's always been one to nose out a bargain." She smiled fondly. "You watch what I do when I come on rounds to check on your ma next month. You watch how your ma changes, now you know she's carrying. You watch your sibs. And you watch yourself, too. You can learn precious much from that."

Lynn rode away. Becca felt a curious warmth in her belly now she knew the blood-tie running between them. Ma would call it nigh blasphemy—a proper woman left all past ties of kin and kind behind her when she went to her husband's house and never looked back or spoke of it more—but Becca felt it as blessing.

Lynn came back next month, and the next. Always she found time to question Becca about what the girl had managed to teach herself, then added her experience to Becca's observations. She even allowed Becca to rest her hands on the unborn baby, to feel it kick.

"It's riding to be a boy," Lynn said.

Becca felt the thrust of tiny limbs under the herbwife's skin, and it made her smile. "He's strong."

"Have to be. He'll be Makepeace Stead's alph some day. That takes a lot of fight."

Becca removed her hands and bowed her head. "Takes more," she said softly. "After."

Lynn put her arm around the girl's thin shoulders. "My son won't be that way. I'll see to that. He'll give them grace, he will; grace to all the young, not just the ones that can run off. In my old stead, we never had a killing, and I hear that's not the rule elsewhere."

Becca shuddered. "Ma told it different."

"Your ma thinks Verity Grange is the world. But the world changes, Becca. You wait and see, it'll change while you watch it. Maybe it'll watch while you change it, you and the rest of the young." Lynn rested her hands on her belly again and beamed over her own fruitfulness. "This one, too. He'll change it. You'll all change it for the better."

But nothing changed. Lynn bore a girl, and there were plenty of girls already born to fill the cradles of

Makepeace Stead. Lynn got lessoned hard that Zacharias' spoiling of his favorite wife had limits.

Becca stood in the roadway, chains of memory looped and linked fast 'round her feet. The weak and hungry wailing from the hill cut invisible razor-stripes into her, bleeding her soul. That was how it had been with her on vigil night, too, but then her thoughts had been anchored to a different hillside: Prayerful Hill. The steads that shared the slope where Lynn's babe now keened never did give that ground a name. Naming made a place more real, harder to forget. The whole purpose of the nameless hill was leaving things behind without a second thought. That was the way it had always been, always had to be. But Prayerful Hill was different. Prayerful Hill was for remembering. Becca forced a breath into her lungs until her chest ached with the effort, but she couldn't move, a stone hard and fixed in place as the bones of Prayerful Hill.

"Becca?"

She couldn't even move enough to turn, but she knew the voice. "Jamie…" It was a sigh, but with all the gladsome relief of a hearty hosanna. He stepped into her sight, a scythe over one shoulder, the sweat of toil patching his shirt. His eyes held every hope she'd ever had of salvation. "Oh, Jamie!" Without thinking, she threw herself into his arms.

"No, Becca, no." He put her away from him gently with his free hand. "This near the house, some might see."

"Do you care if they do?"

"You're too woman-grown to be pardoned for it." He spoke quietly, each word backed by a well-thought reason. "You've passed your changes and your vigil, and I'm older than you. It's not like it was when we were small. By rights we shouldn't even be alone out here. If Paul knew—"

"Pa wouldn't mind." Becca was sure of herself. "If I'm woman-grown, it's my duty to grant you the Kiss or Sign when you ask." Her eyes said, *Ask*.

Jamie shook his head, black hair falling over eyes the color of good brown bread. "You know that's not what I mean to ask of you, when I can." He cast a look back toward the fields the men were working. "I'd best go on. They'll be coming after, soon."

Her hand darted out, holding him back. "Jamie, love, I'm tired of living in wait and want." Her face flushed, showing shame for her bold talk where her heart felt none. "What you've got planned—how do you know the chance of it will ever come to be? To do *that*, to make yourself alph of Wiserways…"

"Not Wiserways." His field-tanned face set stubborn. "Never that, Becca. Paul's not my sire, but still I could never stand against him for this stead."

"There's plenty of his begotten sons who wouldn't have your scruples."

"That's their row to hoe. His word was what gave me the chance of life when I was brought here from the hill. He's never treated me other than as equal to his own gets. The world's wide; there's other steads, other granges, alphs to rule 'em all. Maybe it's even meant for me to face the alph of the stead that left me out to die. If I'm to have you as bride and wife, I'll turn my eyes to one of them, but if having comes priced with Paul's death, I'll sooner set you free."

Her hand slipped down his arm to link fingers with his. "You'll never know how it joys me to hear that. But it hurts, too. I wish we was small again, I do. Back then, it was how kindly you treated all the little ones that made you shine in my eyes."

Jamie pulled a long face and played like she'd hurt his feelings. "And here I thought it was just my ugly face you felt sorry for."

"Ugly? Don't tease me, you provoking thing!" She gave his hand a hard squeeze. "If you're ugly, then I'm— I'm a crone!"

He wouldn't let the teasing go. "Now, now, Becca, you know it's not fitting for a woman to sit in judgment on a man for how he looks. That's vanity."

"It is not! It's—" She caught on to how he was fooling with her. It was his laughing soul and his kindly heart both that had drawn her to him long before she'd felt a woman's longing for him as a man. "Oh, Jamie, if I can't be your wife, I'll beg Pa to let me stay unwed forever!"

Jamie's grin split his face with light. "A fine woman like you, go begging? There's little hope of that, especially with Harvest Home on us. The other alphs will take one look at you and kill each other just for the chance to kiss the hem of your gown."

"Gown!" She feigned a vexed look and tugged at her plain brown skirt.

He set aside his scythe, letting it reap dust, and slipped his arms around her waist. He said nothing, but she could read how his eyes garbed her in the glory of a queen's finery. She pressed herself taut against him and even the rank tang of his sweat was welcome.

"Make it stop hurting, Jamie," she whispered, cheek against his chest. "Make the haunting go away, the ghost that followed me home from Prayerful Hill."

"Still that vision on you, Becca?" His breath riffled her hair like summer wind over the ripening grain.

"It's more than a vision." Something tightened in her throat so she could hardly get the words out. "Visions don't linger or take form. Visions don't burrow into your mind and whisper wickedness. Hear that, Jamie?" She jerked her head up suddenly, eyes wild.

"Hear what? There's nothing to hear."

"The cry from the hill—"

"Hush, Becca. You know it'll only pain you if you heed. Besides, listen; it's quiet."

It was. The infant's mewling had ceased. Maybe it slept. Maybe…

But Becca shook her head violently. "It's not quiet, it's *not*," she insisted. "It's there, crying. It'll always be there, the cry, the hungering, always echoing in me—"

"Hush, Becca," Jamie repeated, stroking her hair. And again, "Hush. Whatever came to pass with you on vigil night, it was only a fancy. Moonshadows do strange things, and the wind's a liar."

Becca stiffened her arms, broke from Jamie's embrace. Her look was hard and stubborn as Paul at his most immovable. "I know what I heard. I see what I see."

Jamie's handsome face held a look of pity for her, but only for a moment. "You know what they'd all say to that, if they heard you talking so."

Becca dropped her gaze. "That I'm crazy."

"But you're not. I know you're not."

"Then what am I?" she demanded, confronting him with fiery eyes. "A Deborah? A prophetess?"

"That's the last thing they'd name you. Besides, it's not prophecy if you see the faces of the dead."

"The witch of Endor summoned the dead." Becca spoke slowly. She knew her scripture-lore better than all her sibs and most of Paul's wives. "Thou shalt not suffer a witch to live."

"You didn't summon any spirits," Jamie pointed out, still reason's voice. "They just came, you say. That's not witchery in anyone's book; it's bedevilment."

"Bedevilment?" Becca echoed the word as if it belonged to some alien tongue. "You mean like...Satan's hand on me?"

"It's all the explanation I can see. And we've been taught that we can wrestle ourselves free of the devil and any worms of evil thought he plants inside our skulls." Jamie stooped for his scythe, then caressed Becca's cheek with a touch so tender it made her quiver. "You're stronger than any woman of Wiserways I know. If Satan tangles with you, look out, devil! Go home, sweet Becca. Let's both go home."

He left her standing in the roadway, watching him until he was a shadow against the light. He took a crosspath that would bring him back to the stead buildings by another route than hers. Her eyes tried to hold onto his image, clinging to him as if he were her sanity. The spell pulled thin as thread, then snapped. The baby on the hill was crying again.

Becca ran, fled the dying sound all the way home. She was halfway across the yard before she stopped hearing the hungry wailing. She tried to cover her pain when she stepped over the heartstone into the house, tried to emulate the older women's stony faces whenever she encountered them, tending to their chores. The ghost of a cry went on echoing through her head. Her mother was alone in the weaveplace when Becca found her. She looked up from the loom and read her daughter's face.

"Still living?"

Becca nodded, then the sobs tore out of her chest and she was in her mother's arms, sinking down slowly to bury her face in Hattie's loose-bearing skirts. Hattie made soft sounds, soothing her youngest, sleeking down the girl's bright yellow hair with her calloused hands.

"Hush, Becca," she said, unknowingly repeating Jamie's words, though not with half their power to comfort. "Hush now, child. Your pa'll be home soon with the other men and he'll know what's been eating on you if you don't dry those eyes and cheer fast. He sees you this way, he'll say you're not fit to be a woman yet, and he'll bar you from the Harvest Home."

"That mightn't be any bad thing," Becca murmured.

"What?"

Becca lifted her head so sharply that Hattie's hands instinctively flew to shield her swollen belly from her daughter's impetuous movements. "I said I don't want to go to Harvest Home!"

"You're woman-grown and you're not due to be in your times for months. Why shouldn't you go?"

"Because I don't want to, and if that's not enough—"

Hattie raised her hands, stilled her daughter's angry words with a gesture. Becca was silent, but she continued to glare. She could almost read her mother's disapproving thoughts: *Willful. Too much bone in her. Lord King help her find a troop that won't call so much bone a sin in a woman.*

To herself Becca thought, *Yes, Ma, but bone's hard. It snaps before it bends. Isn't that how you want me to be? Hard as you? Hard as the others? Hard and dry as bone, with never* a tear for that little lost one on the hillside? Even Thalie, who owes the life of every one of her children to Lynn's healings! Not a tear, not a word, just silent wondering when the baby's going to die! Harder than any bone.

Quietly, firmly, Hattie said, "You're woman-grown, tested and found fit to breed. But a woman's made by God for breeding. You can't breed inside the troop and you know it."

Becca bowed her head before the rightness of her mother's words, all the bone in her broken. "I know it."

Hattie lifted her daughter's chin and forced her to look up. Becca's eyes were green, the alph eyes that made Paul so proud each time he saw them gazing at him out of a Wiserways child's face.

"Becca, you're a good girl," she said, her voice pleading. "You know what's right and what's so, but all the time you're fighting, fighting…fighting what can't be fought, what shouldn't be. Katy tells me there's no one she'd rather have take over teaching the young ones. She says she hopes Paul puts off marrying you away until we need some new blood so you can stay in-troop and run the school when she's too tired for it."

Becca brightened to hear that. "I'm in no hurry to leave Wiserways, Mama," she said.

"You'll be in as much or as little hurry as Paul says," her mother reminded her. "Not that he's so eager to see your back." There was a sliver of something bitter running beneath Hattie's words. "Fighting and teaching, they don't mix. You know so much, child, why can't you know there's no changing the way things are?"

Becca couldn't stand to look into Hattie's clear blue eyes for long. Baby-eyes, they called them. Precious few adults kept that color in this troop, and her mother's expression was always just as open and trusting as any newborn child's; accepting things as they were without question, without thought.

There was no arguing with Hattie. "I'm sorry, Mama," Becca said. "I'll splash some cold water on my face. Pa'll never know I was weeping."

She said nothing about turning herbwife, nothing about the secret store of healing plants she'd been gathering in an unused corner of the drying shed. There was an old book among the few that Katy cherished for the schoolroom, a book that told about which plants were useful and for what. Many of the pictures were of sprigs Becca had never seen, but some she knew. These were her harvest. She'd intended to show them to Lynn when she had enough—the stock of her own herbwife satchel! But she couldn't tell Hattie that. She said what her mother wanted to hear: anything, any promise, just so she didn't have to look into those eyes and think of babies.

"There's my girl." Hattie patted Becca's hands and smiled. "Run along now, and when you're presentable get over to the cookhouse. Selena and Ray are doing noon meal, God help us all! Sin in the making, what they can do to decent food. Hurry, while it's still fit to eat!"

"Yes, Mama." Becca ducked her head, avoiding the benediction, and ran out of the house. Hattie sighed and went back to the pattern on her loom.

Outside all was quiet. There was a steady breeze blowing from out to the west, clouds riding high and white against the sky, but not a sign of rain. The smoke from the cookhouse fire was a horizontal streak of gray that tangled itself in the bare branches of the kindling-oak. Becca turned into the wind and let it redden up her face with its chill freshness until no one could tell she'd been crying. Only then did she go to the cookhouse to offer help.

It looked as if Selena and Ray were preparing for a Grange war instead of the noon meal. Everything was topsy-turvy. Five of the half-grown boys were running wild, screeching at the top of their lungs, stealing the long-handled kitchen tools for weapons in their play. A couple of the stripling males still too young and skinny to be trusted with the grown ones in the fields hung around. Becca knew they were supposed to be helping the cooks, but Ray and Selena lacked the heads to make their charges mind.

"Bet the trestles aren't even set up," Becca murmured. A quick peek into the pantry across from the main hearth confirmed it. Not a single platter missing, not one carved cup out of place, not even her father's special earthenware tankard.

"Becca! Thank God you're here! Pudding's about to—*stop* that, Willie!" Rust-haired Ray grabbed the biggest of the half-growns by his collar and yanked back hard, just as he took a swipe at a smaller boy with a soup ladle. "You wanna kill someone?"

Willie just grinned and wriggled free. His prey squawked and ran for shelter in Becca's skirts, but it took more than that to throw Willie off. Becca swept the little one out of his reach and wrenched the iron ladle from his hand. One-handed, she boxed Willie's ears so hard and so unexpectedly that it took the boy half a minute before he decided to open up and bawl.

While Selena yelled at Becca for hitting him, Willie and Ray came hotly to the girl's defense. The pudding bubbled up and over the rim of the pot to sizzle in a stink in the cookfire.

Noon meal was served late that day. After Grace and the first taste, three or four of the young men said aloud that late wasn't always better than never. From her place at the women's table, Becca was relieved to see that Jamie wasn't one of them. She knew how their words would provoke Pa.

Tom should've known, too. He was firstborn of all, and seated at his father's right hand, as was proper. This day the honor of place worked against him as he lightly said, "Maybe some things are worse than going hungry."

Paul reared up from his place at the head of the hastily laid trestle tables and smacked him across the face so hard that Tom was knocked from his bench.

"Get up." Paul spoke low. At their table, Becca and the other females not busy serving dropped their eyes to their laps and tried not to look or listen. "Get up, I said."

Becca heard a scrabbling in the dust. A shadow at the farthest corner of her eye shifted. She heard Tom panting, the others holding their breaths, all waiting to hear the penalty.

"Get to the bones, boy."

"Pa, I—"

"Not time for words. Not time for excuses, unless you've got a few you want to make to God Himself. You get yourself to the bones. Pray, boy; and when you hear your mother's ringing us home for supper, I want you to hit the road over to Makepeace Stead and ask for Miss Lynn. You tell her you've come to do the rites for her baby out of the Lord King's love. And you *do* 'em! Then you come back home when it's done and tell me about what's worse than going hungry."

Becca kept her eyes down. No one spoke. Then: "Yes, sir, Pa." Footsteps retreated. The women looked up again.

"Why, where's Tom?" Katy asked a little too brightly from the women's table. "It's not like him to miss a meal."

Paul shrugged and went on with his own food while the brother one place down from the newly empty spot poured the contents of Tom's bowl into his own without comment.

The wind blew again, rattling the interlaced branches of the dead trees above the long tables. Becca shivered. She stared at her bowl, sternly ordering herself to pick up her spoon and eat before her father noticed and asked what was wrong with her. The food tasted awful, but she ate.

After noon meal, the men went back to the fields and the women to their chores. Becca had drawn free time, a special privilege reserved for the young females who had tested through their changes but weren't yet bespoke. Free time wasn't really free. It was supposed to be put to some good, productive use by the girls—mostly for preparing as many bits of handy stowage for their leavetaking boxes as time allowed.

Becca was in no hurry to get her latest piece of fancywork out of her box and add some stitchery to it. She lingered near the wood-oak for a long time, watching the other women and young clear away. She would have done more than watch—anything to put off going after her leavetaking box!—but when she offered to help, Hattie was suddenly there.

"We've hands enough to lay to this task, Becca. Too many's as bad as too few. Why are you lingering? Don't you have things to lay hands to? It'll be Harvest Home before you know it, and I'm wagering that you'll be the first of our girls bespoke. Yes, even before the dancing starts and you show those pretty feet of yours!"

Discreetly, in case any of the male sibs were looking, Hattie lifted the hem of Becca's skirt an inch or so to reveal her naked feet, very long and narrow, the skin incredibly white beneath the coating of farm dust. With a smile, Hattie dropped the skirt quickly.

"Where you ever got feet like that—" She shook her head, musing happily. "City feet. Coop feet, just like your brother's. Most of our boys that go into the Coops, you can always tell where they came from just by looking down, but Eleazar…They must think he was coop-born, by now, if he learned his lessons well and applied himself." Her eyes strayed to the eastern horizon. Many miles and many Granges lay between Verity and the Coop city that was sister-linked to it, but Becca knew that her mother was seeing one special face beyond the landline, and distance be damned.

"'Bout time we heard from him again," Hattie said. She spoke with yearning, and a note of hope that faded from her words. "It's been so long, and I did have the last traders through here take word to him that I was fruitful again."

"He must be busy, Mama," Becca said. She slipped her hand into her mother's.

That contact snapped Hattie from her dreams and longings. She looked sharply at her daughter. "And so you should be, too! Not wasting free time and keeping me from my chores. I've a piece in the loom has to be done this day. You fetch your fancywork along to the workplace. I want to see how you're getting on with it."

Becca bowed her head. "Yes, Mama."

There was no avoiding it now. Hattie never issued casual invitations, only commands. Becca felt a chill that never came from the ice mountains. To fetch her stitchery meant going into her dormitory, and that meant going by Prayerful Hill.

Chapter Two

Who's that a-crying in the cold, cold dark?
Only a little lost lamb, my Lord.
Who's that a-coming for to lead him home?
The Babe you sword-saved, my Lord King.

Becca shuddered as she walked along the well-trod path winding through the gently rolling land. In the time of the last Grange war, the low mounds of Wiserways Stead gave her males a hairsbreadth advantage over the western marauders. In a place where the land was mostly flat, any rise let you see who was coming after you while they were still a long way off. The westerners, stripped of the element of surprise, were beaten back almost to the hardrock country, or so the stories told. What they did there, with that pitiful land to live off...

Some things didn't bear thinking about. Becca's thin shoulders shook, exorcising brain-phantoms. She tried to empty her mind of everything, fix a picture of her leavetaking box in her thoughts and let nothing else in, not even the thought of how glad she'd be if she were filling the box as Jamie's bespoke bride. The ruse didn't work. Fancies of the long-gone war were too pernicious. Thinking of scouts climbing the hills to keep watch made her think of another hill and another watcher.

And there it was. Taller than any of the natural mounds near it, taller by a good measure. But no scout had ever climbed the flank of Prayerful Hill to mind the horizon for raiders. You could probably buy a lot more warning-time with what you'd see from up there, but no man ever did. No man dared.

Becca felt her skin grow taut and dry the closer she came to Prayerful Hill. She kept walking, because if she stopped, she feared she'd freeze in place with the fright of it. She would hear the sounds coming from deep inside the hollow place again, the place of prayer and contemplation. Out of the darkness they came, and if she heard them on her lone a second time, if she stopped to listen, if she saw a fresh vision, her heart knew it'd drive her clean mad.

The first time she heard them call, it was a miracle she didn't lose her sanity, that's what she heard her mother tell the other women. When a girl changed— when one of the women noticed the way the men looked at her, scenting the new flow that wasn't yet the blood as only men could do—the women watched her close. If the blood followed the first flow that said she'd become a taking woman, there wasn't a female eye on stead but kept itself clapped tight to the girl until she'd passed her sixmonth with no further sign of a taking woman's flow or the blood that followed. (A female might miss the first, but there wasn't a way under God's heaven she'd fail to catch sight of the second.) And while they waited for the last of the sixmonth to pass, there were other ways the women had of making certain that the girls of their stead were fit to be future wives and mothers. There were tests to let them know a girl would make a proper woman. One such the women of Wiserways set their girls was to keep vigil hard by the Hill all through the hours of one endless night. Taking or not, for once and only once it didn't matter. A stead girl was safe enough on her own that one night—Paul would be a poor alph if he couldn't keep his men under the double lock of his command and the curse awaiting any fool who trespassed on these women's doings.

Safe enough…but only from the men.

Becca's turn fell out in the springtime, the weather remarkably pleasant, the air soft and full of a fugitive sweetness. The littlesingers were awakening from their winter sleep, chirruping and humming in the darkness. Becca spoke the Lord King's blessing over them, thanking heaven for sending such small, insignificant creatures to devour the smaller ones who had besieged the crops since time began.

She said the blessing out loud, but there was no way to cry it loud enough to drown out that other sound, that other sorrowful song. It came for her at the middle hour of the night. It seeped out of the blackness in the Hill, underscored by a cold, muted clatter. It floated on the deceitfully gentle breeze, trailed through a night of flowering stars, and wrapped horror around Becca's heart.

Over and over she said the blessings, over and over she called on the mercy of God and the Lord King, but it didn't serve. The song melted into her, body and brain, and she knew it would never leave.

And in the morning, when the women came for her, they only had to gaze into her face to know what she had heard that night.

"How was it?" Sarah demanded. "Just a wailing, like?"

Becca shook her head. She did her best, through a throat gone tight and small, to repeat the sounds she'd heard coming out of the depths of Prayerful Hill. The older women exchanged glances. She caught Ray making the warding gesture against her, but everyone said Ray was a stupid, superstitious thing. It was a sign to have heard what Becca heard, but it wasn't a sign of evil.

She had heard voices. Over and under and through the dry rattling that burnt her nerves to ash, she had heard another sound: small voices calling out the names of Wiserways women living and Wiserways women dead. The voices calling for the dead were deeper, fainter, older than the strong, piping ones that named the living. None of that mattered to Becca. She would have traded all the years of hearing ahead of her if only the Lord King had stricken her deaf before she had to listen to the voices calling those names out of the Hill.

Hattie's name was one, though the voice was very young indeed, and the name was poorly spoken.

The women told her that it was the pre-vigil fast made some girls hear the voices of Prayerful Hill, but once over, it was done with forever. In her heart, Becca knew they lied. No one could hear what she heard and not show it by some outward sign ever after. Hattie put her arm around Becca's shoulders and told her how proud she was of her daughter's bravery—not running off like some did when they heard the sounds—how proud Paul would be. Hattie thought that ended it.

Becca never told her mother that, fasting or feasting, she still heard the small voices calling every time she passed by the gaping gateway that opened the dark womb of the Hill. It only happened when she walked alone. Company on the road, the laughter of the living drove the voices back underground, but when she went solitary they came after her. And then there was what she'd seen.

The only reason she hadn't run away was that at first she thought the phantom was a real girl, a crazy creature turned out of her own stead to wander and shelter where she might. Some alphs feared the insane too much to give them mercy. They roved the land until the Lord King's will brought them into territory where they were put quiet at last. No telling how far some of them might roam before that kindness touched them. For the pilgrims of madness a place like Prayerful Hill was just another haven, unhallowed by awe or fear.

This girl leaned against the entryway to Prayerful Hill and smiled up into the moonlight. Becca cowered at the vigil place, fingers clenched in prayers never spoke, goggling at her. She didn't seem to be much above sixteen, with long legs that looked strangely dappled in the shadows. Her face, her flesh, her silky fall of hair, even her eyes seemed to drink moonlight into them, washing everything so white all that was left was girl-shaped glow. She bent down to pluck a stalk of grass and nibbled the end.

You didn't touch the grass 'round Prayerful Hill. You didn't linger there, unless you were sent. You didn't stand there smiling when you heard the chorus of plaintive cries, or the dull rattling from the Hill's hollow core.

The girl turned so that she was facing straight in Becca's direction. Becca made herself small and still as stone. The girl stretched her arms languidly toward the moon, making Becca think of the old nursery tale Katy once read the littlest ones about a shining princess who had fallen to earth from the moon's silvery disc. With her arms held high like that, Becca could see the girl's odd, curiously fashioned dress, the skirt far too short for decency. It was torn open across the chest, showing firm, pale, newly made breasts.

They bled. Deep slashes scored them open like buds unfurling to the sun. The blood crawled in black, viscous tracks over her belly, but she acted like it was nothing to her. Then she yawned and slid down to squat with her back against the flank of the Hill. Her legs spread wide open with no thought to modesty, the spattery stains on them showing a clean, bright red.

Becca's linked hands pressed hard against her mouth, stifling any scream. The girl made of blood and moonlight lazily lifted her blue-smudged eyelids until there was no doubt that the burning eyes beneath were fixed on—

Hello, Becca.

Oh no, no doubt, no saving doubt at all!

That wasn't all the ghost-girl said to her that night, nor the only time she saw the vision after. If hearing the voices on vigil night wasn't called a sign of evil, this haunting was bound to be. Paul was an alph of the old ways, and he dealt quickly and summarily with any of his troop proved to carry an evil sign.

You didn't fool with earth-luck, not even for the sake

of your own blood-kin. The tales were too full of warnings for a wise man to err.

So Becca kept her secret well, though from that time on she had begun to feel a thread of separation stretching out between her and the others, a tiny shiver of a gap beginning to widen. She told Jamie, true, but not everything. For all he knew, her vision was no more than a bright, beautiful phantom. She could not tell him of the girl's ravaged breasts, and no man should know about the meaning of the blood.

She was tempted, once, to confide in Lynn. The ghost-girl left her brimful of questions, but the herbwife never had time to listen to more than talk of ailing and healing. By the time Becca got her courage up, Lynn had ridden off. Becca always imagined she'd have other chances to speak with the herbwife about that night, that ghost; she was wrong. Becca knew that the thoughts still troubling her mind would never reach Lynn's ears; not now. Now Lynn wouldn't be caring to hear about another's troubles.

Maybe that was just as well. Becca wasn't sure she wanted to have time alone with Lynn any more; not after this. She didn't know whether she'd ever be able to look Lynn in the face again without hearing the lost cry of the herbwife's child. Becca walked faster, trying to outdistance thought and memory.

It worked, for a time. Her brisk pace jarred everything from her mind except the sound of her breath and the impact of the packed earth under her feet. Rejoicing in her hard-won freedom from those dark recollections, she forced her legs to work harder still. Then, too late, she realized she'd only brought herself into the shadow of Prayerful Hill that much sooner.

Prayerful Hill was well covered with green, even so

late in the growing season. It was just another sign of its apartness. Grass hung down like lank, uncut hair, fringing the opening in its flank. It filled Becca's heart with dread by daylight just as terribly as it tainted her past. She could no more bear to look at it than she could stand the thought of what lay on the slopes of that other hill, even though what made Prayerful Hill a nightmare place didn't lie out in the open for anyone to see.

It made no difference to Becca. She knew what lodged in Prayerful Hill, saw it as clearly as if the grassy slopes were made of glass. Even so, she still had to take this road. Hattie hadn't brought up her daughter to evade obligations over a silly weakness. Becca screwed her eyes tight shut, stiffened her stride, fixed her inner eye on the leavetaking box, and Harvest Home, and her duty.

"Becca! Becca, that you?"

This voice wasn't one of *those*. It was stark human, and the simple sound of her name uttered by a living tongue took all the strength out of her sinews. She thought she was going to collapse in the roadway under the breaking of her self-made spell. But it was Tom's voice, and she knew he wouldn't dare leave the hollow of Prayerful Hill to pick her up, and she wouldn't have the power left to lift herself out of the dust if she fell.

So she stood there, hands splayed at her sides, elbows locked into her hips to brace herself upright. "You shouldn't be a-calling to me, Tom," she told the air straight ahead of her. "What if someone heard? You're supposed to be at prayer. You break that off to touch the mortal world and it's bad luck on the stead."

A mocking chuckle came out of the Hill's darkness. "Bad luck for me, not the stead. You're full woman, sure enough, Becca, spouting superstitions and getting 'em wrong in the bargain. I'll risk the bad luck if you'll hold your tongue about it and come here to me. And if there was anyone nigh enough to hear me 'sides you, I'd've known their tread same as I did yours."

Becca felt a cool, icy dread creep up her feet, twining round her legs like the two serpents that shackled Eve to her alph. Hattie had warned her about the cunning of older males, the ones not yet ready to risk a fight or skilled enough to barter their own particular godgifts for sharing time with the alphs of other troops, the ones not content with the Kiss and the Sign.

The sin was in them, longing to get out, and they liked to lure unsuspecting young women into out-of-the-way places and make them dirt. If they were caught at it, like as not their own alph would kill them, or worse, hand them over for the womandeath. But the girls they took were to blame too, unless proved feeble-minded. If they were in their times for the taking and they turned fruitful, maybe their child would be kept in the troop, Lord King grant the favor. But the girls themselves vanished after, no one said where. And if the man took them in the way of the Abomination!

"Becca!" Tom called again. "Becca, you deadwood, I'm not gonna rape you. That's what you think? In *here*? Nothing you know about men, then, if you think I could raise him with all *these* a-staring. Come on in, it's safe. I need to talk, that's all. Help me."

She couldn't turn her back on him, him having said that. He'd called for help, and everything in her was turned that way—not just on account of Ma's teachings of womanlore. Lynn rode through her mind, singing. *There's too much hurt in this world for us to stand aside when help's wanted.* With Lynn, the helping came first, talk of payment later. Ma said there'd be no talk of payment at all if not for Lynn's menfolk stepping in, being practical.

Becca took a deep breath and whispered a prayer for the Lord King to intercede for her, another for sweet Mary Mother to cast her blue mantle over her and protect a virgin girl. Only when all the words of power were said did she make herself go into the side of Prayerful Hill, to her sib Tom's aid, to the bones.

She smelled them in the dark—the dry, coppery tang of them that was like old blood. Men scoffed when they heard the women speak of the bone-smell, called it fancy. "Flesh boiled away, no place for blood to hide, how can it be?" they asked. But the women kept their counsel.

"Tom?" Becca sent her voice into the shadows like a littlesinger testing its wings. Sunlight from outside showed the fine piled stone facings holding up the entrance to Prayerful Hill. Not every stead could boast a sanctuary this old or this properly made. No iron had ever touched these rocks, as the Scriptural teaching for altar-building laid down. The stone was for show, a later addition to the true foundation of Prayerful Hill. What really held up the man-mounted sod outside was the bones.

"Come on in, Becca." Her sib's voice reached her, somehow weaker than when he'd hailed her on the road. Having her come into the Hill subdued him. "I'm just ahead of you, fifteen, maybe twenty steps. I'm holding out my hand. Don't be afraid."

She stretched her own hand out for his and took a few tentative steps toward the sound of his voice. Beyond that first spill of light from outside, there was only darkness within. The way Tom talked, you'd expect he imagined himself to be perfectly visible. Becca couldn't see him for trying. All she had to hold onto was his voice, and his promise of protection.

"Little more, Becca, just a little—not that way! You almost touched the wall."

Becca gasped and jumped back. There wasn't any worse luck to be had than for an unwed girl to touch the true walls of Prayerful Hill. It meant bad bearings all down the line, like the bones could reach into a body and claim their own will from a woman's womb. Always hungry for something, the bones. All things born were willful—the sin that brought down the ever-fruitful land of Paradise—and some souls born never got the chance to be taught to bridle it. They made the most powerful ghosts.

Becca froze where she was, trembling, not trusting her sense of direction. Any step she took now, *they* might divert. They could force her to touch their walls, and then she'd be theirs. Something like had almost happened once before—

No! No thinking back, not to that, not now! How much more power would she give her vigil-night ghosts if she thought of them here? She closed her eyes and gave a little whimper of soul-struck fear.

"Wait, honey, wait." Tom spoke softer. She heard a muted shuffling, then felt the warm, strong clasp of his hand on her arm. "Cold," he said, wondering at the feel of her flesh. "Colder'n springwater. Poor child, I'm sorry. I wouldn't've called on you if I'd known. Always figured you for one of the bold ones."

"Too much bone in me," Becca murmured, slowly opening her eyes to the dark again.

Tom's hand twitched off her arm. "You got no sense? Don't talk that way here!" She heard the whispery sound of a man rubbing his own arms to cast off a sudden chill, and the thin ripple of girlish laughter.

"Why's there no light in here, Tom?" she asked to cover that second, uncanny sound. "Pa sends you to the bones, a vigil light's supposed to be kept burning so you can see—"

"I know it!" Tom snapped. "Just pinched it out when I heard your footsteps, is all. Had it a-burning the whole time I been here."

He sounded so rock-steady when he said that. *Maybe too full of self-righteousness for it to be true*, Becca thought. The dark of Prayerful Hill might be dreadful, but it was worse to have to keep watch here when you could see the things you watched over. Yes, even for a man. A second thought reared up scandalized in her mind. *You doubting him? You, a woman?* it demanded, hissing the words in Hattie's voice. *You daring to doubt a man's spoken word?*

"I know my duty," Tom went on. "Think it's so easy to come by candlemakings worthy to serve this place? They're Coop-trade goods. But I'll strike a light for you, if that'll make you quit your fidgeting and hear me out."

She didn't tell him no. One part of her cringed from what the light would show, but another stood tall and strong, telling her to open her eyes and see if what she feared was so fearful. Flint chicked against steel, and a small wooden spill took the spark. The flame floated through the blackness to meet the wick of the sanctuary light.

The bones rippled into sight, row on row of the straight ones lining the walls, niche after niche of the odd-shaped ones filled to jumbling fullness, until, despite their ill-sorted shapes, they seemed to make interlocking puzzle blocks of yellow and white and brown. A row of stone bowls ran all around the inner perimeter of Prayerful Hill, deep and wide-mouthed urns for the smallest of the relics—the bones of their little hands, the bones of their tiny feet, and the dust that sifted down.

The skulls had pride of place, stacked high on the wall where the vigil-light was fixed. Not one was bigger than Becca's hand. Discolored by time, a few of them crumbling, touched up with the plaster-dauber's brush for the sake of reverent preservation, inside Prayerful Hill these were the sanctified generations of Wiserways babes that had once lain on that other hillside.

"'And the Lord King Herod heard that the Babe was born in Bethlehem,'" Becca recited piously, as if the bones could hear. "'And he repented of his evil life in that hearing. And he spoke unto his three wise men, saying, *Seek out the Child of whom the star speaks, and bring me word, that I might worship Him also.* But the wise men were made bold by too much wisdom, which was the first failing of man. And they chastised the Lord King Herod, saying: *Thou art a man of wickedness, O King, and all thy worship is a sword. Albeit there is famine in the land, and many mouths, and little bread, that one less mouth might be deemed blessing, we shall not reveal unto you whither this Child lies.* Then the Lord King Herod answered them, saying: *So be it. But with the sword I shall worship Him and serve Him better than any man.*'"

"'With the sword…'" Tom repeated, staring at the rows of infants' skulls. "So that the Babe would never need to go hungry, so that there'd be bread for Him, and for sweet Mary, and for Joseph and all his tribe." He sighed. "You're a wonder, Becca, able to rattle off Scripture so fine that way. Wish I could. It would've been a mercy to me, all this time alone in here, to have something to draw comfort from."

"That the help you said you wanted? Scripture-talk?"

Tom shook his head. He was as tall as Pa and almost as strong, deep-chested, with the huge, heavy hands he'd need to tear himself out a stead of his own some day. It was wickedness, but in her heart Becca prayed it might be Makepeace Stead, and Zacharias' blood on her sib's big hands.

But that was fortune-tempting too, any thought about the future alphs, and the hard rows they'd have to hoe to reach their destinies. She thought of Jamie's hands, so different from Tom's, formed so long-fingered and elegant. Just looking at them, she could imagine how they'd feel against her skin, and the front of her blouse made her breasts go tingling hard. When the time came, could Jamie do what was needful? *He will*, she thought firmly. *He's got to, and where there's need—Oh, Lord King Herod, you who sit on the left hand of the Lord Himself as His own Son sits on the right, lend him strength for a task he'd turn from if he could!*

She put Jamie from her thoughts and looked away from their future. Hattie always said to tend to the now. Becca folded her hands before her and bowed her head, waiting for Tom to speak his mind.

"Miss Lynn's—the baby." Big as he was, Tom sounded like he was choking on a gob of hardened porridge. "I'm to do for it. That—that I can do, but to go over to Makepeace and tell her—to bring her the bones—"

Becca stood tip-toe to place her hands on her sib's wide shoulders. "I'll come."

"Becca!" It hurt her to see how grateful he looked. It ate away everything Hattie had ever taught her about men and the strength God gave them. Just hearing him say her name that trembly way sent another flare of doubt through her, body and bone. She tried to stiffen her soul against it, and she thought she'd won.

But the worm was in her, planted by a phantom with a girl's face, and that was what made her say, "I'll even help you do for Miss Lynn's babe."

Tom's grateful look vanished. His face went hard and rigid. "You know what you're saying? You truly know?"

The worm nestled in her heart, turning it to an alien thing. Her ears were full of secrets whispered to her on that endless vigil night. She heard herself speak as if she were a third person inside Prayerful Hill, a witness to this mad girl daring to talk back to her biggest, strongest sib like he was no more than a girl-child not yet into changes.

"What's not to know, Tom? Doing for the babe, that means bringing its bones to birth. I heard Pa talking to Jerome, the one almost put down Zacharias over to Makepeace. It was just after Selene's last trip to the hillside, he asked Jerome to do him the favor of seeing to the babe, once it was dead, and—"

Tom's hand caught her clean and sharp across the left cheek, making her teeth champ and grate together. She tasted a little blood on her tongue. "*Don't talk of it! Not in here*! You want me to tell Pa? You want to be put out of the stead for a crazy woman? The rogues'd like that. They ain't been fed any female flesh in a long time."

Becca's skin chilled when her sib spoke of the rogues— any decent steadwoman knew the name of her worst nightmare—but the chill never touched her face. She astounded herself when she realized that she hadn't flinched, that she still stood there facing down a sib who might hold the power of life and death over her and her own babes some day.

The moonlight-silver girl's voice uncoiled itself from deep within her heart, a worm of forbidden words and knowledge. *It wasn't rogues did this to me.* The carved petals of her breasts bloomed, dewed with blood. Becca willed herself free of the vision. The cursed worm that would not leave her in peace must come from Satan to torment her so.

Bedevilment wasn't madness, and she wouldn't let Tom turn it that way, to her hurt. Madness meant she'd be outcast, and not even Jamie could save her. It would be a male's word against hers if Tom named her mad, unless....

Very slowly she counted out her words. "You want me to tell Pa you're too scared to carry out all his commands?"

He could kill you! Hattie's voice keened in Becca's head. *Kill you and worse, and leave your body somewhere so the others'd think a band of rogues got daring and lucky, all at once. Becca, baby, sweet living child of mine, maybe you are a crazy woman after all.*

But after the first red flush of rage left Tom's face, Becca saw him bow his head before her as if she were the Lord King himself. "All right, Becca. You want to, you come along, help me do for the babe. But if we're seen, you'll carry the burden of it."

"So I will, Tom." The worm inside her filled her heart with prideful exultation, but she kept her eyes modest and mild. "Lord King witness."

Chapter Three

Sarah was old and stricken in years when she bore Abraham a daughter. And on that day there came before the tent of Abraham three travelers. Then Abraham made them welcome, and set before them all he had, and served their wants with his own hands. And when the three had eaten and drunk their fill, the foremost among them said, "Blessed are you of God, Abraham, for you shall found a mighty nation. Blessed also is your wife Sarah among women, for she shall bear you a son."

Then Sarah answered, "How shall this be, seeing as I am old and have borne my lord only this girl-child?"

Then the messengers of God replied, saying, "Behold, is any thing too hard for the Lord?"

And Abraham took the newborn girl-child from the arms of his wife Sarah and gave her unto the angels, saying, "In the tents of my nephew Lot there are no daughters."

The angels took up the girl-child, who was Abraham's only begotten child of his wife Sarah, and went away with her. And Sarah did not weep to see them go, neither did she question them, nor try to stay them. But Sarah laughed, for her faith was great in the Lord. And so it came to pass that the word of God was accomplished and Sarah bore Abraham a son, and gave him the name Isaac, which is Laughter.

In the grove of dead trees, Becca supported herself on hands and knees as she retched up the last of her noon meal. Behind her she could hear her sib's fluent curses, leveled at himself and her equally. Her sight was all blurry with tears, and her nose ran with searing mucus as another spasm shook her. The smell from the boiling kettle came fainter now, the scent of the wood burning under it stronger.

"You really want to get us both killed, Becca," Tom muttered, stirring the kettle with a hardwood paddle. He threw in another handful of the crumbly stuff he'd brought from the men's special meeting hut, along with the kettle and the paddle. "Noise you're making, it's a mercy they don't hear you clear to home."

"I'm—I'm not making that much—" Becca couldn't help it; she smelled a last whiff of the kettle's special reek and threw up again. For all her aspirations to be a herbwife, Becca couldn't begin to guess at the plants that had gone into the making of that grayish-brown powder, or to suspect when and where the men went to harvest and dry them. By rights, she wasn't even supposed to pose herself questions like that. It was manlore.

But Satan's worm was strong. Even while she was vomiting up everything in her belly, her nostrils full of the smell from the kettle, she wondered whether the powder really did make birthing the bones easier, the way Tom claimed. *Could be it's all just stink and show*, the worm murmured. *I remember when they first*— Becca silenced it.

Stink and show. Most of manlore was just that, if you believed what Hattie and the other women whispered when there were only female children near.

She wiped her mouth with the back of her hand and crawled back cautiously, taking care to keep her skirt out of the pooled vomit. She'd have to wash up before they went over to Makepeace, get the sour smell off her. She stood up and tried to put back the brave look she'd claimed inside Prayerful Hill.

"No one's going to kill us, Tom," she said, forcing herself to sound lightsome. "Who's to know I was here? I'd be mighty surprised if that stuff didn't do more'n smell so bad just to warn folks away from this place."

"Becca…" Her sib's voice went low, warning.

She wasn't fool enough to ignore the signal. Hattie'd told her tales enough of women who were born too harebrained to learn their proper place, who got too swollen-headed the first time they saw a man's face when he took them, who thought they held the magic between their legs that could control a man. Her skin still crawled with the endings to all those tales, so she changed her tune smartly:

"Honest, Tom, don't you fret about it. They miss me at work, I'll just tell them I went with you to pay my respects to Miss Lynn. Everyone knows I'm that fond of her. They'll excuse me. It was you asked for my help in the first place, and I was a help to you, wasn't I?"

Tom laid the dripping paddle to rest against his leg. He didn't seem to feel any pain from the hot water trickling down, soaking his workpants. It was a mark of future greatness, the indifference to pain. The lesser men praised the boys who showed it most, already toadying up to the stead's potential heirs. The smarter boys kept it a private thing, hidden from Pa. There'd been vanishments before this. More than one of Becca's sibs had died in the "friendly" contests between stripling males to see whose body could bear greater hurts. No one commented when there was one lad the less at meals, though after there was always much hushed, hasty talk among the women fluttering 'round the lost one's ma. Pa called it God's judgment and asked no questions, but sometimes he'd been the last person seen with the vanished boy.

"You were a help, Becca," Tom said. "I admit it. Up on that hillside…" His eyes rolled in his head, like the tale-tellers said a man looked when he felt a spirit's breath on his neck. "I wasn't sure she was dead yet, but you—"

"I knew." *Her cry in my head with all the rest of them. Not on the wind any more, but in my skull, calling Lynn's name. Oh, Lord King, if knowledge is the end of a woman's virtue, why'd you give me this dark kind of knowing?* "Studying to be a herbwife, you learn such."

Tom's hearty grin looked pasted on. "My little sib, a herbwife. Sweet Mary witness, you'll be the finest one this grange ever fostered. Now stand back, Becca, and keep sharp watch. Here's one part of this you can't help me with. You get splashed, you'll burn, and then there'll be no explanation big enough to save us." Becca paid heed. She moved as far away from Tom as she could and still stay hidden in the scantling grove. Her sib kicked dirt on the last remnant of the fire, then stuck the paddle under the kettle and used it to lever the whole thing over. It wasn't done haphazard. The water and the rest went exactly where he wanted it to go, in the direction most straightly opposite to Wiserways' territorial fields. The soupy mess gushed over the roots of the trees, but it couldn't harm what was already dead.

Tom knelt behind the upended kettle while the last of the water trickled out. He'd brought a small leather knapsack with him from the men's hut, too. He'd unpacked the poke of kettle-powder from that sack, and the best fatwood kindling for the fire, and a fancy tinderbox Becca recognized as not Tom's, too gorgeously made to be any one man's. He'd laid them all out on a roll of plain blue cloth the color of sweet Mary's veil, but now he took out one last thing.

Becca thought it was cloth, too, rolled up and safe-looking like that. Faded patterns of Scriptural beasts showed in red and black and ochre between the thongs tying it up. Tom undid the knots and unfurled it, laid it flat on the earth a little space away from all the other things. She saw his lips moving over words she couldn't catch while he smoothed every last wrinkle from it. Fully spread, Becca saw the central figure of Christ on the cross, his Mother kneeling to one side, Joseph and his younger wives to the other, and at the foot of the cross a tumble of joyful children feasting on the piled up miracle of plenty, the loaves and the fishes. With the crown of thorns on His head, the nails in His hands and feet, the spear-wound in His side, Christ smiled down on them.

It was a marvelous piece of work, that unscrolled cloth. Becca came nearer, wanting to study the details of it. She caught her foot on a chunk of half-burned wood from the dead fire and nearly fell on top of Tom and the cloth both.

She never knew her sib could move that fast, or toss her so far, so roughly. She sailed backward through the air and fetched up against a tree-trunk, hard. For an instant, she thought he'd snapped her backbone for her, and through the pain came Tom's words, harsher for the fact he had to whisper what he wanted to scream:

"You really *are* a crazy woman! Scared to touch the bones, for bad luck, and going to touch the *skin?*"

"Skin?" She felt like a fool, only able to repeat the impossible word. "What skin? Where's the harm if I touch your—?"

Tom loomed over her, his hands turned to fists. "That's not for a woman to ask. By rights, not even for you to see. Lord King's punishing my yellow heart. My skin?" His laughter was brittle and hollow as a shucked locust husk. "As if I had the makings of a saint in me!"

Abruptly his anger left him. He offered Becca a hand up. "Come on. There's still some to do before we go to Makepeace. You just stand away from my things quiet, think over what we'll say to Miss Lynn. No more shenanigans, you mind me?"

Becca nodded slowly, said nothing. Now that she knew what sort of needle had left that wondrous scene of the Crucifixion and the Feeding of the Multitude, the tattooed skin held her gaze. *What a fool!* the worm whispered. *Thinking you meant that painted hide was his. Do women now believe a man can shuck his skin like a snake and still live? If you do, then he's not the only fool.*

Silently Becca answered the voice inside. *I didn't know what it was 'til he said. I thought he saw harm in me touching his own living skin by chance.*

Not that, the worm replied. *No harm in that, as far as he's concerned. Anything but harm, if his cock weren't still half-dead with terror over bringing home a baby's bones. Men weren't always so weak, in my day.*

Becca's eyes were fixed on the skin; a saint's skin, Tom said. Her mind shuddered for thinking over what martyrdom could have made that skin's unknown, unnamed owner so saintly. She hardly noticed Tom levering the kettle upright with the paddle, reaching inside, taking out the small, bare bones. Only when he laid them out on the skin and folded it around them like a bunting could she look away.

He stowed the rest of his gear in short order, dumped the wooden bucketful of cold water into the kettle, then spilled that out once the metal was sufficiently cool. He rubbed the inside of the kettle with a little wood ash and left it standing there, the knapsack and the paddle tucked inside the bucket beside it.

"Take all that back later," he said, slapping his hands clean on the seat of his pants. "No one'll bother it here." He picked up the carefully tied bundle of skin. "All right, Becca, now it's your time to do for me."

"I'd best wash up some first. The smell—"

"No time. Anyhow, it'll fade in the open air. None on your clothes, is there? Good. By the time we reach Makepeace, you'll be fine."

They walked the road to Makepeace Stead in silence. Their path took them past some of the Wiserways fields where the men labored. When they saw Tom, the older ones stood up from their crop-tending and took off their hats, bowing their heads as a sign of respect for the passing of one of the Lord King Herod's chosen children. Even the man riding the big harvester in the next field over cut off the motor and slid down from the seat to show his devotion.

Walking ahead of Tom, so he could protect her if need came, Becca heard the mumbled prayers. Someone was even singing the old Raven Carol. She thought she knew Jamie's sweet voice and dared a sideways glance. Yes, there he stood, hands folded before him 'round the handle of his scythe, singing for the dead. His work-boss John came up and laid a hand on his shoulder, stony eyes growing uncommon soft at the plaintive tune.

The younger males apart from Jamie—the ones whose final places in the stead and the grange and the earth itself weren't settled—weren't so nice about the outward signs of faith. They left off their tasks when the word spread that Tom was on his way to Makepeace with Miss Lynn's baby, but it was just to take advantage of a break to stretch their bones. They prayed when Pa made them; anything else was womanish, and a young man with dreams of his own stead never dared do anything that wasn't all male.

Even though she walked like a proper modest woman, eyes straight ahead, Becca still managed to catch a sideways glimpse of their faces, to see the way they stared at her instead of Tom and his skin-wrapped burden. It didn't matter that they were her sibs. Scripture held enough examples for a man to twist sin to blessing and back. Their hearts weren't full of faith or fear. It was almost as if out here, in the fields where only males did the tending, you could believe the stories about the rogue bands. Out here no woman of sense could call them tales to fright girl-children; not if she had eyes.

Pretty soon they left the fields behind them and came out into the fallow flatlands, then on into the untouched border country. They headed north for Makepeace. Becca felt the sun on her left side, the coming wintertime already bleeding the life out of its yellow fire. The wind from the ice mountains blew stronger here, or so it seemed. Carefull Stead, where Ma and Miss Lynn hailed from, lay farther to the west. It stood nearer the ice mountains, where the ground was so poor that the few males there had to bribe their continued existence from the other steads of the grange by the secret ways they had with pottery.

The wind from the ice mountains blew thin and cold. Becca hunched her shoulders forward to keep from shivering. She didn't want Tom to turn solicitous on her. The holy awe he had for his task made it safe for her to walk with him alone out here—Pa hadn't stopped her, sign enough he saw no danger—but you never could tell with a male. Hattie'd always taught her that, along with all the other lessons the rest of Pa's wives had pressed on her when they celebrated her Sixmonth and welcomed her as a full woman.

You never could tell with a male. A touch set them off, once they were past a certain age—a touch no matter how innocently meant or given—and then you'd best be ready to serve them if you were in your times, and bear all the blame if your alph was the strict type.

If it wasn't your time to be taking a man in a woman's first way, or if you feared your alph's wrath more than for your own life, you'd better learn the other ways to assuage them and hope it would be enough. But best not to touch them at all. Best to keep away.

"Becca, are you all right?" Tom sounded concerned. Out here in the lands between steads, with none of his male sibs to tease him for caring about a woman's ease, he might mean that concern honestly. But you couldn't tell. You shouldn't dare try to second-guess.

"I'm fine, Tom. Am I walking too slow?"

"It's a good pace. We don't want to be running, like we're in a hurry to get this over with." He forced out a brittle chuckle. "Not that we are."

"Tom, did you hear another cry when we were going through the fields?"

Becca didn't look back, but the way Tom's voice stiffened, she could guess the anger on his face. "What's wrong with you, woman? You like saying too many wild things. Now, and in the grove before, and inside—inside Prayerful Hill, and at home sometimes…What's wrong with you? Talking about such things just to torment a man, or bring ill luck."

"Where's the ill luck in an honest question?" Becca could hardly believe her own audacity. They were within sight of their goal now. In the distance, by the fast-fading light of day, she saw the men of Makepeace Stead, no bigger than sticks, taking the homeward path from their fields. Tom hadn't any power over her with so many witnesses only too ready to defend a lone woman. If he tried anything and she screamed, they'd come running.

And kill him, Satan's worm whispered. *He knows it, same as you. Stand up to him, ask, don't fear him now! It's his turn to fear you.*

But when you have to walk home with him again? Hattie's voice shivered through her brain. *Sweet child, you never do think ahead. You act first and sorrow after.*

"I just thought I heard something is all," she said, subtly quickening the pace so that they'd catch up with the homebound fieldhands. "Could've been the wind."

Tom didn't answer. He didn't say another word to her

all the way to the big house of Makepeace Stead. It might've been that she'd riled him into silence. That thought chilled her. *A silent man's most dangerous.* Her spirit tried to comfort her, bringing to mind that with the mission they were on, silence was only good manners.

It was strange, seeing how quickly the folk of Makepeace recognized what she and Tom had come to do. It was more than strange, the way the homeward-bound men from the Makepeace fields melted aside into two lines to flank them, ceding them the center of the road as they all marched along. When they came into the stead proper, the women came forward to join the lines, hurrying out of a half-dozen different doorways, skirts arustle, eyes dutifully downcast like they meant to read riddles in the dust. The only ones who didn't line up with the rest were two who had babies still clinging to the breast. It was ill luck beyond telling for a living child to come nigh any sign of one of the Lord King's chosen children. The mothers threw their aprons over their babies' faces to shield their eyes and hustled them away.

Walking between the lines of Makepeace men and women, Becca and Tom and their burden were skillfully steered to the place they sought without them having to break the holy silence to ask directions. Lore was clear as good water when it came to the rites surrounding how decent folk must notify a mourning mother of the Lord King's blessing: Do all you can to shield living babes and fruitful women from sight or speaking of the bones, lest their power should reach out and claim another soul for the Lord King's mercy; don't speak at all of what's brought you to the stead until you're asked.

They came to a halt in front of a grand house. In the solemn silence, while they waited for someone to address them directly and free their tongues, Becca got her first real look at an alien stead. She'd thought all steads were more or less alike, differing only in size and situation. She'd tried to learn more, earnestly questioning her mother and all of Pa's wives who'd been brought to Wiserways from elsewhere, interrogating any older female sibs who'd danced at a Harvest Home.

But the wives were vague in their descriptions of the steads where they'd been born and raised. Some acted fearful to talk of their past homes. "*Now* ought to be enough for any sane soul to chew on," Hattie taught. "Smarter folks than you have been choked dead on yesterdays."

Up to this moment, Becca assumed she'd learn more of the world only when she went to the Grangewide Harvest Home this year. She'd learn more yet when she became an herbwife, but that was too distant a dream to give her much satisfaction.

Your ma doesn't know you at all, the worm whispered with its moon-shadowed girl's face. *For all her cautious talk of putting away yesterdays, she'll never understand how you're the kind who'd sooner try to choke yourself on too many tomorrows.*

Now that they'd reached Makepeace, Becca took in everything she saw greedily, forgetting to keep her head down and her eyes lowered. At Wiserways, a stranger would have no trouble choosing out the main house from the others at first sight; only one building looked that important. Things were different at Makepeace, leaving Becca grateful that the steadfolk had come out to guide her and Tom as they'd done. There were a lot more stone buildings here than at home, some of them an obvious meld of ancient ruins shored up and topped off by newer construction. She saw one structure so tall that its top story and roof were visible above the lesser buildings in front of it. It looked big enough to be a depot. But a depot here, in an ordinary stead? She thought it was only at Grange—

Someone was staring at her. All Becca's rambling thoughts stopped dead, facing something more immediate.

He was a young male, a little older-seeming than Tom. His body looked like it was carved from square blocks of stone, all rough edges and blunt strength. Standing still, he leaned forward as if he smelled something good on the table. There was a wash of sallow color all over him, suntanned skin and russet hair stained with yellow, even a sprinkle of yellowy flecks across his cheeks and the bridge of his pug nose. Bright green eyes held hers—green like a sickly plant, not the healthy green of good growing things like Pa's eyes and her own. She felt a bitter fire inside her spouting up into a blush of shame on her cheeks.

But it wasn't shame; not really. Her mouth went hard and small, and she felt her fists tighten while Satan's worm whispered louder in her mind than Hattie's voice ever sounded, *How dare he?*

Because he's a man, her common sense replied. *And you provoked him to it, you walking along that heedless way in a strange stead, gawping at everything. Good thing Tom didn't see you!*

And so what if he did? The worm was shriller, feeding on the unholy rage it kindled within her. *Don't you have the right to look? Don't you have the right to see, to learn? Didn't Miss Lynn herself tell you that these two eyes of yours are the best teachers you could have?*

And where's Miss Lynn now? Hattie's voice came in, soft and smug. Behind her, Becca heard Tom shift his bundle, heard the dry, muted rattle and scrape of swaddled bones.

For once, good sense shouted the worm down. Becca jerked her head away from the young male's gaze and stared at the ground, at the wooden steps leading up to the porch of the great house in front of her. She heard muted chuckling and knew it came from the man who'd stared at her—who probably was still staring. Already she'd forgot what he looked like. Only those balefire green eyes stayed in her mind.

Hollow footsteps sounded on the porch. "Welcome to Makepeace, neighbors." Becca raised her head to reply, but Tom was edging his way in front of her, eager to speak up and have done.

"Thank you, Zacharias. Hope our welcome holds."

It was the set way to warn your host that you brought sorrowful news. The ritual words made Tom sound older than he was. Becca thought she gleaned a hint of self-importance in her sib's voice. Maybe he wouldn't need her after all. He could pack her off with the Makepeace women and never call for her until tomorrow, when they'd be heading home. She'd go back to Wiserways without seeing Miss Lynn at all.

And come all this footsore way for nothing, just to stiffen Tom's spine? Every step away from Wiserways seemed to let the worm speak louder in her. She tried to make it hush, but it wouldn't, no more than the ghostly voices she'd heard that had first heralded it out of Prayerful Hill.

The truth doesn't hush for anyone, man or woman. Becca couldn't tell whether it was Hattie or the worm had taught her that.

Becca kept her gaze fixed on Tom and Zacharias. It was acceptable and safe for her to look straight ahead. The Makepeace alph was a tall man who looked taller for being up on the porch. He wasn't built burly, the way her pa was, but there was plenty of strength in those lean arms and legs. Strength and quickness, or he wouldn't be alph here—and maybe something more dangerous than strength and quickness in him, too. Zach had a fox's face, sharp and scheming. Becca had never seen a fox, except in Katy's books, didn't know if they still lived, but she knew foxes were supposed to have the Devil's own wicked cunning.

Now Zach turned his fox-face sharply from them and snapped his fingers. A girl somewhat younger than Becca came out the front door of the house with the welcome plate. She kept her eyes lowered in the proper way as she came down the steps and offered it to Tom. She kept them so well lowered that she never saw how Tom's arms were full.

Tom was flustered. It would be the deepest insult to turn down the offer of food, but blasphemy to treat his burden like an ordinary bundle, juggling it awkwardly from arm to arm or setting it down on the ground. He didn't know what to do any more than the girl, who started trembling while she waited for the touch of a hand taking something from her proffered plate. Becca's mouth quirked up a little. She wanted to laugh, but she didn't dare. It looked so silly, her big-shouldered sib turning red in the face because he was sure to humiliate himself one way or the other before all Makepeace Stead with his bad manners. What would Pa say when word got back?

And just look at Zach! Becca thought. She saw a nasty twinkle in the tall alph's eyes. *He planned this. Soon as he* heard we were the ones bringing in the child, I'll wager he planned this so. He always did envy Pa. Bringing Tom to shame's his coward's way of doing the same to Pa, I know it. Becca remembered her mama saying how they'd both come off the same stead, Pa and Zach, but Pa had the strength to win Wiserways openly, after a plain and honorable single challenge. They still taught the boys the story of it, with special mention of their father's merciful ways after. No one talked much about the way Zach had come to rule Makepeace Stead.

Times are you've got to break a dish to save breaking a bone. Becca stepped boldly between Tom and the girl and took herself a handful of the dried fruits. "We're obliged for your kindness, sir," she said, looking Zacharias straight in the eyes in a brazen way that left her shaking inside. "It's not many would be man enough to treat the bearers of ill news so fine."

"What ill news is that?" Zach's eyes narrowed as he fell back into the ritual words. He wasn't grinning now. Could be he'd send word to Wiserways about the uppity way Becca had behaved, but it wouldn't be the same as reporting Tom for a stumble. Pa would just laugh and say that you couldn't expect miracles of good sense from a woman.

Becca's reply was set for her by generations of use: "Lord King's chosen Miss Lynn's babe, sir."

Zacharias folded his hands on his bosom and bowed his head. "The Lord giveth and the Lord King taketh away."

"Who shall know the shape of His sword?" The response rose from the lips of every Makepeace soul assembled there.

"We give thanks for His gifts, and submission to His will."

"*His ways are not our ways. They are true and unknowable.*"

"Blessed be the name of the Lord."

"*And of the Lord King also.*"

Zach's arms dropped to his sides. This much of the ceremony was done. "Miss Lynn's waiting. Come on in."

Becca fell in behind Tom. As they climbed the steps and went into the great house, she heard a rumble of speculation behind her. *Let them talk!* The worm was jubilant.

Inside the house, Becca couldn't keep her eyes from wandering. She'd never seen the like of this place. Her bare feet glided over fine-sanded wood floors, brushed the cozy nap of carpets far prettier than the old braided rag-rugs that were all she knew at Wiserways; thinner as well, and tickly under her soles. The walls were different too, covered with something smooth and slick, colored more hues than a sunrise.

There was even a likeness on one wall. The only likenesses she'd ever seen were all blessed: Mary and her Babe, Jesus on the Cross, other Scripture folk. You could recognize who was who easily—the scenes were set, the poses never varied. The blessed likenesses had come to Wiserways so long ago that no one now living recalled the name of the stead that had made them, or if it was in-grange, or even if it still existed. Pa kept them put by in the storeroom and only brought them out for holyday services.

The lady in this likeness wasn't Mary or Martha or Magdalen or any of their kin. She was naked as any newborn. You couldn't see more of her than just below the shoulders, but still you could tell. There was the hint of a hand near the bottom edge of the frame reaching up to cover her breasts, and another hand not hers at the right edge of the likeness, a hand holding out a folded cloth to cover her shame.

But the lady didn't seem to know any shame. The tilt of her head and the set of her shoulders made her nakedness a simple offering instead of something wicked to be hidden away until it was her time. Her long auburn hair blew on an imagined breeze and her hazel eyes looked out of the likeness with a calm that as good as said: *This is how I am. Your rules aren't mine.*

Becca felt a deep longing when she met the lady's eyes. There was none of Mary's glorious joy or boundless sorrow in them, nothing worshipful or fearful. There was only *Here am I*, an acceptance of how things were, and knowledge of who she was. And the miracle was that *Here am I* was enough for any eyes to say.

To look at the world like that...To tell anyone who asks, *Take it or leave it*...To be free...

Tom had to call Becca sharply, twice, before she came away from the likeness. "Thing like that to have hanging where a young woman can see it!" Tom spat out his disgust only loud enough for Becca to hear. He was down the far end of the entry hall already, left standing by himself in front of two big doors. One was dark and old, glowing with uncounted years of careful oiling. The other was a new addition, a replacement, the wood still raw and unstained but meticulously carved to match its sib.

Becca scurried over to join Tom. "Where's Zacharias?"

"Told me to wait here." Tom sounded sullen. "Ducked

into one of those side doors in the hall. He said he was going to fetch a girl to take us in to see Miss Lynn. As if he couldn't be bothered!"

"No need to rile yourself, Tom. Maybe it's their way."

"Leaving visitors standing outside a closed door? Pa wouldn't treat a caller so, and he's twice the man Zacharias ever was. Old man Zach acting like he's too good to show us in himself, after all our troubles?" Tom's voice rose with indignation.

"Shh. Someone'll hear you."

"Next you'll be telling me it's a Makepeace way to set up a challenge on hearsay. It's a free land under heaven! I can say what I like about Zach, long as it's not to his face, or where his people can hear me. And maybe someday it *will* be!"

He held the skin-wrapped bones closer to his chest, but there wasn't any reverence or tenderness in the gesture. The contents of the packet let out a chalky complaint at the rough handling, and the bottom folds of the bundle were starting to come undone.

If he's not careful, they'll slip out and go skittering all across this floor. The thought hit Becca like a midnight horror. *What'll Pa say to a tale like that? And Tom already put to penance for impiety.* Her eyes filled with fear and pity for her hot-headed sib. Couldn't he see that this was another trap Zach had set for him? Why? She couldn't say. She'd been taught too long not to question the ways of men.

Maybe it's time you started then, the silvery whisper twisted itself around her heart. *And the ways of women, too.*

Gently Becca reached out and touched Tom's hands,

Esther M. Friesner

being cautious not to brush the bundle in them. "Tuck it up some, Tom," she murmured. "Down there, see?"

"Good Lord!" Tom saw, and hastily readjusted his burden. "I'm in your debt, Becca; more than for this."

"No reason to lose our manners just because Zach can't find his." Her mouth turned up in a conspiratorial smile. "Best way to drive a rival mad is to ignore him, but hold yourself better."

"Where'd my little sib get so wise?" Tom asked, regarding her with true respect.

Becca laughed very quietly. "Nowhere. That's just womanlore I told you, gotten up in different clothes. You could learn something from it, old Tom."

"From womanlore?" It was his turn to laugh. "Clever, though. Pa says there's nothing a man should watch out for more than a clever woman."

Unless it's a clever man, Becca thought, recalling Zacharias. *Cunning-clever. And that green-eyed one out there, he must be one of Zach's first sons. He's got the look on him, Lord King shield me from such.*

A whisper of cloth-shod feet came up on Becca's left hand. She turned to see another young woman, just out of girlhood, with the nervous look of one who'd reached Changes but hadn't yet had the blessing of Sixmonth.

"I'm Dassah," she said, her voice pipey as a reed flute. "I'm serving Miss Lynn's wants this week. You come to see her, I hear. I'll take you in." She spoke to Tom, as was proper, but she kept darting her eyes to Becca.

Doesn't want to look too long at the bones, Becca reasoned. *Not even when they're wrapped from sight. Was I ever that jumpy over omens when I was waiting on my Sixmonth? Poor child.*

Becca saw how Tom stared at Dassah, even if Dassah didn't want to look at Tom and what he carried. *He's hungering after asking her for the Kiss or the Sign, I see it plain. Not likely Zach will invite him to the liberty, though. She's a pretty thing. I wish I had a face so delicately made, and how is it that her skin's so sunless pale? And her hair…* It was long and silky-fine, the same rare shade as the likeness lady's, more of Zach's siring at work. Much as Becca mistrusted the Makepeace alph and all his doings, she caught herself wishing he'd been her sire, too, for the gift of that firelight hair.

Dassah opened the big doors, sliding them back into the walls with a rumbling. The three young folks stepped into a room washed clean with sunlight, crisp with the scent of the drying herbs that hung in head-down sheaves from the rafters. Becca blinked, blinded by the last westering rays pouring in through the wide windows. It seemed as if that whole wall of the house was glass.

There was a rocking chair like Ma's at the center window, facing the view, plump cushions slopping over the arms and pressed out between the back dowels. Becca recognized Miss Lynn's hair from behind—and anyhow, even Zach wouldn't send them in to see the wrong woman. Tricks like that would be enough to shame a man before the whole Grange, alph or not.

Dassah led them toward the chair, mouse-quiet. The figure in it never moved, gave no sign they were heard even when Tom stumbled a little over the floorboards. Something unnatural was in that stillness.

Becca sensed Tom hanging back. The closer they got to Miss Lynn's chair, the slower came the sound of his heavy feet to her right. Then they stopped altogether. She looked back over one shoulder and saw how white he'd turned. He was hugging the bundle close again, but this time with all the sacred awe and terror Pa might wish.

His lips moved, forming the words, *I can't*. Over and over, with never a sound.

Becca didn't smile—he might take that wrong, though she'd only mean it to reassure him—but she did her best to set him at ease just as silently, with a nod and a look and a subtle calming motion of her hands. She would take care of things. She would make the first, most delicate overture to Miss Lynn.

And then let your Lord King grant that Tom grows into an alph! the Devil's girl-faced worm crowed. *One who'll remember this day, this debt, how gingerly you've got to tread with a woman who's lost a child. Look at him! You can see by his eyes that he's remembering the tales of wild women, the ones who ran mad into the wilderness when their little ones were taken from them. Think there's only rogue-band stories the women tell to frighten girls? The men have their own horrors. You do this for him, Becca, and you'll have a bridle on one male at least; a bridle stronger than any service you'll ever have to do for his body. You take it, and you hold firm!*

Becca shook her head hard. She wanted the worm out of her, the little voice of evil that would lead her to her death if she harked too closely. *Something's wrong inside me*, she thought. *Something worse than bad Changes, or the voices out of Prayerful Hill. Oh Lord, maybe if I talk to Miss Lynn about it, she'll be able to help me. Only first I've got to do this for her.*

Dassah was hanging back with Tom, her skinny arms showing gooseflesh beneath the short sleeves of her homespun dress. Becca wet her lips and went up to the rocker all alone. She stopped about two armlengths behind it and said, "I'm bringing you tidings, Miss Lynn." They weren't the words that custom taught were fitting for this hard time, but custom set the fitting words in the man's mouth anyhow, and Tom wasn't up to shouldering his part just yet.

"Tidings?" The voice was fuzzy, almost fresh-woke. Hattie always said how sleep was the greatest healer.

Becca took in a long breath. It was easier standing here, behind the chair, seeing nothing but the top of Miss Lynn's head, all else shielded from her sight by the rocker's back. "The Lord King's will is God's will." The formal Scripture-talk sounded hollow, but it was the best way to lead into what she had to say—unless the Lord grant Tom the loosening of his tongue first. And wouldn't Miss Lynn be expecting to hear something like this by now? The wonder was that the babe had lived as long as it did on the hillside. If any other stead had wanted it, they'd have come at the first cry, but when a babe wept for more than a day everyone knew what its fate would be. It was only a matter of time. "His will is over all His creatures."

"God's will be done," came the set reply, spoken by rote like it came out of a dream. So many occasions called for a woman to voice her acceptance of what the Lord had decreed for her, the two of them might have been speaking of anything.

Becca bit her lip. Silence had spooked Tom, but Miss Lynn's distant way of talk was what left Becca's scalp prickling. *Like grief's sucked her hollow. Like I'm talking to empty meat.* Her spirit wailed for leave to flee the room, so dark despite the sunlight. *No.* Stubbornness made Becca stand her ground. *It's got to be said and done.* Becca set herself to say it all out at once, to cast aside the cup Tom's cowardice had forced to her lips. "Miss Lynn—your baby's out of hunger and cold. The mercy of God rides the Lord King's sword, and He—"

The shriek was harsh and seemed loud enough to shatter the wall of windows. The rocker shot back, tilted over, crashed down on the floor and spun around, striking Becca's legs as she jumped away. Dassah moaned and fell to her knees, covering her face with her apron. Becca heard Tom say, "Jesus God," as if his whole throat had turned to sand.

And there stood Miss Lynn, a crazy fire in her eyes, her long hair loose and streaming like a warrior-angel's banner. There she stood, breast bared, a *living* babe in her arms, sucking her milk; a babe some other stead had cast aside, brought here like Jamie'd been brought to Wiserways, because this stead stood in need of a manchild. "Damn you!" Miss Lynn shrieked in Becca's blanching face. "God's judgment take you and all you love, you idiot girl! Talk of the Lord King's sword so near my little one? God grant it cut you to the heart! Get out! Get out! Don't ever come into my sight again, you devil!"

Becca felt the tears spring to her eyes, hot and sharp. She let loose a little wail of despair, pressed her hands to her ears, and fled, Lynn's curses flying after.

Chapter Four

In his sire's steps he trod,
Where the dust had drifted,
Gave his sweet soul up to God
When his sins were lifted.
Wherefore, though we hunger here,
Praise we those who perish.
Of their blood our souls we clear,
And their teachings cherish.

Becca sat on the floor in the small, darkened room, her back wedged into a corner, arms wrapped tight over a bent head buried on updrawn knees. Through her sobs, she thought she heard a faint squealing. She felt the weakest breath of new air lift the wisps of hair around her ears, and even with her eyes so close-shut she saw the suggestion of light from the hallway wink into the room and then away. The darkness came back.

"Becca?" Small feet shuffled nearer over the wooden floor. Little hands touched her back and shoulder, bringing with them the smell of dried herbs, but it wasn't Miss Lynn's voice. "Becca, it's me, Dassah. You don't have to hide in here by yourself. Father didn't look angered with you any when I saw him at supper. He put your sib in an honorplace at table. I saw. He even asked after you. Becca, are you all right?"

One prying hand crept down, worked its way in to feel the tears on Becca's cheek. She heard Dassah's flutey voice give a startled "Oh!" as if the girl were knothead enough to expect dry eyes after such a scene.

Thinking back on it tore more sobs from Becca's chest. Instinctively, she threw her arms around Dassah's neck and wept into the younger girl's bosom.

Dassah was no more able to give comfort than fly, but she stumbled along, trying. "Don't cry. Don't cry." No reason given why not, but still the numb repetition. "Don't cry. Please stop. Don't cry."

"I didn't know!" Becca choked out. "How was I to know she had a newborn on her lap? I'd sooner cut out my tongue than name the Lord King's sword near a baby! Why didn't you tell us when you brought us in to see her? We'd've taken the bones to your senior woman instead, had her give Miss Lynn the tidings later. Why'd you let us do it, Dassah?"

"*Us?*" The worm laughed. *Tom never opened his mouth. It's you that your pa's going to question when Zach sends you home tonight with this tale. And it will be tonight!*

Dassah was shaking. "I didn't know either. Nor our

senior woman—I asked her at supper and she said so. Nobody in all Makepeace knew Miss Lynn'd come by a babe."

"I thought I heard crying on the hillside when we left Wiserways." Becca spoke her thoughts aloud, as if Dassah weren't there. "I guessed some other woman from a different stead had—" A convulsive shudder from Dassah made Becca tap her own mouth closed. The girl was like to shake her sanity loose at the smallest mention of anything that touched on breeding.

No, I never was that skittish waiting on my Sixmonth. Never. Not even knowing how Ray had dealt with her own girl, Margaret, when she—

Suddenly, fully aware of how badly Dassah's fears had crippled up a healthy young woman, Becca's own vanished. *Oh, pride! Pride!* The Hattie-voice might be right, but pride didn't look like such a bad thing right now; not if it let her stop this snivelling and get to the bottom of things. Not even the thought of what Pa'd do to her when she came home mattered more. All the tears were gone.

"Dassah, if no one knew *then*, they surely must know *now*. Secrets like that don't keep. There's always suppertime talk. How did Miss Lynn come to have that babe in her lap?"

Dassah's skin was icy. She wouldn't say.

Anger burned off the last of Becca's fear. Something stank worse than field-ripe piss here, and she'd find out what if she had to twist it out of Dassah. "You know as well as I that she'd wouldn't have been able to ride out to the hillside herself. Not so soon after a birthing."

"Father wouldn't hear of that." Broken-spirited misery in that saying.

Esther M. Friesner

"And none of your women would go to the hillside without cause, willingly. Nor bring back a babe without your pa's leave, I'll wager. But you can hear the cries from the slope when you're in the fields. That's the whole point of choosing that hill. I hear tell that four big steads can hear the tidings from it, and sometimes two smaller steads beyond, when the wind's right. But only your men could've heard the cry I did. I didn't see any stead girls working the fields when we came by."

"Father doesn't want us in the fields this close to Harvest Home." The words came out like a confession of sin. "Our sibs—the older ones—get too excited with thinking about what's waiting for them at the festival time. Father says we'd best avoid the chance of sin. Last year he had to step in against Jubal."

"Step in?"

The birdlike voice fluttered down until Becca had to strain to hear: "Killed him."

"You mean Jubal went off on his own." Becca gently reminded Dassah of the fitting way to speak of such things.

"I mean he *killed* him!" Dassah's shout out of the dark was a slap. She pushed Becca out of her arms. "In front of the whole stead. He had Jubal's arms tied, so he couldn't fight back, then he wrestled him to a neck-snap, like it'd been a fair challenge. Fair! Father killed Jubal and made all of us watch, down to the youngest, so we'd remember."

"But—but that's a sin so great that—" Becca paused. There was one case in which open killing of a valuable working son wasn't a sin but a holy duty.

Dassah shared that knowledge, sensed Becca's unasked question. "My little sister." Her voice dwindled back to its shyness. "Jael. Father did justice, but why he felt the need to make us watch—Little Jael. She wasn't even into Changes."

That was bad enough, but Becca caught a hint of something worse to be revealed. She ventured a guess. "And Jubal was—her brother too? Not just a sib?"

"Hers and mine. It didn't stop him."

"Sweet Mary!" Sourness tingled down from her throat to her belly, but she fought it away. She couldn't let these stories of cursed wickedness get between her and what she had to know. Becca set her teeth and steadied herself before forcing the talk back to what she sought: "Someone brought Miss Lynn that babe. Who?"

No reply.

"Who did it, Dassah?" She groped in the dark until she found the girl's wrist and squeezed it hard. Hard and intent, she told her, "Baby didn't just walk itself up to this house. Your daddy'd have runners and riders all over Grange blaring out the miracle, if so. He's a big one for flaunting appearances. Only thing he likes to hide under a bushel's muck." Becca sounded solemn and grown as she parroted all the hearth-talk she'd overheard about Zacharias. "If you don't tell me, then when I go home I'm going to tell my pa about your kin, Jael and Jubal. That's not the sort of tidings gets spread too readily, is it? Nor what your daddy'd like to have spread. I know my pa's ways pretty well"—it was a good lie—"and I'll wager that when he hears this he'll steer all his sons away from breeding into Makepeace Stead!"

"That isn't fair!" Dassah wailed. "I never meant to tell you about it. I just wanted to stop you from crying and waking Father and the rest who're going to see you home."

Becca ignored Dassah's distress, pressed the question. "Who did it, Dassah? Who brought her that baby, who knew she had it with her and didn't warn us? I meant what I said. I'll tell about why your father killed Jubal!"

"Father did it!" Dassah screamed. "Father and Adonijah between them, they brought the baby home!"

"Adonijah? Which one—?"

An arm came out of the blackness and struck Becca awkwardly across the head. Whether Dassah intended to hit her so hard, or at all, didn't matter. Maybe the Makepeace girl was only groping for the wall, trying to push herself upright, get away from Becca's questions, run out of the room. The blow itself smarted, but not that bad. What was worse was the way it sent Becca tumbling from her haunches into one of the walls, then toppling forward. She flailed with her arms to stop herself; no good. Her chin skidded over the floor until she fetched up sharp against a big piece of furniture, anonymous in the shadows. Her temple knocked into a massive knob of hardwood—a carved footpiece, likely—and her eyes saw bursts of gray and red that faded out into a deeper black. Behind her, dying fast, she heard Dassah calling her name.

⊱⊰

"There," Miss Lynn said, taking the hot, damp cloth from Becca's forehead and replacing it with a fresh, cool one. "I hope you're satisfied now, Becca. There's no more talk of taking you home tonight. I never saw Zacharias half so put out. He doesn't care to have his plans undone, least of all by a fool girl who plays catch-and-kiss with a bureau leg."

Becca blinked at the sound of Miss Lynn's beloved, freeheart laugh. It was the last sound she'd expected to hear again in this life. She tried to sit up and say something, but the herbwife used both hands to push her back down flat on the sweetly scented, hay-filled pillow.

"You rest and hush. I've checked your eyes; the pupils say it's safe for you to sleep. You're in my own bed, so take your honor politely and don't make any trouble." The old jesting talk was back. Becca must have shown how incredulous it all was to her, for Miss Lynn added, "I'm sorry for what happened before, child. Dassah's been and told me that no one who should—that you didn't know. It took every fiber of nerve in that child to speak up, too. Poor little soul, we'll all breathe easier when her Sixmonth comes. Only two more months to go, now."

Becca took the cloth off her forehead, wincing when it flopped against the bruised side of her head. She couldn't resist exploring the full extent of her hurts. Her cautious fingers touched a thin wad of cotton resting a little above her left cheekbone.

"Don't you fool with that pad, girl! The ointment underneath is all that's holding it on. You haven't got more than a bump and a scrape. It'll heal faster when you can uncover it in a few days and let the air hit it. Until then, my special comfrey cream will help it start mending clean. Going to be some black-and-blue, though." Miss Lynn clucked her tongue. "Better say yourself some prayers that it's all faded away by Harvest Home."

"I don't care if it is," Becca murmured. Jamie's face was before her. "I'm not ready to be bespoke. I'd soon as not go to Harvest Home."

"Oh?" Miss Lynn's glance was impish. "Which one is it?"

Esther M. Friesner

"Which?"

"Not a sib born, I know, but there've been more than a few babes brought home from the hill to Wiserways. Time goes by and who can tell brought from born?" Her smile was for Becca, but the girl knew where the herbwife's thoughts were. "You can tell me. I can't read minds, though the way your face gives up everything it doesn't take a mind-reader to know you're thinking of a young man. That much I can see; his name's the mystery. Go on, tell. I keep more secrets than you'll ever learn."

"Jamie." It felt good to say his name. It was like letting clean air into a sickroom.

"Ah." Miss Lynn nodded. "He's a handsome one. Wise, too; wise enough to hold himself low until he's strong enough to stand a challenge. Maybe in a year, eh?"

"Maybe." Becca felt the cold, close sensation of a dark hand on her. To speak of a young man making his challenge was fortune-tempting, too. She didn't like to think of her Jamie struggling in the dirt with some faceless alph for mastery of a distant, unknown stead. She knew that fight might mean the making or the death of all their shared dreams, and she shuddered away from it. She'd never seen a challenge fought out—Pa's challenges up to now had come when she was too young to witness—but she'd heard tales. There were always tales to hear.

It didn't bear thinking of Jamie locked in such a struggle, dead if he lost, death-guilty if he won. Becca turned the talk from things she couldn't bear. "Miss Lynn, about what happened when we came to see you—"

"Told you to hush."

"He could've *told* us! Zacharias could've said—"

"Didn't I say hush?" A sliver of wildness scaled up Miss Lynn's words. Her eyes shot some of the same madness that had startled Becca half to death in that sunset room. In a more level tone the herbwife said, "I've already had words with Zacharias, child. Not his fault. He allowed he'd told Adonijah to warn you off, but that boy had other things on his head. Not much room in that head to start with. He's been punished to improve his memory. No one's going to run to your pa, tale-bearing. Everything's settled and forgotten. Now will you rest?"

Becca tried to speak up again, but a look from Miss Lynn made her turn the unsaid words into a sigh. She worked her shoulders back into the pillow, let her limbs enjoy the unwonted softness of a really substantial mattress. The bedclothes had a smell of sweet clover— one of Miss Lynn's concoctions added to the rinse-water, likely. Under the sheet and blanket, Becca wore only her shift. She closed her eyes and tried to imagine herself lying down among the stalks of rye, stealing a moment off field work to dream.

Dreaming of the stalks parting, of Jamie's face smiling down on her, of his voice giving music to her name, of his warmth, his scent, his hands—

A baby's cry tore the dreams away. Becca bolted straight up in bed, crying out, "Oh, God! Help!"

"Shoo, child." From the bedside chair, Miss Lynn whispered her calm. "It's only my Jesse, wanting his milk."

The baby was in her lap again, crying with infant rage at not having his every wish met immediately. Already he had the imperious look and sound of a born tyrant, his helpless hours on the hillside forgotten.

And will he ever remember? Will he ever know, when he's grown, how close he came to death? Will that change how he treats his own babes, if he rises high enough to have them?

Esther   M.   Friesner

Becca's head ached with unanswerable questions. She had to lean back and rest her mind as well as her swimming eyes.

Miss Lynn looked down fondly at the small brown face, flushed ruddy and screwed up as tightly as the tiny, trembling fists. She draped the child's swaddling blanket loosely over its birth-bowed legs and miniscule mark of male sex, then lifted it to her bared breast. The dark head, thick with black curls, nuzzled in greedily.

"Isn't he a wonder?" Miss Lynn said, speaking her thoughts aloud. "Not every woman births a son this strong. God forgive me any pride I feel, but I can't help it."

For birthing that baby? In whose dreams? Becca let the worm have its way, too tired to battle the evil thoughts that Satan's creature forced into her mind. *What sane person'd ever believe a child with those looks came from a mother like Miss Lynn, with Zach for his sire? The baby that died on the hillside—her true child—you could see her mother's face in her, even so young, even dead. But Makepeace must need sons, and no other stead needed daughters, so she's bones. Woman's luck so young...*

Soon everybody would be talking about baby Jesse the way Miss Lynn did, like he'd been Makepeace born, not hill-brought. Stories about his birthing would crop up in the mouths of older women who still wanted some attention paid them, or who needed allies to swear to their usefulness in a winnowing time. They'd claim they'd seen him born of Miss Lynn's body, spin the tale out until even those who knew the truth would lose the thread of it. There were bonds aplenty between stead crones and young mothers who'd given their true babes to the hillside and taken home a different infant.

Boy for girl or girl for boy, and sometimes one left, none taken home. Sometimes the other way around, just any old child to fill a fruitless womb or a hearthside cradle the Lord King had emptied for His own reasons, all according to the needs of the stead. And who decides those needs?

Zach spoils me, Miss Lynn said. But not enough to let her keep a healthy babe of her own bearing when Makepeace Stead had enough daughters born. Becca could almost picture the alph's sharp face as he carried the newborn girl away to the hillside, his eternally calculating eyes weighing the infant's life against what he saw was the future. The Coop city traders weighed out goods and grain the same way, and nothing alien ever tipped the balance.

And is your pa that much different? the worm asked, gleeful, though her breasts still glimmered with blood. How many infants has he carried down that same path? Your own mama's fruitful, but does Wiserways have room for daughters or sons?

Go away, Becca told the worm in her mind. Leave me be. We do what we have to do. It's hard to be a woman, but it's harder to be a man. It's hardest of all if you're alph of a stead. Then you're the one responsible for the mouths and the bellies and the future. No one can help Pa with what he's got to do.

More parrot-talk, the worm sneered. And did your pa ever seek help? Share the burden? Share the power? He wouldn't like the taste of that. Who ever saw the proof of all you've said? Who— But Becca had fallen asleep.

This time she woke to Miss Lynn saying, "Get away, Adonijah. She's resting. I won't have you rousing her for nothing."

"All I wanted was to beg her pardon." The answering voice was thin and whiny, but low-pitched. "That's the least I can do when it was my fault. She's had all night to rest."

Becca opened her eyes and saw Miss Lynn standing in the doorway, her body blocking all sight of whoever was out in the hall. Early sunlight came in at the windows, showing just how cubby-small the herbwife's bedroom was. The bed, a chair, and a chest of drawers crowded up most of the space. Becca's folded clothes waited for her on the chair. She felt a little chilly; the blanket was off the bed, probably kicked away when she'd tossed in her sleep. She looked for it to either side, then held the sheet to her bosom and leaned over the footboard. The blanket lay pooled beside the cradle where baby Jesse lay asleep, content.

Miss Lynn was saying, "Apologies'll keep until she wakes. Now get to the fields before Zach sends—Oh!"

The herbwife staggered away from the door. In the tiny room, she hooked her heel on the tangled blanket behind her and came near to falling into baby Jesse's cradle. Becca's arms shot out to steady Miss Lynn, but in one last stumble the herbwife's foot struck the cradle's rocker. The cradle pitched and spun wildly. Jesse woke up shrieking.

"You stark crazy, Adonijah?" Miss Lynn screamed out the door. She swept Jesse into her arms. "Pushing me like that, almost make me land on my son? Didn't Zach lesson you enough over what you did yesterday?"

The door swung all the way open. Adonijah leaned against the jamb. With a giddy, sick feeling, Becca recognized him as the same solid, square-built young man who'd stared at her so shamelessly the other day. Now he came swaggering into Miss Lynn's room as if it were his own. Those yellow-green eyes drifted lazily around, treating the women with as much interest as the furniture.

"You didn't say I was crazy yesterday, Lynn," he drawled, not bothering to call the herbwife by her title of respect. "Yesterday I got every blessing your mouth could give. *Every* one." His lips twisted into something too evil to be named a smile.

Becca saw Miss Lynn blush, saw Adonijah relish her shame. He was wearing work clothes that looked relatively new, with a refined quality to the material that set them apart from homemade goods. When an alph wore Coop city manufacture, that was the way of things. When a young man of the steads wore such, and not hand-me-downs, it was a message.

Adonijah reached out a thick hand for Jesse, still yowling in his mother's arms. Miss Lynn held the struggling babe closer to her, sheltered the little one's body with her own. Moving away from Adonijah, kneeling onto the bed, she made as if to pass the baby into Becca's care, her eyes frozen on Adonijah. Becca was fascinated. She'd never seen white-cold fright like this in the face of any woman.

Then Adonijah laughed and let his hand fall. "Who's crazy now? You put too much behind what other folks do and say, Lynn. Your baby's too young to be any threat to me, so I'm none to him. I just wanted to see my newest sib and to tell Miss Becca I was sorry for not having warned her about him yesterday." His ill-luck eyes flashed over Becca's sheeted body and left her burning. "Sometimes a man gets distracted in his mind."

"I accept your apology." Becca was surprised at how calmly she spoke to him. *Like I was looking down on him from a Coop tower!* she marveled. *Like I was a senior woman and him a stripling boy.*

"Big of you, Miss Becca." Adonijah's mouth twisted again and he doffed an invisible hat to her. "Kind of you to say so. No hard feelings."

Every word of his and every gesture mocked her somehow. That same mockery made her pull more dignity around herself. She heard Pa's voice in her own—Pa at his strictest—when she replied, "No hard feelings. Now I wonder if you'd be kindly enough to leave. I have to be getting on home."

"Pa'll be pleased to hear that. He's holding Nahum off work just to see you and your sib back to Wiserways. Shame what happened. If you'd've gone home last night, the honor of seeing you there safe would've been mine." His teeth were the only part of him untouched by that all-over sallowness. They flashed strong and white and sharp between thin lips. "So, I'm dismissed. Then I won't take up any more of your time. The Lord watch over you, Miss Becca."

"And over you." She watched him back out of the room, watched while he pulled the door shut, all the time feeling that if she took her eyes off him, some protective spell would be broken. She could sense Miss Lynn doing the same, adding her might to the unspoken charm of shielding they laid up between themselves and him. Only when the latch clicked, Becca relaxed and became aware of the shooting pains in her spine and shoulders from holding herself so stiffly erect before him.

O Lord, she prayed. *O Lord, keep that one far from me!*

Prayers. The worm chuckled. *Words.*

They're all I have, she told it in the sorrow of helplessness. *All any woman has.*

All I had, too, the worm agreed. *Maybe it's time you sought more.*

Chapter Five

I'm going to dance with my love tonight,
With her silver hand and her teasing eye,
Dance with the lass with the honey lips,
Have a taste of heaven before I die.

"Stand still, Becca. You can speak to your own pa without shaking, can't you?" Paul pushed himself back from the desk with its piles of sum-books and its scatters of inky quills. He rested his head on one hand, looking wearier than if he'd just put in a full day's fieldwork.

There was a small, high window in this room, unshielded by curtains or blinds, but this near to Harvest Home it didn't provide enough light by which a man could do close work. A small lamp, manufacture of Miss Lynn's old stead, helped make things more clear to see, even some things better kept in shadow. The little clay lamp's flame picked out every crease of fatigue on Paul's face, the droop of his eyelids, the patchy stubble on his cheeks, the hints of gray coming into his hair.

"Lord, this time of year's a trial." Paul sighed and rubbed his reddened eyes with only partly scrubbed up fingertips. "Times I wish Katy'd just do the accounts for me and be done with it."

"Why don't you let her, then?" Becca spoke up without thinking.

Her sire smiled at how the sound of her own words made her jerk up short. "Now that's my girl," he said. "Bold to speak your mind. But why're you goggling like you'd said something sinful? Some questions don't hold any harm. Katy's this stead's teacher and can spin figures better than cotton thread, but she's not me. I'm honor-bound to keep my word to the city traders. Said I'd be the only one responsible for what these books tell, and I meant it. Why're you so frighted of asking that, Bec'? You never were the one to walk tippy-toe over eggshells. Only since you come home from Makepeace. I thought you women just went through two sets of Changes, but the way you've been since then—"

Becca looked down, studiously minding her fingers as they twisted and pulled at themselves. Only Pa could speak of Changes so freely. It wasn't proper for a male to do, and he'd discipline any man caught with such shaming words in his mouth, but who'd ever lesson Pa? Who'd do it and live?

"There, now." She heard his gruff voice go gentle. A shadow shifted over the floor and the chair beside the flat-top desk creaked. He stood before her and lifted her small, round chin. His skin felt like thin horn, but the touch was near womanly. Green eyes like her own kindled a deeper shade of emerald in the lamplight.

"I ask your pardon, child. It wasn't my place to speak so in front of you. I like to forget you're a woman now. It pleasures me more to think that you're still a little one, too little to be marrying out of Wiserways so soon."

His arm stole around her shoulders, heavy and comforting as a big winter quilt. She couldn't help shrinking in some, by reflex. There wasn't one action a man could make—not a one, down to the veriest gesture—that the older women hadn't described in detail to their living daughters: What it was, what it should mean in a natural man, what it *might* mean if the man weren't so natural, what a woman could or should do about it by way of encouragement or escape. An arm around the shoulders, sire to girl-child, that ought to have a warm and joyful meaning, but there were stories—

There's too many stories! the worm shouted. Yes, it was shouting inside her now, the Satan-sent worm that ate at her heart, that danced in her head on blood-dappled legs, flaunting its bleeding breasts. Nothing quieted it, for all the prayers that Becca had tried. *Too many tales to make you afraid! Too many foolish tongues clacking and too many ears ready to have such swill poured into them! Dassah was like that, reading doom in every dust-speck. Are you made of the same flimsy stuff as Dassah?*

"Becca?" Again the unwonted womanly touch of the alph's fingertips. He could cradle her whole face in one hand. "Hattie said you wanted to see me about something. Now you're here, you're silent as a stone. What's troubling you? Not what happened at Makepeace?"

She shook her head.

"That's good. Day I care about Zach's squallings, that's the day I take myself off and leave Thalie be the alph here!" He chuckled over his own joke. In a more serious tone he said, "Out of all the children that the Lord King saw fit to leave me, there's always been something about you, Becca. God alone knows what it is or why. Oh, don't pull into yourself that way! You don't think I mean anything evil by it, do you?"

"No, Pa."

He clicked his tongue. "Still so shy. Times I think your mama didn't read any but the most forewarning parts of Scripture to you. When I tell you how esteemed I hold you, there's no more but a father's love in it."

And what could you do about it if not? the worm asked.

"I don't deserve anything special, Pa."

Paul smiled at her. He'd cast off a little of his weariness when he left the wrangling account books lying idle on the desk top. "So you say. A person's not always the best judge of what's inside his own skin. Look at Zach if you don't believe that. If pride was sugarbeet squeezings, he'd be the first man sweetened to death."

The thought of anything sweet touching Zacharias made Becca return her sire's smile. "Hope I'm not like him."

"You? His name's not fit to share breath with yours. You listen to your pa, girl. I've lived some and I've seen some, so I know what I'm saying. There's something that draws God's notice to the children I've got by your mama. Hattie's not fruitful as much as I'd like, but when she's in her times I make damn sure who answers for it if she's blessed. Did your brother Eleazar ever think he was better or higher than his sibs? No, and yet the traders had their eyes on him from the time he was a half-grown boy. They even went so far as to—"

Paul stopped, cast his eyes all around the room even though the door was fast shut. Like a little boy plotting his first ambuscade, he asked Becca, "Can you keep secrets?"

"Yes, Pa."

"Then I'll trade you even, words for words, something nobody knows but me, if you'll tell me straight out what's been troubling you this while. A secret, mind!"

Useful things, sometimes, secrets, the worm murmured.

Becca ran her tongue over her teeth, buying a little time. It was the worm had brought her here, had driven her crazy enough to ask to speak privily with her pa. Now she knew what had made him crazy enough to agree to hear her out: Like Eleazar, chosen by the Coop traders for the privilege of city life, she was Hattie's child. For Eleazar's sake he held all Hattie's children special. If he did truly care for her as fondly and as purely as he claimed, maybe there'd be no price to pay for what she had to tell.

"Pa, I'm carrying sin. I can't go to Harvest Home."

"*What?*"

"I tried to speak it out with Ma." She spoke faster, louder, getting all the fearful words out before the sight of her pa's stunned and angry face scared her dumb. "I told her what the trouble was, how it came to me at my vigil time, and she sent me up to old Gram Phila. Gram was who named it sin. She was the one told me to see you."

"Gram Phila—" Paul's gaze wandered upward involuntarily, up to the eaves of the big house where Gram Phila kept to her own room, her wants served by a girl-child without a name. She was the oldest woman of Wiserways, the stead crone, the oldest living soul of either sex. She was the only one who still recalled the name of her predecessor, or the cunning means she'd used to kill the old man and take over his post. If she named something sin—

"She said I should make confession of it and be free."

Paul relaxed visibly. Becca felt her own heart ease to see it. As alph, it was his place to watch and ward over his stead and all who dwelled there. He was just as responsible to God for the accounting of steadwide sins as he was to the city traders for the accounting of crops. If it was sin on Becca's spirit, Gram Phila would know, but she'd also know whether it was sin that could be washed clean by confession or by blood.

By blood, the worm whispered. *A woman would know all there is to know about sins of blood.*

Becca saw the unspoken thanksgiving flood over her sire's face. *Could be he does care for me as much as he claims,* she thought.

Or tells himself so, the worm hissed.

Hush! she commanded it. *You hush with your wicked sayings and your evil gifts! I'll confess to harboring you and I'll be free, just like Gram Phila said. I'll drive you out of my heart and you'll be gone!*

And will you drive out the voices from Prayerful Hill too? the worm asked. *Can you or your all-powerful sire do that, when they and I are so deep a part of you? For so we are, Becca, and you can call us by other names and swear on a thousand Scriptures that you want none of us, but we're here. Inside you. Of you. Lodged in the learning of your eyes and the doubts of your heart forever. Call us by our right name, woman. Call us your own.*

Becca started talking to drown out the worm's words; it didn't help. The worm danced on the bare feet of a young girl, spinning a cocoon around itself woven of the wailing, swirling sounds she'd heard on her vigil night, the hard-edged sights she'd seen inside Prayerful Hill and in the cauldron grove with Tom, the arrogant mastery of Adonijah's leering face that haunted her. When she sat at her fancywork with the other girls, making themselves the gowns they'd dance in at Harvest Home, cooing over the supple softness of city-brought goods, she saw Adonijah's narrow eyes searing her skin in every stitch of the needle.

He'll be at Harvest Home too, the worm reminded her. *You know what he'll come asking. And there's no nay-saying a man that night, if you're virgin and not in your times.* "Let us give thanks," *the preacher'll tell you women, but it's the men have all the thankfulness to say!*

She couldn't bear that. Not however much she was told it was her lot, not with Adonijah. She'd be safe a time while the maidens' dance lasted, and the striplings' brawl, and the wrestling matches on the threshing floor with the Coop city traders looking on.

But when the wedded women doused the torches and all fires but the big Grange blaze were covered, when there was only the moon's cold grin to witness, then she'd have to go with any man that asked and serve him in the ways an unbespoke virgin could. *It's nothing*, the older women said. *It's simple gratitude and plain courtesy.*

You don't want to go shaming Wiserways.

It's quickly over.

Yes, if you heed your lessons and know what to do.

I never wanted it too quickly over, when I was young.

Selena, you're a caution! What pleasure could a woman have from that?

Oh, I don't know. It justs sets me to remembering how it is when I'm in my times. Try to tell me you don't enjoy it then, too!

You're making little Rusha blush.

Let her blush! Who'll see it in the dark?

That's how I came to Paul's notice, in the dark at a Harvest Home.

Pride! Pride!

The echoes of the women's voices died away, leaving only the worm's mockery of their laughter. *If you were sure it was Jamie you'd find waiting for you in the dark, you'd be the first into the wagon bound for Harvest Home!*

Becca spoke on, ignoring the worm, ignoring the voices of the older women. She heard herself telling her pa about the thing that haunted her, the evil creature that had come into her spirit, though she never told him the strange, blood-spattered shape of it or how the haunting had first come to be. She finished her telling and waited for the alph's power to banish it with a single word.

Paul sat down at his desk again and adjusted the lamp wick so that there was a little more light. "That's all, child? A voice in you sowing doubt?"

Becca nodded. "Wicked doubts, Pa. Satan's own. Sometimes I can't sleep nights for listening."

Paul folded his hands one atop the other. He didn't look at his daughter while he spoke, but stared up at the small window that did the job of illuminating the room so poorly.

"When I was some two years older than you, my brother Nathan died," he said. "He had a year on me—

nineteen, he must've been—but we were full brothers, not just sibs, born on this stead. My mama said Gram Phila birthed us both, and that we were of her direct line, but how much of that was true—" He sighed. "That year, a month scant of his twentieth birthday, Nathan challenged our pa and lost. He had the strength and he had the weight and height on the old man, but still he was the one had his neck snapped for him. We all watched that fight, and afterwards I recall hearing Zacharias going on about how *he* would've done different than Nathan and won the stead, but I don't recall him ever making a try. Nathan was a good man. Zacharias was a sly one and a scoffer, not fit to touch the dust of his feet. But Nathan was dead, and Zacharias lived."

Paul looked away from the high window, looked back at Becca with eyes that were reflections of her own. "That was the year your Satan-sent worm came and lodged with me."

"You, Pa?" Becca couldn't picture the moonlit girl coming to her sire's bedside with her taunting whispers. Maybe Pa's worm took another shape. She had come to make confession to him. To have it all reversed this way left her uneasy in mind and body. She cursed herself, wishing she'd come up with a better way to escape from Harvest Home and Adonijah.

Ah! the worm breathed. *So that's your true reason for coming to him; not me. If Jamie's boss-man John hadn't said he needed him to mind the fields, and he was going, you'd never have told your sire a word about me.*

"Doubt," Paul was saying. "That's your Devil-worm. You were raised on Wiserways Stead the same as me. You were properly lessoned, told what was right and needful, wrong and sinful. That never changes, what our children learn; as is right! When you teach a child righteousness, Satan hasn't got a chance. Then a time comes when it's not the schoolteacher who asks the questions, and they're not always asked out loud. Because you're well brought up, you know some things aren't to be asked, but old Adam's strong in you. You say, 'Can't be *me* wanting to ask all this *why, why, why,* 'cause I know it's only asking for sorrow. So it must be Satan in my soul, creeping in with this wickedness.'"

"Why your brother had to die," Becca said quietly.

"That was one of mine." Paul held out one hand to her and she took it in both of her own. "But I realized I couldn't go blaming Satan for what was in me alone. I knew that if I did, soon I'd be shifting blame to the Devil for every cursed word I said and deed I did, not just for evil thoughts."

"So…it's me after all. But Gram Phila said—"

"How many years since she knew what it's like to be young? I know what's pained you so, child." Paul leaned forward in his chair and laid his other hand on hers. "Miss Lynn's babe, that so?" He didn't have to wait for her nod. "I knew. What you call the worm, it's been telling you how it's not fair, it's not kind, it's not right?"

She hesitated some before nodding again.

"Well, maybe not. Maybe it hurts you down to where you think you're going to catch a fire in your bones with the pain, maybe it's not kind or fair at all. But I'll tell you the lesson I learned that threw my own doubts back into the depths of Hell where they belonged: Just 'cause a thing's not fair or kind or pleasant doesn't mean it isn't right."

He gathered her closer to him and made her sit on his lap. Tugging mischievously at one long blond braid, he said, "Your sole sin's that you're growing up too fast. Wish it was a true taint you're carrying so you'd not have to go to Harvest Home yet."

"So do I." Becca's tone was hollow. Her sire would need to be deaf and blind not to understand there was more weighing down her soul. Paul had ears and eyes, and the wit to ask. One simple question from him and she blurted out the whole story.

"Adonijah, hm?" he said when she was through. He put her from his lap and looked thoughtful. "Zach's eldest living son, I'm bound, or likely to make himself so, if he's got his father's slippery nature. Well, you put by your worries, Becca. You go lightsome to Harvest Home with the rest of us, and don't you fear. You stay by my side always, as long as it takes and as long as you want, and if we see Adonijah coming up, I'll spin him a tale about how you're helping me with business and can't be bothered. Not as if there won't be enough girls from the other steads to hand him into Paradise."

Becca's face grew hot, hearing her father talk that way, but no preacher could have measured the true gratitude she felt just then. "Would you, Pa? Do that for me?"

"As much as I'm able. Not that I'll stand by for you shirking a woman's proper duty to the others, mind!"

"I can bear that, Pa, long as I don't have to have that Adonijah—"

"No need to name him, darling. I said I'd keep him off you, didn't I? Which reminds me, I promised you a fair trade, secret for secret. I'll show you one reason that yellow-eyed cub of Zach's won't dare talk back to me— short of the fact I can crack his neck like a barley straw."

Paul scraped his chair backward and pulled open the bottom right-hand desk drawer. It was deeper than the others and looked to be stacked full of loose papers, many of them yellowing. Then Paul reached in and lifted them all out atop a wooden tray. Under the tray lay a brown metal box.

"False bottom," Paul explained, opening the box. "Look—but don't tell a soul what you see."

Becca looked into the box. She had seen pictures of such things in Katy's books. She had read stories—a special treat reserved for those children who excelled in learning their lessons, a trip to the small back room of the outbuilding where Katy taught, the room where the precious storybooks were kept safe. She recognized the thing in the box from those stories, though she could hardly make her eyes accept what they saw. Seeing a herd of beef cattle come rumbling over the fields would be easier to believe.

"Pa, how'd you come by a gun?"

Paul chuckled, enjoying the effect his revelation had on her. "And you know it for what it is. That's learning a man can be proud of in his girl-child! You wouldn't recollect it much, the time the traders came and took notice of Eleazar. Just a little bitty thing you were then, still dirty-bottomed and hiding in your mama's skirts every time a stranger came by. Yeah, the traders from our city sat up real straight when they heard that boy of mine go through his book-learning, and they studied him real close when he worked half-stripped in the cookhouse, seeing if his body was half the promise of his mind."

"I didn't think things like strength mattered," Becca said. "Not in the cities."

"Matters *all* over." Paul smacked a fist into his open palm for emphasis. "Getting soft was our death once, and we're not about to make the same mistake twice. We *remember* what happened. Or we die. Out there toward the mountains, beyond where we're civilized. God alone knows what's waiting. And if the mountains split the way they once did and spew out more monsters, all the mind in the world won't last a minute without strong arms to fight them back! Coop or Grange, we need strong men to stand with us, beside us, behind us."

"Yes, Pa." Becca sounded trembly as a new shoot of grain. Paul's face had reddened, a little muscle along his jawline twitching. Her meek words brought him back.

"Sorry, child." He smiled sheepishly. "Didn't think such talk would fright you. You've studied your history, Katy says. You know all about this."

"Some." She was in the back room of the school again, younger, staring at Katy's few saved volumes like they were a treasure trove. In memory she stood tiptoe, reaching up for a bright-covered book, pulling it off a high shelf, except that book wasn't the only one to fall—

"Well, at least your Mama's taught you about the rogue bands, and staying close to home." Her sire's mention of the rogues was ice water thrown over Becca's memories. "It's not just lone women they prey on, you know. Band gets big enough and runs into innocent travelers fewer in number, that's all. Even traders from our city, which is why they don't much care to risk themselves apart from the big fall and spring caravans. It was in springtime they favored Eleazar. One of them was so taken with the boy, he wanted to bring him into the city then and there!"

"Is that when he left?"

"Oh, no." Paul patted her on the head, mightily amused by how innocent his cleverest girl-child could be. "There's order in the cities too, Becca, same as here. All things are equal before the Lord and the Lord King. That man who was so witched by your brother, he was nowhere near alph. Fact, he was a puny-looking thing. If I didn't know better, I'd say he was one of the abominations."

"But they don't allow such in the cities, do they, Pa?"

"They do not. High walls don't change the people inside, or make them any less decent and godfearing. They deal with 'em same as we do."

Becca nodded, recalling a time her Pa probably didn't think she could recall. She'd still been too young for fieldwork when it happened, but not too young to listen and know. One of the lesser men and one of her sibs— barely a stripling—were caught together in a way that—

Abomination!

Becca wasn't sure then what the word meant, but she heard it spoken often enough in the hours that followed the discovery, and she witnessed its effect. Whispers crackled through the stead like brushfire. Men and women together roused Gram Phila from her attic lair to pronounce the ritual sentence from Scripture. The sentence was carried out in the fields. The children were told to stay in the big house seeing-room, with only one of the younger maidens set to mind them. Still Becca managed to hark out the truth of what had happened. *Abomination!* She wondered if they managed it quite the same way in the Coop Cities, and if so, how they executed their judgment on the guilty.

Paul didn't have time to waste on pondering the problems of city dwellers. He seemed more eager to tell Eleazar's story to a receptive hearer. "Puny or not, that fellow's leader heard him out, said maybe the boy had possibilities, but there wasn't any rumors of a web in their city needing new blood. The first man argued with his leader like I never saw a man do and live."

He shrugged away the unfathomable ways of the Coop. "Said that if they waited, something might happen to the boy or some other—now what was that word?—*elic*, I think—some other elic'd snap him up. It's hard to follow them when they get to talking about how they live in the city, but I hear say it's much the same as out here, only different namings for things: webs and elics and coops and Lord King knows what all instead of steads and troops and bloods and granges."

"That the only way they differ, Pa?" Becca asked, still staring at the bright, oily flank of the gun. "Names?"

Another shrug. "We're all men, here or there. Don't go swallowing those hearth-tales whole of how they live sleek and warm in the cities. Your head's too level to get overbalanced with wild stories. I tell you, they're people, same as you and me."

He cleared away a passing frog in his throat and continued. "Anyhow… So your brother's man pleads his case fierce, but the leader stays firm. As is right," Paul reminded her. "But he does look some put out at the thought of a rival elic getting Eleazar, so he takes me aside. We struck a bargain, man to man. I was to pledge him that I'd not send Eleazar off with any independent traders as might happen through Wiserways before reaping time, and by the harvest he'd tell us yes or no, take Eleazar with him or not."

"But if different men came to trade that autumn—?"

Paul beamed with the memory of that long-gone city trader. "There was that in me knew that no matter what he'd have to do to get it, that fellow'd be the one leading the trade party out here come harvest, puny or no. And so he was! But not knowing that yet—just waiting to make sure Eleazar came into his elic—he said that he'd send me word by a trusted man if a vacancy developed suddenly in his group. When I got that word, no matter when, I was to pack off Eleazar to the city with his strongest sibs for guard."

"I see." Becca watched how the lamplight rippled over the barrel of the gun. It was an old one, older even than some of the weapons she'd read of in the stories. (That little book that had fallen off the shelf when she tugged out its neighbor, did that hold pictures of guns like this? It had soft sides, tattered yellow paper, and what was written inside....) The gun held Becca's sight. Maybe it was a new thing made to an old design—she couldn't say. "That was why he gave you the gun, then. To protect Eleazar on his way."

"Except no word came until Harvest Home, and then he was back, like he'd promised. He took Eleazar off with him and never seemed to recall he'd left this in my keeping." Paul scratched his head. "Even the city men get careless. I didn't see any need to remind him."

He picked up the gun and rotated it slowly so that she saw it from every angle. Becca didn't cringe, in spite of all the tales she'd read and heard about such weapons. Didn't Pa tell her not to heed tales? Something in her hungered for more than a look at the gun. She wondered what her father would say if she asked to touch it.

She inched closer, hoping to manage matters so that her hands brushed against it by accident. Her mind filled with questions about what such an alien thing might feel like. How heavy would it be? How awkward or how graceful to hold? She got near enough to look more closely into the metal box. It held a knot of soft cloth that smelled like the harvester's insides—oily—and a little metal can. A small, lumpy brown envelope lay there too, and a folded sheet of ambering paper. She thought it would be harmless if she reached for them instead of the gun.

"What're you after, woman?" Her pa slammed the box lid shut so fast that he almost caught her fingers.

"I just wondered—"

"Eve wondered too." He rattled off the old truism. "More than was healthy for Adam. You've got no need to be trifling with bullets. Next you'll spill them all over the floor and if I miss picking up one—just one!—*then* where's the secret of what I've got here?" He tapped the box and it rang.

"Bullets?" She'd read about those, too.

"Rope in those eyes, young one, before they fall out of your head." Paul opened the box just wide enough for him to slip the gun back inside. "You're not the only one on this stead who knows what this thing is—though you're the only one 'side from me who knows it's here. Me and Eleazar. Now get along. Or don't you have any chores?"

Becca had chores aplenty. In the succeeding days, she went through the motions of fieldwork and housework with a lighter heart. She sang as she worked on her dress for the maidens' dance and even helped her sib, Lenora, with a tricky bit of needlework on her frock. For the first time in weeks she felt young and free again, with the coming festival something to anticipate joyfully, not to shudder from and avoid. Pa would protect her. She was as special to him as Eleazar had been to that unknown Coop city man, and he'd look after her the same way.

Feeling Pa's wing over her made her bold. At noon meal one day she raised her eyes up from her plate and gave Jamie a look that Hattie would have called straight-out brazen. He met her eyes for an instant, then looked away fast. *Like he'd been the maiden and me the man*, she thought. But then common sense broke in, reminding her that Jamie had always stickled to the proprieties. Exchanging invitations with their eyes before all the troop wasn't something they had any right to do.

Still, she wanted him to share her relief and her joy. So close to harvest time, the women were supposed to keep their fieldwork to a minimum and stay close to the home buildings. The treasured machines were trundled out— Wiserways had come by two harvesters through some stroke of lucky trading years ago—and Paul didn't need to call on so many human hands in the fields. Jamie was a good driver, so Becca waited until house rumor said it was his day to ride the machine, then stole herself off to the barn where he'd have to bring back the harvester at day's end.

She heard the chug and crunch of the homecoming machine, smelled the reek of its burning fuel. The earthen barn floor was chewed up with the marks of its treads, full of the oily stink of the tools and truck needed to maintain it. Its mate had a barn all to itself, but she'd made sure which one Jamie was driving. On Wiserways there was never any question about putting things back in their exact and proper place, from the most precious pin to the biggest field machine. She stood back in the shadows and waited.

She watched him drive the harvester in, cut its power, hop down with the same heartstopping grace she'd seen in his every movement since the time she was old enough to notice such things about a man. Though the weather was cooling fast—fast enough for Becca to have put on her shoes—he was still stained with sweat. She saw him fumble through his pockets for a kerchief to mop his brow, muttering about how it must have fallen out when—

"Would you like to use mine?" she asked, stepping out of hiding.

"*Becca!*"

Why was there no pleasure in the way he cried her name? She took a step back, suddenly ashamed without knowing any reason for it. Jamie's expression reflected the horror in his voice. This went beyond surprise. Pain bit into Becca's chest. She'd intruded, but she never thought to have her Jamie treat her like an intruder. Then, abruptly, that terrible look fled his face, replaced by the soft, loving gaze she cherished. "Becca, how'd you manage—?" He came into her arms, embracing her with his warmth and the pungent scent of his body.

No one was around. There was little chance of discovery. "Kiss me, Jamie." She wanted something safe to cling to, something even stronger in her eyes than Pa's promised protection. He gave her what she demanded, tenderness on his side, raw hunger on hers. There was no middle ground in that kiss. She wanted more.

But—

"No, love." He put her questing hands away from him. "There's risk." His eyes seemed tired, his whole face wrung out with some unguessable strain.

"I doubt there is," she replied, and told him all she'd gleaned from Pa about how highly she was held in the alph's esteem. "Even were we caught, he'd grant a mercy."

"For you, maybe." Jamie's hands stroked back the wisps of golden hair escaping from her braids. "For me only if I was old enough to claim the Kiss or the Sign from any woman."

"You'd best not claim it from just *any* woman when

you're old enough," Becca teased. "You do and that's the last of my mercy on you."

Jamie wasn't smiling. "When I'm old enough to command such blessings, you're all the key to Paradise I'll ever need. Pa says he'll keep Adonijah off you, but there's other men—"

Becca knew. Becca had always known, but turned away from thinking of it. She'd told Pa she could bear it, but it still made her feel stained. What waited for her at Harvest Home wasn't anything she'd seek, given the choice.

Choices aren't for women, the worm whispered. *That's what they taught us, and dragged up Eve's sorry choice as proof that they were in the right. They've always blamed as much as they dared on women's choices, as if they'd done no harm with any of their own.*

"I'll only do so much as I must," she told him. Then all the fear and all the longing in her gushed up from the pit of her soul and came out in one wild cry of despair: "Oh Jamie, Jamie, let's run off 'til Harvest Home is done! My brother's in the city. We could go to him. Could be they need new blood in their troops. They'd take us. Pa says city life's 'most like ours, but it can't be so. He's never been, he can't know. Maybe you and I can—"

He silenced her babblings with a kiss that was no more than a sop. She felt nothing and no one behind the pressure of his lips. Her heart wouldn't have it; she gave him back far more than he offered her, and her love-longing clothed it all in sweet lies.

Then he said, "You know that's silly talk, Becca. This is our place, not the Coop city. Wait. Bear with it. You know I won't hold you any less dear for doing—doing what you've got to do at Harvest Home. And I know that you—you'd feel the same for me if I—" He made a funny sound in his throat. "I won't be young forever. Things will change for us. We've got to bide until they do."

"Things will change for me sooner than that, if I'm bespoke at Harvest Home." She couldn't help sounding sullen.

"You said Pa wouldn't—"

"I said he'd keep me from Adonijah. But that one's his sire's favorite, too. You didn't see how he went dressed like a king at Makepeace. If something should happen to leave this stead beholden to Zach's—"

"Lord avert it," Jamie said quickly.

"Lord avert it," Becca agreed. "But if so, and I'm the price of helping Wiserways, special or not, Pa'll pay me over. You remember the Scripture tale of Jacob and Rachel."

Jamie did. "Jacob came to Laban's stead looking for a wife. He wanted Laban's pretty daughter, Rachel, but Laban gave him Leah. Then an evil came and stole off most of Laban's herds, so Jacob offered to trade the other alph fresh stock for his pretty daughter, and Laban did what he had to do to save his stead from hunger." A strange bitterness touched Jamie's eyes as he said that. "The way we all do what we must."

Becca hugged him to her tight, yearning to work a woman's magic that would press his body into hers forever. Nothing mattered to her but taking the sorrow out of his eyes. "Never mind, Jamie-love," she murmured in his ear. "Harvest Home will come and go, and I'll do all I can with Pa to have him keep me home another year. By next year you'll have rights to me—maybe even breeding rights, if you work hard enough; who knows? And in another year or so…" She wouldn't mention a challenge; he'd just know.

"A year," he repeated, and this time all the hunger was in the last kiss he gave her before they parted.

She didn't have the chance to see him privately again. The actual harvest came around and the women were told to keep from the fields. "Something to do with manlore," Hattie explained to little Susanna, who was just old enough to feel the blood of Eve's fatal curiosity rising in her veins.

All the women, young and old, sat together in the seeing-room. The men had taken all the boys with them into the fields, short of those at the breast and those who still just toddled along, clutching their mothers' skirts. The final weeks before Harvest Home were a kind of holiday, especially for women with field duties, but that didn't mean all work stopped. Work never did stop, on a well-run stead. Leisure courted the Devil. You had to keep busy, whether with hands, back, or mind. Learning was as much of a duty as weeding the rows of kale and carrots. When other work didn't call to be done, a virtuous woman took or gave lessoning.

That was what Hattie was doing with little Susanna and her like-aged sibs, teaching them the beginnings of custom and law. That is, she taught whenever Susanna didn't interrupt her with another question. The child was Thalie's first, with her mama's chestnut hair and eyes a mix of Thalie's brown and Paul's bright green, but with none of Thalie's discretion. "Why?" she demanded again and again. "Why can't we help with the harvest?"

"We're not needed," Hattie told her. "If we were, we'd be sent for."

"That's not right!" Becca looked up from her book and heard her younger sib pipe a strident protest. "Other times we *have* to help, even when there's enough men to do the chores. Teach us not to fear hard work, they say then, in springtime. Why's springtime any different from fall? Why do they take the growing boys into the fields now, when they tell them to stay home for their own good all summer long? Why?"

Hattie rolled her eyes. Her belly was big, and Miss Lynn had said how near her time was. "Thalie, love…"

Before Susanna could get another *why* out of her mouth, her mother grabbed her by the back of her dress and dragged her out of the seeing-room. Pretty soon everyone heard the sound of a switch teaching manners.

Gram Phila cackled. She had the best place, a chair near the hearth. This holiday-time was special for her too, one of the few occasions she came down out of her aerie under the big house roof-pole. The nameless serving girl who tended the stead crone sat on a cricket-stool at her feet, ready to fetch and carry and tuck up the blankets layering the old woman like petals. The few words she spoke for courtesy's sake came out harsh and raspy. Mostly she held her peace.

When Susanna and Thalie came back, the girl-child took her place quietly in the group around Hattie's chair and never asked another question. Hattie went on with her lesson.

"Becca, you'd best join us." Selena motioned her over to her own circle of young women, all unbespoke maidens, all safely through their Changes, not a one of whom had ever attended a Harvest Home before this.

Very reluctantly Becca gave her book back into Katy's keeping. The teacher had brought out a goodly portion of her precious horde to while away the hours until supper needed making and the men came home. This one had fine, grand pictures in it, and tales so wild there was no danger a person would believe them for a minute. Yet they still could captivate, those swaggering stories.

Becca especially favored the picture of the metal-clad man slaying that fearsome dragon-beast. The story made him out to be a man of God, slaying Satan in monster's shape, but Becca kept putting her father's face on the knight. Sometimes the monster he slew had the face of Adonijah. Sometimes a second book laid its ghost over the one she read, handwritten lines obscuring knight and dragon both. She shivered, blinked hard, and the ghost was gone.

"Now I know a lot of you girls think you know it all," Selena was saying as Becca settled into her place on the beaten bark floorcloth. "You've served your sibs once or twice and you think you've got the whole male populace eating out of your hand."

"Not what Lenora had 'em doing out of her hand," Marion whispered, tittering.

"Eating, though…" Del snickered.

Selena ignored them. She reached under her straight-backed chair and lifted a small wooden box into her lap. "You're all good and dutiful girls, and there hasn't been a woman out of Wiserways these many years but has made a good marriage and was a credit to this stead. Breeding shows, and upbringing, and that's pure education. The men who'll see you dance at Harvest Home might be alphs already or alphs someday. You catch their eye, you gauge their status, and if they're somebodies, they could be the making of your futures. Remember that!"

"I bet Lenora's thought of nothing else for months," Del hissed in Becca's ear. "Like to wore the paint off her bedpost for practicing."

This jibe Selena did not ignore. Her hand flashed out and slapped Del's cheek scarlet. "At least Lenora knows what counts, young woman! When you're old and unclaimed and a winnowing time comes—Lord King forbid!—then maybe you'll wish you'd spent some little time with the bedpost yourself!"

In a milder tone, she addressed the rest of the maidens' circle. "Now doing for a man's all fine and right, but there's ways and ways to do. You're going to learn the ways that make you stick in his mind better than if you were in your times and were his first woman. You're going to be more than a good time in the dark at Harvest Home. You're going to make the man who chooses you lose sleep and yearn after you until he comes to your Pa and makes his offer."

The box in her lap opened on leather hinges. She took out several accurately carved objects and passed them out to the girls, one apiece. Their expressions ranged everywhere from shock to boredom as they turned the wooden phalloi over and over in their hands. Every vein, every surface change, every small area that could be called distinct from its neighbor was painstakingly colored and numbered accordingly to make it an important individual feature of the whole.

"I hope she doesn't tell that old story 'bout the girl who expected the real thing to be painted and numbered like this," Del muttered.

"Why? How does it go?" Lenora asked.

"Sure does beat hell out of raggy dolls," Marion

whispered loud enough for Becca to hear. "Not lifesize, but it don't signify. Look at Lenora with hers. Don't you just know what she's thinking!"

"Pay attention, now," Selena admonished, and the lesson began.

Chapter Six

Little baby on my knee,
Hush, hush, hush-a-bye,
In my breast no milk for thee,
Sweetest babe of mine.
Mary sweet heard her lament;
Hush, hush, hush-a-bye.
For her Son's sake milk was sent,
Sweetest babe of mine.

"You get out of here!" Thalie jammed her fists on her hips and tilted her head back to glare at Paul. Becca hurried through the seeing-room with a basket full of clean cloths, but she couldn't resist slowing her pace some to watch the little woman face down Pa. She had to smile, what with the flustered look Pa was giving his youngest wife. He knew as well as any man that only one thing would give a woman the backbone to speak to him that sharp and short, but it still came as a surprise.

"I thought she'd gone to her room," he managed to say. His big hands worked the brim of his straw hat into a tight curl.

"Well, the Lord had other ideas and the baby shared 'em. You want us to haul her upstairs to suit you?"

"Yes—I mean, no, but—in there?" He nodded toward the closed door. "There's no bed in that room, hardly space to turn around. Will she be all right?"

Thalie laughed in his face, adding to his stunned and stupid look. At the door, Becca dragged her feet some more just to hear the young wife say, "Where'd we birth 'em before beds? If you want to be useful, go keep watch for Miss Lynn. Though, God knows, I don't reckon she'll ride here faster than this child."

Becca slipped through the door and shut it quietly behind her. It was like passing into a different world. Outside, in the seeing-room, all the windows had been left unshaded to let in as much sunlight as possible. In this room—more of a den or closet—the single window had been curtained with a double fold of bedlinen. A cooling breeze still managed to work its way through the cloth, but the light was comfortably dim.

Hattie lay on a thin mattress that the women had dragged in from one of the bedrooms. Becca cast a worried look over her mother's pale face. She set down her basket, then took a folded cloth from it and made as if to dab away the traces of sweat still on Hattie's forehead.

"Leave it be." Gram Phila spoke out of the darkness. Her voice crackled like the scum of ice on a frozen puddle. She sat on the only chair the tiny room would allow, her nameless handmaiden sitting cross-legged at her feet. "She's been made as easy as she deserves. In sorrow we shall bear our children, the Lord decreed. So be it."

"So be it," the echo came. It came from Ray, who sat on a pillow beside the basin and pitcher to Hattie's left. It came from Selena, who leaned against the birthing frame and tested the joints for strain. It even came from Gram Phila's girl, whose eyes seemed to see too much and nothing.

Becca's lips moved, but she said no *So be it*. These past eight hours had been more hard-lessoning than she'd ever wanted to receive. When her mama was taken with the pains, she and little Susanna had been the only girls present in the seeing-room. The other maidens and children were helping in the cookhouses. Harvest time was time for putting food by, and every hand was needed. By rights Becca should have been there, too, but Katy told her that for once there were hands enough; Becca would be more use helping Susanna catch up with her reading. They'd been sitting with heads bowed over the same book when Hattie lurched to her feet with a groan, a puddle forming where she stood.

Selena took charge immediately, ordering the younger child to run out to the fields, manlore be damned, and send one of the men after fetching Miss Lynn.

"I'm afraid," Susanna had said, chin trembling.

"What do you have to fear?"

"We daren't go into the fields while the harvest—"

"This is a birthing time! You're too young to know all that means. Man'd have to be straight loony to stand on ceremony when it's a question of birth."

"Selena, don't send the child," Hattie said. "With the

men, you never know. It's not like it's my first. You could midwife this one yourself, and there's Gram Phila, and—"

"And who's to make it right with Paul if this is the one time you need herbwife help? Such things do happen—God forbid—and afterwards it's too late to make amends. Could be as I will be the one to bring your babe to birth, but at least we'll be able to say we sent for Miss Lynn. We'll be clear of blame. Get going, child!" This to Susanna. "I'll back you up if there's any trouble."

"I could go instead of Susanna," Becca said. She didn't say how grateful she would be if they'd let her go. Ever since her mama had risen from her chair, the back of her bearing skirts drenched with the outpouring of her broken waters, Becca had been wanting nothing more than to escape.

"You stay," Selena directed. "We'll need someone to fetch and carry within the house, and the rest of the girls and women have enough to do with the preserving. You'll be wed and gone and passing through this time yourself soon enough. This is one lesson you'd do well to get now."

So she stayed. She helped Thalie drag down the mattress for Hattie, she brought fresh water and ran to one of the cookhouses to set a kettle boiling over the fire. The wife supervising that place accused her of intruding on the winter preparations until Becca told her the reason why. She was promised all the boiled water she might need, and sent back to her mama's aid. She climbed up the attic stairs to tell Gram Phila she was wanted. She helped the nameless girl bring the old woman down the stairs, helped Selena set up the birthing frame, helped Ray hang the doubled sheets over the window, helped wherever she was asked or saw that help was needed.

Through it all she tried to be deaf and blind to Hattie. The panting and the soft moans, the subdued voice asking for a sip of water, the shuffle of feet pacing back and forth, back and forth over the small stretch of floor left clear in the little room, none of these were Becca's mama. As the labor worsened and Hattie asked to sit on the birthing frame, Becca took up a post by the window, hiding her face behind one edge of the folded sheet with the excuse that she was watching for Miss Lynn's coming.

Kindly Ray clucked over her fragile ploy. Ray was the smallest, the plumpest of the stead's mothers, the one most children came running to for comfort when they had hurts to be kissed well or tears to be dried. She couldn't cook to save her life, but she brought a warmth with her everywhere, greater than any kindled on a cookhouse hearth.

"It's no punishment, Becca." She stood right behind the girl and spoke so that no other ears could hear. "It's only what waits for us all. Oh, I know how bad it sounds and how frightening it looks, but you mind me: It's a pain worth feeling. You just watch how your mama looks once she holds that babe in her arms. Shoo, she labored to bear you the same way, and you ever see any grudging in her eyes when she looks at you now?"

"Ray…"

"Yes, child?"

"What if I'd been born a boy?"

"What?"

"I was let live because I was a girl when Wiserways needed girls. What do we need now? What if this babe's not the right—?"

Strong fingers dug into Becca's arm. No comfort or

kindliness shaded Ray's voice, hard as sharpened flint. "One more ill-luck word like that in this room and you'll wish you'd never been born at all. Get out! Make an excuse and go. Lord King send you everything you wish on your poor mama and worse besides. Get!"

Ray's hands dragged her away from the window and propelled her toward the door. "Becca's going to fetch us some more clean cloths," she told the rest, smiling. A last whispered curse flew out of the room after Becca as Ray slammed the door.

She killed as much time as possible fetching the cloths, trying and failing to drive Ray's words from her mind.

Some words don't die so easily, the old, feared voice of the worm slithered through her mind. *No matter how hard you wish they'd go, they linger. You try to push them away, to bury them deep as bones, but they remain. They wait until something comes to scrape away the earth thrown over them and let in the light. Then there they are, waiting. You remember the words, Becca. You know you remember.*

I remember lots of words, Becca thought.

Not like these. Not like the words you read in that little book. My words. You were bright, for a little one. Not much older than Susanna, were you? Katy knew you were smart. Even a teacher who loves learning recognizes when too smart's the same as dead, for a woman. So she took that book away. My story. How much did you read before she found you there, puzzling over the words written in my hand?

I know all I need to know. The thought was fierce, a wall against the worm. *What's past is done. You're past. It's got nothing to do with my life.*

Or everything. You remember reading all that I remembered? About how things used to be, the tales my grandma handed down from hers? But things changed. The world changed. Women changed. Oh, not all at once, but eventually. We couldn't take a man except when our poor, scared, starved bodies said so—not even if we wanted to take him! Try it and he'd tear us so bad that most died of it. So we learned to wait for the sign that said we were ready, that we were—"taking" women, you call it. In our times. By my day, it seemed like we were all alike again—different from how we'd once been, sure, but when everyone shares the same difference, it's the throwbacks had better watch out.

I don't know what that word—

Yes, you do. You know more than you're comfortable knowing, but you wouldn't have it any other way. You know that too, Becca.

Becca began to sing as she folded cloths into a basket, trying to drive the worm's voice from her mind. Only it wasn't any worm; it was a girl who waited in a spill of moonlight, her body streaked with blood. No matter how loud the song on Becca's lips, shed blood was always louder. The ghost-girl hovered in her mind, holding the ghost-book to her breasts.

Wouldn't you like to know the ending of my story? she crooned, holding out the book for Becca. Every letter had been redrawn in red. Katy loves books, would never destroy a one, once it came into her care. Don't you ever wonder if it's still there? Wouldn't you love to know?

Becca picked up her basket and ran. As little as she wanted to go back into the birthing room, she couldn't stay away, even if there was no ghost to harry her: There'd be too much talk. Back in the room, she remained at her mother's side. She kept her eyes fixed on Hattie's face because it was preferable to meeting Ray's hostile glare, even by accident.

"She's sleeping some," Selena said, standing over her. "Got a little respite from the pains, as happens sometimes. Could be Miss Lynn'll meet this child after all."

"Lord grant it," Becca rattled off.

"Lord *King* grant it," Ray prompted. It was no curse to speak of him so long as none spoke of his dread sword. Some claimed it was even a fortunate thing, calling on him with reverence at a birth so that he'd look kindly on the child and turn his choice elsewhere after.

A knock at the door roused Hattie from her doze. Thalie stuck her head into the cramped room. "Sun's almost down. The men'll be coming back soon. Paul says maybe Miss Lynn was at another stead, not Makepeace. If so, they'll have to dispatch their own runner to fetch her."

"Which other stead?"

Thalie shrugged. "No way to tell. If it's a far one, or if she's got business there that's still not done, who knows when we'll see her?"

"Least they could do is send a junior herbwife," Selena said, getting huffy as a hen. "Send *somebody*."

"But you could midwife as good as any junior herbwife," Ray reminded her. "Why need—?"

"It's the principle of it. Well, never mind. Hattie, love, how are you?"

"Starting again," Hattie said, panting. "Strong."

"Help her stand. You, Becca, let her lean on you. You too, girl." She pointed at Gram Phila's handmaiden.

The nameless girl did as she was told, stepping under Hattie's right arm as docilely as an ox going under the yoke. They walked the floor with Hattie for only a short while before the woman demanded to sit on the birthing frame.

The frame looked old enough to have served Gram Phila when she'd been the young wife of some forgotten Wiserways alph. It resembled an outhouse with the walls and roof torn away, half the seat gone too, nothing but four tall uprights and the cross-pieces sufficient to link them stably. It was fragile to the eye, made of what looked like a clutch of saplings lashed together with rawhide. Only no saplings grew near Wiserways—true tree country lay farther east, by Hallow Stead—and the lashings never showed the stains of sweat or slopped water the way rawhide did. As Becca helped her mother to hoist up her skirt and perch on the narrow seat, she felt the cool smoothness of the framework and knew it for citymade. The false rawhide holding it together, forming the hand-holds for a laboring woman, must have been the same.

Selena knelt in front of Hattie, lifted her bunched and sweated skirts, and made a quick examination. She rocked back on her heels and said, "Can't be helped. You two girls run out to the cookhouse where Becca set the kettle and fetch that boiled water. Don't spill any on yourselves, mind! I can birth this child, but we'll need Miss Lynn for sure if you sear off your hides."

Becca had to hold herself back to keep from flying out of the room. Gram Phila's servant loped after her with an easy stride and an indifferent attitude. She kept behind Becca all the way to the cookhouse, though she could have caught up with her and passed her if she chose. Unlike Becca, her legs weren't hampered by long skirts. The dress she wore was little more than a man's checkered shirt, fitting loose and hitting just above the knee.

The cookhouse was deserted, despite the fact that the day was waning and the men would be wanting their supper. There were no big meals at harvest time, what with all the work of putting food by to occupy the women. The men ate cold takings out in the fields, sometimes adding to their fare with such small creatures as they surprised between the rows of rye and wheat grass. They would brag about their catches at supper, show off the miserable small skins, and act as if they'd done a grand thing. Only last year old Garret had taken Becca aside and offered her one of those paltry little scraps of gray fur in exchange for the Kiss of Thanks. She refused and ran—she knew he had the right to ask for that favor, with Pa's consent, yet shunned the thought that he sought to buy her, like a Scripture harlot—but later she saw that same bit of fluff spread out on Marion's pillow like a trophy.

"What are you gawking at? Course they've left this cookhouse empty. You know they're all hiding sooner than meet with us. Chores are just an excuse. A birthing woman frights 'em all worse than death himself."

Becca's head jerked back over one shoulder. Gram Phila's girl grinned at the effect she'd made just by speaking out loud.

"What's wrong now? You believe the stories about how they yanked my tongue when I was born? Not much! That'd be smart, all right, put the old woman up in the rafters with a mute to keep her company. Why, you'd have her go stark mad before the next one up ever had the chance to kill her." The girl chuckled. "Not that that'd be easy. She's still fair sharp, old Gram, and she's taught me fighting skill enough to make up for what she can't do for herself."

"You know how to fight?"

The girl showed her teeth in something near a human smile. "As well as any man. Maybe better. They need to pick up a stick or a rock to kill, if they can't get the neck-snap on you." The grin widened. "I don't. Want me to show you?"

Becca's plain terror made the nameless girl laugh. "Not kill *you*, you great fool! Think it through: What'd I gain by that except have them kill me? Unless I ran off, and I'm not dumb enough for that. They say the rogue bands carry more than sticks and stones, and they don't keep a woman longer than she's useful. Which isn't that long, Gram says. I'm not dying split; not me."

"If you do want to," Becca spoke slowly and carefully, "how will you teach me fighting?"

"Willing to learn, are you?"

Becca tried to look indifferent. "Gram Phila's the stead crone, and that means wisdom. If it's a skill she's mastered well enough to teach, must be a skill it wouldn't hurt me any to learn."

"You're a smooth one," the girl mused. "All right, I'll lesson you, but you've *got* to keep a closed mouth about it."

"Swear to God and Lord King witness."

The girl spat. "Lord King. God does for me. Next thing is, I'll clear it with Gram—no problem there, just courtesy—and she'll fix it so you're the one who brings us up our food. That's when you'll have your lessons. Deal?"

Becca gave the girl her hand the way she'd seen the men do. "Only one question," she said. "Why are you willing to share something like this with me?"

The girl's thin mouth contorted with a joke she wasn't telling. "Words fly up faster than birds. Think we don't hear all the talk, up there in the rafters? How you did for Miss Lynn's baby, what happened over to Makepeace, how your brother's gone for a city man, how Pa keeps a warm eye on you, all that and the whispers—let's just say that Gram Phila sees something of herself in you, Becca. You won't be the one to kill her, but you might be the stead crone after that, killing her killer. Revenge tastes sweet and smooth, even if it's just second-hand and it only feeds a ghost."

Becca shuddered. She'd had her fill of ghosts. "But I'm going to Harvest Home," she said. "Someone might ask to marry me, and I'll go elsewhere to live." *Lord* forbid! "How can I be stead crone here at Wiserways then?" *And* would I want to?

Those teeth again, sharp and white, like the God-cursed face of famine or Adonijah's greedy leer. "Told you we hear a lot. You don't want to leave Wiserways, deny it in truth if you can. The way Pa favors you, he might offer a good deal to any man that asks for your hand: You get your keep here and your husband to visit you only when you're in your times. Fostered wives; it's been done. Katy the schooler'd back him up, 'cause she wants you to stay too. Who'd pass up the chance to have another wife without need to shoulder the burden of feeding her? Oh, you'll live and die on Wiserways, sure. Gram says so."

Becca caught herself praying that God would bend His will to Gram Phila's prophecies. It *did* make sense. Even if Becca couldn't picture herself sneaking up on whoever would be the stead crone's successor, the bare notion must seem reasonable to the no-name girl. The inevitable pattern of every steadwoman's future held some killing. Better to hold death's hand as an ally; better that than to meet him someday in the sudden dark, a victim.

"You want me to swear I'll avenge her? Is that the price for lessoning me how to fight?" Becca asked.

The question amused the girl. "And why not swear to avenge me too? When Gram dies, I die. No thanks. Vengeance comes too cheaply. You can pay me off in dearer goods. I teach you, you teach me. I hear you're a good teacher; that's why I'm making this offer to begin."

"What could I possibly know that you—?"

The girl's face was so pale that her lips were no different color than the rest of her skin. Her hair was also a sickly, faded yellow, haloing her face with wisps escaping from the small, tight bun binding it back. Only her eyes had some beauty—a brilliant blue-green that sparkled with all the animation of a furiously active mind.

They fairly glowed as the girl replied, "Teach me the Sign of Gratitude and the Kiss of Thanks. Lesson me how to worship a man's body so that, when it's done, it's him that worships me. Bring me one of those wooden things the women use to learn about men. Show me how to move so a man's eyes follow you and his blood heats for you. Teach me the ways that make 'em want you more and more, and what makes 'em fight to the death to keep you."

Becca's cheeks burned. The girl's eyes were blazing now, the pupils dilating in the shadowy cookhouse. The fire under the kettle of boiling water turned her face into a fierce mask, half white and half red.

"I don't know if that's fit for me to teach," Becca told her. "Gram Phila might not allow it."

"Fuck Gram Phila." The girl slapped down Becca's hand even as it rose to cover her own mouth. "Don't come all maidenish, damn it! You know you only do it for show."

"Talk like that's wicked."

"*Your* lips are clean. *I'm* the one said it, and I'll say it again, if I like. It's safe; no one here to hark but you and me. Time you heard straight speech, if you're going to turn out strong enough to survive."

"What you said about Gram—"

"Who's got the better right?" More flicks of hair stood out from the no-name girl's face, firelight burning through them.

"No one's got the right to use such language about Gram." Becca heard her mother's prim tone come creeping into her words. "Especially not you."

"You come minding me that I'm alive because of that old bitch and I'll toss you right into the hearth! Did I have choice? I was born extra, a babe for the hillside. Maybe I'd've died there, but maybe someone would've picked me up, taken me to a different stead. To a *real* life! Not to dwelling all my days up in rafters with a crazy old crone, and not even a name to call mine. So yes, *fuck* Gram Phila and all she ever did for me. Suck out the days I've had, drink my life, tied it fast to hers, that's what she did. I'm her watchdog now—that's the only reason she taught me fighting and killing, to keep her alive that much longer. When she dies, I die: They'll kill me. The new crone will bring her own nameless girl-child—or boy, if it's a man who wrings Gram's neck for her."

She was a hard knot of fury as she said, "Now tell me you didn't know *that*."

"I knew." Hattie's empty self-righteousness deserted Becca. She had overheard enough cookhouse talk about Gram Phila. "When I was seven, one of the senior women vanished. The others said she'd been planning to kill Gram Phila and take her place."

"I remember her." The girl's lipless smile grew more chilling by the minute. "After, I fetched a man to bring her corpse away. I was too young to do more. I was seven, too, just like you. Even then I felt his eyes on me." The corners of her mouth pulled back farther, tasting the memory.

"You only seven! Did the man try anything? Did Pa know?"

"Gram Phila did." The girl's laughter became an old woman's relishment of the past. "She didn't let him touch me, but she used the promise of later, when I hit Changes, to keep him as her eyes and ears among the men."

"Who—who is it? Which man?"

"He's dead, so what's it to you? Unless you think there's someone else needs to know."

"No. No one." Becca swelled with questions she wanted to ask and didn't dare. "Oh, don't worry yourself about what *Pa* might say." The name was pronounced with contempt. "The less he knows about Gram Phila's doings, the sounder he sleeps. Gram was a pretty decent herbwife in her day."

"'Herbwife'?" Becca saw no connection. Could be the no-name girl was crazy after all.

"And if what she fed me didn't work to stave off my being—blessed by his seed—the hillside don't ask any questions." Her eyes devoured Becca's look of revulsion and were avid for more. Strange things grew in attic shadows. "Anyhow, we've got another spy these days. It's not Gram's way to wait and see what the future brings. She makes her own. I've learned that much from her. I'm enough for a man to use and forget, but if you teach me how to be more—how to please him so he *remembers* me—odds are I can save myself that way, when the old bitch dies. Even at seven I had something that held their eyes. That big sib of yours who went to Makepeace with you—Tom?—he's got the alph's mark on him."

"It's ill luck to talk that way about a man."

"Who's to hear?" The girl's eyes focused on a future only she saw. "I've been putting myself in his way whenever Gram sends me on downstairs errands. You teach me the right skills and I'll manage to do more for him than pass the time of day. *He'll* remember me. He'll be alph some day, and he won't let them kill me. An alph has that power."

An alph has all *power,* Becca thought. *And for Tom to be alph of this stead means that he and Pa—* She didn't want to think about that. Let the no-name have her fantasies. It wouldn't hurt anyone, and it might serve to soften her captivity. Lesson for lesson, they agreed. So be it.

"Fine," Becca said, rustling up a couple of thickly quilted potholders from the cookhouse sideboard. "I'll teach you whatever you want, only right now we'd better get this water back to the house before Selena comes after us with a stick."

They toted the covered kettle between them, taking care not to let it swing too wildly, watching out so their legs didn't brush it. Some of the younger men were about the place, standing in their threes and fours in the dusk, being damned sure never to let the little groups dwindle to twos and cause speculation. They ate where they stood, cold hand-food scavenged from the stead larders and storeplaces. Becca caught sight of Jamie standing with Sam and John and Noah, passing a bottle around among them.

Willie scampered past, carrying a torch to light the lanterns. The autumn air was unnaturally still, the boy's feet sounding startlingly loud as they pounded over the dirt paths, crunched across the occasional swath of gravel.

A bony old plowhorse was tethered in front of the house. Becca would have spilled the boiled water in her hurry to scramble inside and greet Miss Lynn. The no-name held her back, laid a finger to her lips, all her perilous free talk folded up and stored back under her tongue. Her eyes spoke for her in the lantern light: *Hark and learn.*

They walked into the house calm and proper, eyes on their chore. Someone had lit the lamps and stoked up the fire in the seeing-room. Paul was the only one there. Why had Thalie allowed him to return? Becca's glance edged past her pa's boots as he sat in the big chair before the fire, though she couldn't resist stealing a quick look at his face. Sorrow was there, and the marks of wear and weariness carving their signs deeper yet into his mouth and eyes.

"You're a little late, Becca," he said.

Late. A swarm of words squirmed up in her throat. Gram's girl had a face of stone. A sharp smell glided through the air, the sweet-sour bite of alcohol. Paul nodded toward the closed door across the room.

"Go see your mama."

The kettle was deadweight between the two girls. The no-name stopped at the door, made Becca set their load down, then leaned against the wall and slid down to squat beside the jamb. Becca pulled the knob, but not before trading one last look with Gram's strange, fearsome handmaiden.

And in that small eternity, her thoughts came together, pouring over a past now so clear, so very clear—

"*I was seven too, just like you.*"

Seven when I was seven, born the same year. Born for the hillside, because Wiserways didn't need any more girls. But she looks older than me; could it still be so? First come, first saved, but what if—? Pa favors my mama and the children she bears him. Even if she was born first, the last girl Wiserways needed for awhile, when I was born female it changed. Pa changed it!

"An alph has that power."

An alph has all power.

Becca's life tore out of her hands the same way some unlucky soul was sent to tear that girl-child out of her mother's arms. "*But you promised me, Paul! You said she could live!*" The alph's decision to make, the alph's decision to change. The Lord giveth, the Lord King taketh away. And if that was so, the girl *had* had a name once. But instead of the hillside taking her, she'd been passed upstairs to serve Gram Phila all the days of the old woman's life.

Could it have fallen out that way? The part of Becca's brain where thoughts turned into words rejected it. The part where feelings reigned—hunches, instincts, "a girl-child's fool notions"—that part said yes and yes and yes. It only took a look into the nameless, once-upon-a-time named eyes to know.

You owe me, Becca. A twitch at the corner of the girl's tight mouth confirmed it. *You're too smart to deny what you know. Or too foolish. That's why you're free and living, and why I'm locked away to plot my own survival when the time comes: Because your mama's womb breeds smart ones, fresh young shoots of the Knowing Tree. And isn't it wonderful, the taste of knowledge? The one taste that lingers forever on the tongue.*

"Becca?" Miss Lynn opened the door. She was smiling. "Come in, child. You have a new sister to welcome."

The herbwife conducted her inside, shut the door after. Hattie lay on the floor, on the mattress, her back propped up with a mountain of pillows. All the thick smells of blood and sweat had been scoured away, flung out the door with the old bedclothes and the vanished birthing frame. The sheet was down from the window, a slip of purple and gray sky caught in the casement. None of the other wives were present.

"About time you got here," Miss Lynn chided gently. "We had to use what water there was left in the house jugs to wash her clean. I did what I could to guard your mama and the babe from turning birthsick. I suppose it'll do."

"The kettle was too hot—" Becca began to fumble out excuses.

"Never mind. I've birthed babes when I've lacked worse than a little boiled water."

"Becca—" Hattie's hair was combed back and tied with a lucky blue ribbon. The babe in white swaddlings lay nursing at her breast while she beamed at both her daughters. "Kneel down and see her proper." Love made Hattie's voice melt with tenderness.

Becca obeyed. Miss Lynn found herself something to do, a hustle and a background hum while the new mother acquainted her children with each other. "Her name is Shifra."

Miss Lynn couldn't resist putting in, "For the Scripture midwife, right, Hattie? One of those who said how lively the Hebrew women were to have their babes. Near too lively for me, that one!"

A dreamy smile glowed over Hattie's face as she hooked a finger into the outer corner of Shifra's mouth, breaking the baby's suction on that nipple. She shifted the child to suckle at the other breast. "This one was in a hurry to be born. Angels must've told her there was a good life awaiting her here, bless her heart."

Becca saw her own hand float out to touch the tuft of golden hair peeping from under the hooded swaddlings. The sight and smell and feel of the baby were all a strand of marvels. The newborn twisted a little at her touch, but Hattie's breast held her attention.

"Paul's so pleased," Hattie said.

"He is?" Becca spoke too loudly, let too much surprise into her words. Her mother gave her a quizzical look.

"Well, of course he is! Say a thing like that…Soon as Selena told him it was a girl, you could've heard him whooping the good news across the whole entire stead!"

"If he's so happy—" Becca thought better of letting words follow out her reasoning. —*then why does he look so sad out there in the seeing-room? Oh Lord, don't let it be that he's had a change of heart! He takes this sweet babe from my mama's arms now and, I swear, I'll be the one to kill him!*

Miss Lynn held out her arms for the baby. "She's done nursing. You sleep now too, Hattie. They'll be moving you both upstairs come morning." The herbwife laid the little one in the cradle near Hattie's head. She helped the mother to get comfortable for sleep, then turned down the lamp on the other side of the mattress and pinched out the remaining lights. "There. No chance she'll knock into that one in her sleep. See me to my horse, Becca."

"You riding back? But it's full dark!"

"Your pa's got men down the road, waiting to join up with me and see me home safe. He thinks of everything."

Outside the room where Hattie and Shifra slept, the house seemed empty. The nameless girl was gone, the kettle gone with her, the chair before the fireplace empty. Becca took one of the clay lamps from the mantle to light their way.

"I guess we needed girls," Becca said as Miss Lynn mounted up.

"Why do you say so?"

"Because Pa let this one—Mama kept her."

"Becca, have you got the brains of a rock?" Miss Lynn leaned down, spoke intently, a formidable vision in the flickering lamplight. "Talk like that! You hush before your pa hears. We need *all* children. Every birth's a rejoicing, a fulfillment of God's command to people the earth. You think Noah's kin counted boys from girls when they replenished the world? You think the Hebrew women held back from giving birth when Pharaoh said he'd cast their boy-babies into the Nile, or when they wandered in the desert and hadn't a bite of bread to put between their teeth? Even then, in the wasteland, they were fruitful according to God's law! And according to His will, they accepted the Lord King's judgments."

"But the Lord King, he only came after. I don't understand—"

"You don't have to." Miss Lynn sat up straight and jerked on her horse's bridle. "It's Scripture teaching and it's life. None of your understanding's going to change it. You just have to take it as it's meant to be." The nag turned and clopped leisurely down the road toward Makepeace, her rider stiff as any pole of the birthing-frame. Miss Lynn no longer sang as she rode, and she set off into the dark without a drop of natural fear.

Becca tried to cast the puzzlement out of her mind.

Miss Lynn had changed down to the roots since the "birth" of her baby Jesse. This harshness, this harping on Scripture rules, made Becca's head hurt.

Hunger was in her belly. She shelved all thoughts except where to scrounge up a staying morsel or two. There was no way she'd be able to brave the path back to the dormitory, passing Prayerful Hill by night, without something to ballast her stomach. Everyone made free with the larders this time of year, no one checking the old supplies too closely when the new were about to pour in. She headed for the nearest storeplace.

It was one of the yearlong huts—the sod houses redug fresh each autumn just before Harvest Home while last year's were destroyed right after that festival. There were other kinds of storeplaces on Wiserways land, bigger ones, permanent holds, aboveground and underground granaries and root cellars carefully guarded. The yearlongs were mostly underground structures with no windows in the sod dome and a plank floor over the main storage pit. A stick or two of furniture was stowed inside, the slimmest of accommodations for whoever had to do work there.

Steadlore said that each yearlong could hold enough seed to support two adults and two children through the winter, but no one ever tried to prove it that Becca could recall. Neither could she learn why the little storeplaces were built up and destroyed year by year. *Take it as it's meant to be*, Miss Lynn said. That was the answer given to a lot of things on Wiserways Stead. The huts held most and were most closely guarded after Harvest Home when they held Coop trade goods and the like, but at cycle's close they were nigh bare and open to anyone with a mind to foraging.

It was getting on for bedtime when Becca entered the hut. Most folks had eaten already, and the men were too tired at this time of year to do much prowling. She pulled back the latchstring on the door.

Ray jumped from the table when Becca's light spilled into the room. Her plump hands grabbed for the clay jar full of hard crackers, then set it down again when she recognized the girl.

"Sorry." Becca tried to back out of the room, but Ray hurried over, made her sit down.

"You've got a sister, I hear. Rejoice."

"I do." Ray's renewed kindliness put Becca on her guard. "Mama's named her Shifra."

"A good name." Ray took her own place at the table, pushed the cracker jar across. "Hungry?"

"Thanks." Becca took a cracker, nibbled it until it softened in her mouth. Her hunger had lost its edge. The air between her and Ray felt full of mysteries. The older woman's earlier anger was gone. Becca saw only her pa's sorrow twinned in Ray's face. She had to ask the reason. Miss Lynn should have known that it wasn't in Becca's nature to take things as someone else claimed they were meant to be. She had to reach up and pick the fruit of knowledge, had to taste it, had to *know*—

"Ray, what's wrong?"

"Wrong? Nothing—"

"I don't believe you. Did I go through Changes and Sixmonth or not? Don't I count as a Wiserways woman for all that? Tell me, Ray."

"All right: Susanna's dead," Ray said.

Becca gasped. The taste of the Knowing Tree was sharper than any blade.

"Paul killed her."

Chapter Seven

Praise the Lord, O ye peoples,
And praise His name, ye nations of the earth.
He hath sent forth His young men in strength,
And His maidens in sweetness.
He hath set the boundaries of life and death with an even hand.
Who shall dare to raise himself up against the Lord,
Or who shall deem himself eternal in his powers?
Who shall claim the pride of years,
Or who shall evade the reckoning of time?
For the Lord setteth up and casteth down,
The Lord rules the changing of the seasons and the peoples.
The high are brought low, and new powers arise.
That which went before is destroyed,
Even to the seed, utterly forgotten.

"It's lucky for Selena, that's all I'm saying." Del settled herself more comfortably on the cushioned floor of the covered wagon and rooted through the provisions hamper while she talked. The lurching of the wheels made her words come out as humpy as the road to Verity Grange, and made Marion's answering giggle sound like a case of hiccups.

"Lucky for *her* that Thalie came into her times?" Another blurt of laughter sputtered from Marion's lips. "Sure, same as it was lucky for Lenora to have hers come on just before Harvest Home! The look on that girl's face—"

"And how she tried to hide it from Pa?" Del leaned over the hamper to nudge Becca. "Were you there for that?"

"No." Becca tended to her fancywork. She'd been elsewhere for that scene, somewhere she maybe had no business being; surely taking something she had no right to take. She wasn't in the mood to discuss Lenora's misfortunes. The old, old book she'd hunted down in Katy's storeplace was a weight of blame in the pocket under her topskirt.

"Well, I wish you had been! Out in the cookhouse, it was. I tell you, Lenora's face went from flames to ashes! She said no and no and no again until she saw the sheer *knowing* in Pa's eyes. That shut her mouth." Del slammed the hamper lid and shoved it back against one of the wagon sideboards. "*Soap!*" she exclaimed like a triumphant battle-cry. "That ninny actually thought that the smell of citymade soap would cover for her. It was *your* mama's soap she snitched to do it. I'm surprised you didn't know."

"As if that'd deceive Pa. Or any man with all his

senses." Prisca laid her crochetwork in her skirt and joined the discussion.

There were eight of them in the covered wagon, eight of the marriageable girls of Wiserways Stead, and every one had her opinion. Only Becca and Sarah June kept theirs quiet, for the time. Becca had her mind on other things, and as youngest, Sarah June was as skittery as Dassah of Makepeace over the festival to come.

"I don't know." Red-cheeked Rusha hugged her updrawn knees close. "I've heard tell that there are ways you can fool a man about such things."

Marion snorted. "You can hear tell *anything*, if you waste enough time lollygagging around loose tongues. Why, once I heard some fool talk about ways a woman can take a man when her times aren't on her, and I don't mean the Kiss or the Sign!" The other girls all demanded to know who the simpleton was who'd uttered such an impossibility, but Marion waved them off. "I told you, you can hear anything. The truth's another matter. When a woman's in her times, there's no way on this earth you can trick a man into thinking she's not. The smell alone brings 'em from miles. Isn't no fieldwork gets done, for all the young ones turning frisky and the old ones praying maybe this time their alph will let one of them have his turn."

"And what good does all their friskiness do 'em?" It was Del's turn to let loose some laughter.

"They can dream. And no need to tell about *those* dreams, Del! Not even the fear of Pa keeps the boys from sneaking off and doing for themselves then. I bet he's giving thanks that this happened near Harvest Home, so's he could get most of them off the property and on the

Verity road before they wore their hands down to the wrist!"

"Marion, you got a nerve, criticizing *me!*" Del snapped. "You've got a dirty mouth and a worse mind." Her sib just giggled again.

Selena's oldest girl still living on stead spoke up. Her name was Apple, after a picturebook pretty, though she didn't look as fresh or juicy or tempting, or even as pleasantly sweet to the eye as her namesake. "That's allowed, this time of year. Good luck for the next. Tend your own business, Del. Marion's a good girl."

"How good?" Del purred, her eyes slitting up slyly. She put a twist in her words, a twist so plain and strong that it would take a raggydoll to miss her real meaning. "I think it's purely wonderful, the way you've always taken her part, Missy Apple. Why, whatever would this poor child do without you behind her every step, making sure no one says a harsh word to her? You'd think the two of you were more than sibs, the way you watch over her so close and constant."

Rusha tugged at the baggy sleeve of Del's blue cotton sweater. "Del, that's a wicked thing to say."

"Wicked?" Del's brown eyes opened wide.

"Accusing your own sib of such evil—"

"Just because Apple's such a *good* sib to Marion? Just because she's still on stead, at her age? Just because she's been to near as many Harvest Homes as Pa, and never once a man desperate enough to say the word for her? Could be a man can scent more about a woman than when she's in her times. They can sense more than just the fact that your body's ready to take 'em."

"What are you jawing at?" Apple's big, unlovely hands clenched in her lap.

"Some women want men, is all I mean," Del replied, smiling sticky-sweet as beet sugar. "Some don't."

Paul was not amused when he had to stop the Wiserways Stead caravan to break up the fight in the maidens' wagon. He was still less pleased when none of his daughters would say what had started the rumpus. Del tugged her stringy brown hair forward to cover some of the scratches on her face and stayed mum. Apple bent to the knitting she'd brought to occupy herself, ripping out and redoing several perfectly good rows.

As soon as the wagon got moving again, Orissa changed her place, discreetly stealing out from between Apple and Marion to sit near her younger sister Rusha and her sib Becca. "You *ever*?" she whispered. "You *ever* hear the like?"

"Poor Apple." Rusha sighed and hugged herself tighter still. "Lord King spare me all the burdens she's got to bear. I couldn't stand 'em. Was I to get so old, and no one to ask for me—the shame of that alone'd make me want to die."

"And what Del said, well, of course there's bound to be that sort of talk when a girl goes unwed so long." The sisters nodded their heads in sage agreement.

Sarah June swallowed her anxiety deep enough to lean across Becca and confide, "I hear that Pa asked around all the menfolk to learn whether she'd been niggardly with the Kiss or the Sign."

"And…?" Orissa wet her lips in anticipation.

"And nothing. She's always been a proper woman. Else she wouldn't still be here, would she?"

"What *I* heard was how the first time after her Sixmonth that Apple came into her times, she came home fruitful." Prisca had caught some of the whispers on the left side of the wagon and decided to contribute her mite. She was almost of an age with Apple, and just as unbespoke, but so long as the elder girl remained on stead, Prisca was saved from the infamy of Apple's position. "It was about the time of Harvest Home, and the man Pa set to mind the women was a day too old and an eyeblink too slow to catch her with one of the young men. That's what I *heard*, anyhow."

"Bet he was a day too *dead* when Pa found out," Orissa said with malicious glee.

"Fruitful? Truly?" Sarah June was most satisfactorily scandalized. "How could that happen?" Prisca's scornful snort made her flush and quickly amend, "I mean, why wasn't it common talk? That's *one* thing you can't hide from anyone, man or woman."

"Oh, after he dealt with the senior man, Pa sent her off somewhere when it started to show." Prisca shrugged as if her explanation were the most obvious thing in the world.

"What became of the young man?" Sarah June asked. She looked relieved to have someone else's troubles to shiver over. "What'd Pa do to him?"

"Nothing I ever heard about. *She* wouldn't give his name, and Pa didn't press. No sense losing a good field hand just for following the urges God gave him; not when it was all Apple's fault, anyhow. A proper woman minds herself. Pa sent the babe all the way to Hallow Stead hill when it was born, they say. I *think* someone there may've taken it, but that's only gossip."

"Gossip or no, poor Apple." Rusha glanced across the wagon bed to her ham-handed sib. "And now with all this new trouble her ma's got to suffer—"

"Nothing Selena didn't bring on herself." Prisca pursed

her lips. "Becca, you were there. Didn't anyone tell Selena what she was risking, sending that poor child to the fields at harvest? *Becca*!" She gave her a hard poke in the arm.

"Leave me be!" Becca swung back just as hard, with an open hand that cracked across Prisca's cheek. Tears burned inside her eyes but refused to fall. "None of your damned business what Selena did!"

"What you said—*Pa*!" Prisca didn't seem to feel the blow, though it had been hard enough to leave a white print that was fast turning scarlet. She stuck her head out the back end of the wagon and caterwauled, "Oh, *Paaaa*!"

Later, Becca walked at the very tail of the Wiserways caravan, behind the grain wagons. Paul walked beside her, his rucksack swinging heavily from his right shoulder by its one unbroken strap. He had given her a kerchief like his to tie over her face and cheat the churned-up dust of the road. It made their words come out sounding muffled and alien.

"I could mend that busted strap for you when we camp tonight if you'd like, Pa," Becca volunteered cautiously. She could see the hard outlines of an oblong shape pressing out the canvas bottom and knew it had to be the box from Pa's secret drawer. The metal box with the gun. So he was going to keep his word to her about warning Adonijah off. Even poor Susanna's little ghost couldn't compete with the thankfulness she felt toward her sire then.

Paul's jaw was tight. He ignored her offer. He didn't slacken his stride to accommodate his daughter. Becca was a sturdy marcher, but paired with Paul she had to do half-again time to keep up. The silence between them made the marching even harder.

"Pa, if you're that angry with me, I could go home."

Esther M. Friesner

"By yourself? With the steads between here and Wiserways so down on their people that there'd be no men to spare to shield you?" Paul lifted his face kerchief and spat into the dusty golden stubble lining the road. "'Sides, you'd get lost. You couldn't even take the highroad, this season."

Becca knew he was right. The road that folks traveled to Verity Grange from Wiserways at Harvest Home was different than at other times of the year. It went roundabout, skirting other steads by a goodly distance. In the growing season this route they now followed was little more than a path between fields.

Each member stead followed its own traditional way to Verity during the autumn pilgrimage, none of them taking the direct road. It was pure courtesy for the in-grange caravans to avoid one another, a courtesy to the land and the precious beasts who would need their grazing. Too many steads sharing a single road would strip the side-country bare in no time, leaving latecomers' draft animals to starve, playing hob with the water supplies. Wars had been fought for less. A little more inconvenience, a little more time spent on the way to Verity, were a fair price to pay to keep the peace.

"I could get home safe." Becca's face turned as hard as her father's, a stone mask part determination and part mulishness. "It's mostly flatland between here and there, even if I keep off the highroad. I could see trouble coming a long ways off."

"And trouble could see you!" Paul seized one of Becca's dangling yellow braids and tugged like it was a plowhorse's rein, just hard enough to make her stand still in the road. The caravan went on at its steady pace without them.

"Pa, the wagons—"

"They don't move so fast. We can catch up. What I'm afraid is the Fool Killer's going to catch up to you first. Now you hark to me, girl: All that talk you brought me about Satan making his own private stead in your soul—I'm starting to believe it. Ever since your sister Shifra was born, you've been carrying yourself fey. I can understand you being spooked over your first Harvest Home, but haven't I promised you I'd keep Adonijah away? Still, you go about your chores jumpier than a thief's shadow. Gram Phila been telling you frights about your first time with a man? I'll forbid you to go up attic any more if that's so."

"Oh, no sir!" Becca would say anything to hold onto those precious visits, the lessoning she gave and received under the rafters. Learning all she could from Gram Phila's no-name girl, she'd come to understand why Eve chose to eat of the Knowing Tree first, leaving the Tree of Life untouched until too late. "Only thing Gram ever said…touching that was how third time's the charm." Her forehead knotted. "But when I asked what she meant by it, she just laughed."

Paul's sternness relaxed some. "Well, that lickerish old—Never mind, child. Gram's all right. But all of your brawling in the wagon, and swearing—What call did you have to go using such language to your sib? A curse on a woman's lips is like a cupful of mud."

"Prisca provoked me."

"Prisca provokes everyone. Why d'you think she's still on stead? I hear tell that Hallow's got an alph who lost one ear in a fight. If he can only hear half her fractiousness, could be he'll take a fancy to her and relieve us of the yoke." He started walking again. Casually he asked, "How'd she set you off, then?"

Esther M. Friesner

Becca doubled her stride, pretending to be in a great rush to overtake the caravan. She didn't want to tell about the talk in the maidens' wagon, especially not if it meant mentioning Susanna's name. She could still hear Thalie screaming at Selena, vowing to take her co-wife's blood in pay for her daughter's.

"You said you'd stand up for her with Paul! She was killed for running your damned errand! Lord blast you barren, you didn't even need an herbwife to birth Hattie's child. You just wanted to keep your own skin safe in case something went wrong. Ray told me!"

And Selena, crumpled up like a hank of wet cloth, letting her nose run from all the tears she'd shed ever since she'd heard that Susanna was dead: *"I would have done it, Thalie! I went after meeting Paul as soon as Miss Lynn came, to tell him to forgive the child. But it was over by then. If I'd've thought they were so sharp to guard their cursed harvest doings I'd never—"*

"Manlore killed my baby? Is that what you mean? Don't you bring down your own damnation by blaming what puts food in your mouth! I wish there was a man here right now, to bear witness to what you just said. Save me the trouble of killing you myself. Bitch! Godless bitch! I'll make sure you have the death that you deserve."

But of course there was no man present. All the men were back out in the fields and the storeplaces that day, readying the caravan for the trip to Verity Grange. Paul wouldn't listen to unfounded accusations from one wife against another. It took five women to testify to the same thing before a wise stead alph would take action. Female feuds were too common, especially between wives, and the lore on past mistakes too detailed and deep to ignore.

There were more than five women in the room to

witness Thalie's threat, Selena's foolish words, but nothing would come of it. Not one would come forward, not even the most pious. It would take more than one child's death, however unjust, to make them turn over one of their own number to Paul. There would be other children. As if to prove it, Thalie came into her times that very night.

"Becca? I asked you a question."

"Oh, just silliness, Pa. You know I've got a temper. Prisca was taunting me over how I'm clumsy with my needle. I don't have my dancing dress fully done 'til yet."

Paul looked dubious, but he allowed her to return to the maidens' wagon. There were no further squabbles. The caravan was within about a day's journey of Verity and an atmosphere of suppressed excitement took the place of all the petty quarrels among the girls. That night, when they made camp, Little Sarah June was so het up that she started to say her prayers out loud and couldn't stop.

"I'm all for piety in a woman, but this goes too far," Paul said. A number of the other men stood behind him when he came to the maidens' campfire to settle things down. "Sarah June, the Lord's heard enough out of you for one night and so have I. I'm leading you to a dance, not your doom. Now you sleep and grant the rest of us some peace besides."

"Yes, Pa," Sarah June quavered. But it didn't take long for her to resume the rapid recitation of more petitions to God and the Lord King and sweet Mary Mother, this time in a raspy whisper that would get on a saint's nerves.

"I'll help calm her, Pa," Becca said hastily, seeing Paul come striding back to the maidens' fire with fire enough of his own in his eye. "Let me make us a smaller campsite just over there a ways. I'll sit with her until she sleeps."

Paul grunted his consent. With capable hands, Becca made a ring of hearthstones a good distance off from the other fires, laid down a small bed of wood, then borrowed a burning brand from the maidens' fire to kindle it. Wrapped in her blanket, looking like a woebegone worm, Sarah June shuffled over to huddle up beside the new blaze.

"Sorry, Becca," she whimpered.

"No need for any sorries." Becca tucked her sib's blanket more securely around the younger girl's shoulders. "This is my first Harvest Home, too. We've all got times we're frighted. Waiting on something new to happen's worst: waiting for Changes, waiting for Sixmonth, standing a woman's vigil, going to your first Harvest Home, serving your first man in thanks, birthing, dying— all of it's living."

"I guess." The girl didn't sound convinced or happy about it.

Becca wrapped her hand in a pocket kerchief and picked up a clay cup she'd set to warm at the edge of the flames. "Here, love." She held it out to Sarah June. "Take it, cloth and all; it's hot."

"What is it?" Sarah June stayed snug in her cocoon, hands out of sight, bright eyes suspicious.

"Just a little herb tea I set to steep. It'll soothe you and let you sleep." She smiled. "Let Pa sleep, what's more important. Go on, you can trust my dosings."

"Oh, that's right." The girl was reassured by a thought. "You're lessoning to be an herbwife, ain't you?"

"Lord grant it. Now drink."

Coaxed and comforted, Sarah June sipped the tea,

then curled up with a sigh. Her eyes drifted closed, then opened suddenly. "Becca, won't you sleep too?"

"In awhile. I just want to sit up some and see the stars."

"The stars? Huh!" The idea struck Sarah June as so outlandish that she turned her back on it and Becca both. Before long her sides were rising and falling with the slow, regular breath of sleep.

Becca sat back, her own blanket over her shoulders, and looked around her. The other fires were ringed by sleepers. The only waking souls were the sentries Pa had posted. For himself, Paul had a fire set apart and manned by those men senior enough to owe him more than a few debts of gratitude. The road to Harvest Home wasn't blessed for challenge, but sometimes an alph made enemies desperate enough not to care whether they died too, so long as they took him down first. So Pa slept under loyal guard, as was proper.

Becca looked up at the night sky. The flickering campfire light stole a measure of the stars' full beauty, but it couldn't touch their power to exalt her heart. "You were always there," she breathed up into the silver-strewn bowl of heaven. "Even before. Even then."

The book was a pressure against her thigh. She gave Sarah June's slumbering form one last glance before she dared to pull it out. It looked so much smaller than she remembered it from that long gone day when it had fallen into her hands by accident. This time there was no accident in how she'd come by it. If Katy ever found out, she'd have Becca's hide.

The paper between the pasteboard covers was brittle and so yellow it looked almost brown. The ink had faded and in some places was just a blur. Most of the pages were blank. The younger Becca had thought that what was there filled the whole book. More than a few words were lost, sometimes whole sentences, but there was enough to read. As Becca's eyes strained to make out the scrawly letters, little by little she came to wonder if maybe there wasn't *too* much to read.

…has to die tomorrow because they found out about her and we've got to watch. I'm afraid, Mama. What if they find out that I'm the same? I don't understand…wrong with me. Ever since I can remember, all I've heard is how there aren't enough people left to work the soil. Nora and I could have so many babies, the way we are…don't they see? Why…want us?

Finding soil that'll yield…a task in itself. I've overheard Conrad explaining to the boys about how once upon a time, before the Flood, the earth was sweet and…food like there was no end to it. But after the waters rose and the Ark sailed away, the salt sea covered…and made it barren. I don't believe what he said about the Flood, but the land…living with…that that's true.

I miss you, Mama. It feels like you've been gone so long. I miss…I can talk to, so I'm writing this down now…how good it'll be to share it with you makes me feel a little better. If only I didn't have to think about tomorrow, and Nora—

I can't talk to Conrad any more. Conrad's all right, but the older he gets…like a stranger. All the talk I hear from my girl cousins…how he'll be the best man to lead us one day soon. Once…Uncle Ira overheard. Ever since… don't like the way he's been looking at Conrad. He doesn't think I see, but I see plenty. I see…looks at me, too, and I really hate that. Mama, hurry home.

Uncle Ira says that he's heard about another troop of people living over those hills to… He suggested that maybe we should leave this land and go see if they'll have us. There are still places where the earth bears...bears a little more easily, anyhow... funny: The men talk about the land being barren, but... something growing any place we've come. No land entirely naked when we find it; it's just our crops that don't seem to want to grow...the right crops. Remember how you said you'd noticed that too, just before you set off east?

Maybe if there's still people living in the cities... give you the answers we need...silly to think of city people knowing anything about which seeds will take in this land and which won't, but if you find them—

You will find them. Mama, you've got to find them. From what I hear, I think that you and I are the last ones to remember...stories of how things were before. Some of my cousins don't believe...were such things as cities. No one settles anyplace for long...say that's the natural order of things.

...changes...frightening. One Sunday, when Uncle Ira preached to us...sounded strange. I went rooting through that box of books you left me and I found the black one you said was my grandma's, and her grandma's, and... how many grandmas ago?...Uncle Ira's words, only not the way he'd said them. When I took him the book and showed him ...the words wrong, he grabbed it away from me and said, "Things change. What with all I've got to do, worrying about how to put bread in your mouth ...safe from marauders and rogues, can't you just be a grateful woman and not meddle with things that don't concern you?"

Whole paragraphs were lost after those words, and then:

...knives. The women did it themselves. Elaine even put a knife into my hand and shoved me...I wouldn't. I just let it fall...screamed at me. I wish I'd...give the knife to Nora so *she could either put an end to it or take some of her tormentors with her, but…too much blood…*

…said it was a sign that she was evil. No other woman in our group can have a man…except maybe once, twice a year. We thought we were being so careful, too, hiding the blood when it started to come to us that often, pretending we weren't able to…the men except like the others can. But Nora wasn't careful enough. That's how I found out she was like me in the first place, surprising her washing…blood when I knew she'd just been available to the men the month before.

…blood enough when they were through with her. Evil. I know where the real evil lies: Envy. Fear. They see how the men dance attendance on them when they're in the right times… year to take them…not fools. They figure if a man could have his choice, he'd be a thousand times more eager to feed and guard a woman who could serve him any time of year over one he can only have once or twice. And then where would they be? So they called poor Nora evil and they killed her.

It wasn't always this way. That's what you used to tell me, Mama, the same way you told me fairy tales out of the book box. (…proud of me. I convinced Uncle Ira not to burn all the books in…way he burned the black one. I said that maybe the people over the hill might be willing to trade for them.) I think you said it like it was just a fairy tale, or a wish to keep your spirits up, but…don't think so. Was the world always this hungry? Did the hunger always make people so cold? …cut Nora's breasts, Mama…no more remorse than if she were a rabbit to be flayed…her thighs where the pad had slipped and stained and given her away. Blood washing over blood, so much blood—

You should have taken us with you to search for the city, Mama. You shouldn't have left us here behind. Now I'm the last one left who's different...hard to live this way. Maybe I'm not writing this to save for your return. Half my heart doesn't believe you're ever coming back, no matter how much I tell myself to believe you will. Maybe I'm writing this because what I really believe is that you're dead, and I know that Nora is, and I'm too alone to care any more whether I live or die...what I'll have to become if I live...Uncle Ira...

And there was no more.

Becca pulled the blanket around her as tight as it would go, moved herself close enough to the fire so that her hair picked up the burnt smell, and still she felt cold. She thrust the book back into her pocket, fighting her first urge to feed it to the campfire flames. How much of that terrible testimony of the past had she read as a child? Enough to fetch the long gone ghost out of the bosom of Prayerful Hill. Enough to place a silvery phantom of blood and moonlight before her eyes forever.

It wasn't always like this.

Things change.

Not if you talked to Pa or Mama. And the thought of change sometimes frighted Becca more than even the worst of things the way they stood.

"Who were you?" she whispered into the dark. "What was your name? Did they catch you the way they caught Nora? Did your mama ever find the city or did she—?"

She looked back up at the stars, wondering whether they'd shone so bright for the lonely, frightened girl who'd left only her words behind. If she slept that night, she couldn't remember any dreams. By next night the stars above were mirrored by the campfires from Verity Grange and the following day the Wiserways caravan was there.

Chapter Eight

Lady in your dress of green,
Tread your measure like a queen.
Bright as sunlight, sweet as spring,
Love you more than any thing.
Heard you tell me, good and true,
Whole of heart you loved me too.
Hard my pillow, loud my moan,
In my bed I sleep alone.
In my dreams it's you I see
Wed to him that sired me.
Sweet your hand and soft your eye,
Love you 'til the day I die.
Freeze my heart and hone my knife,
Slay my father, steal his wife.

As soon as they made camp at Verity, Paul told Becca and the other maidens to stick close to their tent and not to go hoydening around the grange without at least one of their male kin hard by. Those girls whose first Harvest Home it was laughed over their father's stern "preacher-face," even little Sarah June. The older ones, Prisca and Apple, only sat there and twisted their mouths up as if they were keeping something tasty hidden under their tongues.

The next day, Paul sent the girls to present themselves to the grangewomen who'd be overseeing the dances. He delegated ten of his sons and six of his men to accompany them out of camp. The younger girls tittered and twittered about slipping free of their sibs' vigilance and doing a little exploring on their own. It wasn't wilderness, with rogue bands lurking behind every tree, was it now? No, it was Verity Grange, and every alph's eye ruling like steel over his own people. No one would offer them any insult if they broke harness. No one would dare.

So they came down the hillside almost dancing, the girls matched two and two, the males arrayed in a staggery human fence around them. Apple and Prisca went first, still with those galling little crabapple mouths. Becca linked arms with Sarah June and kept to the rear of the group.

"Shall we, Becca? Shall we?" Sarah June dragged on Becca's arm, whispering her willingness to join in the grand plan of escape that Orissa had proposed. "Del said she'll stop short, grab her middle, and start to carry on like she's got the bellyache. Isn't anyone can feign like Del."

"Another name for lying," Becca said, but she smiled.

"And then, when she's got all the men distracted—Lord knows, could be they'll think she's coming into her times!—then we'll all scatter."

"Pa'll have a hissy."

"That's all he'll do. He can't punish all of us. That'd mean going straight home before the dances and the matches, no chance to show us off, or strut proud over our sibs, or—" she spoke softer still "—ship Apple off stead."

"We're none of us too old to whip," Becca reminded her.

"And leave marks?" Becca's little sib smirked. "That'd help Apple's chances just fine! And doesn't he always pride himself how a good alph doesn't need to use a switch on his children?"

Becca shook her head. "Apple and Prisca will never go along with this."

"Yes, they will." Sarah June was so earnest that her big blue eyes burned like a summer sky. "They said so, swore by the Lord King and all!"

"Well, in that case—" Mischief kindled in her heart. It would be good to get free, to be on her own again. She wasn't used to living so constantly cheek-by-jowl with her female sibs, except nights in the dormitory. Out in the fields she worked apart and liked it that way. If not for the lessons she was getting from Gram Phila's girl, nothing could have made her stay cooped under the great house rafters voluntarily, not for a minute. As for the long journey in the maidens' wagon and the enforced togetherness of the maidens' tent, she saw it all as a foretaste of hell.

"I'm with you," she told Sarah June. A last qualm—

What if I chance to cross paths with Adonijah?—was quickly stilled. It was broad daylight, and she would stick with Sarah June; if ill luck did set him 'cross her path, she'd be safe enough in company. She wanted to be free more than she feared his evil shadow.

"Watch Del, then. She's right behind Apple, up front. She'll signal when—"

Right then Sarah June walked smack into Orissa's back.

"Here! What's wrong with you?" The little maid gave her sib a good hard shove in the small of the back. Orissa never seemed to feel it.

"Look," was all she said. "Just look there."

Apple and Prisca snickered into their hands as the small, astonished cries went up from every one of their kinswomen. Wonder was voiced over a greater wonder, the marvel beyond any Scripture miracle, the power of sheer size past anything of their own imaginations' building: Verity Grange.

Shielded by the broad backs and tall bodies of their male sibs, minds preoccupied with their bold escape plan, the maidens had come into the heart of Verity without really being aware of the presence of the place. Where the grange's borders touched the raggedy edges of the stead encampment areas, you couldn't tell much difference between Verity and what they knew. Grange wagons and neglected outbuildings looked much the same as some of the temporary shelters the Harvest Home visitors had set up for their own use. A little farther in, the Wiserways young folk had passed by storeplaces of wood and stone little grander than those back home. The mind recorded familiarity and turned to other thoughts, making smug assumptions.

Then, sudden as summer lightning, the heart of Verity Grange, and all assumptions shattered.

Buildings taller than three, four men, all built of stone with real glass windows.

Field machines with the paint brand new and bright, lined up in a row like pies on a trestle table. Cans and cans of fuel for them hard by, too big for a lone worker to tote, and the smell of it strong on the air.

Pens of beasts that Becca and her sibs only knew from books—actual beef cattle! Whose dream had they sprung from?—filling the air with their alien stink, their fierce, terrifying bawling.

"Becca, what if they get loose?" Sarah June clung close and hid her face with fistfuls of Becca's skirt like any nursling.

"Hush, they're safe pent up. They can't get free." Becca mouthed words she didn't believe. The pictures in Katy's books never hinted that cows could come so big, so *loud*! She saw some of them bigger than horses.

Shoulders jostling, hands linked, the girls walked slow and solemn through the midst of miracles. Prisca and Apple were the only ones who kept their heads held proud, though they cast their eyes earthward for the required form of modesty. Even some of the males carried themselves skittery, eyes here and there, fearing the next horrible surprise that might come leaping out at them around the next corner. If not for Pa's orders, they would have turned back gladly.

The meeting with the grangewomen was brief—just long enough for pure business and no pleasantries. The maidens waited in a large building—but all buildings at Verity seemed large to Becca—and were made to sit in a chill, high-ceilinged room with groups of girls from other steads. The grangewomen told all the males in no uncertain terms to remain outside. Hard benches were set in rows in the center of the room, like for the Lord's services. Looking around, Becca recognized Dassah of Makepeace Stead. She tried to wave, but the girl kept her head down, her shoulders hunched forward. Becca would have gone over to greet her if Apple hadn't seen her start from her place.

"Where do you think you're going?" she demanded, hardly moving her lips. She snagged Becca's waistband and yanked her back down.

"I see someone I know. I wanted to go and—"

"Sit. In this place you do what the grangewomen want and leave the rest go by. I won't have you dishonoring Wiserways."

Becca wrenched herself away. "Dishonor? For giving a friendly greeting?"

"At Harvest Home there's times set by for all things, and proper women respect 'em. This isn't the time for your silly flibbertigibbeting. Your friend will keep. Now *sit*."

"Old vinegar," Becca grumbled, but she obeyed her elder sib.

One by one the girls were taken into one of three back rooms, elder ones first. For once Apple and Prisca wore discomfited looks when they emerged to rejoin their sibs. When it was Becca's turn, she was taken into the far right-hand room, told to strip to her shift and sit on a contraption that looked much like the birthing chair. A brisk, efficient grangewoman with the spicy-keen scent of an herbwife clinging to her clothes asked Becca a lot of questions about her Changes and her Sixmonth. Then she was given an examination that was none the less humiliating for all it was done with so quickly.

"Your mama ever have any troubles with fruitfulness or bearing?" the grangewoman asked, washing her hands and going over to a table covered with papers.

"Not that I know. She was brought to bed of a girl-child not long since." The hot color on Becca's face was starting to turn from shame to anger, even though she knew this ordeal was no more or less than what her sibs had suffered.

"Rejoice," the grangewoman said automatically, her eyes on the papers before her. "Hmm, and at her age. Well, that's good news for you. Ever served a man? Not just the Kiss or the Sign."

"Served...?" By now the anger had won out. "I'm pure virgin, unwed!"

The grangewoman set down her papers. "Well, no need to shout it. You're not the only one; it won't improve your fetching price in all quarters. Some steads don't care about such things, and there's a few where the alphs prefer to trust newborn proof of a girl's fruitfulness more than any family history before they wed her."

"Can I go now?" Becca wanted to tear the grangewoman's papers out of her hands and shred them.

"Hm? Yes, yes, get dressed and go your way. Send in the next girl." Becca was dismissed without further ceremony.

In the waiting hall, she had to sit and stew while the rest of the Wiserways maidens went through the same ritual. At last they were done and sent on their way. As Becca was walking from the hall, she tried to catch Dassah's eye again. The Makepeace girl lifted her head—

she couldn't help but see Becca—yet her eyes seemed to look right through her. In that glassy stare Becca felt as if an icy claw reached through her chest.

The way back to the Wiserways encampment went a lot faster than the way into grange. Nearly all the girls were in a hurry to get back to familiar territory. It took the rest of that day and part of the next for them to recover from their first brush with Verity. It might have taken longer, if Prisca and Apple hadn't made themselves so almighty provoking and superior about how *they* couldn't see what all the fuss was for, it was only a place like any other.

"Just like they were grange-born or something." Del sniffed as they sat inside the maidens' tent doing makework chores. No one said so aloud, but the fact that Apple and Prisca were elsewhere in camp made their captivity almost pleasant. "Now they're noising it that we're too frighted to show ourselves until the dance!"

"But we don't need to go into grange until then," Rusha said softly. "Do we?" She and Sarah June both looked like they were hoping for a no.

Becca laid a calming hand on her small sib's shoulder. "Course we don't, love. No business at all for us to go there until it's dancing time."

She felt Rusha shudder under her hand. "I wish it wasn't even so. I wish I was still a nursling, that I do, and home with Ma!" She spoke vehemently, and no amount of hushing from Sarah June would make her lower her voice.

"You don't worry about that, missy!" Apple's voice came into the tent sharply, crisp and cold as morning wind. She pulled back the entry flap to stick her plain face inside. In her hand she held a man's shirt with the mending needle still jabbed through the fabric. "You'll have worse to mind if Pa hears you go on that way."

"Who asked you, Long Ears?" Becca snapped. She could feel all the fear inside her shy little sib like it was living water filling up a skin to the bursting point. *So much to fear*, she thought angrily. *Too much, when you're a woman.* She recalled what she'd read in the stolen book—her ghost book, as she thought of it—and that unknown girl's scrawled words so full of despair. The fear hadn't changed. Apple herself must have felt afraid more times than not. What if she never found a man to have her? What if she grew old, unclaimed? What happened to stead spinsters if a winnowing time come to Wiserways? So why did she have to add to her sib's misery? "You tend to your own business!"

Apple put on that mean, knowing smile. "I'm not talking to you, Becca, so hark to your own preachings." Her eyes dove in on Rusha, and there was no mercy in her look or words. "You just let Pa hear you carrying on like that, denying your natural born woman's part, shaming Wiserways, and you'll be lucky if you see the dance floor. Shoot, luckier if you see homestead again!"

Rusha gave a little moan and fell into Becca's arms. Becca bridled, opened her mouth to flay Apple's hide with her tongue and threaten her with worse for later, once she got Rusha comforted. She never had the chance for hard words. A shadow rippled down the tent flap, covered half of Apple's face and blacked out all the outside light.

"How does it come that you're playing alph for me, daughter?" Paul's rolling voice never sounded so sweet to Becca. She saw Apple blanch, saw her sib jerk her head out of the tent, then heard as lively and biting a dressing-down as any of the stripling males ever got for damaging valuable field tools. Paul finished it off with: "Maybe you just better be the one to stay in the tent until the dance, Apple. The light's spare in the dancing ring, at night. You'll have a better chance of it, that way."

Del couldn't hold in a nasty snicker. Both Sarah June and Rusha gave way to unthinking whoops of joy to hear their self-righteous sib told to her face that Pa himself didn't favor her chances this Harvest Home either.

Becca heard Apple mumble something about having to sew Daniel's shirt and wanting to give it back. The swish of her retreating skirts in the dust was as close to a dead run as she could manage. Then Pa was along outside the maidens' tent calling for Becca to come out.

"I've business in Verity," he said. She felt her stomach sink as he added, "I'd have you with me."

"Pa, I was going to work some on—"

"Not on your dancing dress? How big a fool do you take me for, expecting that excuse to last forever? Lord King witness, Bec', you're a right Penelope with that dress." His eyes shone with pride when she blushed. "There's my girl. Not many maids'd know enough to look shamed over my speaking of 'em that way. Penelope's just a name to your sibs, but you've got the learning to know it for more. Only book-learning, though. Time you had world-learning too. Come along, child. I'll keep you from harm."

So Becca found herself trailing a pace or two behind her father as they took the path from Wiserways camp into the mad, wild, terrifying, wondrous heart of Verity Grange. This time there was a shaving's worth less terror for Becca. The noise and bustle and strangeness seemed to have lost a little of their power to petrify. When they walked past the livestock pens and a cow lowed just over her shoulder, she didn't even blink, let alone bolt.

They went deeper into Verity than she'd come with her sibs. Here and there was dressed stone underfoot, or a high walkway of logs. She marveled at the opulence, the magnificence of it. A look at Pa's pinched, disapproving face told her that here was a display of wealth bordering on the sacreligiously prodigal. She tried to trim her own expression to jibe with his, but the wonder-thirst was too strong. She kept her eyes downcast more to hide this from Pa than for any rightful modesty.

They stopped outside of one of the tallest buildings she had ever seen, even in Verity.

"Wait here for me," Paul said.

To be left standing there alone! She should have felt fear but didn't. "Yes, Pa," was all she said.

"I won't be long. This is where the Coop traders meet." He patted the heavy rucksack at his side. "Time we cleared the books for this season."

She watched him vanish through doors shiny as a littlesinger's eyes, clear as water. She didn't think to ask whether she could accompany him inside—if that was allowed, he'd have said so. In truth, she was happy to be left here, on her own for the first time in days. She took her post and tried to keep her heart from singing out loud for freedom's joy.

Becca kept her eyes lowered and her back to the wall of the building, at first. Pretty soon, though, her gaze rose by degrees. With half-lidded eyes she managed to watch the comings and goings of every person on the street. It didn't take much doing to realize that this whole section of Verity was the traders' own. Her plain stead clothing stuck out like a stand of green millet in a blooming clover field, yet none of the passersby cared to pay her any notice. They were all taken up with their own affairs.

Most everyone who passed wore city garb, with its eye-enticing colors and impossibly fine texture. Becca longed to touch it, to have her fingers prove what her eyes already believed. She heard accents so strange that it took hard listening before she could credit it was her own native tongue the cityfolk were speaking. Some had high, warbling, female voices, too. Impossible that they could be women, though. Not one skirt flicked a hem past her feet. They all wore boots and breeches and tunics with long, drapey, turtling hoods to cover their heads.

Becca was wondering whether she'd go to hell just for imagining the feel of her legs swinging free in city breeches when Pa came out to reclaim her.

"Got a prize in my pocket, Becca." He patted his shirt, looking smug. "All that sweating blood over the accounts paid off fair and fine. Wiserways' reputation's solid enough for the Coop to want us doing them a favor. Test seed. Like to feed ten times as many mouths per acre if it works the way they're telling me."

"That's wonderful, Pa." Becca yearned to see the seeds that promised so much, but it was likelier that she'd sprout wings. Such a special gift would be quickly sealed behind a fence of manlore, only offered to woman's eyes when it had fallen from miracle to commonplace.

"Fancy that was worth our walk, do you? Not scared any while you waited for me?" he asked, smiling. She shook her head. "Good girl. This sector's reserved for cityfolk. Any of them'd die before offering a steadwoman offense, even one standing lone, like you. I knew you'd be secure. And you knew to trust me." His whole face warmed, but Becca looked away.

You never know, with males.

They set off back for their stead's encampment. While passing through the grange market a piercing, piping voice hailed Pa. "Paul! Hi, wait up some!" A bizarre little man came lolloping across the marketplace to greet them.

Becca glanced at her father, silently asking who this strange man was. At first she thought that distance made the fellow look so small, but when he caught up to them she saw that he was a full head shorter than she.

"Weegee, I'm joyed to see you." Paul gave the little man both his hands the way he'd greet one of his smaller children. "This is Hattie's Becca. You recollect me mentioning her to you? Bec', this is Weegee of Hallow Stead."

"Honored to meet you, Mister Weegee." She dipped her head briefly, more out of reflex than respect. She couldn't find it in her to fathom how this little bit of a man could be her father's friend and equal.

Snapping brown eyes under ragged brindle brows flashed over Becca from head to foot. Weegee's lips were framed by a dark brown mustache and a small, pointed beard such as the girl had never seen outside of storybooks. What she could see of his hair, mostly hidden by a shapeless tan hat, was the same sprinkly mix of brown and gray as his eyebrows.

"No *Mister* to me, girl. Nor no honorifics in your mouth that don't come from the heart neither."

Becca's father laughed to see shame and confusion

flash over her face. "Lord, Weegee, times are I think those stories about you having second sight are true."

"So they are," the little man returned solemnly. "I can read hearts and minds and the future, all three."

"*You* say." He patted Weegee on the back, stooping some to do it. "But what you pulled on Becca, was there any second sight to that? Truth, now!"

Weegee winked. "No more than the sight it took to see that she balked at calling a littlebit 'Mister.' You felt like you were raising up one of your pesky sibs, didn't you, girlie?" He reached up to chuck Becca under the chin. His hands were soft and smooth, sweet-smelling and unmarked by any sign of hard labor.

"Answer the man, Bec'," Paul directed.

"Can you really see what you say, Mis—Weegee?"

The little man rocked back on his heels, his canny eyes taking in all the hubbub of the grange marketplace. Seemingly offhand, he asked, "You like to read, child?"

Paul answered for her. "Only the best student my Katy says she ever had! Isn't hardly a book on stead she hasn't spelled through twice."

Oh, Pa, if you only knew! Becca thought. The ghost book was with her, now as always. She didn't dare risk leaving it behind in the maidens' tent, even in her traveling box.

"I asked *her*, Paul." Weegee lowered his voice and moved closer, so close that Becca smelled the pungent mix of clover and tobacco and a sharper scent she couldn't name—much like the sour yellow fruits she'd seen the Coop city traders offering at one marketplace stall. "You read any tall tales, Becca?"

"Some."

"Some like what're called fairy stories?"

She thought of the man in metal and the great scaled beast in the picture. She thought of the ghost book writing: *It wasn't always this way. That's what you used to tell me, Mama, the same way you told me fairy tales*— "Yes."

"Then you know to call me—what I am—by my right name."

"You're"—she looked to her father for any prohibition, but he held his expression neutral—"a dwarf."

Weegee had the most perfect smile she'd ever seen. "Good. Bold and bright, and full of questions too, I'm bound." He looked up at Paul. "Another Eleazar, eh?"

Paul jammed his hands in his pockets and puffed out his chest. "Why not? They're full brother and sister."

"Oh, don't I know that! This big head has to hold a lot of knowledge if it's to carry this little body all the way to a peaceable death."

"You'll outlive us all, Wee—" Paul stopped, wrinkled up his nose, then sneezed loudly. No surprise: The marketplace teemed with enough exotic smells and more than enough traffic-churned dust to make anyone's nose twitch.

Becca watched her pa yank a kerchief out of one shirt pocket. A small drawstring pouch came flying out too, its contents spilling in the marketplace dirt. She gave a little cry and fell to hands and knees along with her pa. No one had to tell her that what had spilled was precious. *Test seed*, Pa had called it, acting like it was a holy mystery in that soft cloth bag instead of hard, white, peg-shaped kernels.

Seed was seed. You didn't waste it. Becca's keen eyes picked out every grain lying in the dirt before her fingers flew to gather it all safely back. When she'd picked up as many kernels as she could, she offered her father the contents of her cupped hands.

He ignored both her and the precious seed. He was still down on all fours like a beast, even though there wasn't any more scattered seed to gather. And while he picked up invisible grains between his big fingers, he conferred secretly with Weegee in the midst of the marketplace bustle.

"—things go at Hallow?"

"Bad…for some. The women with nurslings are already looking for hidey-holes. Thazar's mother, she's carrying herself like it was all over already, lording it with the other wives, making sure they know whose arse to kiss if they want to save their young ones."

Paul shook his head, picked up another seed that wasn't there. "Fool woman. I know Thazar. He's a good lad, always does what's right. He won't play favorites for anyone, not even his mama. You sure he'll be the one?"

"Who else have we got? Unless some off-stead buck comes along. Which I doubt. They all got a good look at Thazar in the ring last Harvest Home. If they want to die, they could do it as well on their own steads."

"Poor Jed."

"Well, Thazar knows how to make it quick, which is more than Jed did for his sire." The dwarf's eyes narrowed. "Never could forgive him for making Da take the long dying."

"Your father deserved better, Weegee." Paul got up and poured the few grains he'd gathered back into the pouch, then dusted off his hands on his pants. "But how many get what they deserve?"

"Pa—"

Paul finally deigned to notice Becca, standing there with her offering of seed and dust. Instead of looking pleased with her industry, he spoke harshly to her. "Lord King take you, have all my daughters got a plague of long ears on them? Where's your business listening in to our talk, girl? I've a mind to—"

Weegee laid a hand on his forearm. "Take the seed from her, Paul." His voice was as soft as his skin, and his eyes were fixed on Becca's face. "Speak her gentle. Oh yes, speak her kindly and sweet, this little girl-child of your getting. She's holding much and more."

Becca wanted to scream. She wanted to step back, turn, and run all the way home. A new fear was in her heart, a dark dreading that this little man out of a storybook was going to lay his unnaturally soft hands on her next. His voice had lost all of its pert life, had dwindled off into a spooky, quiet drone that set the short golden hairs along her arms to tingling. She wanted to shout a warning to her pa, tell him to snap the dwarf in two and protect her the way any good alph was supposed to do for his women. But she knew Pa wouldn't heed, and she knew that the little man's words were heavy with a power to change her whole world forever.

"What are you hiding, child?" Weehgee asked, never taking his eyes from hers. It was a question and it wasn't. "It's a mystery too deep for any of my sight, yet I know it's there. Eyes on this one, Paul. Be her shield and her rock, Barak to her Deborah. There's to come an end to killing, and a new time of singing to the moon, and all the rivers seeking out the sea—"

Weegee started shaking. It wasn't a fear-tremble, but a downright spasm that clattered his teeth and jerked his bones in a half-dozen different directions. He fell to the ground thrashing. Becca watched with fingers pressing her lips white. The seed fell from her hands as her pa knelt beside the little man, yanked a much-gnawed wooden stick from Weegee's belt, and jammed it between the clashing jaws just so.

A crowd knotted in fast. Becca heard more than one mouth say, "That's Weegee of Hallow. Lord King help us, he's taken by a seeing again."

Someone else answered, "Too strong for that small body and all his years, those seeings."

"Truth hits us all hard."

A dry, scornful laugh put in, "Isn't always truth in what he sees. I hear his ma schooled him to such things, so he could live on. She had a name for 'seeings' too, else his sire would never have let him live to see his second dawn. Every time there's winnowing talk down by Hallow Stead, he has another 'seeing' and the wind passes over his head."

Becca wanted to single out that last person, but she didn't dare turn to seek the speaker. Her eyes had to remain firmly downcast. Even if Pa was presently too taken with looking after Weegee, there'd be plenty of tongues willing to report her later if she overstepped a maiden's bounds. She decided to make the best of it and knelt to regather the twice-fallen seed.

Hallow Stead folk came by at last, drawn by the crowd's cries. Paul left Weegee to his own kinfolk's care and hustled Becca back to the Wiserways encampment. He didn't even think to ask for the seed back, and she was too breath-stole to remind him. She slipped it into her underskirt pocket for safekeeping, hearing the hard kernels slide down the sides of the hidden book.

Most of the way back they went in silence, but when the maidens' tent came in sight Paul seized her hard by the elbow and growled, "Not a word of any that you heard him say, Becca. Not one whisper of it, loud or low, understand?"

"Y—yes, Pa. Nothing Weegee said—"

"Good girl." He dropped her arm and wheeled away, leaving her to return to the tent alone. She tried to be obedient and good, tried to forget what had happened, but the bruise on her elbow turned black and the little man's face still stared her in the eyes until beard and brows and flesh boiled down to the silent accusation of a skull.

Chapter Nine

It is full merry in Heaven,
It is full heavy in Hell,
But how it is on earth, my love,
The two of us must tell.
I chose you for your beauty,
I chose you for your grace,
I chose you for your wisdom
That knows a woman's place.
She's wise who does not scorn love,
She's wise who bows to fate.
She's fool who fights God's wishes,
She's doomed who learns too late.

"How does my dress look?" Del asked. Becca had never seen her sib so anxious. Del the self-possessed, Del the most skillful feigner Becca had ever known, this same Del was now unable to feign even for an instant that she was anything more than a panic-stricken maiden. She had been sick once this night already, and she was not the only one.

For as little supper as any of them had eaten, it was amazing how much they gave back. If one of the elder steadwomen didn't come to empty the nightsoil pots soon, the next weak-bellied girl would be in a sorry case. The others did what they could to tidy up their stricken sibs and to keep all word of it from their sire. There was no telling how he would react to the possibility of his girls doing something to shame Wiserways.

"You look lovely, Del," Becca said. She smoothed her sib's snowy skirt unnecessarily. "There'll be alphs fighting over you before we've finished our first measure."

"Liar," Del called her, but it was fondly said. The maiden's eye lost some of that fear-glaze.

Becca managed to smile back. She too was feeling ill, but she forced herself to subdue a rebellious stomach. *I will not be sick. I will not! This tent smells vile enough already without me adding to the soury stink.* She prayed that their turn to dance would come soon, before the heat and tension and reek made her go the embarrassing way of her ailing sibs.

The tent where they bided was hotter than the Wiserways' maidens' tent, for all it was so large. The material was thicker, and it was old and black. No light could penetrate the heavy sides from within or without. Beyond the closed flap, the maidens of Hallow Stead were just finishing their dance on a fine plank floor surrounded by magical city-brought lightposts whose art stole a circle of daylight and plunked it right down in the midst of God's natural dark. Bright as those eerie lights shone, not a flicker could invade this tent. One lone lantern hung from the ridgepole, and that was all they had to see by.

Becca struggled against the sensation of being crushed by the weight of overheated, close, foul air. Her dress was damp under the arms and a fine trickle of sweat was inching down between her thighs. She wondered whether half the rumored wildness most maidens put into their dance wasn't just relief at finally being back out in the open air, free and able to breathe once more.

Music wormed its way in where light could not. An indistinct, half muffled run of melody crept into the black tent like a thief. Strummers and shakers and fluters had been gathered from every stead allied to Verity Grange— scrawny youths and swaybacked relics whose sole true right to live was grounded in how early and how apt they'd showed themselves to master music's own soul. *It would be a fine thing to be a music-maker*, Becca thought. She strained her ears to pick up any raveled thread of sound from outside.

But women made no music. It wasn't right, nor blessed. Oh, they could sing all they liked, if they'd a mind to that. It was hard not to sing, sometimes, when a job of laundry called for you to scrub and scrub and scrub until your mind would purely shatter itself mad without a song to anchor it to a more pleasant reality. Women could sing. Holy Deborah had sung beneath a miracle tree and Mary Mother lulled her baby silent while Herod's angelic messenger led them into the Egyptian land of plenty. You expected a woman to sing.

Instruments were another story. They were manlore. Becca leaned nearer the sealed opening of the tent and wondered what a bone pipe would taste like, resting against her lower lip, or how a shaker would heft when the tiny pellets inside their clay shell rattled until you nigh believed they were bone too.

Too many bones. Her hands clutched into fists in her lap, palms sweat-slick. She wiped them on her skirt. It wouldn't do to have Prisca's hand slip out of hers in the ring-figure part of their dance. She wished this dance, this night were over. *I wouldn't feel so if Jamie were here.* But Jamie was home on Wiserways Stead, and Becca felt as lone as the unknown girl whose book she'd stolen.

The book was back in the maidens' tent, packed in her traveling box because she couldn't wear a pocket tonight. Her flimsy white dancing dress had as little substance as the cotton shift under it. It would be cold when Becca and the rest stepped out onto the floor, but there was never any question of maidens wearing heavier garb at Harvest Home. *I heard the grangewomen remark on how chill the weather's turned,* Becca thought. *"Not like in my day,"* one said. *"Then we were pleased to have such airy dresses for one night, at least. This time of year was always near as warm as high summer. Now I'm feared these girls will catch their deaths before they catch their men." How odd. Seasons change, but years? So much change that the old women notice and remember?*

The tent flap was cast aside, the distraction breaking off Becca's thoughts. An old woman stood there, her skirt plain grangewear but her headshawl a shimmer of city goods. Backlit by the bright lights of the dance floor, she held a small lantern high beside her face so that the waiting maidens would see her to be as human as they. Once, tales told, a grangewoman had scared a whole tent full of maids to death because she came in upon them suddenly, unheralded and untouched by any homely light. They thought she was the death angel herself come for them, and their hearts all stopped cold.

There was nothing the least angelic about this crone. "Wiserways Stead, is it?" she rasped. No one dared answer. "Speak up or rot where you sit. I asked were you Wiserways Stead?"

Becca could have sworn she heard Prisca's tongue scrape over her dry lips before the rotten-ripe maiden replied, "We are from Wiserways."

The old woman snorted. "Grow you rude out that way, I see. Well, come along. There's only you and Quarter Stead to see, and then the wrestling. Swear to the Lord King, if we don't get you girlies moving faster, them young sinners'll kill each other off before they're even sent for. Barak's had three quarrels to bust up so far, and praise be we've a patient man for our alph's all I'll say. Haste, now." She made encouraging motions with her free hand, even to swatting little Sarah June lightly on the rump when she loitered in the tent doorway. Beneath the gruffness and the dried mushroom wrinkles, Becca thought she sensed a friend.

Silence met the maidens as they stepped onto the floor. Not a whisper crept forth to meet them. The air itself was a taut strummer string, waiting for the finger of God to pluck it into music. Becca's toes curled at the unfamiliar feel of finely sanded planks gliding away beneath her heel and ball. She gave a fleeting wish for her shoes, though she knew they were as forbidden as a good, warm dress this night. The coop-brought lights were brighter than she'd ever imagined anything but the sun could shine. She blinked stupidly in the white dazzle. Under the glare she had no hope seeing what waited in the blackness beyond the dance floor. *How can the cityfolk sleep if they blaze away God's sweet night like this?* she thought.

A small hand slipped into her left, a larger one clasped her right firmly. Linked between Sarah June and Apple, she rustled forward, part of the white wave of Wiserways maidens taking their places for the first figure of the dance. No sound came from the world beyond the lights, not even a hint to let keen ears tell where the music-makers sat biding. Becca could see nothing but the floorboards and the lightposts, no one but her sibs. In spite of their company, she felt bone-naked and alone.

You never are alone when you dance, child. Her mama's voice came softly into her mind on the wings of a nightwind. *Hark and she'll be there, the holy protector of all maiden dancers. Open your heart to her blessed love, Becca. Take sweet Saint Salome into your soul, step bold and never fear.*

A breath of lost homestead evenings toyed with the wisps of yellow hair tickling Becca's ears. Old words returned, told out by leaping firelight: *The Lord King Herod was once a man much sunk in wickedness—* Apple's dry hand and Sarah June's moist one vanished from Becca's grasp. The blinding lights faded into the glowing bud of the seeing-room hearth. Becca was a child again, nestling close to her mother's skirted knees, hearing the Scripture tales go around the circle of winterbound women.

And he did much wrong, and was flown with wine, and would not heed the good words of his counselors. Thus it was that God beheld the Lord King's iniquity, and spoke unto His angels, saying: "I will destroy this man and rid the world of his evil."

But there was one among the heavenly host who dared to speak before the Lord's face and say, "Nay, my Lord, as salvation even now lieth in a virgin's womb, I say unto Thee that this man must not be slain, but rather saved."

And the Lord said unto His angel, "He will not heed any word that may save him." And the angel replied, "Then he must be saved by other than words."

And it came to pass that the angel of the Lord descended unto the earth and visited the Lord King's daughter, even the royal virgin who was called Salome, the daughter of Herod. And the angel bid her in God's name arise and dance before her father, saying: "Thy father will heed no word of good counsel to his own soul's saving. Wherefore it must rest with thee to bring him unto the light and the love of God."

Yet Salome protested, saying: "How may my father heed me, a simple maiden, when he will not hearken to the good words of his wisest counselors?" And the angel answered, "They have poured wisdom from their lips into his ears to no avail, but thou shalt write thy counsel on the living air where all must see it, and with the flesh of thy body thou shalt witness more of God's own truth before thy sire than might all the wisdom Solomon ever uttered."

Then the maiden Salome arose and bathed and annointed herself with sweet oils and fragrant unguents and put on her veils and went in to where the Lord King sat drinking wine. And the maiden Salome put off the jeweled shoes from her feet and did dance the truth of God before the face of the Lord King Herod. Then did the Lord King read in the steps of the

maiden's dance all his wickedness in plainer sight and seeming
than in the words of ten thousand good counselors.

And the Lord King was ashamed. He put away his wine
from him, and his evil ways, and he threw himself upon the
mercy of the Lord God, which is infinite, crying out unto
heaven: "Forgive me, O my God, who am the most miserable
of sinners." And the Lord heard his supplication and sent His
angel to be a sign unto him.

The angel spoke and said: "Arise, O King, for thy
salvation and the salvation of all mankind is close at hand,
even in a virgin's womb. Arise, for by the grace of God and
His only begotten Son your sins shall be forgiven."

Then the Lord King rose up, and his soul was clean, and
his heart was light within him. And the Lord King did send
for the princess Salome, for he made a holy vow to reward
her for her dance which had saved him. "Anything that she
may ask, I shall give her, even unto the half of my kingdom."
But the King's messengers came back again, saying: "We can
not find the princess Salome."

Then the angel of God spoke a second time unto the Lord
King, saying: "Do not seek to find her, for she is gone from
thy sight forever." But where she had gone, no man did ever
know.

Becca's mama stopped her Scripture then and linked
knowing looks with Pa's other wives. No man, but every
woman knew where sweet Saint Salome had flown! They
knew, and all the little girls might beg and tease forever
to be told the secret: They would never have it out of
their mothers in words. There was just the *knowing*, more
powerful than the shielding words "Lord King grant it,"
more secret than all the hidden doings of manlore.
Someday you'll know, child, was all Mama ever said. *But
remember, she who danced for the Lord King's own saving is*

*never nearer than when her small sisters stand up to tread
the dance in her holy name.*

The breath of the saint filled Becca's chest as she stood
there on the dance floor. She drew it in greedily through
her nostrils and swung her hands high, exultant. Taken
by surprise, her flanking sibs raised both their hands as
well, and the motion rippled out to the ends of the human
chain until all the Wiserways maidens stood stretching
their joined hands to heaven. Prisca, in the leader's place,
was startled for a moment. Cold and sharp as a dash of
meltwater in the face, she made brisk to seize back
control.

A crisp bob of her head and the music-makers struck
up the dance tune that had always belonged to the
maidens of Wiserways Stead. The dance itself might
change, but never that music. Becca heard tell that it had
come down to her generation through the harsh and
hungering times, hidden in plucked strings and hollowed
bone-flutes and sometimes just the wire-thin whistling
of one man's lips. The music came from *before*, and it
would ride with Wiserways maidens as far as *ever*.

The maidens stamped their right feet in unison,
brought their left around behind, stamped those, cast
their clasped hands up and back, dropped free one of the
next, twirled and bounded across the floor to join again
into an outfacing ring. Arms encircled waists, each resting
on the next girl's hip. Bare feet flew, flashing white and
rose and gold and brown against the amber boards,
flicking back beneath the shelter of their skirts as if
ashamed of being too fair. The music rocked and tilted
the world. Flute and shaker, strummer and sticks raced
ahead of the dancing feet, spinning a spiral stair from
earth to heaven just a step ahead of the whirling dancers.

Esther M. Friesner

Now there were sounds from beyond the lights, other sounds than the burning lash of music. Becca heard them, the low voices in the dark. Her eyes had grown accustomed to the dazzle of city-brought light the same way she'd grown used to the overwhelming size of Verity Grange; she was not grateful for the favor. She filled her mind's eye with the painted image of Saint Salome, afraid that if she looked beyond the dance floor she would see too much. But the blessed dancer's image would not tarry for one who called on her out of fear, not piety. Becca's glance strayed farther out, seeing, despite herself, what she never wished to see:

Devouring eyes on her, on all her sibs as they danced. Male faces gaunt with wanting. All the men of the steads allied to Verity, both young and old, a host of hungering presences ranged back in shadowed rows around the dance floor. They bided out there in the darkness that was powerless to veil the leap and pulse of pure desire. Their hunger was forced out in a throb of words, a rumble of rising speculation.

Becca prayed for a miracle to burst over her, deafening her to the sounds of their greed, blinding her to the plain carnality in their faces. Bad enough to hear them toss their wanting whispers from lip to lip, worse to be able to see the looks that went with those whispers.

Alphs made or in the making, all men will long for you some day. Selena's last lesson murmured through Becca's mind as she crossed the floor to take Prisca's hand for the ring-figure. *They'll look you full in the face, but that's not where their thoughts are tending. You'll know. Not a one of them will see you dance, but he'll be spinning dreams of having your body hot and naked against his own, you in your times. That's proper. That's the purpose God put you here for, to drive them mad with that one imagining. Every stone a man ever laid atop another, every step a man ever took to lead his kin out of the hungering years, back to the light of God, there was the promise of a woman's heat behind it, waiting to reward him, waiting to kindle his seed and no other to life.*

Proper, all the weight of lust that Becca felt heavy on her out there in the darkness. Proper, the way their eyes glowed with wanting her and her sibs. A promise: That was all she was, all any of the dancing maidens were. A promise that spoke deep in a man, chafed his blood and urged him on to be stronger, braver, more cunning than his brothers so that *his* seed and not theirs would root in every woman he could claim. And if only the strong, the brave and the cunning lived to make the bones of the unborn, the children who came after must surpass their sires. That was the holy law, immutable, that shaped the world. Stone on stone, lifetime on lifetime, each step upwards in turn like the progress of a maiden's dance, until the generations lifted themselves clear of the devil and came back at last to Paradise.

On a stairway of spread-legged women?

Becca gasped, caught poised on tip-toe by words that couldn't—shouldn't—exist in any proper maiden's mind. The bleeding, mocking ghost of Prayerful Hill danced before her eyes in the midst of the maidens' ring, the worm of doubt Becca had thought she'd exiled. She came down hard on both feet, deliberately, as if that would jar the phantom out of her. Her sibs stared—this was not part of their dance—but Becca just spun fast enough to whisk her white skirt wide as a blown blossom, trying to whisk the apparition away. The ghost giggled in her skull.

She danced harder, driven, doing all she could to

stamp away the evil, unsettling knot the ghost and the ghost book had tied inside her. She heard the slither of whispers in the dark too clearly now. The worm reached out and drew in whole threads of words, all distinct and chilling.

"—better legs than Hallow girls. Look there, the littlest one. Hardly seems old enough to have passed Changes."

"You let Paul hear you talk that way, Jared, and Quarter Stead'll have a new alph who got his way in cleared for free. Paul'd never put up one that wasn't man-ready. You know what a stickler he is."

"Young like that, they're easier taught government. That's how I admire to have them. I do believe I'll have a word to say with Paul tonight."

"Keep your milk-taste. I like them better like that one there, the bright haired one near the center. See how she flies! You know the saying: A fire on the dance floor, a fury in the bed. Yes, if my dealings go well with the Coopfolk, I wager I'll have more than just a word to say to Paul about that girl."

"No. That one is mine."

Rough laughter greeted those words, so quietly spoken it was a perverse wonder that Brecca heard them. She slowed her steps to meet the music, but she could not tear her hearing back to only heeding the melody. She knew that voice, but lest she try to lie herself serene again, the worm used its unearthly powers to make one man out there say loud:

"*Yours*, Adonijah?"

And more laughter came that lasted until the music ceased and the Wiserways maidens' dance was done.

Chapter Ten

Where are you going?
Down to the river.
What will you do there?
I'll meet my lover.
Is his heart yours, then?
Yes, it's mine.
How will you love him?
The Kiss and the Sign.

Their dancing done, the Wiserways maidens were conducted from the floor by a different crone than the one that had brought them on. As she followed her sibs away, Becca heard the music-makers bringing their instruments to readiness for the Quarter Stead girls who had yet to dance.

The old woman led them by a twisty route that took them far from the massed male spectators, down streets lit only by the harvest moon, and into a grove of trees. Becca had never seen the like. Every tree was vital, she could tell by the livewood scent of them, though their leaves rustled dead and dry overhead. Her bare feet slipped over small round things in the grass between the towering trunks. Any child knew that lofty age had to go into the making of trees so tall. She darted out a hand to caress the bark as she passed, thrilling with the secret thought that perhaps here was a living witness of the hungering times.

More than a witness, one that had survived.

The way through the grove was too short, too soon done. The golden lights of a long, one-storied building welcomed the dancers and their guide. Inside they saw all those who had danced before them. The girls sat on the floor, stead by stead, invisible boundaries set clear to see in the spaces separating group from group. Cityware lights hung from the rafters, though these burned with a gentler brightness than those ringing the dance floor. Fire gleamed in the massive stone hearth at the far end of the hall. The blaze was half-hearted, poorly tended, but thick walls kept the cold outside at bay.

The Wiserways girls quickly staked out their own parcel of floor space. The crone who had brought them in deserted them without a word as soon as she had the last maiden herded over the threshold. "There's slippers to borrow in the bins, if you feel need of 'em," was all she told them. Then she took herself off downhall, pulling a chair up to the fire and falling into gossip with the four other Verity matrons already there.

No chairs for the girls, though; no chairs and no chance to talk with any but the self-same band of sibs she'd been pent up with for days. Becca tried to steal a pleasant word with a dark-skinned girl from the gaggle nearest her own, but her overtures were shut out with a stonewall silence.

"Leave her be, Becca!" Apple hissed, tweaking Becca's ear. Her voice was hushed; no one in the hall save the chaperones seemed willing to speak above a whisper. "And don't go making your usual hoorahs. Biding 'til we're called for, quiet, that's all we've to do now. You go kicking up wild and you'll learn how hard these old barkskins by the fire can thwack a fool's head for her." Apple's smug grin as good as added that any vengeance Becca might be thinking to trade for that ear-tweak would count as "kicking up wild" and be punished accordingly.

Becca turned her back on Apple, though she knew her graceless sib was right. She spoke from experience, as would Prisca, both of them having come to Harvest Home in years past. Much as she despised Apple and Prisca for being so sour-hearted and mean, a lonesome little flicker of fear inside her longed to ask them the truth of what was awaiting them all, out there under this night's lambent moon.

It was one thing to take lessoning from Mama and the other wives, demonstrating just so on the carved phallos how she would give a man the Sign of Gratitude and the Kiss of Thanks. Yet how would it really be when what she held wasn't artful carvery but living flesh? On stead, she'd never been called upon to serve a man, maybe because the men felt Paul's eye heavy on them any time they looked to his favored child. Before, she'd been glad of it, but now she nigh wished she'd some measure of knowing to draw on, to lend her bone for what she'd have to face tonight. She huddled herself small against her overbold imaginings.

Tales the wives tell sometimes tell too little or make up too much, she thought. *The Kiss and the Sign when I'm asked, yes, but sure there must be more? What happens after the giving? Will there be aught the man might give to me, and must I take it? What's to do and who's to blame if he wants more and I say no? Sweet Mary Mother, grant that I can find Pa quick, once they turn us out of doors. Give me the words to make him believe I've done enough of a woman's part to satisfy the honor of our stead, so I can claim his protection, like he promised. Heaven witness, it's not just Adonijah I'm feared of this night!*

The Quarter Stead girls came in, led by the crone who'd first brought the Wiserways maidens onto the dance floor. They took over a share of the floor near Wiserways, but Becca made no attempt to scare up chat with any of them. Her doubts made her too restless. She got up and stood at a nearby window, letting the unfamiliar cool of glass press against her brow. She lost all reckoning of time. Outside, all soon grew darker. The rafter lights cast false ghosts of brightness against the pane.

"See anything, Bec'?" Sarah June sidled near, leaning close and tight against her elder sib's side. Becca looked into the young one's frighted eyes and remembered how often she'd comforted her and Rusha when they woke screaming from night terrors in the dormitory. Only chance that had brought her into her Changes later than most—chance that had put her in her times at last year's Harvest Home—had saved her from having to face this ordeal as young as they.

"Can't see much, love." Becca returned her gaze to the full dark outside. "For a time I thought I saw a glow out that way"—she gestured west—"but it's long gone."

"That'd be the wrestling ring." An aged voice came up behind the two girls at the window. It was the grangewoman, the one who'd just brought in the Quarter Stead maidens. Becca hadn't heard her creep up close enough to speak. "Shouldn't be too much longer before they're done with the bouts and the after-business."

Sarah June frowned. "Weren't the bouts done when the lights went out? How can they wrestle in the dark?"

The old woman laughed and pinched the girl's cheek. "Lord King bless you, there's a question that comes with answer known! In that much of a hurry for the real joy to commence, child? When I was a maid, my mam often said how Wiserways bred 'em lickerish young." Her small black eyes twinkled at Sarah June's confusion of blushes.

Becca put her arms around her sib. Poor Sarah June burrowed her face into the shelter of Becca's embrace. Hardfaced, she snapped at the grangewoman, "You've no call to go measuring us to your own twisted rule. My sire hears you talk like that about us, you'd best have a hidey-hole to hand. My mama often says how old women are broomstraw: useful enough, but plenty more easy to come by if some's wasted."

"*Becca!*" Sarah June jerked her head up, shock outdoing shame. She cast fearful eyes from her sib's angered face to the crone. "Becca, she's *Grange!*"

The old woman tried to force a scowl over her features and failed. Instead she chuckled and touched Sarah June's cheek gently. "Flower-fair, don't you tremble. Grange is just air, so far as I'm concerned. Your sib won't gather any trouble for me." A broad grin pushed her sags and wrinkles into new patterns. "You're a brave 'un—Becca, is it? Put me in my place all proper, standing up for your little sib here. Sweet Mary keep you that strong, child, and you'll come to much."

The crone's unexpected grace caught Becca by surprise, disarming her. "I—Ma'am, I didn't mean—"

"Stuff." The old woman waved away Becca's words. "You meant what you said, right enough, and right you were to say it. There's no harm in strength like that. God witness, I've had call for it in all my travels, and you've a further way to go than I." She offered a knobbled hand like a clutch of dead branches, and in a voice of seeing-room formality, said, "Ivah of Verity."

Becca took the handclasp with care, as if afraid the thin fingers would snap off if pressed too tightly. "Becca of Wiserways, Paul's get."

"Get? They still drum that into your head? Shoo, and me long since forgetting whose seed got me." A wink nipped across one eye. "Ungrateful woman that I am." She looked to Sarah June again and added, "I'm heartily sorry for any offense I caused you, precious one. Honest questions deserve plain answers, especially now when the waiting hangs heavy. Forgive an old fool?"

Sarah June recovered some self-possession. She stepped away from Becca and managed to nod, but couldn't get a word out.

"That's good." Ivah sighed and stared out the window, blinkering her eyes with both hands to peer into the night. "Not easy, a woman's lot, but times like this I don't doubt a man's is harder. So you'd know about the wrestling? Well, 'long as the lights are on, with the Coopfolk watching, the bouts are clean and ordered as the maidens' dance. Any man you ask will tell you that the wrestling's fair and ends with the formal bouts. Stead against stead, all strictly ranked by age and weight, the traders passing 'round their flasks to our men just as if they'd all grown up of one blood and breeding. Wagers fly and are paid, and when each bout's done the winner takes the loser's hand in fellowship."

Ivah turned from the window and lowered her hands. Muted and secret her voice then, holding its saying hidden from all ears but Becca's and Sarah June's. "But when the wagers are settled up, and the strong drink gone, and the Coop city folk have picked this or that young'n to take off with 'em when Harvest Home is done…then the dark. Then the true striving."

Becca didn't—couldn't understand. Ivah's words were for her, yet Ivah's eyes wandered wide, spanning the brightly lit hall. Dancing with ghosts: Mama always called it so when Becca's sight roved. Feeling shyer than even Sarah June, Becca tugged at the trailing iridescence of Ivah's shawl and asked, "What do you mean, please, the true striving?"

Ivah's ghosts came home to dance in a sudden rise of tears. They trembled in the cups of Ivah's pink-rimmed eyes, but not a drop spilled over. "Why, save you, child, what other striving do men ever know? To kill."

A half-strangled wail of terror escaped Sarah June's lips.

"*Ivah!*" The name cracked across the hall. A blue-clad grangewoman sprang out of her stiff-backed chair and bore down upon them like a riled-up beetle, plowing straight through any maidens' groups in her way. The steadgirls stared, glad of the distraction.

She took Becca and Sarah June by the elbow and hustled them off. Their self-appointed conductor looked older than Ivah, yet vigorous enough to give the lie to anyone who named her ancient. Small and incredibly plump, she rolled rapidly back to her hearthside seat, bearing the girls with her.

"The idea!" she snorted. "Going to fill your poor little heads with her mealymouthings, lending you horrors that aren't there. As if you hadn't enough to think on just now!" She plopped herself down in the chair. Chubby hands fanned her face as energetically as if she had just returned from a footrace.

"Praise the Lord King my ears are still keen. I declare, that woman'd make dewfall into hailstones and rain into the Flood itself! Sit, girls, sit." She planted hands on knees and leaned forward as a bewildered Becca and Sarah June sank down obediently at her feet.

"Now listen, for there's no need my repeating it. You're women tested and tried—Lord King avert a mischief touching you!—else you wouldn't be here. You're old enough to know things straight out. Things are as they be, and rightly, nor all Ivah's portentous riddle-speaking will change 'em. You've naught to fear. *Naught*, hear me? This ain't any sort of a winnowing to touch a maid. It's your brothers must fear this night, not you. While the lights shine, the striplings wrestle fair, and them as conquer take the hands of those they best. But when the dark comes, the losers flee, for if they don't, they're dead men."

She seemed to take satisfaction in the startlement that crossed the girls' faces. The other grangewomen closed their eyes like basking turtles, but Becca sensed that they too were drawing some perverse contentment from the effects of their companion's tale.

Because they know something you crave knowing, the

worm whispered. *It pleasures them to parcel it out by bits and scraps, the sole treasure age has left them. And if it sets a crease between your brows, sucks out a little of the youth they envy you, so much the better!*

The grangewoman spoke on: "When the Coopfolk call an end to the bouts and take the lights away to save 'em, *they* think our men come here straightaway for you lot, or to fetch the torches for later. Well, they don't. There's a business yet to do, and if the Coopfolk *do* know what it is, they sew their lips and tend their own knitting. There's none to force our boys into the ring, you know. One stands up to try a bout, he good as says he's got hopes to face his sire down some day. Now if he loses poorly, who's the less for it if later, by dark, there comes a better man to teach him the full price of pride?"

"Kill him?" Sarah June's lips parted. "Who does it?"

"Any who can catch him, child."

"Even one who's not alph of his stead?" There was no sign of pity for the losers in the womanchild's expression. Revelation and excitement sharpened her face. Becca was appalled.

The plump grangewoman nodded. "The haughty shall be brought into the dust," she intoned.

Sarah June leaned forward, her small hand stealing out to grip Becca's. "Then those who come for us tonight, they'll all be alphs, else alphs some day?" The thrill running through her blood seemed to shoot into Becca's skin. Ambition lit Sarah June's eyes bright as city-brought lights. "Only the strong?"

"Oh, better than that, my dear." The grangewoman settled down into her own unnatural fatness, complacent. "For betimes it's the dark takes off the winner of the bout. Stand up like that, win too well, and where's the lad's sire who's fool enough to wait for the death he begot himself? It takes wisdom as well as strength for a stripling to pass through this night. Some are too wise to show their mettle, some too sly to risk their weakness." She tossed her head to lead their eyes back toward the window where Ivah still stood. "Now her boy, he'd the strength but not the wisdom, else this day she'd be the great noise of Verity Grange." A tiny smile tugged at her pursed mouth. "Instead of me."

"Only the best will dare come 'round to seek you out, child," said another matron. Her eyes remained shut as if in sleep, so that her words seemed to come from an oracular statue out of olden tales. "None of the chaff or the gleanings, but the sweetest of all our harvest. Alphs, else young men too strong or lithe or clever to fear whatever the dark may hold. The unworthy who've got sense enough will take themselves off to safety. You'll not be pleasuring any but the finest men in all Verity Grange tonight."

Sarah June came near laughing for joy. "I thought I'd have to thank every man and boy as came to Harvest Home!"

The matrons echoed her laughter and one ruffled her hair. "Bless you, sweet love, think you'd fallen in with a rogue band? Strong and sharp-witted our men will be, *and* mannerly. We haven't lost a maid at Harvest Home since the war with Righteous, Lord King avert another."

"Now go back to your sibs, dear hearts," said another of the grangewomen, shooing Becca and Sarah June away. "You'll be told when it's time."

"Calm now, baby?" Apple's question bit into Sarah June when they rejoined their group. "Or will you still be wanting your mama to hold your hand tonight?"

"Hush, you deadwood." Becca couldn't help but put herself between her little sib and harshness. "You'll be lucky if there's anyone except your mama willing to hold *your* hand."

"Oh, Apple, now you've got her mad." Prisca feigned a frightened face, her words laced with acid. "Don't you know that if you raise your voice to Sarah June, you bring down Becca's wrath? So loving she is with that pretty dollbaby."

"Yes, indeed." Apple latched onto her sib's insinuation. "Fool I am to forget what the whole stead knows."

"What? What wickedness are you old hags saying?" Sarah June demanded. Her small face colored up high.

"Ignore them," Becca said evenly. "It'd joy them too much to see us get in trouble with the grangewomen." Deliberately, she stood up and walked away. She could hear Apple and Prisca still mewing after her. She crossed the hall, threading a path between the other crowds of maidens. There was nowhere for her to go, but that didn't matter so long as she put space between herself and her sibs.

"Becca?"

A hand twitched the hem of her dancing dress. She looked down. "Dassah!" Becca fell to her knees and clasped the Makepeace maiden's hands. "Oh, Dassah, I'm so joyed to see you again!"

The other Makepeace girls didn't look as if they shared any of Becca's joy. One and all, they wore faces stiff as starchwater masks, their mouths pinpricks of censure. A chill hung over this stead's maidens that had nothing to do with the weather outside the hall.

"Can we—can we walk apart some?" Dassah asked.

She spoke so low that Becca had to ask her to repeat the question.

"I suppose." Becca looked around. "No one upbraided me for it, or Sarah June. Come over by the windows."

The two girls stole away from the Makepeace maidens as if their going were a crime. Becca drew Dassah to the windows that didn't look in the direction of the wrestling ring. Even though the darkness on that side of the building was now complete, her imagination peopled it with young men and old locked in a killing dance.

"You look well, Dassah," Becca said, hoping to cast off the mantle of gloom she sensed clinging to the Makepeace girl. "I asked after you from Miss Lynn. She said you passed your Sixmonth fine. Rejoice."

"Rejoice." The word came out of Dassah's mouth cased in a shell of irony. "Now I'm a full-grown woman of Makepeace Stead." It sounded like a sentence of death.

"Well, not for much longer," Becca replied, hearing her own voice turn false-sounding and fey. Another ghost was standing between her and Dassah, a cold and faceless ghost that made her want to flee. "After this night I'll wager that there'll be alphs aplenty asking to have a word with your sire." She spoke the words every maiden was supposed to want to hear, desperately wishing for them to work their heart-lightening magic on Dassah and make her smile.

"No man will have me," Dassah said. She stared unseeing at the windowpane where reflections of the hanging globes of light floated like bubbles of hope just out of reach.

"What kind of fool talk is—?"

Dassah's eyes suddenly flashed back to life. Their fires burned like the taste of winter-frosted metal, their gaze clamping down on Becca's spirit like the jaws of a trap. She couldn't have moved if she tried.

"Becca, stay with me tonight," Dassah begged. "When they bring us out for the men, don't let me go alone."

"Sugar, we can't do that." Becca tried to lay a hand on Dassah's silky hair, but the other girl's whole body seemed to crackle with a power deadly and invisible. She pulled her hand away. "Pa's wives told us that the grangewomen contrive it so we go singly. I'd say we could meet up as soon as we're out of their ken, but neither one of us knows Verity. How could we find any meeting place?"

"I can't go out there alone. I *won't* go out there alone."

"Dassah, it won't be so bad. There's nothing to fear." Becca never thought she'd hear lies rise so readily to her lips. "Even little Sarah June's not frighted any more by what she'll meet out—"

"Is she going to meet her sire, Becca?" The question lashed from Dassah's lips. "Is she going to meet him woman to man? Has she been told face-to-face by her own father how she's to run straight to him? Did he walk her through Verity and show her the very place where he'll be waiting, or tell her what'd happen to her if she didn't mind him?"

"Her…*sire?*" None of what Dassah said seemed to hold any more sense than dreams. All Becca could do was repeat the words stupidly.

"My sire." Dassah struck the window sill with her fist. She looked up at Becca and her eyes swam with tears. "I thought it was a joke when he first told me—*ordered* me. At first, when he called me to him, I was joyed. I thought that maybe I'd done something special on the trip here to merit his praise. He never was one to play with his girl-children—or even to speak with us, if he had his choice—so I felt honored by his notice. Honored!"

Becca wished she didn't have to listen to the girl's hollow laugh. "What you're saying, Dassah...It's...it's not...it's abomination greater than any—"

"And who's to prove it?" Dassah spat. "Whose word? Mine? Mine against the alph of Makepeace Stead? Tell me who'll believe me! Name one soul who'll heed and help, and I'll shout it from the rooftops of Verity! But it wants five women to swear to a thing against one man's given word."

Becca could only shake her head, denying what was undeniable. "This can't be. Maybe you misunderstood. Not even Zach—"

"Why not?" Dassah countered. "He's alph; his wants and his will are all the law we live by, for as long as he's got the power to keep it so. If I were a man, I could stand against him in challenge. I might lose, but dying that way doesn't seem so bad to me now."

"What did he say to you?" Becca asked, not really wanting to know.

"He said"—Dassah's eyes lost all their life—"he said how proud he was to see what a pretty thing I'd grown to be. He said he was avaricious of pretty things, Lord King forgive him. He said that he wasn't one to share such, no, but he was one to crush even the prettiest thing if it showed itself heart-rotted with treachery and ingratitude against the hand that fed it. And then he kissed me."

"Dassah—"

"We were in his tent right here, soon after camp was made. He didn't kiss me with a father's love, but just the way I'd seen him kiss my mama or one of the other wives. And then he told me how it would be and how I'd be rewarded if I showed myself a grateful child. Any children I might bear—"

"*Children!*" Becca was aghast.

"—they'd never see the hill, no matter what; he swore it. My silence for their lives. Last of all he took me to the route where he means to find me waiting for him tonight. Where he'd *better* find me waiting, he said."

She tilted her head back and the city-brought lights turned the streaks of tears on her face to silver. "Sweet Mary!" she sobbed, keeping it still too soft for the grangewomen to take notice. "Oh, sweet Mary Mother, why was I so feared of not coming through my Sixmonth clean? Why'd I pray to pass it? Talk of girls who didn't make Sixmonth's just a lot of scare-tales. Not a woman alive but's come through that time from when her Changes first come on her until half a year's proper passed. It's all an empty rite. Why'd I waste my prayers? Better I should've prayed for the mark of blood to take me. Better if the women had given me a secret death. Better any death than what's waiting for me tonight, O Lord!"

"No," Becca breathed. She took Dassah in her arms as tenderly as if she were a babe to be saved from the hill. "No dying's better. I'll stay by you. Your sire shan't touch you. We'll find my pa. I know where to find him." Dassah's fear-wide eyes flashed at her and she made haste to add, "It's not like that between us: He's promised me his protection from—from one we're agreed's no proper man, that's all. He'll shield you too, you wait and see. I know he—"

"Against another alph?" Dassah demanded. "Stead against stead? Against another *man?*"

"Hush now," was all Becca could say, stroking Dassah's hair. "It'll all come 'round right. Hush."

The door at the end of the hall opened while they stood there. The grangewoman who entered announced, "All's done. It's time." A stillness fell in the wake of her words. The quiet of several score held breaths was like the shade cast by the death angel's wing. Becca felt Dassah shudder once in her arms.

Wordlessly, Ivah took a strange, smooth reachpole and extinguished the hanging lights. The matrons by the hearth cast handfuls of earth over the flames and all was blackness.

In the dark, Becca heard the rustle of dozens of skirts, the scuffle of scores of feet, bare and shod. She pulled herself and Dassah back against the windows, praying to sweet Saint Salome to cast her veil of invisibility over them both.

It wasn't the night for the answering of a maiden's prayer. Strong hands grabbed her shoulders, dragging her aside. She clung to Dassah, whose sole sound was a low, distraught, animal moaning. Little by little the girl was being pulled from her grasp. Becca tried to hold her fast, but there were too many hands laid to the task of opposing her.

"Dassah!" she cried. "Dassah, wait for me! I'll find you! I won't let you go alone!"

Then her hands were empty, and there was the cold night wind on her face, and she was thrown flat in the dirt under the ancient trees.

Chapter Eleven

Here's how you lesson a woman:
When she's milkfed, her ma does it.
When she's mischief, her pa does it.
When she's maiden, he who'll be her master does it.
That's manlore.
Here's how you break a woman who won't lesson:
When she's milkfed, her ma does it scoldwise.
When she's mischief, her pa does it switchwise.
When she's maiden and brays she's masterless, he
    who's got mind and muscle to put truth to her does
    it, and he's to be her master.
That's manlore too.

Becca wandered through the grove, calling Dassah's name. The moon's light sifted through the trees, turning the fallen nuts to nuggets of gold in the half-frosted grass. She stumbled back toward the long building, hoping to find the Makepeace girl lingering near it. Instead she found Ivah guarding the door, the reachpole in her hands.

"Need help finding your way into Grange?" the older woman asked.

"I—I was looking for someone."

"The only ones you need to find tonight are in the streets, and they're waiting for you."

"It's a friend of mine I'm seeking. She's afraid—"

"Not that pretty sib of yours? I thought the other wives settled her stomach for her. She looked downright eager to be about this night's work when they were done."

"No, it's not Sarah June. I said a friend, a girl from another stead than ours."

"Well, she can be from the moon for all I care. You're to go singly. This night's not for hen-chat. You've no business meeting your obligations in any but the ways laid down by lore."

"What if—" Becca began, a canny look in her eyes. "What if I run into another maiden in the streets this night by chance? There's aplenty of us."

"And Verity Grange is aplenty big enough, even counting just the streets we've set aside for you. Still, chance meetings happen; and when they do, it's your duty to turn a blind eye, a deaf ear, and put swift feet under you to move on. Every maiden stands alone this night, I said. Or didn't your mama lesson you right?"

"I was lessoned as good as any," Becca replied stiffly.

"Then take yourself off that way." Ivah tossed her head toward the moonlit streets of Verity. "I know what you're up to, buying time with all this empty jabber. Lord witness, I wish you were through this night—you and all your sibs—but things are as they are, and there's no use fighting what's always been and forever will be. Now get, or I'll give you some encouragement." She wagged the reachpole meaningly.

Becca didn't need or want more reason to get a move on. *I don't care what she says,* she thought fiercely as she ran through the grove, down the path that led to Verity. *I'll find Dassah and I'll stick by her tonight. Worst that can happen is they'll separate us, but then I'll find her again. Yes, and again, until we can either find my pa or they send us both back to our tents. They'll call for Pa then, more'n likely. Let them; it's all I want. He'll believe me when I tell him Dassah's tale. He knows what Zach's like, and he'll do what he can to nose out proof against him. I recall him saying once how an alph can't do a better job of work than rooting out abomination. Oh, and this is abomination past all excuse! Maybe when all's done there'll be a way contrived to make our Tom alph of Makepeace. And if he takes Dassah for his wife—*

Her mind was preoccupied with spinning out a future cut to the measure of her own desires. She didn't notice the shadow biding in a sidestreet she loped past until it stepped out and siezed her firmly by the sleeve, making her stop and turn.

"Bless you, sister. Have you been fed?" asked the strangerman.

And so it began. She never had the chance to find her sire; the men found her first.

It was easier by the third time. After that, Becca no longer felt compelled to seek out a rainwater tun for scrubbing her hands and mouth clean raw. The next man she thanked would only undo the moment's stolen feeling of being free again, and clean. A splash of water was enough.

The smell was the worst part of it, near as she could tell. The stickiness wasn't too bad; some bearable, like getting gluey griddle batter on your hands. Selena'd been right about how it didn't have such-a-much taste and slicked right down your throat if you gulped fast. For the rest, she minded every lesson she'd ever had from Selena and the others, doing all she could for all who chose her to speed them on their well-earned way to Paradise.

Only one of the men gave her any trouble, and that more from his strange behavior than any desire to work mischief on her. He was a funny-looking fellow, by what she could see of his face in the moonlight. Most of his hair was gone and sight of his red, rounded cheeks provoked her with the notion that she knew him from somewhere, that she ought to recognize him. She was seated on the ground leaning against a rough brick wall when he found her—stumbled over her was closer to the truth. When she arose to make proper response to his mannerly greeting, she saw that he was only a shadow taller than she.

"Bless you, sister, have you been fed?" he asked. His voice was wobbly and uncertain as a growing boychild's.

"Your strength has brought me sanctuary, your kindness has fed me, your honor vouchsafed me salvation." Becca had lost count of how many times that night she'd droned out the set answer. It got so that she wished the men would drop all this play-acting and just let her get on to doing their business for them. She chose to shut her mind and play at dreaming while she performed her proper duty.

The first time, she tried pretending it was Jamie she served, but that did more harm than good. Jamie would never treat her so, like she was a thing—oh, a pleasing thing, sure; a handy, comforting thing, yes—but no more than that. To these men she was a cool dipperful of water on a hot day, a staying meal on a hungering belly that doesn't care what it devours so long as it's fed. That wasn't—that couldn't be Jamie. She let his image go. The dawn would redeem her. Until then she would go through the motions so that none who met her might run carping to Pa.

She hushed the worm when it asked her whether all this would be any different when she was made a wife.

I'll be Jamie's then, she told it proudly.

That wasn't what I asked, it replied.

She ignored it and returned her attention to the round-cheeked man claiming her duty. In the same flat, obedient voice she used for *yes'm, yes'm* when Mama lectured her about some fancied fault, Becca recited her proper part for the round-faced man: "I would show you thanks and gratitude." That made it his turn to say how he'd have her serve him.

He jumped away from her so lively that for a moment she mistook the abrupt gesture for an indication that he'd take the Kiss of Thanks from her lips. She gathered up her white skirt to keep it as clean as possible while she knelt, but his pudgy hands clamped on her shoulders, hauling her upright.

"Oh, no, no, no; not that, missy!" The words fluted high and chittery. The agitation Becca heard in them startled her out of her hard-won detachment. Blinking, she extended her hand to him, thinking he wanted the

Sign instead. He turned his whole plump body away from her as modestly as a maid first come into Changes.

"Please." He waved her back toward the wall. "Please sit. I've no desire for anything but talk with you."

"*Talk*? This night, at Harvest Home? What's wrong with you?" The words bolted from Becca's lips before she could reflect on what she was saying. Too late, her fingers flew to stifle such offense, and a flush burned her cheeks.

But he laughed. It was such a gentle, homely sound. Becca couldn't recall the last time she'd heard true heartfree laughter since coming to Verity Grange. His hand was smooth and cool as his fingers stole into her hot, sticky palm.

"Bless you, missy, what tall tales have your steadwomen told you about men? I've been served and comforted and thanked enough this night to make me relish a little *in*gratitude 'long about now, else I'll drain to dust." He slid down the wall wearily, dragging her along to sit beside him. "There's just so much a man can do."

Becca's lips pursed in puzzlement. "Then if you've been proper served, why linger? Why not go back to your stead's tents?"

His eyes were wistful. "Think they let us escape any more'n they let you maidens? Oh, these Verity matrons are truly a rock and a rod to stand firm and drive back into the fold any who'd like to stray."

"I know," Becca mumbled, recalling Ivah.

"Tried to sneak out of Grange, did you?" He asked it mildly. "I know, I know. Every year there's more than a few maidens who'd sooner not be Ruth to however many men take Boaz's face tonight. Meet 'em at a barricade, did you?"

"A barricade?"

"Oh, they're not much by any standard—just a teetery few sticks of wood lashed together—but they're warded by stone-faced grangewomen who'll peck the hide off your back with their questions: *What's your business passing this place? Surely you're not running away from a good maiden's rightful duty at Harvest Home? Doubtless you've merely lost your way?* And all your excuses turn to flimsy things under their hard eyes. No use trying to hide in any of the grange buildings, either. They make certain to lock all the doors and windows you might try."

The chubby little fellow sighed. "Duty, duty." He shook his head. "Wisht my ma'd never brought me up so strict to my duty. Could be then I'd have managed a way to wink those old harpies into turning a blind eye to any as seek to slickery past their guardposts. Unwilling service doesn't do anyone honor. Some of my boys, they've been working like oxen for weeks now, getting all ready for the Coopfolk and all the steads coming into Verity. Shoo, don't I know as they'd most likely rather steal a little sleep this night, could they. But duty…" He tilted his head back wearily and shut his eyes. He couldn't see the sharp, quizzing look Becca gave him.

Her mind's eye held a plump, complacent old grangewoman's image, the self-same one who'd lectured her and Sarah June on what the young men truly did after their wrestling bouts. One face, that old woman and this grown man. What had she said? About how wisdom sometimes bested strength?

"You're alph of Verity!" In Becca's mouth it sounded like the charge of some crime.

"And named Barak, by blessed water." He opened his

eyes and smiled sweetly at her. "Knowing that, will you talk with me now, missy?"

Feeling tinier than Sarah June, Becca gulped and bobbed her head. Her hands folded themselves primly in her lap and her lips pressed tight together, as if she were awaiting some lesson she'd as soon not hear.

The harvest moon swam in his eyes, so very large that the hurt he felt had nowhere to hide. "I see," he said. "You'll do it from fear of me. Well, better that than have you cast your net for me a-purpose. I've walked that path times enough this night. But you *will* talk? Not just sit there tight as a lowtide clam?"

Whether it was the sadness in his look or her own accursed curiosity, Becca couldn't help but blurt, "What in the Lord King's name's a low-tide clam?"

Barak laughed with a whole heart and suddenly it was all easier. There was that about Verity Grange's unusual alph that set Becca's triphammer heart free. Then he began to talk.

The moon vanished and the hard wall at her back no longer pressed rough and cold through her dancing dress. As she and her sibs had danced for the men, this man now made wonders dance for her alone, solely with the words of his mouth. He could speak about most anything under the sun, making Becca see it too. He could talk of happenings past and take her there, even if she had no more notion of the things he'd witnessed than a—why, than a lowtide clam! He even welcomed her questions. The back of her head held the knowledge that here was a man who'd done a man's given business—he'd killed to claim his place as alph of Verity and killed since then to keep it—but when he spoke, it didn't seem possible.

And he knew more about the Coop Cities than any man she'd ever met, including Pa.

"Course I knew your brother Eleazar. Saw him and the party he traveled with when they passed through here— how many years gone is it? Well, no mind. It's not such a ways our Coopfolk have to come to reach Verity. It's them of the other Coops I pity every time I see the lines of their beasts and wagons against the horizon. They've got to cross the ice mountains, they do, or so our Coopfolk tell me. They say as their rivals would give a pretty to be trade-linked to Verity, which is why *our* Coopfolk care for us so dear. They've a panic of losing us."

"Losing us? But I thought—" Becca paused. Suddenly she realized that all her notions of what linked stead to grange and grange to city were as misty as an autumn morning. If ever she'd asked it, she couldn't recall. A hardspun thread of practicality from her ma's blood most likely had yanked her back from the asking. Hattie would say such questions were useless knowledge for any girl, improper nosy for any woman.

But Hattie wasn't here.

Barak cupped his hands around her own, friendly. "Have I frighted you, missy? God witness, I never meant it. Could be it's as I've heard my ma lesson: The world's too big for a woman to grasp; one hearth's sufficient unto the day for you."

"No! No, I'm not frighted at all, sir, not a shaveling. Oh, please, if there's more to tell of the cities, I'm perishing to know." Becca responded so eagerly that it drew another ready chortle from her peculiar friend.

"Eve, little Eve." He beamed indulgence and condescension upon her and patted her plaited hair.

"Please, if you would," she repeated. "It's not on

account of idle curiosity, truth it's not! You see, I've this friend from another stead and—and her life's turned evil on her. If our Coop City's so fond of us, could be they'd grant her the grace of going there. You're alph of Verity, sir; you must know the chief Coopfolk. Couldn't you have a word in their ears on her behalf, for mercy's sake?"

Barak's brows rose. "Why, child? What's your friend done?"

Yes, what has she done? the worm whispered. What's her crime? Did you ever think he'd see it any other way? For that matter, hark to how he asks! He doesn't believe this treats with any 'friend' at all! He thinks it's you.

The worm's truth was a pang. Still, Becca managed to reply, "She's done nothing, sir."

"Well then, a good girl's got nothing to fear." He chucked her under the chin. "It's all right, missy. There's no need for pretense. Some of us don't view it as sinful when a woman wants to learn more of the world; not unless what she wants to know's not proper for her. Now tell me: What's the name of such a bundle of curiosity as you? Could be I'd best warn your sire of the vixen he's rearing."

"I'm Becca of Wiserways, Paul's get," she replied according to custom, empty of hope for her friend's sake. She'd deceived herself about Barak: To her eyes, the Verity alph's empty, benevolent smile was another potential door to safe haven slammed and locked in Dassah's face.

"Lord King bless and keep thee, and raise up the children of thy womb full-fed." Barak raised one hand in a formal gesture of benediction, the words of his blessing sounding awkward and antiquated. His solemn expression made to match the heaviness of words, and handsign melted from his ordinarily jovial face the first chance it could. "Now you can tell Paul as how you've been rightly proved and consecrated and can go get yourself some rest."

"Sir—?"

"What? Don't they lesson your steadgirls aright? Oh, wait. I've to mark your brow, too, else where's the proof your sire might demand?" Barak took a pinch of earth in his palm and spat it into mud, then dipped a finger in the mess and leaned forward to touch Becca's brow. The mud traced a cool downstroke just above her nose, then a second line crossing the first.

"There," he said, pressing his thumb to the juncture of the lines. "My mark, so he'll know you didn't just do it for yourself. Now run along and show that to your sire and tell him the words I pronounced over you. You take that first righthand turning, then go by two more streets and left past the barricade. You shouldn't have any trouble finding him. Last I saw, he was in parley with a pair of the Quarter Stead comers down thataway." He giggled. "Words were he was congratulating 'em on how they did in the bouts, but truth's likely he's as worn as I, and looking for an excuse to shun the maidens. Harvest Home's a young man's festal night, made for the barley that's heavy in the head. Us nigh chaff-straw fellows have enough to do with cheering up the wives we've already got. Although I suppose I'll have to take me another one this year, for show, or my ma'll have a word to say to me about *duty*."

Automatically, Becca's hand drifted up to touch the mark on her forehead. Only fear of smudging it made her stop in time. "I don't understand, sir. What is it that this mark and your words will mean to Pa?"

Barak's hand came up under her chin again, only this time his fingers merley stroked the smooth skin. The touch made her legs tingle, despite herself. "Why, it's a great favor I've done you, Becca, and my own poor Sign of Thanks I've given you. I've marked you with the cross, sure sign of haven to every decent woman since the evil times first fell upon the world; and I've blessed you with the words that set your womb apart in surety from others less fortunate. Since those dark years, when all was madness, and the Lord shut up the doors of the womb as punishment for womankind's sins, it was only those females as the alphs cherished special who lived to bring new life into the light."

Becca bowed her head. She knew the stories, told of a cold night when the girls were growing fractious. It seemed like a true devil got into them, Mama always said; a demon whose coming meant their Changes would soon touch them. The girls turned sharp-tongued and forward, upsetting all the house. It wanted a few good lessonings— truth-spoke tales of what bided for stiff-necked women who thought they were better than their place—before they'd settle down:

—and she was split, and a long time dying! Thought the Lord had closed up the doors of her womb with stone, not mere flesh like all the rest—she held herself that proud— but she learned otherwise. Learned what a mob of single-minded men can do to stone, if they want. They say you can hear her groans to this day, out in the milo fields where the wild men found her.

—learned to her sorrow that her ma's good lessoning wasn't all tall tales of rogue bands when that lot got through with her. Didn't live to learn much more.

—worst of it was that she lived on after. I saw her myself, when I was a baby on homestead, but I'll never forget it: A face like clay, cold and gray, and the monstrous babe she bore still clinging to her withered breasts, one greedy mouth on each, a-sucking her milk until it ran pink with her blood!

A pang of nausea creased Becca's belly. There was no banishing those tellings. Their horror stuck like burrs in memory. Barak saw her clench her teeth with the effort of driving the terrors off. Still gentle, still kindly, he asked, "Why are you troubled? That mark, those words I gave you, they're purest manlore. Isn't a civilized male alive won't recognize their power. They mean that I've granted you the right to turn away any man you will, this night. Doesn't that please you, Becca?"

"Oh, yes, more than—!" No, it would give him the wrong notion if she were too grateful for escaping a woman's rightful service. Truth could be remade, like an old dress prettified near new. Meekly, she replied, "I am your servant, sir. It would be unworthy of me to turn aside your favor."

Now I can find Pa, get him to help me look for Dassah, she thought.

Barak regarded her all of a puzzlement. "Deep, you are. Such a simple, open face, yet what's behind it? Cleverness. Calculation. You've your secrets, Becca, and I vow they're more than womanlore can explain. Well, go your ways. I think I'll give thanks to the Lord King you weren't born male, else I'd not be leaving this meeting as a living man. Godspeed." And he was gone.

Becca didn't waste time pondering his parting words. She was mortal glad to see him go. Not a thing he'd said or done but unnerved her, almost as bad as the worm's evil whisperings. Verity's alph was a compendium of peculiarities that would have sent Mama howling into Pa's arms for the warm shelter of a natural man. A fine one he was to speak of cleverness and calculation! If those weren't the twin swords he'd used to bring down the former alph of Verity Grange, Becca didn't know breakfast.

The crinkly feeling of mud drying on her brow reminded her that at least her patience with him had purchased her freedom from Harvest Home. And all for the price of hearing his wondrous tales! If only he had offered her more of a chance of hope for Dassah…Well, he'd done the next best thing. Smiling, Becca went in search of her friend and her sire, wishing that all her life's bargains would be struck so well.

She quested up and down a number of streets, hoping to find Dassah first and bring the girl under her protection. Surely the arms of Barak's cross could extend far enough to shelter more than one woman? But she couldn't find her. Around one corner she found little Sarah June, on her knees before a man of Pa's years. Becca went on her way faster, even more resolved to bring Dassah's plight before her sire, praying to sweet Mary Mother he'd believe it and help her save the girl.

When she did find Pa, waiting for her at just the place he'd promised, and it all happened as Barak told her it would. Pa took one look at her brow, heard the words of blessing, and bid her return to the tents. He didn't look sorry either, though the two younglings from Quarter Stead wore long faces and excused themselves in a hurry.

Pa laughed. "They're afraid Barak's going to grant the cross to every maiden here. They're off to have them what fun they can before that happens."

Tentatively Becca asked, "You're not…displeased, are you Pa?"

He only beamed at her. "Didn't I just tell you as how I'd hopes not to lose you this year? There's no shame in a girl coming back unbespoke from one Harvest Home." He made a wry face. "Not that I'm telling you to take Apple for your model, now." They both shared a chuckle over that. His eyes were warm with true fondness when he added, "Now go back to the tents, Becca. There'll be no trouble at the gates for you, once the grangewomen see the cross."

"I know; they passed me straight through to reach you," she said. "But Pa—I can't go back to the tents. There's evil business to be stopped this night."

"What?" Paul wasn't beaming now. "What evil's that?"

The word came out little more than a whisper: "*Abomination.*" Even the speaking of it dirtied Becca's lips.

Paul scowled darkly. "How'd you come to know this? What have you seen?" His ominous look froze Becca's tongue, but he had no patience with her silence. He took her roughly by the arms and shook her. "Who's bent on bringing the Lord's curse down on us all?"

Gradually, in whispers and words jerked out piecemeal, Becca told her sire all of Dassah's tale. It got harder toward the end, for the grimace transforming his face into a demon's mask grew more terrifying with each sentence she uttered. She felt as if she were stoking the fire for her own burning.

At last, after a seeming eternity she was able to say, "—and he's keeping her to himself this night. Pa, we've got to find her! We—"

"Quiet." Paul didn't have to shout his commands to

his daughter. "Quiet and calm yourself, then hark to me: Who else knows what you've said?"

"No one—no one so far as I know. I don't think Dassah told anyone else about—"

"So it's just the word of two maidens gone addle-headed at their first Harvest Home against the word of an alph."

"Pa! You think I'd lie about such things?" Becca didn't know whether to be more hurt or more furious.

"I'm your sire, child; I know I've raised you truthful, else I wouldn't have raised you at all. I'm just telling you what the others will say. Oh, I believe you, all right! I know Zach, too. Even when we were boys he had a fondness for taking what he should never have had. Now he's alph, Lord knows how many times before this he's misused the ruling power God gave him. But all my knowledge and all your testimony won't weigh enough in the balance to bring him down."

"We have to do *something*," Becca wailed.

"And so we shall. I'll search for your friend this night. I won't be alone, either. I'll scare up another man to walk with me—tell him some tale or other to bring him along—and if luck's with us, we'll find her and her unnatural sire both. With true luck, we'll catch him at his business." Paul smiled grimly. "And we'll put an end to it."

"But Pa, if you do, and there's no alph of Makepeace—" Becca knew what that would mean and she shuddered for Miss Lynn's sake; for the sake of all the women and babes. "Can't you just—just take her from him? Force him to give her up to you? She's a sweet girl, pretty; she'd make a fine wife, she—"

"Are you daft?" Paul demanded. "There's no abiding

such evil. Wine's called sweet, too, but it was made into a hellbound road by Lot's lustful daughters. Where there's abomination, a righteous man's honor-bound to root it out—all!"

"No, please, not Dassah. It's none of it her fault."

"By whose word?" her father challenged.

Becca felt her fear fall away. "By mine," she replied, standing straight and looking him in the eye. "My life for hers. I know some justice, and it's only the stead's own alph can render judgment on the stead's women. If you take Zacharias in his sinning, he's alph no more, so he can't condemn her and none of the others have that right."

"Is that so?" A glimmer of the old smile touched Paul's lips. "And what about when there's a new alph made in Makepeace?"

Becca recalled Selena's lessoning on when it made a woman stronger to play weak. She dropped her stern look and gave her pa a sideways, teasing, purposeful glance. "Then it'd all be up to Tom, wouldn't it?"

"Up to—" Paul thumbed a lock of hair away from his brow, his face astonished and admiring at once. "Why, you scheming—! Lord witness, there's a future I never foresaw, though why it shouldn't be…Becca, you're a wonder! It's Tom himself I'll find to walk with me, and when all's done I'll testify there was fair challenge made and met. My Tom, alph of Makepeace!" he crowed.

Tom, who owes me a wagonload of favor for the help I gave him doing for Miss Lynn's babe, Becca thought, well satisfied. *He'll take Dassah for his wife, and spare the others, and all will be well.*

"The Lord willing, it will happen so," she said.

"Bless your cleverness, yes. You can go back to our camp easy, child. You've done a good night's work for a woman; now let the stronger shoulder your burden. Sleep well, and the Lord King's angel guard you."

He set her on the proper path and she took it with a lightsome step. It was all she could do to keep from singing. Only the decency of her upbringing laid a bridle on her tongue. A time or two a strangerman hailed her, only to beg her pardon when he saw Barak's sign on her brow. She thought she'd burst with the joy of those encounters, as if the power to turn a man away rested in her and not in the little smudge of mud.

There were many couples hugging the shadows in the streets as she passed, and courtesy taught that silence from any passerby was the only practical form of privacy they'd have. She thought she caught a glimpse of Prisca once, and believed she heard Apple's harsh voice raised in a strange cry, but she was too well-bred to look or hark any closer into the matter.

Wouldn't you like to know? Truly? She hushed the worm and walked faster.

At least I don't think I spied Dassah and Zach anywhere, she thought.

The shortest way to the tents brought her back into the grove of oak trees near the long hall. Their rich, musty scent was a welcome sore missed after the hours spent amid nothing but the sharp smell of dressed stone. Her feet kicked up small rustles of dead leaves. She thought she heard other crunchings behind her, but good manners let her ignore however many pairs now shared the little woodland through which she passed. Her thoughts were on her bedroll, back in the maidens' tent, and finally getting her feet warm again.

Hard hands siezed her. She gasped, too startled to scream. Too late she recalled how the grangewoman had driven her from the grove; this was no place for any honest steadfolk tonight. Strong fingers dug into the tender flesh of her upper arms as she was flung back against a tree bole. Her ankle twisted as she trod on a clutch of tumbled acorns under the leaves.

Pale green eyes squinted at her, meeting her appalled stare with unholy glee. "Bless you, sister. Have you been fed?" Adonijah's voice turned the ritual greeting into a travesty and an abomination.

Chapter Twelve

Moonlight nights, moonlight nights,
Angels come out on moonlight nights.
Open your window, open your soul,
Welcome the spirit that makes you whole.

Adonijah pressed her hard against the tree trunk with the full weight of his body. She squirmed uselessly, hampered by the long skirt of her dancing dress. When she opened her mouth to cry out, he covered it with his own. Not any Kiss of Thanks she'd given that night was so odious to her as this kiss. His tongue tasted hot and sour and there was an alien reek to his breath. She tried to nip him with her teeth but he pulled away, laughing.

"Forgotten the right words, Becca?" He pinched her face so roughly that her teeth scraped blood from the inside of her cheeks. "I'll help you, then. Wouldn't want your pa to hear as one of his girls was found wanting. Repeat after me: *Your strength has brought me sanctuary, your kindness—*"

"Let me go!" To her ears, her shout sounded loud enough to fetch a dozen souls. None came. No more lights glimmered through the trees from the long house. The windows were dark and cold, the sockets of a row of skulls. The matrons of Verity had business elsewhere. Adonijah laughed again.

"Let you go? Not likely. I've sought you long, ever since they first told us they'd gone to fetch the maidens. You're the only one I'd have this night, Becca. You should be flattered. All I am I've saved for you, and I'll not let you go until you've served me as tender and lovingly as Eve did Adam for the gift of the apple. You and me, Becca, we're the only man and woman in the world this night."

She cried out again, louder. She called for help and none came. He repeated his first offense against her body, compelling her to open her mouth. His tongue slithered over her teeth. Wild fancies filled her mind, trying to distract her from the coarse reality invading her: *Adam and Eve and the apple*, she thought. *And the snake.*

Bile rose in her throat. His weight and his hands pinned her arms behind her. With a fierce effort, she got one free and struck him with her fist, but the blow was negligible. Gram Phila's girl hadn't yet taught her near enough fighting tricks to be of any help to her now. Wildly, she wished she'd had more lessonings, more practice, more time. All she knew was kicking, and Adonijah overlay her so straight that she couldn't even bring up her knee to give him the sharp reply he deserved. What her mama taught was true: *What can a woman do against a full-grown man?* When he finally broke the seal of lips to lips, she gasped for breath.

"Well, Becca? How shall we begin? The Kiss or the Sign? Or have your matrons taught you any special tricks? My pa's heard tell that whoever's to be next alph of Wiserways will fall heir to the true Eden."

"Your pa..." Becca spoke bitterly, thinking of poor, scared Dassah.

"What's my pa to you?"

"The man I'd most like to see reach Paradise," she said, turning her head away. *After he's dead. For it's from the high gates of Paradise that the angels plunge the souls of the damned deep into Hell.*

Adonijah couldn't tell her thoughts; he took a man's meaning from her words. "So, aiming that high? You forget those ambitions. The old men's days as alphs are nearly done. You'd do better to hitch your dreams to mine, if power's to your taste. Speak to me sweetly, Becca, and I'll make you glad." His hand closed painfully hard on her breast. It was a sign of taking possession, not of tenderness.

"You have to let me go, Adonijah." The words rode a dry sob. She despised herself for how weak and pleading she sounded. "You must."

"Why? Won't you serve me, else? Don't make me drag you before the Verity matrons. It'll only humiliate you and your pa and all your kin. You'd be made to show me your deepest gratitude in front of witnesses, then, to prove you're a proper woman. Or you could still refuse, and die. Have you heard how they grant death at Verity? Seems their alph's a clever man and learned more than a few new notions from the Coopfolk—"

"*Look!*" Desperate, she found the strength to thrust

him a little distance from her and jabbed a finger at her brow. "Look here, Adonijah, at what's manlore! Barak, Verity's alph, himself marked me with this sign and set me free. My pa saw it, and two witnesses with him. Touch me while I wear it and you'll be the one to learn how Verity grants death!"

Her chest swelled as she spoke. More of Mama's teachings came back, this time to strengthen her courage: *We must be grateful for manlore, hard though it sometimes will be, for most of it was forged in the hungering times, a powerful shield for the powerless.*

The moonlight amid the trees was faint, but enough for her to see every feature of Adonijah's hated face. Enough for him to see by, too. Surely he could not deny he saw the saving cross on her brow! Now he must let her go and slink away, defeated.

But Adonijah only whistled low, and many pairs of feet came crunching through the dead leaves. Four and five and six young men—none of them seasoned or muscled enough to give an opponent pause in the wrestling ring—all sifted out of the darkness to stand behind Adonijah. Four more came up to stand at his right hand and another two at his left. A great ravening overlay their faces, and a naked longing in their eyes made them seem like dead men come back to lick their dusty lips with envy over the living.

"Will you greet my friends, sweet Becca?" Adonijah asked. His green eyes glowed nigh yellow. Deliberately, he spat on his fingertips and smeared away the mark of the cross on her brow while she writhed in his grip. "All are good young men, these twelve, clever sons of many steads. I met them over the course of the years, when business took me and my pa on rambles. I've nigh come

to call them more my sibs than any of my sire's gets.
They're no more like to triumph in the wrestling ring
than I, nor ever give their stronger sibs or their sires any
troubling thoughts. Still, they do the bright-minded work
on their steads, and do it well. Their words are trusted.
They'll testify in truth that when you knelt to me, there
wasn't any sign on your brow but the Lord King's own
radiance that blesses a grateful woman."

Becca stared in horror at the young men ranged
around Adonijah. When it came from another's lips, truth
was no hidden worm, but a terrible dragon. Even as she
wondered why these youths would bond in friendship
with Adonijah, she read the answer in their eyes.

—and she was split, and a long time dying.

Why had she been blind fool enough to dream that
the rogue bands dwelled only beyond the plowland, in
the wilderness? Whatever Adonijah did to her, his
creatures would do likewise. You could read the patience
of a weak man's wisdom in every one of them. Wait their
turn they must, but have it they would.

Panic iced her bones. Air rushed into her lungs, and
the scream that burst from her mouth was the blackest
essence of terror. It stole the light from her eyes, set her
free from the small, powerless body that Adonijah so
coveted. Her senses stayed with her, but fogged over so
that she seemed to be in two places at once—within
herself and feeling nothing, beyond herself and watching
all they did to her as if it were to someone else.

Their hands grasped her arms, weighed down her
shoulders until she felt as if she were drowning in a sea
of clutching, greedy fingers. Her dress caught and scraped
on the oak bark as Adonijah's pack forced her to her
knees. She struggled desperately, knowing with the fear

that goes beyond rational thought that if they succeeded in dragging her down, she would be lost forever, body and soul.

Adonijah siezed her chin fast as she went, compelling her to tilt her head back so far that it would have hurt had she been all there to feel it. He was speaking to her, a smirk crinkling up his pale green eyes. She cast his face and his words both into the shielding fog around her.

Her head filled with the old songs her mama used to sing to her when she was milkfed and they still shared the warmth of one bed. Mama's voice was so loud in her ears that it left no room for any silly man's jabber. Becca closed her eyes, smiling because Mama sang so sweet for her alone, and this was one holy of holies Adonijah couldn't violate.

"*Look at me!*" He wrenched her chin so hard the pain penetrated, searing away the merciful fog with a flaming red sword. Becca whimpered and squinched her eyes tighter shut. "Damn you, woman, you're going to know it's me!"

She opened her eyes too late to pacify him. She saw his hand upraised, ready to fall across her face in a blow she could not escape. He'd mark her, just as Barak had done, only with a badge of shame instead of honor. No man ever struck a woman but with good cause, because she was lacking; everyone knew that. Tears sprang to her eyes, tears of self-pity for thinking of how Mama would mourn and Pa would turn his proud love from her. In the unnatural slowing of time that began when Adonijah's hand swung toward her face, she dreamed she saw Pa himself come forward through the trees to witness her punishment.

And the Lord King made her witness to a miracle.

Pa's own hands shot out, sieizing Adonijah's upraised arm. The younger man yelped loud at the wrench the Wiserways' alph gave it, twisting it behind his back to an angle that God never intended. All around her, Becca heard the rapid crunching of dead leaves as Adonijah's cronies broke ranks in panic. She covered her face with her hands and wept for joy. Through her sobs she heard the solid, meaty, unmistakable sounds of a thrashing. Something heavy fell into the leaves beside her. She pulled away from the tumbled body, not wanting to look at Adonijah even now, shamed, defeated, maybe dead. When she did raise her face, it was to see that Adonijah still lived. Her pa would never bother kicking a corpse in the belly.

"King blast you to bones, you keep away from my daughter!" Paul aimed another kick at his fallen opponent. Adonijah groaned and rolled as far away from Becca as he could before he loosed the holdings of his stomach into the leaves. Blood glittered from his mouth and the split skin of his cheek and temple. One eye was puckered shut, the other starting to swell. More heaves shook him, though he had no more to spew but bile.

The two striplings who had been with Pa on the streetcorner came out from behind the trees and hauled Adonijah to his feet. Grinning, they held him steady for Paul. In an awful parody of what had gone before, Becca's sire used one hand to tilt Adonijah's chin so that the younger man had to look right at the alph with his one half-open eye. Paul looked smug; Becca could see how much he was savoring the moment. It didn't last. The alph's fist crunched into Adonijah's face. Blood rushed from his crumpled nose. His body slumped, suspended between the other youths. With a curt nod, Paul signaled them to let him drop. They obeyed, then vanished through the trees as silently as they'd come.

"Baby, are you all right?" Paul gathered Becca into his arms and let her dry her tears against the coarse cloth of his shirt. His rough fingertips gently touched the spot on her brow where Adonijah had eradicated Barak's cross. "That filthy— I've a mind to call him before the law on this; him *and* his sire that never taught a son of his the price of blasphemy."

"Pa, please don't." Becca huddled closer to her sire. "You've lessoned him plenty; he won't forget."

"But the cross, Bec'! He spit on the cross itself."

She shook her head rapidly, wishing she could shake loose the memory of the past few minutes. "On his fingers, Pa; he only spit on his fingers. Oh please, can't you just let it be? You saw the pack he runs with."

"Cowards," Paul sneered.

"They're all respected men in their steads," Becca said. "He told me so. If there's trial, there's testimony. They'll all band together to twist things. They'll turn it against me, Pa, somehow. They could, if they'd a mind to."

Paul hugged his girl. "You put too much weight on cleverness, Becca. Guess that's because you're so sharp yourself. There's nothing a body has to fear from any one of that lot. I saw them as they ran—rabbits all. Those fine young men you saw with me, between 'em they're sib to four of Adonijah's mites. They just laugh whenever anyone says how bright that scrawny lot are. Adonijah's the only one among 'em with any brawn. One spine-snap in the ring and there's an end to all their brightness, even were it fit to blind the sun."

Becca knew it was so. Strength bested sharpness more

times than not; Barak was just the exception to prove the rule. She took comfort in the certainties of her life. Still, the look she'd seen in the eyes of Adonijah's followers haunted her bad. "Pa, promise me—"

Paul gave her another squeeze. "If it'll pleasure you, child, we'll say nothing more about this than *that* one cares to noise up." He jerked his head at the fallen Adonijah. "Though when his pa gets a look at how bad his boy got chewed, I'll wager the pup spins his sire another fine tale to bind up his pride."

Becca gazed at her defeated tormentor's body and shuddered. Even in this forced repose, streaks of blood and slime already drying on his face, he scared her. She wanted to be away, to run back to the Wiserways tents, but a stubborn spark in her mind held her bridled to the spot.

Adonijah's pa…Zach…Dassah.

"Pa, when you came here, did you see—?"

Shouts burst from the grange. A streak of flame smeared the sky. "Lord God, what's that?" Paul exclaimed, his hands tightening protectively on Becca's shoulders. The roar of fire washed over the oak grove, and its blazing light fell on father and daughter like a judgment.

"Paul! Paul!" One of the two striplings who'd held Adonijah helpless came barreling through the trees. Even in the ruddy light his face looked sickly pale. "Come quick! The granaries are burning!" He wheeled on one foot and plunged back the way he'd come.

"Jesus *damn*!" Paul flung himself after the younger man, leaving Becca behind without a second thought, without a glance. For her part, the girl took one last look at Adonijah and knew her choice was made: Gathering her skirt shamefully high above the knee, she raced to catch up with her father.

It wasn't easily done. Paul's broad body crashed through the clinging branches of the oakwood without care or pause. Gasping, Becca pelted along behind, though whiplash-skinny twigs clawed and clutched at her arms and legs, licked at her face and eyes.

She shrieked when her foot came down wrong and twisted out from under her, the same foot she'd wrenched earlier on a fallen acorn. Pain lanced through her ankle. She sprawled awkwardly, embracing rocks and kissing dirt. Her father must have heard her cry, but he ran on. She stumbled to her feet and hobbled in his wake the best she could.

The pain subsided to a throb by the time she was among the grange buildings. Paul was nowhere to be seen, but that didn't signify. She could take her pick of guides. The streets of Verity were thronged with running men, young and old, Grange and Coop. Torches flickered past, lesser kin to the vast blaze now leaping from the hillside. Near as Becca could judge, they were all heading west, but her head was so turned she couldn't be certain. She hugged the wall for fear of being trampled. Torchlight or no, the men had eyes for nothing but the flame.

Becca passed many huddles of maidens as she made her halting way behind the menfolk. She thought she recognized some of her sibs, thought she heard them call her by name, but she neither harked nor slowed. The fire was leaping higher on the hill, a call stronger than any other. Her ankle still hurt, but not so badly. If she gritted her teeth, she could lope on it some.

She passed a place where two streets crossed in a broad plaza. Here were torches, and here a mass of hard-faced grangewomen, grim and brisk. Working together, they rolled tun after tun of rainwater into the square. Other teams of Verity matrons dunked leather buckets into the rainbarrels and handed these to the running men with harsh, sharp words of warning not to spill a drop. Becca saw Ivah sweating behind a barrel she was rolling in on its rim. She ran to help the older woman, but got a curse for her pains and stern orders to get out of the way.

"This is no place for infants! Get back to your stead's camp where you belong!"

But Becca knew different. Where the fire flung itself into the face of midnight, that was where she belonged. Where she could see a sight she might never hope to see again in her lifetime, that was her proper place, all her mama's cautioning be damned. No one paid mind to a maiden who rushed along in the river of grangefolk. She rode the river until it broke on the rocks of the burning granary.

The heat hit Becca like a shovel full in the face. The wispy hairs around her face curled back from the blast. The granary was a single tower, pierced with small slits that shot out yellow tongues. The crowd surrounding it kept their distance, except for crews of men who ranged themselves in orderly lines starring out from the tower like the spokes of a wheel. Buckets swung up and back along those human spokes, arcs of water flying through the air in a vain attempt to dampen the blaze.

"Whose silo's that?" Becca heard one man ask.

"Not one of ours, thank God," came the reply. "That's all I care about."

"Yes, but what if the fire spreads to some of ours? You know where they are?"

"Damned if I do. All looks different, in the dark."

"It'd be easier to keep track if they kept each stead's silos grouped together, not scattered all—"

"Well, no arguing with Grange ways."

"How'd it start?"

"If I knew—"

"Look! Look there! More flames from that other silo!"

"How in—? It's nowhere near this. Sparks wouldn't fly that far over, skip the ones between. Besides, there's no wind but what's coming off the blaze."

"Lord help us all, that's Makepeace Stead's granary, same as this! I can see the marks on it from here, in all this light."

"Makepeace?"

"What's that thing crawling up the side?" A man pointed at the newly ignited silo. This one had no window slits, only a spiral of wooden slats pounded into the outer walls going all the way to the top. Flames licked at its base but hadn't yet climbed above the height of two grown men.

"Lord King save us, it's a demon!"

By the first inferno's light, Becca saw a ragged ghost, skirts asmolder, face a smoke-blackened devil's mask. It carried a slender stick of burning wood in one hand, and with this makeshift torch it was calmly and deliberately setting fire to the steps behind it as it ascended the tower. Its other hand clasped a drinking skin, but if it held water it must have been drawn from Hell's own river. Slat by slat the creature stopped and turned and tossed a sprinkle of liquid from its flask down onto the rungs below before applying the torch. Each slat burst into avid flame.

The apparition was almost to the topmost rung when it misjudged a distance and sprinkled its own skirts. A falling spark from the torch puffed the cloth into a sudden blue-white blaze. Torch and flask both fell as the creature stood swaying on the rung, cloaked in fire. Hands that swiftly turned to blackened claws groped for heaven. Hair became a torch more glorious and more ghastly than any ever kindled by man. For a heartbeat the burning figure seemed to blow back and forth in some mysterious wind. Then with a scream that drove a spike through Becca's soul, it fell.

The men swarmed forward with more water buckets. Cityfolk came from another direction, carrying strange objects that gushed fire-killing foam. Between foam and water, the second silo fire was soon extinguished, though the first could only be contained until it burned itself out.

Becca started forward.

No, Becca. The face of the lost girl's ghost swam before Becca's eyes, backed with a halo of flame. *There are some things we don't need to see.*

Becca didn't heed. Little by little, she threaded her way between the lines of men until she could see what manner of devil had fallen from the burning tower. Bone grinned through the split and blackened skin. Flesh still bubbled like the surface scum of the men's bone-birthing kettle. A stink such as was meant to haunt dreams of damnation flooded Becca's head.

Only the size of the body hinted at its identity. Only the charred and smoking remnant of a dancing dress suggested that it had been a woman and a maid.

This is nothing human. Becca clung to the thought, lashed her sanity to it, denied all other possibility. *This is no one I could ever have known.*

Only later, after she had gone back to the shelter of her own stead's tents and crawled into her bedding fully clothed, did Becca overhear her sire telling one of the other men how sad it was that madness had claimed Zacharias' daughter. The words pushed her beyond denial and she buried her head in her arms and wept.

Chapter Thirteen

Babe, my babe, won't you come with me
The hills of Heaven for to see?
Run through the sunshine, dance through the rain,
Lie down with sorrow and get up with pain.
What's that lying on the hills so white?
The snow that the storm clouds left in the night.
What's that shining so bright and clear?
The tall white gates of Heaven near.
Who's that weeping where the black birds fly?
Only a sinner who's bound to die.
Why do the black birds circle the hill?
Hush now, my baby, hush and be still.
Earth is a grievance, life's a sorrow.
Save your joy for a lost tomorrow.
Angels dance on the head of a pin,
Open the gates, let my sweet babe in.
Once I knew where God had gone
I had the faith to carry on.

> *Cry for the sinner, weep for the dead,*
> *Here's a place for my baby's head.*
> *Pillowed on white like a highborn king,*
> *Hushabye, child, to the song I sing.*
> *Mama, Mama, give me your grace!*
> *Babe, don't let me see your face.*
> *Hide from the wolf and stone the crow,*
> *Tears my heart to let you go.*

"So Apple's got her a suitor? Isn't that fine!" Becca's mama glanced at her over Shifra's downy head and mouthed *finally*!

Becca jammed a finger to her lips, stifling giggles. Proper-minded Hattie only mimed the word that everyone else on stead was saying aloud.

"Hallow's a fine stead," Katy put in. She held up the shirt she was mending as if to inspect the needlework, but Becca saw it shake with the young woman's suppressed laughter. "And Prisca will be company for her there."

"Those two chosen. Miracle on miracle," Thalie said drily. Her face was still pinched with bitterness, making her older than her years, though Hattie had told Becca she was sure the woman was already fruitful again. "If Paul's wise, he'll make the matches while Hallow's alph still lives, else he'll never find another one fool enough to take those girls off his hands."

"Thalie!" Hattie hugged Shifra a little closer to her breast, her whole body stiff with indignation.

"Not a young alph, anyhow; none of the new ones," Thalie went on. "So many changes since Harvest Home. It's like watching a cloud's shadow pass over a field of barley at reaping time." She closed her eyes and recited:

"One generation passes away and another generation comes."

"That's as ill-omened a thing as ever I heard from the lips of a grown woman. You ought to be ashamed!"

Thalie shrugged. "I don't mind omens. No more."

Selena spoke up from her place, as far from Thalie's chair as the seeing-room walls would allow. "Well, it was a good Harvest Home for our girls, wasn't it?" Her words danced out light and brittle as flakes of wood ash. "And sweet little Sarah June too, bespoke so readily! How precious young is the dear child?"

"Only two years more than my Susanna," Thalie said, looking nowhere but at the job of sewing in her lap. "If I recollect it rightly. But what's time to the dead?"

Selena went sallow and fell hushed.

Ray leaped into the conversation with the same speed she used when tidying her worst kitchen messes from sight. "Our Sarah June, brided to Barak of Verity himself! A grangewoman made so young. There's pride for us all there."

"Pride." There was no telling how Thalie managed to pour so much souring into one word.

"Don't you fret, Becca," Ray went on, leaning over to pat her hand. "You'll be bespoke next year sure. There's no hurry."

Becca forced herself to breathe naturally. Thinking of next year's Harvest Home clamped a cold band around her chest. Less than a year to wait now, and already she was dreading it. Bad enough she had to walk with ghosts on Wiserways Stead; now there was a burned and blackened phantom whose eyeless, ash-filled sockets would follow her every step she took on Verity Grange lands.

Oh, Jamie! Jamie, don't let the year run away from you! There's change in the air—everyone's noticed it. The old alphs are making way for the new. Somewhere, surely somewhere there's a place, a way for you to take a stead for yourself— for us? Jamie, my dreams are full of evil, pale green eyes when they're not full of flame and ashes. Save me, save me from my dreams!

"Feeling well, child?" Katy asked, solicitous. "Your times sitting well with you?"

Becca shifted in her place uneasily. "All right," she mumbled. While she was grateful for Katy's words, which had saved her from her own frightsome thoughts, she wished the woman wouldn't speak so openly about a state she found to be inconvenient at best, at worst disgusting.

"Came on you a shade earlier than due, it seems," Selena remarked.

"Selena's a wonder," Thalie said in that scornful, dead tone. "Manages to keep a tally on her own times and on those that don't concern her."

Ray was again swift to try damping down the crackling air of the seeing-room. "Right after a girl's first Harvest Home, there's bound to be some shifting. After my first, I didn't come into my times again until three months late, but the women of my stead let it pass for natural. It didn't do me a speck of harm neither."

Hattie balanced Shifra on her lap and stroked the infant's back until she burped. "Here, Becca. Tuck up your sister in the cradle and fetch me Gram Phila's mending." She passed the baby to Becca's arms and added, "See you're quick about it. Any questions she asks you about Harvest Home, answer brief as manners allow. She'll have all the tale soon enough, when it's time for her to give our brides their last lessoning."

"Yes, Mama." Becca took Shifra to the big cradle hard by the hearthside, grateful for the excuse to be far gone from Ray's companionable chatter about such embarrassing matters as her times.

Laying her sister down to sleep, Becca inhaled the sweet, milky smell of a clean baby. Tenderly, she offered the infant her finger and smiled to feel the tiny fist close powerfully around it. Gazing down at Shifra that way, Becca harked to her heart question whether it would be so bad a thing to be made a wife, even if never Jamie's. As bride and wife, coming into her times wouldn't mean fleeing from the men, and discomfort, and that eerie, restless feeling in her belly, but—with the Lord King's blessing—fruitfulness. A child. A child to fill her arms, her heart; a child to still the yearning in her womb.

Soon, Jamie, she thought, urging all her need from her soul to his. *Please grow bold soon, or I'm afraid I'll be wanting a babe—any man's babe, so long as it's mine—more than I'm wanting you.*

"Becca!" Hattie's sharp summons jerked her aware.

"Just going, Mama," she said, and fled up the stairs to Gram Phila's nest among the eaves.

The stair treads up attic were no longer strangers to her. She knew their every creak and settling from the many times she'd stolen away to seek out Gram Phila's nameless handmaid and keep their hidden bargain. The bare wood felt smooth and comforting underfoot, worn too satiny by the generations of Wiserways to even dare admit splinters existed. She reached the ancient hardwood door at the top of the stairs and knocked.

"Enter and be blessed, in the Lord King's name!" Gram Phila's voice was strident and steady. Just hearing it without seeing the old woman, you'd never lay an age to her.

Becca pulled the latch-string and went in, filling her nostrils with the welcome odors of the attic. Dry wood she smelled, baked by the hard summer sun, and the bookish scent of all the old, mysterious boxes stacked in their ordered ranks against the walls. Gram's girl claimed that not even the crone knew what they all held, though the old woman stubbornly refused to allow Katy to investigate their contents. There was the tang of metal from the platters and goblets and utensils set apart special for fetching up Gram Phila's food, but not the veriest taint of eatables gone bad. Not a crumb, not a drop, not even the ghost of a good meal's aroma lingered in the attic.

Dust motes danced in sunlight from the single, round window centered in the triangle formed by the great house's gable end. Many times Becca and her nameless friend had sat there while Gram Phila snored away on her pallet. You could gaze down through the spotless pane and see the front yard of the house, and off west across the fields. The round window had its twin at the attic's other end—you could see the glazy circle from outside plain as plain—but inside it was hidden from view by the boxes. The under-gable living space itself held the form of a squarish C, hugging the little walled-in landing at the top of the stairs.

"Come nearer, child." Gram Phila sat by the window, her old bones bent into the hold of a rocking chair. Rag quilts lapped her, until all the setting sun could touch was her dried-apple face and gnarly hands. A white cloth bonnet like a baby's cradling cap hid what little hair she might have left. The strings dangled down beside her withered cheeks.

Becca did as she was told, making a dutiful curtsey to the crone. She glanced about, but saw no sign of the old woman's handmaid.

Gram Phila's eyes sparkled. "Not here," she said, and when Becca gaped, the crone's laughter was like a trodden littlesinger's shell. "Oh, that's my power, child, to read a body's mind. Didn't you know it?"

"I'd say more likely it was sense, ma'am," Becca replied, recovering.

"Would you?" The crone cocked her head, delight twitching her wrinkled lips. "And you'd be right. You've a keen eye. It cuts like a knife, straight through to the bone. We know a lot about bone, you and I. Now tell me where my Martha's gone and I'll make you a fine present."

"Martha?"

Gram Phila raised her cold-knotted hands. "Ah, so there's another secret for you to cherish, girl. I know you're carrying enough hidden things these days to people the earth. Yes, I've named her Martha—and why not? Between us, there's many long days and nights to pass. Shall I treat her as less than an animal? Even Miss Lynn's rattle-boned old horse has a name. For form's sake, she's nameless as all the serving girls who went before her; but in the truth of our exile she is named. Share this with us, child, but don't tell. What we know up here dies at that door. Not a word belowstairs." This last came hard-said, brooking no choice about it.

"I won't tell, swear by the Lord King." Becca touched her chin in thought. "If she's not here, she must be doing a needful chore. Emptying slops, maybe?"

Gram Phila teetered with cackling. "So, just so. I knew you for wise. Tell me, Becca, is it true what flutters up here about Harvest Home? Apple and Prisca and Sarah June bespoke?"

"Yes, ma'am, true enough."

"And you marked out by Barak?"

Becca nearly tripped on her own tongue, in haste to deny. "It's only Sarah June he's asked for, ma'am."

"Not bespoke, girl; *marked*. With the Jesus sign in earth and all." Gram Phila sketched a small cross on the air before Becca's forehead. This time there was more scare than surprise in the girl's reaction. Soft as snowfall, Gram Phila asked, "What do you think of a stead crone's powers now?"

Carefully, picking over each word, Becca managed to reply, "I think there was talk enough of what happened at Harvest Home for some to have drifted up here. I'd be more surprised did it happen *not* to reach you, something that big. Your—Martha's your second ears, isn't she? And being so still in her comings and goings, having no name, she's as good as invisible to most folks' minds. That's how she hears so much for you. I think that between her ears and yours, you've lessoned yourself to hear as skillfully as Miss Lynn's lessoned herself to look. And I think it's a wise woman who lessons herself best to do both."

"That wise woman's you, is it?" For an instant there was a glint of pity in Gram Phila's eyes. The crone reached for Becca's hands and stroked them. "Watch and hark, child; hark and watch. It's the dreamers who die, with their eyes and ears of stone. A star dazzles 'em and they miss the pit another digs in their path. But those who carry fire in the mind, they live through the hard times, and the hungering times, and all the times of pain. They know there's many a lost path that's only overgrown, waiting to be found again some day."

"But if the path's overgrown"—Becca spoke almost too quietly to be heard—"if it's hid from sight, won't it take more than keen eyes to find it? Won't it—can't it need dreams?"

"Oh, keep your dreams too, dearie," the crone agreed. "Only don't depend on dreams alone. Times are the eyes see too much for the heart to bear; that's when dreams can heal you. Times are, for all your wished-for wisdom, you can know too much."

A creak of the big door's leather hinges made Becca whirl about. Gram Phila's girl stood there with a freshly scrubbed chamber pot balanced on one hip. The old woman pushed away Becca's hands.

"Now tend to your business and stop your troubling me," she snapped. "Just because your times are on you, don't play the limp stalk. Work! Work's a woman's saving."

Becca bobbed another curtsey and rattled off an asking for any seamwork to be done, but she hardly heard her own words or Gram Phila's answer. Even while the crone's girl fetched a few shifts and stockings and a quilt that wanted a mend, Becca kept hearing Gram Phila's voice echo through her head. She felt unnaturally warm, but that could be another taking of her times. All that talk of fire, and paths lost, and the death of dreamers—

—*and dreams. Do they die too?* the ghost whispered, wearing the face of the long-dead girl from Becca's vigil night. *Then what's the voice on the wind that blows from Prayerful Hill but the breath of madness? No ghosts, Becca;*

no wandering souls to call your name. We are only dreams. All that's real is what you can lay a hand to, and it's a wise woman learns that lesson straightaway!

Something burned deep in Becca's chest. It struck no spark, gave no glow, yet still it radiated a powerful heat steadier than any hearthfire. Hard as stone it sat within her, more fiery than the sun's own soul, and all it was was the single word denying the ghost's harsh, bitter ruling on what was and was not reality.

No. And again, and louder and brighter in the cupped hands of her soul: *No!*

Dassah had smoldered with that same spark of denial, refusal, and it had leaped from her soul on wings of actual flame.

—and burned her to ashes in a fire of her own kindling, the ghost whispered. *Is that what you want, Becca? Is it?* An image of her infant sister's sleeping face flashed in Becca's mind. *No seed takes root in a flame-scorched furrow. No fruit grows from a fire-eaten tree.*

Gram's girl shook her by the arm. "Hey! Wake, you. You'll have a tumble down the stairs, else. You've no need to be going so soon. Gram wants to see what I've taught you."

"What *I've* taught, you mean," the old woman said with satisfaction. "Through my Martha I've given you as fine a lessoning as ever you'll want some day."

"Some day?" Becca murmured to herself. "Now." She recalled Adonijah, holding her pinned against the oak, and dearly wished she had him there to show him what she'd learned since Harvest Home.

"Set down your load, Becca," said the crone's girl. "Fight me."

Becca started to protest that her mama would be

waiting below, impatient to have Gram Phila's mending
to hand and done with. A queue of other reasons why
she should not bide up attic any longer tumbled into eager
places behind. A girl in her times, tussling all over the
attic floor with another lass? The wives would each and
all have a seizure if they heard of such wildness!
Wrestling, fighting, knowing how to save your neck and
break another's, that was manlore.

Manlore, the worm whispered.

Becca set down her bundle of clothes.

"Why not?" She smiled.

The bout was short but lively. Martha made the first
move, springing for Becca catwise to fight with nails and
teeth. (The first lesson she'd taught Becca was that
women fought without the formal rules of the challenge
ring, taking any advantage they could lay hold of.) The
leap caught Becca astonished—a bold feint unlike any
she'd ever had from the lean, silent girl. *Surprise!* Any
fool knew how often that could be the winning of a fight.
All the times she'd heard that said came back at her more
swiftly than Martha's leap. Time slowed. She could count
every tooth in the other girl's head, see every speck of
grit under her nails. In the drawing out of moments,
Becca's body took charge from a mind struck stunned.

Surprise! But not to me.

Time flowed true again. She sidestepped without
thinking about it and laid hold of Martha's thin shift by
nape and waist as she sailed by, adding a little extra lift
to the girl's lunge. Thrown off, Martha skimmed her face
over the attic floor while old Gram Phila cackled.

The crone's laughter scarce died before Martha was
up, crouched, eyes narrowed and mean. She made as if
to repeat her first leap, but checked herself as Becca went

into that sideways glide again and met her halfway. A
bare, brown foot came up into Becca's belly. Strong hands
knotted themselves to the front of her dress as Martha
pitched herself over backward into a roll, taking Becca
with her. Becca's mouth opened to skreek until that same
unthinking fight-sense closed her throat.

Yes, scream and bring the whole household up here!

Another Becca spoke inside her head, the same
wicked, unnatural womanchild who'd embraced the
notion of this fight in the first place. A decent maiden
would have been long gone, back downstairs at her
needle. Becca bit her lip for silence as she hit the floor
on one shoulder. A dog-tooth dragged through and she
tasted a little blood.

Martha was up from the floor first, master of the
moment. As Becca still gathered breath from her tumble,
Martha flung herself across her chest and scrabbled to pin
her hands spreadeagled from her body. The girl didn't
weigh much, but enough to keep Becca from rising again.
The soft breath of the girl's triumphant laugh stirred the
hair around Becca's ear.

Adonijah had gloated too.

Becca jackknifed sideways at the hips. Her skirts flew
up as she linked her ankles and swept them like a scythe
to knock Martha off her. The blow made Gram's girl lose
her hold on one of Becca's hands; it was enough. Becca
made a fist and drove it stiff-armed into the girl's chest,
just between the scanty breasts. Martha's breath flew out
in a gust as she fell back on her elbows.

Move and countermove, strike and parry, the separate
incidents of the silent battle melted into the continuous
weave of a maidens' dance like no other. Neither gave as

much to the match as she might, knowing an ill-dealt blow could bring death. No true trial, this, yet it held all the raw, perverse, bloodbright beauty of unfeigned battle.

The dance possessed the dancers. An alien joy filled Becca's body, casting out the helpless, biding woman her mother would have known. Anger too came surging up in her:

Why couldn't I do this with Adonijah? Why did I let him lay a hand on me? I didn't know all this then, but even so, I should've tried, I should've fought more, I should've—

Rage at her own past impotence turned her fierce. Time vanished in a red haze, only to return when she was astraddle of Martha—Martha wild with the mortifying knowledge of undeniable defeat. Becca's ears could hardly hold all the curses Gram Phila's handmaid stuffed into them. She looked down at the skinny girl as stunned as if some unseen hand—not her own doing—had placed the two of them so.

"Well!" Gram Phila clapped hands to knees. "I only hope you've given her as good lessoning as you got." The crone was out of her chair, moving with surprising agility to yank Becca off her opponent and to help the loser up. "How shall we call her now, Martha? Is this Becca or Judith?" The old woman's jagged grin was fearsome and wonderful to see.

Becca clambered to her feet unaided. She wiped the sweat from her face with a dirty sleeve. Her mouth tasted salty. For some reason her eyes were tearing and her nose was making a streaky mess down her face. Deep gasps of air turned into an embarrassment of hiccups. Gram Phila and her girl both laughed at her.

"Who'd think it?" Martha crowed, well over her

humiliation. "You don't look like much, Lord witness, and maybe that's best. Let them know what really bides under that yes-sir-please-sir face and no man in all the granges 'round would take you willingly into his bed."

"Not bad," Gram Phila agreed. Then, more practically, she added, "Go wash before you see your mam again, child. I'll wager you're a better hand with fights than explanations."

"Change clothes, too," Martha put in, already bent over to gather up the pile of mending. "I'll fetch these along to your ma and make your excuses for you."

"But Mama's expecting *me* to—"

"Change clothes first," Martha said firmly. "You're in need. Mary Mother, why You ever let the Lord visit times on a woman—!"

Becca yanked her skirts around and saw what Martha meant. The bloodstain was a sign that her times were nearly done, for which she praised the Lord. Still, it was a messy blessing. She colored red in the face.

"My other skirts are all in the dormitory. It's nigh time for the men to be coming home from the fields. I daren't go there to fetch them."

"I'll walk with you," Martha offered.

"And I'll bring my own mending downstairs," Gram Phila said, accepting the pile from her handmaid. "If I can't spin some tale or other to pull your mam's teeth from her head without her knowing they're gone, I don't deserve to live another hour. You two go on. Ah, take that cloak by the door on you, Becca; it's got a fair deep hood to hide your face. Everyone on stead knows it for mine. Even do you meet up with a stray man, he'll take one look at the cloak and doubt his own senses. It's been long and long since I was in my times. Scoot, now!"

Becca grabbed the cloak from its peg and cast it over her stained clothes. She and Martha legged it hotfoot down the attic steps, Gram Phila's cackly laughter in their ears.

Chapter Fourteen

If I can't find a heaven in your arms, love,
At least I'll find a heaven when I die.
It's nights like this that I'm most cold and lonely
With nothing more to warm me but a sigh.
So don't believe my heart has been unfaithful,
And don't believe that I have not been true,
But if you can't take me with you to heaven,
I've got to find my heaven without you.

"I shouldn't even be here," Becca said, drying her face with another girl's towel. She tucked the damp side under, rehung it on the washstand, and said a silent prayer that the towel's true owner wouldn't notice it had been used.

"Neither should I." Martha grinned at the dormitory ceiling, then sat up suddenly, swinging her feet over the side of the bed she'd claimed. It was Prisca's, and Becca knew her sib would have a royal fit if she saw Gram Phila's girl occupying it so lordly. "But who's to tell we've come and gone?" Her gaze swept the long hall with its double row of beds, each with a storage chest at its foot and a washstand beside it. "So this is how you live! And me up attic full of night-fancies, thinking it was so fine, so grand! I've been pining after dust."

Becca folded up her soiled skirts and thrust them into her own clothing chest. She'd gotten the worst of the spots out; she'd make time to wash them thoroughly, apart, after her times were over. "I wish I hadn't taken so long fussing over the stains," she said, thinking out loud. "I should've just let you fetch a change of clothes for me."

"Never would've found your things in all this," Gram's girl replied affably. "Each place looks like its neighbor. A body could almost think you girls were just as easy to trade off, one for another. Don't fret about the time; by this hour your sibs are all busy with supper fixings."

"Not the smaller ones."

"*Them.*" Martha's voice was ripe with disdain. "Day comes I can't scare one of those little bits to within an inch of her life if she so much as goes *peep* out of turn—"

"*Martha!*" Becca slammed the lid of her chest. "Don't you dare threaten any of my little sibs!"

A look more sneer than smile shaped the lips of the other girl. "Tender to the babies, are you? Even when it's a swap between whether you get caught out here in your times—with whatever's the punishment for that—or if some snot-nosed brat blubbers a little but keeps her mouth shut?" She shook her head.

Becca took the basin full of wash water and tossed it

out the open window. She wiped it dry with her own petticoat, then borrowed a little water from several of the other girls' pitchers to refill the one she'd used.

"There," Becca said, ignoring Martha's provoking ways. "No one'll be any the wiser now. I'm done; we can hurry back. I'll give you Gram's cloak at the backstairs, you'll take it up attic, and I'll go wash my face and hands all over again, like I was getting ready for supper. Come on."

"Coming." Martha got off Prisca's bed without bothering to tug the covers into any semblance of their former smoothness. As Becca hastened to pull the rumpled bedclothes taut once more, she thought she heard the girl snickering at her.

Becca snuffed the one discreet lantern she'd dared to light just inside the dormitory entryway and closed the door behind her. Carefully, she cast her eyes up and down the road before venturing a step. Her ears pricked, keen to catch any rumor of someone coming along. The air was crisp and cold. It crept beneath the deep bell of Gram Phila's hood to lay a shivery hand across Becca's neck. She gave the path another look—

"Oh, *move*, damn you!" Martha shoved Becca hard enough from behind to make her stumble out into the road. "I've given up enough of my time for you; damned if I'll forfeit my supper. Old Gram, she'll gobble up my share as well, some days."

Becca pulled herself up tall, trying to retake her lost dignity from the girl. "No harm in caution," she said stiffly.

"If Mary Mother had half your caution, Jesus'd still be a bulge in her belly," Gram's handmaid shot back.

Esther   M.   Friesner

"Let's hustle back to the house. Nightfall's come on and I don't favor the dark."

Becca refused to admit it aloud, but she had no fondness for the dark either. Though it hid this wrongful coming and going of hers, it hid worse things, too. Her hands formed fists beneath the shelter of the cloak as Adonijah's face returned to taunt her. Such a one liked the dark just fine, blessed it, stood kin to it. Becca set her sights on the faint glow of light coming from the great house and put air beneath her feet.

The glow from the house windows was so faint it was scarcely more than Becca's own faith in the lights being there. In truth, she knew the house lights couldn't be seen from the dormitory. Only after supper would the Wiserways maidens be given their lanterns and sent on their way to bed, a glowworm weaving through the night. There'd come a time when the strung out lanterns would cluster into a tight knot of light—the place where the path passed Prayerful Hill—then trickle out again into the long strand of bobbing bright yellow bubbles.

It was never easy to walk past Prayerful Hill. It was less to endure when you walked in cheerily lit company with many, but when there were only two, and neither with any lantern, and scudding clouds running between you and the light of the moon—

Becca wondered what Martha would do or say if she slipped her hand into the girl's grasp. Prayerful Hill huddled beside the path like some apparition out of the old tales. Becca couldn't lay a name to the feeling of ice and liquid fire that the shadowy bulk of the bone-built hill summoned up from her innards. Too often the sight of it sent her mind flying back to a night when the

Wiserways girls gathered in their dormitory to sit up late and tell scare-stories. A younger Prisca sat in state, pouring out horrors before the faces of her younger sibs who lapped them up greedily—so good to hark to terrors that were only tales, not realities!—and begged for more.

Not Becca. The evil doings of the scare-tales were all real to her. The story of the young alph who walked out on a lonely road to seek his true love's ghost sank talons of dread deep into her heart.

—and as he walked, he came upon a woman huddled over by the roadside. He greeted her proper, he did, and asked her name. Then she lifted up her face to his and he saw she was all teeth and eyes, all burning eyes and bloody teeth. And she told him, "I am the first woman to bear a babe after the barrenness fell over us all, and the hungering times fell heavy on the earth." So he gathered his courage and said to her, "Well, Mother, then you're a blessed seeing for me, because yours was the first of the new fruitfulness." And she answered, clashing those keen, keen teeth: "Blessed?" Oh, how his fine, thick, black hair went all white to hear that bone-scraping laughter! And she sat back on her haunches and pulled her cloak aside to let him see the babe she'd borne—the first babe borne out of the barrenness—the babe she'd borne…and…EATEN!

Prisca would lunge for one of the smallest girls right then, making her shriek. All the others screamed, too, giddy with delicious fear. All but Becca, who pulled her head deeper into the circle of her arms, shut her eyes tight and tighter, and willed for the awful image in her mind's eye to go away.

That was what Prayerful Hill reminded her of still, sometimes: the ghastly, imagined conjuring of that scare-tale image, the first mother made after the hungering times. She huddled beside the road under a cloak of sod and grass, gnawing over the clean-boiled bones of her babies.

"Martha—" Becca's hand stole out from beneath Gram Phila's cloak. No matter what the girl thought of her, she needed a touch of living flesh to stave off the demons.

"Shush!" The girl stopped stock-still in the roadway. She cocked her head an instant, then grabbed Becca by the shoulder of the cloak and dragged her aside, off the path, into the frosted grasses left unmowed since Harvest Home.

"Down," she said, tugging at Becca as she dropped flat herself. Becca did likewise, feeling the cold earth through the wrap of clothes and cape. She pulled the hood even farther forward, though her face could be no better hidden. She wished it were a cave deep enough to swallow her entirely from sight.

"What—what is it?" she asked in the scratchiest of whispers.

Gram's girl squeezed her hand. "Heard something. Think I did." She nodded toward the hill.

"In there?" Becca peered into the darkness. If there was any light kindled inside Prayerful Hill, it would have to be seen. There was none.

"I'm not sure. Hush. Hark." The two girls crouched in the roadside grass, their breaths a seldom silver net on the air.

Then Becca heard it. It was a voice, familiar and different as a dream. It wasn't coming from inside the hill, but from the flank beyond. It rose and fell, music on the night, and note by note she sifted out its identity.

Her heart went cold when the riddle lay finally read: his voice, Jamie's.

Gram Phila's girl hissed after her and tried to make her hang back by clinging to the cloak; it made no mind. Becca crept toward the sound of Jamie's voice with all her strength, all her determination. What was he doing, out alone in a holy place when he had no business being there? Why was he speaking out loud like a crazy man? When all his sibs should be making ready for their supper, why was he here? Becca crept around the flank of Prayerful Hill, in the very folds of the dreadful, all-devouring mother's skirts, to follow a voice that called to her heart.

Other shapes reared up in the darkness, freezing her to the earth. Man-shapes stood tiered on the side of Prayerful Hill where no man stood willingly. They stood in a circle around one beaten-down shape that spoke, that pleaded, that raised its hands to the sky and cried mercy. Becca dropped noiselessly to her heels, just another rock against the hillside. She was still as bone.

But she could see him. There he was, her Jamie, her beloved. Clouds ran before the wind, letting the moonlight peep through. There was no doubting him now; no doubting any of it.

No doubting it was Pa she saw standing there, with eleven of his oldest, most faithful men. Their heads were bare, despite the cold. She knew every face among them. Some of them she knew had even been given the privilege of lying with Pa's wives, to sire children for the health of Wiserways. No doubting who they were, nor doubting the glitter of the knife in her sire's hand.

No doubting the shine of blood already patching Jamie's face from cuts above and below his eyes. Blood dribbled from his nose, seeped from the corner of his mouth, from his deeply gashed lower lip, cross-raked with the clearer lines of his tears.

And no prayer or hope of ever turning blind to the thing that lay in the grass beside him: the stripped and slashed body of a man with holes for eyes and a pool of blood in the well of his mouth.

"—for what he did to me!" Jamie cried, pointing at the corpse. "No, you didn't make him suffer near half enough for that! You want to know the way of it? All right, no need to cut it out of me; I'll tell: He'd been planning it long, but he waited until you were gone, off to Harvest Home, before he made a move in plain sight toward me. He told me to go out to the fallow lands, said there was a reaper there he'd taken out because it didn't work right. He said he had other business to tend, that I should give the machine a look, see if I could fix it. Well, I went—John was my field boss and I never thought to question him—but when I got there, he was waiting for me in the reaper's shadow. We were far from the house, far from any of the other men, lone—" His words skirled with grief and pain, broke into fragmented sobs. "When I saw what he meant for me, I tried to run. He caught me and struck me down. When I came to—it was too late."

"And after?" Paul's voice was flint. "After he'd used you like—" He spat the thought away. "Why didn't you say anything after?"

Jamie said something too low for hearing.

"What?"

"I said he made me afraid!" Jamie's anguished shout went through Becca's heart like a blade. "He said he'd call me liar, tell you I was the one to blame, say I'd given myself like—like that to someone else than him. He had it in his records that my sib Simon hadn't pulled his weight of work. He said if I spoke one word, he'd lay the blame on us, on me and Simon, claiming it was all our plot to blacken him. He said he'd say that we—" Jamie was gasping.

"Go on." No mercy showed in Paul's eyes.

"He said he'd say that we were the lovers, Simon and me." Something went out of Jamie's body. It slumped as if the life-breath had already fled.

"Lovers." Hearing how her pa pronounced the word, Becca could almost taste the poison of it on her tongue. "Is that what *he* called it?" Paul nodded at the corpse.

"Yes."

"But we know the true word for it, don't we." It wasn't a question.

"Abomination." A sound uttered so low that a breath might have blown it away.

"What did you say, boy?"

"*Abomination*!" Loud enough, now.

"Abomination," Paul agreed, and a confirming murmur went around the circle of other men. "Abomination such as brought down the world."

"But it wasn't any of my—!"

"You were with him, Jamie. No one else was there when Mark and Joab found you two together." The men named shifted some where they stood. "No one can gainsay their testimony."

"And what about mine?" Jamie cried out in despair. "Doesn't it mean anything? I didn't want what happened!"

"That first time, maybe not. But it wasn't the last."

"He said—he said that once he'd—had me like that,

there wasn't any going back. If I wouldn't come to him when he sent for me again, he'd tell you to summon a herbwife to examine me. She'd know the signs."

"So you became his creature out of fear." Paul sighed.

Becca felt a tingling in her hands. She looked down and saw that she had them clenched so tight in prayer that they'd gone bloodless. A fresh wind blew and pulled the clouds back across the moon, leaving the hillside in darkness.

From out of the night she heard the men's voices, each taking it in turn to speak, each offering counsel. Every measure of counsel offered was the same:

"Paul, why tarry? The women will be wondering. You know the penalty."

"There'll be need to clean up after, too. Supper's biding."

"Look, I've got to change this shirt. That bastard fought me! It's all over blood."

"What are we waiting for? Let's have done."

Becca saw her sire's hand rise suddenly, the hand that held no knife. His voice seemed to fill the icy bowl of the sky. "You know what I've got to do, Jamie."

"What you did to—to him?" Jamie's voice was so lost, so small that if her own fear hadn't frozen her, Becca would have run forward to shield his body with her own.

Is it fear that freezes you? the worm asked. *Or are you just too wise to want to die?*

Her pa was saying, "No; his death was what he deserved. He brought it on himself by the words of his mouth when Mark and Joab took you in your sin."

"Then—then I'm not to die?" The hope rising in his voice was piteous to hear.

All Paul said was, "Take that away." Six of the men came forward to pick up John's mangled body. They moved off toward the fields with their burden. Five were left to stand by Paul. He nodded, and they stooped, reaching for something in the grass. While they did so, Becca saw her father approach Jamie and stroke his hair.

"My son." The words were heavy with a tender weight of love and sorrow. Then he clutched Jamie by the hair and yanked his head back without warning. The knife blade slipped across the young man's throat swift as a whisper. Jamie didn't even have the time to cry out. The blood was still rushing from his neck when Paul let him drop.

One of the five—Joab—stood up and said, "Why'd you do that, Paul? You know the lawful penalty—"

"It's death," Paul replied shortly. "That's satisfied."

"Death by stoning," Joab maintained.

"Growing learned, Joab?" Becca knew that dangerous tone in her sire's voice and dreaded it. Would Joab be so wise? "I know the writ as well as you. He's to be stoned and he's to die. Does it matter if one brings the other, so long as both are accomplished? Well, stone him now, if you've a mind to it." He stooped and picked up a fist-sized rock, then threw it hard at Jamie's body. It made a dull, meaty sound when it hit. "There. Feed the law." Without another word, he strode away in the same direction as the other men had carried John's corpse.

"Feed the law?" Joab stood with hands cupped to his mouth, crying out after Paul. "Mock the law's more like it! Does this whole stead have to suffer God's judgment because you were soft-hearted to the boy? And him not even your true get, hill-fetched!"

Paul stopped, turned. He didn't raise his voice, yet still it carried, swift and far as an arrow's flight. "Under this earth there's bones enough—bones of my true begetting, if that's what you want—bones that speak. You know what they say, Joab? Many things, but never—never once that when it came to the welfare of Wiserways—that I let a soft heart overrule what had to be done."

He took a step toward Joab, who now stood with his arms dangling limp at his sides. "I don't charge you with ignorance. Could be you've just forgot. Go to the bones, then; ask them to make you remember."

Joab shook his head slowly, his mouth working. "No," was all he could rasp out. And again, "No, Paul. Please, for pity's sake, don't make me go—"

"For pity's sake," Paul repeated. "Go."

Becca saw Joab shiver as if he were a girl-child. So rapt was she by this new evidence of how the bones could strike even a grown man's heart to flint, she didn't realize that the shortest way to the opening of Prayerful Hill would bring him right on top of her. If she ran now, they'd see her, and if she held her ground, she'd be discovered. She closed her eyes tight and in her soul offered up a prayer to Mary Mother that Pa would grant her as swift and merciful a death as he'd given Jamie.

Then she heard Pa call out, "Wait!" Joab's footsteps stopped. "Never mind. You needn't go." He sounded weary, beaten. Joab began to speak, babbling thanks mixed with vows never to speak out of turn again. Becca could hear his boots moving away from her, back toward Paul, and all the time he praised the alph's mercy and swore him loyalty.

Paul's sigh carried all the way to Becca's ears. "Save your breath, Joab. Use it to put strength in your arm, if you've still got your heart set on a stoning. Or if you do know pity, then save it to say a prayer for this boy's soul."

Becca didn't wait to see whether Joab and the rest would stone the poor bloodied body. She wrapped Gram Phila's cloak around her tight and ran as quickly and as silently as her feet could go. The frost had numbed them badly, even through the thin shoes she'd slipped on to go outdoors, but it was nothing next to the cold that seeped in beneath her flesh. She flew past Martha on the road and never looked back. The other girl's startled breath gasped out behind her, a dying echo.

She ran all the way home, dropping the crone's cloak by the backstairs, and kept on running. She raced up to her mother's room where she, too, slept while in her times and flung herself on the bed, hugging the quilt to her heart. Outside the night had gained another wandering ghost. Every phantom was another weight bending Becca closer to the earth. She wondered if she'd have the chance to shout *No more!* before she broke in two.

She felt the room, the house, the stead like layers of stone around her. Soon her kindred would be sitting down to supper—the women demurely serving out the food, the men fresh-washed so that no one might guess from what errands they'd come. There would be smiles and pleasantries. It would be a meal like many others. No one would know.

And Pa will look up from his thanksgiving prayer and ask if anyone's seen John or Jamie, Becca thought. *He'll feign like he doesn't know a thing about it, the same way Katy feigned that time with Tom. Everyone will ask the same question, at first, but it won't take long for them to know the truth. They'll never let on, though, especially not the women. That wouldn't be proper, to talk of such things. Mary Mother, forgive me, but I can't be a proper woman now. Lord help me, I can't face the lies no more!*

She put her face down in the pillow and wept. They were all the tears Jamie would ever know. She wept for the nameless babe he'd been, saved from the hillside, from the arms of death itself.

(*Saved?* One hillside was like another. Death was patient.)

Becca wept on, her tears for Jamie and for all the other chosen children of the King: for Miss Lynn's girl-child and Thalie's Susanna; for Dassah dancing in her shroud of flame; for Pa, who'd loved his son, and given him his death; for all the infant dead of Prayerful Hill.

For Jamie and for dreams.

Chapter Fifteen

...if it be a son, then ye shall kill him.
Exodus I:16

After Jamie was gone, Becca thought the cold came in stronger than at year's wane. Waking, she wondered whether this feeling was another brain-wraith of her own conjuring or if it was truly so. She went back and forth about her business with the feeling that something dark had cast itself over all the stead, Gram Phila's cloak grown huge by the crone's uncanny powers.

"What's wrong, child?" Mama asked that question more and more as the days made weeks and the weeks plaited themselves into a brace of months. Part of Becca's heart yearned to have her cast herself into Hattie's lap and wail all her grief away, but the part that had grown shell whispered that there was no true mother's concern in the asking.

That long, pale face you wear these days doesn't look proper for a maid, the worm sneered. *Now the harvest's done and the new planting time's still a ways off, the load of work's grown lighter; everyone's joyed, and shows it plain on their faces. Everyone but you. Your eyes are full of bones. A look like that, even if it doesn't turn you into a walking dead, proclaims you poorly bred. That might give the other wives cause to lord it over Hattie. There's no mother made but wears her children like a string of gilded beads or a strand of mud pebbles. That's all she really cares about: how your bearing shines back on her.*

No, Becca thought, her hands turned to fists. She was laying out a fresh lend-gift of clothes for Shifra on Mama's bed. The child was growing out of all knowledge and the other wives had needed to scramble to scare up what would fit her from their own stores of infant wear. *She does care for me more than for how I adorn her! My mama loves me!*

Then why didn't you tell her instead of Selena when that came over you? the worm teased.

Because...because it would only have grieved her needlessly. When I... When it came over me so soon since the last time, I went to see Selena. At first I thought it was just my imagining, but the way the men leered after me—But it was so. I could almost scent it myself before I felt the flow. Selena just laughed and said such things happen. Said it happened to her after she bore her first babe, her times getting all muddled for a spell, coming on her earlier than looked for. It happens to most women, once or twice, no harm done. It would've been a darker tale if this had come to pass before I was through my Sixmonth, she said. That wouldn't be natural.

They're fine ones for knowing what's natural, your kin, the worm drawled. *From the Lord's own mouth to their ears, and no appeal! So you're safe—or safe as any woman can be who's in her times.*

Hush! She folded up the last of shirts and went downstairs.

Pa was among the women when Becca came down. She bowed her head and dutifully went to her place beside Shifra's cradle. The driving urge to hold a babe of her own had lost its luster when Jamie died. She still loved her little sister, but now she grew easily bored with the drudgery of infant care. With the cold come in, and her in her times, she found herself stuck with the baby more and more. Until her times were off her, she shared sleeping space with her mama. It was no longer a treat. Her heart ached too keenly for her to enjoy serene nights, and she felt that Hattie's eyes were on her too much. She longed for the crowded privacy of the girl's dormitory, but Mama said it was out of the question.

"Your pa's too wise to the ways of young males, the strong pull that a taking woman's scent can have on them. You were never bred up to deny a man—and that's as should be!—nor strong enough to keep one off when he means to have his way. Common days, fear of God, and knowing what's civilized keeps the men from falling into sin, but when a woman's in her times…" Mama didn't have to say more.

"At least our times don't last forever," Becca whispered to the sleeping baby. "Mary Mother witness I'll be glad when mine sort themselves out to their normal space again. Twice yearly's more than enough for me. And for now, I'll just be grateful when the blood comes and this part of it's over." She brushed the downy cheek and smiled.

A commotion snapped her attention to the doorway. There stood Selena's Willie. It could only mean one thing: news. Audacious as striplings grew, none of her sibs would have the face to burst in on their sire and his wives like this, unbidden, unless there were great tidings.

He strode into the room, heading for Paul. Only when he passed near Becca, he paused. Underage and scrawny as he was, Willie sensed the difference in the big seeing-room; her difference. His nose twitched, his mouth hung a little open as he breathed. It was comical to see, yet at the same time gave her cold creepings of the spine. She raveled herself up into a tighter ball of shadow behind the tall headboard of her sister's cradle.

"Well, what is it, Willie?" Paul demanded. "A badger in the stubble rustle up too loud for your liking?" The wives treated themselves to a patter of soft laughter at the jest. Everyone knew that Willie and his like-aged sibs were being given a first taste of keeping the night-watch out over the reaped fields. The tallyless number of false alarms a stead had to bear while the up-and-coming boys stood guard was an old, old joke. In their eagerness to prove themselves, everything spooked them to a run.

Willie opened his mouth even wider, then reeled up his jaw and tried to speak. The nest of older wives—past fruitfulness, still spared from a winnowing for whatever cause—buzzed with sweet, wicked speculation. *They* knew what was tying up the boy's tongue. *They* had borne and raised enough sons for the fields of Wiserways to know how fool-headed a male turned when his blood recognized Eve's call; only his brain couldn't catch up fast enough.

They took it in turns to slew their eyes from Willie to
Becca, and their tongues darted more artfully than their
needles until all the wives shared gladly in the mischief.

Selena was the only one present who didn't chortle
over the boy's discomfort. Becca wondered how soon it
would be before she took her son's part. Not long.

"*Willie!* You answer your pa, else you'll be back on a
tether in the cookhouse tomorrow."

Willie gulped something down a dry throat and
dutifully replied, "Yes, Ma." His gangle-fingered hands
snarled into knots before him as he said, "There's one
outside who's come to see you, Pa." Another dry swallow.
"Says he wants your blood."

All laughter ceased. The death-hush fell soft and thick
as recent snows. Katy gave a little whimper and started
up from her seat. One of the older wives arose and forced
her back down again.

"The children—" Katy began.

"They're sleeping." The older wife had a voice of dull,
gray metal. "Asleep they'll bide. You'll witness and accept
what comes, as the Lord King in his mercy will decide,
but you shan't stir a foot to shame your man."

In her place, Hattie was breathing hard, almost
panting. Her eyes filled with a desperate light and she
turned a face strained with unspoken words to Becca. She
needn't speak; Becca understood. *The storeplace.* Her
hands slipped beneath Shifra's small, warm body silently
as she tried to gather up her drowsing sister.

The baby stirred and began to cry. The shrill sound
tore the air.

Paul was on his feet. Becca saw the look he passed over
all his wives—old and young, chosen and come to his
hand with Wiserways. There was no reading any human

feeling into that look, save only the knowing that a task was at hand that he alone must do.

"Who is it, Willie lad?" he asked. Not a ripple unsteadied his voice. He might have been asking about the weather. "Did you know him?"

"No, sir." The boy looked truly miserable. "I was at watch with Levi when we saw him coming down the road past—past the hill." No need to say which hill. "We hailed him, and he answered right away, stating his business. But he said he'd give his name when he came before you. So Levi stirred up the watchfire to call in runners from the other posts and spread the word along, and he—the man—he sent me here to tell you." Impatience to be gone suddenly possessed the boy. His bare feet danced on unseen coals. "Would you be wanting me to rouse my sibs for this, Pa?"

Paul laid a staying hand on Willie's shoulder. "We'll see about that, boy. We'll just see." He started for the door. On the sill he turned and gave command to the eldest among his wives. "Michal, keep order here. It'll be mine to choose the place, and I'll have it before the gates of my own house. I'll send Willie in to fetch you and the rest out to witness, when it's time. Until then, no one's to stir, is that clear?"

Michal bowed her neatly braided head. "Lord God strengthen your arm, husband. Lord King grant this one walks the same road as the others before him."

Paul smiled. "Lord King grant it." He lifted her chin and kissed her on dry lips that hadn't known such a mark of favor for many years.

Becca attempted to use the moment's distraction to hush little Shifra and spirit the infant out of the room by the back door. It would be no task at all for her to climb out through a handy window and race for one of the abandoned storeplaces. For a wonder, Pa hadn't ordered all the yearlong ones destroyed after this Harvest Home. A couple had been spared with a thrifty eye to shoring them up with stone, adding to the roll of the permanent ones. Only Becca knew that a goodly part of Pa's optimism was rooted deep in that small pouch of experimental seed the city traders had gifted him. No one said a word, for fear of ill-wishing, but stead knowledge was that Wiserways had never had so bountiful a harvest as this. It augured well enough for next year to justify Paul's plan for expanding storeplaces.

Next year lay at the end of a night a century long. All that mattered was that a storeplace was also a good hidey-hole for Shifra if—

"Where do you think you're going?" Michal's words came down across Becca's back sharp as a switch.

"I thought I'd fetch the baby a clean diaper. She's messed herself; that's why she howls." Becca was amazed at how glibly the lies came to her tongue.

No use. Michal crossed the seeing-room and wrenched the infant from Becca's arms. "Then why not fetch it to her, instead of her to it?" An expert hand thrust in among Shifra's swaddlings. "Dry," Michal pronounced. She gave the baby back to Hattie. "No more of that."

Eyes downcast, Hattie unbuttoned her blouse and gave Shifra the breast. If she wept, no one could see.

"Paul's a good man," Selena said.

"Strong, too," Katy added, making her voice bright with hope. "None stronger."

Thalie raised one eyebrow. "All the years you've been kept on this stead, how would you know?" Her eyes swept the room. "How would any of us know how he measures up to what's come calling this night? These walls are our world. What's beyond them is beyond us. For all we know—"

Michal didn't deal in slaps, but fisted blows. Thalie was knocked from her chair almost into the hot embers of the fire. Ray was with her almost instantly.

"You crazy old woman!" she shouted at Michal, cradling a weeping Thalie against her bosom. "Where's your brains? Where's your *ears*? You the only one in all Wiserways doesn't know this girl is *fruitful*?"

Michal blanched. "I didn't—She should never've spoke like—Oh sweet Lord, you going to tell?"

"Her *face* will tell plain enough," Ray spat.

"No." Thalie cupped a hand over her reddening cheek and pushed away from Ray. Cross-legged on the floor, she said, "I caught my foot in the hem of my skirts and fell. If that brings me to any grief with this—" she touched her belly "—so be it; the Lord King's will be done." Her laugh was savorless. "I'll breed again soon enough. Could be it's a mercy."

"A mercy?" Hattie's voice seethed up from a black place deep within her soul. Hot and thick, the echoing she gave Thalie's words, and as like to sear flesh from bone as any manlore cauldron. She rose from her place and put Shifra back into Becca's care without ever taking her eyes from Thalie. "Now you mark me, woman." She spoke slowly, each word laid down as incontestable as a corpse. "You mark what I tell you here, with witnesses to testify. When this night's work is done, if your sweet *mercy* comes to pass, then I will lesson you to learn the true meaning of mercy. I will surely wait for you in all the shadows of this stead. I will wait, and when next you see your fruitfulness as blessing, I swear by almighty God, I'll come from out the shadows and with these two hands I'll tear that blessing bloody from your womb."

The little golden hairs along Becca's forearms stood up tauter as each sentence her mother uttered added to the horror of the curse. Ray drew away from Thalie quickly, fearing contagion. The other wives held still, just their eyes growing wider to show they heard. Only Thalie stayed as stone.

"Before or after," the young wife replied dully. "You or another to tear it from my womb, my arms, what difference will it make? It's only another child. Have the cursing of me, Hattie; it's no burden. The Lord King laid a greater on us all, long ago."

The door opened. Selena's Willie was back. "Pa says you're to—" He paused long. He could taste more in the air than the call of Becca's readiness. Involuntarily, he shuddered. "He says you're to come stand before the house now," he finished, and bolted.

Their bare feet passed in ordered procession over the plank floors of Wiserways. Becca went with them, clinging to her mother's side as if she were still the dirty-faced brat in leading strings. Fear crept up out of her belly to damp her ears and veil her eyes. She was abruptly aware of a world of scents closing her in: the musk of her mother's sweat-stained dress and the tang of Thalie's near-singed hair; the burning rush-dips casting their ailing light along the endless way from the seeing-room to the great front door; the assault of chill, fresh air when that door opened and the women came out into the night, and the moist, cool, ripe smell of the fallow earth. The waiting earth, and Shifra's powdery sweet aura of a living babe pressed warm against her shoulder.

Gram Phila was already there, seated in a straight-backed chair with her handmaid crouched at her side. Becca tried to catch the other girl's eye, in vain. Toes curled tight, hands clutched to knees, every strand of nerve and muscle in the nameless one was pulled tight to spring at the slightest touch. Her eyes burned keen. Hers was the only face there smiling; a famished smile.

The women arranged themselves in a single line beside the stead crone, the big house at their backs, gazing straight ahead with strictly schooled, indifferent eyes. Across an open space before the house was an answering line of men: Paul's sibs, Paul's sons. By the light of hastily kindled torches, they had all gathered to bear witness, as was right. Only the youngest boys were absent, boys too young yet to do duty in the fields and be an asset to Wiserways. These still slept in their dormitory, tired from a day of play. Katy's son slept there, and silly Tamar's, and Simon, the son of Metria's last times before she was touched by a woman's second Changes. Becca could picture them all, though she never had set foot in the boys' dormitory: tousled heads and sleep-flushed cheeks, nightshirts a-tangle over legs just starting to lengthen, getting ready to take the first stride out of childhood.

Two figures alone stood free of the lines of men and women. Two men stood in the uneven light, in a square whose borders someone had gouged into the hard-packed earth. Becca knew them both: one her sire; the other, Adonijah. The wonder of that recognition was that it wrenched neither terror nor astonishment from Becca's soul.

Time was when Becca was small she'd climbed an old dead tree too high and tumbled out headfirst. However bad she knew the hurt would be when she hit, however bad it was, in the moments of her fall to earth it was as if she'd left her body and flown with her spirit to sit among the angels. From high and outside she watched the stranger-girl fall from a dead tree's branch and break her collarbone. There was no terror as the ground roared up to meet her, there was no pain when she struck it.

So now, that same unfeeling isolation. *This is what happens*. Not the worm in her mind, but not her own thoughts either. *This is just the way it ravels out, and neither help nor hindrance for it*. The two men and what they would do were far away; they could not touch her. Adonijah had come to kill her sire, if he could, and take Wiserways Stead for his own. Becca was too numb to pray against the unthinkable. *This is how things are*.

The hill is how things are! Satan's worm, Becca's self, howled indignation. *The cauldron is how things are, and the godly lies, and what will become of Shifra if Paul loses, these abominations are how things are! But oh, are they so everywhere? In the cities? In a world more wide than Katy has the scope to lesson, must they be?*

What matter? Becca's stony spirit replied. *My life is here.* And she almost believed it.

In the ring, loud enough so that all present might hear, Paul hailed his challenger. "Adonijah, welcome, and welcome be Adonijah of Makepeace Stead on Wiserways ground this day." The words were a set piece for times like these. Their stilted, ceremonious intonation made the listeners aware of just how old and time-honored was the ritual contest to come.

Adonijah answered in kind: "Greetings, Paul, and may it be after Adam's way with you, Paul of Wiserways Stead."

"Of earth, to earth."

"Of bone, to dust."

"The Lord shall uplift and sustain me."

"The Lord shall bring down the mighty."

There was a pause in the exchange. In his everyday voice, Paul said, nigh gently, "Adonijah, what passed between us at Harvest Home is done. Don't lose your life for pride's sake."

Adonijah grinned. "Frightened, old man?"

Paul's folk sucked in little gusts of breath that came out quick enough in scandalized whispers. Adonijah's jab drained even the hope of gentleness straight out of Paul's face. "Very well." His jaw was set. "You've chosen to play the fool, and pay the penalty in a man's coin. You've brought one to stand up for you and tell after how it all happened? I'll have none of Zacharias' coming 'round here after, swearing as how I murdered his son."

"No." Adonijah's lip curled. "You'll have none of that." He kept on staring at Paul with that jackal leer of his, but motioned for someone behind him to come forward. Of the six young men who stepped into the torchlight, Becca recognized every one. They were half the complement of Adonijah's hunting pack, and the tickling chill at her nape told her the others must be near.

"So many?" Paul looked dubious. "One's all you need by lore."

"One at least." Adonijah's teeth glittered. "More if I like." Paul's men muttered among themselves, the torches swaying. "Will you fear them as well? It's only me you must battle, and then be free for no less than a month's time before the next may challenge you. Or me."

"I fear neither them nor you," Paul said, and for the moment turned his back on Adonijah.

There was some minor business to settle before the fight began. Paul's strongest, swiftest sons were sent to carry word to every stead and to Grange itself that a challenge had come to his hearth. Next to Becca, Katy was all a-fidget. To keep her mind from the innocents asleep in their dormitory beds, she took refuge in her role as teacher.

"See there, Bec'?" She pointed to where more of Paul's men and boys were rolling away a pair of black barrels from some unguessed storeplace. "Those are iron-made. *Iron!* I hear as they were saved from the hungering times, when men still scavenged. Lord King witness, they look old enough, but we've kept them well. Wiserways' tidings have always been kindled in them. They'll fill each one with stuff that will burn with different colored smoke when lit—manlore contrivings. Could be the smoke will reach the outer steads long before the runners do, but their sentries will mark the color and recall it when our folk finally come to tell them the winner's name."

"Grange is far." Becca put her thoughts into words. "That means all this will be done with before anyone there knows it's begun. There couldn't be any stopping it."

"Stopping it?" Katy frowned. "Becca, who'd dare?"

Becca thought of Barak, who had been so kindly to her. Surely the alph of Verity Grange must have the power to halt a stead striving? Wouldn't he want to know that one as unworthy as Adonijah was trying to bring down her sire? Paul was godly, but Zach's get had rubbed away the cross. Could such a blasphemer be allowed to vie for mastership of Wiserways?

Only smoke flies through the air; not words. Becca's

thoughts were bitter. *By the time Barak learns the end of what's happening here now, it will be settled. Not even the alph of Verity Grange can meddle with what's over and done.*

Paul pulled a kerchief from his pants pocket and wiped his hands. He tossed it aside and spoke the words the Lord King's scripture recorded of Pilate's lips, casting aside all personal blame for whatever might happen after. He stripped his shirt off and Tom came up quickly to take his sire's garment. Two of his younger sons knelt in the dust at his feet to remove his shoes and socks while one of the older men got down on all fours to provide his alph with seating while the boys accomplished their task. If Paul lived, their services might be kindly remembered. Becca was old enough to have had lessoning on what coin an alph used to repay favors.

Her pa was only one man, and sometimes, for whatever purpose, he shared.

Adonijah kicked off his shoes and pulled off his own socks without help from anyone, but he left his shirt on. Becca heard one of her male sibs whisper that Adonijah must be half in love with death to give Pa such a raw advantage. Easier to grasp hold of a man's clothing than his skin. Easier then to draw him into a rib-crusher, or a twist to bring his neck within your power. One snap, then—

Becca prayed, heart and soul, that it would fall out as swift and simple as that.

Then one of the older men stepped into the clear space where Paul and Adonijah waited. He raised his right hand to the night sky. "In the name of God!" he cried, and let the hand drop, then leaped gratefully back into anonymity.

Becca was as taken by surprise as her sire when Adonijah's leap came so suddenly. It minded her of Gram Phila's girl, a simple-minded tactic. Her sire was expecting the usual order of fighters circling 'round, sizing each other up before they closed. In spite of his first surprise, his reflexes were too good for Adonijah's daredevil ploy to buy the boy much advantage. He took Adonijah's inrush of clawing hands square on the chest and brought his own linked fists up hard to break that grip. Paul's knotted hands slammed Adonijah's chin, sent him staggering back, blinking. The striving had begun.

Becca felt the air around her change as man and youth settled into the time-fixed sequence of such bouts. Apparently, Adonijah had spent in one effort anything new he had brought to the battle. To left and right Becca saw the faces of Paul's wives relax. Tension washed from their bodies. They recognized the spectacle spinning itself out before them as an old tale. Other males before him had taken up the part Adonijah now played, but the end had always been the same.

Katy was actually smiling. Even Hattie let her mask of solemn witness drop, its straight mouth crackling up at the edges. Becca stared. For her mama to smile now—prim Hattie, who worshipped the stead proprieties, loved them more than she loved any child of her bearing—it was like some other woman bursting into peals of thanksgiving song.

"Young," Ray murmured. Selena nodded agreement. Though Adonijah managed to catch Paul in several minor holds, the stead alph broke these like so many afterthoughts. He wasn't even sweating. He, too, knew how this match must end; he had time. "Very young; ill counseled to come to this, I'll wager." Ray's words were

269

taken up and echoed by the rest. Paul's wives, young and old, all felt easy enough by this to grant the doomed boy the luxury of sympathy.

All but Thalie. Becca saw how her hands clenched every time Adonijah managed to get a hold on Paul. The young wife's eyes were a kindling and a blaze, her lips parted and her breath rasping as if she had the power to force her own meager measure of strength into Adonijah's body by main will. Becca looked away, burying her face in Shifra's downy neck.

In the ring, Paul siezed Adonijah by the shirt front and yanked him close. Adonijah lashed his head forward sharply, the front of his skull smashing Paul's nose. The wives gasped as blood spurted. Paul bellowed with pain. Zach's fox-faced son grinned and danced away while the big alph wiped at the stream, smearing his forearm red.

"Surprised, old man?" Adonijah called. "You'd best keep your distance from me. I might hurt you again." He opened his arms as if to a lover. "Here I am!"

Paul's eyes burned. Adonijah's taunts were intended to goad him to a charge. He was too seasoned to let any man but himself control his actions. He held his distance.

Adonijah shrilled the night with laughter. "That's right, old man! Hold onto your life while you can. But before the dawn comes up you'll be meat for the plow to wedge into the earth, and all the sowings of your seed with you! Your sons will serve me and your daughters do my pleasure. And your wives?" His mockery writhed on Becca's bare skin like a plague of littlesingers. "When they talk of you abroad, they say the grave's already got you from the navel down. Show charity to these poor women, Paul, and give the earth the rest."

Paul filled his lungs. "I'll give the earth enough," he

answered, his voice so soft that old Gram Phila clamored to know what he'd said. Before anyone could tell her, Paul sprang with death riding on his shoulders.

Adonijah made the weakest of attempts to escape. The impact knocked him flat to the ground. Paul tried for a throat hold, but that was rage making him simple. Stripling boys still under their mothers' eyes learned how to break that one with upflung arms or their sibs didn't let them live to get a second lessoning. Adonijah stiff-armed it off readily enough. It didn't seem to matter, though. Paul had his full weight pinning Adonijah to the dirt. Twist and rock the young man might, but the contest was now down to pure weight and muscle and bone.

"Fights like a woman, for all the brawn he carries," Michal murmured. Becca could hear every note of scorn.

I wouldn't have done it so, she found herself thinking. *Fighting someone that much bigger than me, I'd keep out of close combat until the edge was worn off his strength. Why in God's name did Adonijah court so quick an end? He's fast on his feet, he could have sidestepped Pa's charge, run him out some more. He didn't. Does the fool want to die?*

Her heart knew he didn't. No fool, Adonijah, but a fox. That knowledge did to Becca what witnessing all the night's striving could not do: It touched her bones with fear.

In the square of light, Adonijah was pummeling her sire's chest with both hands while the men stood by. Some even laughed. The final judgment seemed a sure one, the certainty of Paul's victory already lending a festival lightness to air so lately burdened by doubt and foreboding. Only Adonijah's minions kept still, showing neither sorrow nor shame for their leader's fall, his weak, defensive struggles. Paul hooked a leg beneath his adversary, ready to roll him over and give the final backward twitch to snap a stubborn spine.

"In God's name, Paul, show mercy!"

Heads turned. The shout had come from one of Adonijah's pack, a skinny get with scraggled hair and scanty beard. Even Paul looked up, still pressing Adonijah down securely under him. As if in gratitude for the respite, or as a last vain effort to protect himself, Adonijah's hands crossed on his own throat.

Only for a moment. They fell away from his collar and balled back into fists. The left struck Paul so lightly that it only made him glance in that direction, as if someone had tapped him to get his attention. The right hit harder, a strange blow that landed beneath Paul's left arm. Becca frowned, watching. Was Adonijah trying to push her sire off him that way? Why not bring both fists to bear together, then? And for as trifling as that strike seemed, why did Pa let out such an awful cry?

Why did he clap his right hand across his chest to his upper ribs? Becca tried to recall any lessoning she'd had from Gram Phila's girl about where you could hurt a man most. If Adonijah had chanced on one such secret place, it wasn't one she could recall. Except that underhand hit hadn't looked like chance—Adonijah wasn't the sort of man to hope and hold with chance when he risked so much of himself. He'd aimed it just so. There was no doubt in Becca's mind that he'd meant it to land how and where it did.

There wasn't space to think of chance; the striving had resumed, though to Becca's skeptical eye it now had the false, suspicious gloss of child's play. Adonijah was flailing at Paul again in that silly, powerless way. The heartsick women of Wiserways had too much of their own desires tied up in Paul's winning to question why a healthy young man like Adonijah should put up so sorry a fight. Becca could almost hear them reasoning away the evidence of their eyes: *He's young, he's unseasoned, he was never trained, it was the whim of a moment, young men often die for their whims—*

The steadmen were no better. The old were fearful of any change, and the young? They held their sire's triumph as needful only because each one of them saw himself as the man who must at last bring Paul to die. No offsteader should dare try stealing that future glory from them.

Everyone watched, but no one *saw.*

The rain of Adonijah's glancing blows had no more worth than to rile. Their insistent pelting quickly distracted Paul from whatever small, sharp hurt his foe had dealt him with that bizarre, seemingly uncalculated underarm jab. He settled his weight more heavily onto Adonijah's body and again turned his concentration to rolling the youth over like a turtle. He had a death to get done with and wives to cheer after.

The world fell down a nightmare sky where time slowed and motion went insane. Was Becca first to see it, that tremor running down her sire's arms? His jaw began to sag, his mouth to slacken. The large hands clamped to Adonijah's shoulders regained color at the knuckles as their strength trickled away. Becca pressed the baby tighter to her breast as Paul's left knee buckled under and he fell.

Or had that been Adonijah's doing, a keen, crisp move that tucked his own knees up tight and sharp beneath Paul's splayed legs, pitching the older man over to the left? Adonijah rolled the other way, free, and was on his feet while Paul was still tumbling in the dirt. A barefoot kick connected with Paul's already bleeding face as he tried to get up. Becca saw how he stumbled even before the blow landed.

It didn't seem right. It didn't seem real. Was she the only one to see it, or had it all come to pass so swiftly that the others couldn't tell? And if it had happened one way or the other, would they know, so wrapped up in their own desires for how the contest should end? Becca never felt so lone. No matter how much force Adonijah had packed into that kick, she knew her pa had the strength to take that and more. If this were the fighting artistry Adonijah truly commanded, why hadn't he turned to his skill that night of Harvest Home?

Can a man learn so much in so little time? Could something other than natural cause be making Paul move with the slow deliberation of an ailing man?

O Lord King, why couldn't they *see*?

The Lord King's ways are not the ways of man. Hattie's phantom self invaded Becca's mind with the only reasoning she could summon to answer all her questions. Again she was a child, hearing the older woman's voice mete out lessonings. *As David with Goliath, as the Israelites before Jericho-town, sometimes the Lord and His best-beloved King choose to let us witness miracles, to Their greater glory.*

No! The worm in Becca's heart shouted down Hattie's Scripture-assured authority in a voice of boiling flame. *Pa's no Goliath, nor no town of sin! He's done no evil. It's Adonijah who's the evil—*

Shifra squirmed against Becca's warmth and gave a little whimper. Becca looked down at her sister and all the voices of Prayerful Hill rose up from the infant's small, damp mouth to shriek away all of Becca's own certainty.

They welled up in a dark and gusty chorus, layering

the air with all the times that Paul had sent them newborn to the hill because they were male when female was desired, or vice versa. They keened for those who had gone to the bones half-grown, for breach of lore or merely because they'd sinned against full health or cleverness or obedience. They wept for the girls whose Changes had not come over them after the proper way of women, girls who bled too much, too often, so that they had to die before their presence destroyed the proper order of the world. Thalie's lost Susanna found her voice there, and she was not alone. For every death, Paul had a line of lore or Scripture reasoning to back his will, but Becca knew that cold strings of spoken or written words hadn't been those babies' executioner.

It was a simple song they sang, the babes and children of Prayerful Hill: *His turn, now.*

His turn, Becca thought. *And maybe what he did was evil too, but still*— Oh, Pa!

And through tears that made the torchlight swim, she looked back into the ring in time to see Adonijah's foot skim the back of Paul's leg in a snare-and-trip move so primitive that even stead girls practiced it on the sly. A push—a touch, in truth—and Paul fell to the ground. Adonijah jumped with both feet this time, full on Paul's chest. The screams that went up from the women covered any sound of breaking bone. Another kick to the head then, and another, given with vindictive glee that iced every cell in Becca's body.

By the time Adonijah deigned to heave Paul over onto his belly and take the alph's battered head between his hands for the last wrenching out of life, it was done as if the younger man had something better on his mind. The snap of the neckbone was less victory than formality.

Adonijah stood over Paul's corpse and wiped sweat from his brow with one shirtsleeve. "In God's name," he said.

"His will be done," came the answering mumble from the steadmen. One went to cast his torch into an iron barrel that belched out thick smoke tinted a deep red. Over the miles, until dawn broke, the other steads would see it only as a black cloud rising. The untouched barrel would have smudged the sky with white.

The men of Adonijah's picked band were already moving through the night, and all but one of the widows of Wiserways tore the darkness with their grief. Their groans and screams climbed the path to Heaven with the trail of bloody smoke.

Becca had no time to mourn her sire. Sorrow must wait. Only one thing mattered now. While there might yet be time for any hope, Becca ran with Shifra into the night.

Chapter Sixteen

Down in the meadow where the bad snakes bite
I caught my love with Lillith on a cold, cold night.
Down in the meadow where the fruit's like flame
I gave my love an apple; another got the blame.
Down in the meadow where the sad snakes grieve
It's amazing what a man or a god will believe.
Down in the meadow where the man-snakes crawl
I'm not ashamed I did it at all, at all, at all.

"She's in here."

Becca knew Thalie's voice. She heard it before the wash of torchlight invaded the deep storeplace pit where she'd crouched for what seemed like hours. She tilted back her head to meet the light and squinted with the pain, but she didn't cry. There were two men with Thalie, one of Adonijah's crew and one of the older steadmen.

The latter wore a thin-lipped look of grim satisfaction. Outside the storeplace, old debts were being paid out for a roll of slights and scantings ancient but unforgotten. The steadman looked old enough to have belonged to Wiserways since before Paul claimed it as alph. He could probably recall Paul's sire.

So old, Becca thought as he dropped into the pit beside her and linked his hands to give her a leg up and out. *I wonder how many times he wished for the courage to do what my pa did, to dare make himself more than just another pair of tilling hands? But he never did, and he must have envied Pa for being more than he ever was. Maybe in his dreams he was more, but—Sweet Mary Mother, how he must relish my poor pa's death!*

He wasn't the only one. Adonijah's man was transformed, his flat face beaming with nigh holy exaltation. That was to be expected: With Adonijah the new alph of Wiserways Stead, all manner of rewards would fall to those who had stood by him from the start. Little need to wonder in what kind this one would claim his fee, judging by how he stared at Becca.

Then he caught her scent and his face fell.

"Best take this one straight to 'Nije—Adonijah."

The older man nodded, wrinkling up his nose as the full, unmistakable tang of a woman in her times hit him. He glowered at Becca as if she'd done something wicked on purpose.

Just because he can't have me, she thought. *As if he ever could! Our blood's too near for that. Just the Kiss or the Sign—God deliver me from sharing either with him!* She glanced at the young one and shuddered. *Safe from you, too; for now. In my times and all, I'm Eve's own. None can have me now, except...* Her stomach shriveled within her. She began to pray.

"Not so fast!" Thalie held up her hand. Her face was fevered, eyes shining with unnatural brightness. She dipped her torch down into the storeplace pit, flame sweeping away any chance of secrets. "Where is she?" she demanded when all that came to light were scattered gleanings of grain and a toss of cloth too small to hide a baby.

Becca didn't reply.

"*Where is she?*" Thalie's hand tightened on nothing, but the longing was in her pinched face: the longing to close her fingers on Becca's throat and squeeze out answers. "Curse you, where's Paul's last-born child?"

Becca kept still.

The younger man seemed to fear Thalie as a burned child veers from the fire. All deference and pause, he stammered out the suggestion: "Could be—could be maybe we've already found it."

Thalie made a hoarse sound of disgust. "Think I wouldn't know it? I tell you, she wasn't among the rest." She gave Becca a hard stare. "If you think you're doing any good for your damned Scripture-hen mother, think again. She'll tell you herself to bring out the babe and abide by the Lord King's judgment in all things." A wild tatter of laughter fluttered from Thalie's mouth, startling Becca. "Yes, His will be done, she'll say! Likely those very words were on her lips like a grace when Paul first had her, or when she gave some other fool the Kiss of Peace. His will be done, and if I do less to comfort her than she ever did for me, may Herod's holy sword strike me down!"

"Come with us, Becca." The steadman was quietspoken but firm. "Please."

She walked in their midst from the storeplace out into a world where dawn was just beginning to lighten the fields. Becca bit her lower lip, willing herself not to see whatever the coming light would thrust before her eyes. It was futile. Too much had happened recently, and none had come yet to clear the dead away.

The first she saw was Tamar's son, Hiram. He lay on his back, eyes open to the sky. He'd been trying to make for the safety of the outer fields when the men caught up with him. His nightshirt was a shroud of cloth too long for his little legs, a hand-me-down from some older sib. His head lay at too sharp an angle on his neck; at least there was no blood.

There was blood aplenty further on, as they neared the house. Selena's Willie lay sprawled across a wheelbarrow in the yard, his skin a sickly yellow where the blood had drained away beneath the field-got tan. Whoever had caught him hadn't had an easy time cutting his throat. The slash was jagged, the boy's face and arms a welter of lesser gashes. Two other boys of around Willie's years slumped against the side of the big shed as if they had hunkered down there for a game of marbles. Their heads were caved in.

Becca caught herself breathing hard through a gaping mouth as Thalie and the two men led her closer to the house where Adonijah waited. There was an ungodly stillness lying over the place, and an absence of any smells save the perversely fresh and heartening perfume of a clear late autumn morning. No smoke rose from the cookhouse or the ovens. All that tainted the sky was the dying trail of crimson signal-smoke dispersing on the easterly breeze.

O my Lord and Mary Mother, let the women come, Becca prayed. *Let them be here before me to take away their dead. Sweet Lord, only grant that I don't have to bear witness to this, and on my soul I swear—*

She never got to finish her prayer. They rounded the corner of the house and found Katy and Ray kneeling over the littlest ones. The children had been laid out in a single row, stripped of their clothes now piled in a laundry basket nearby. The women looked up when they heard the four approaching. Ray's face was a solid streak of tears, her hair a disheveled fringe around her face. In her lap she cradled the broken body of a little girl not three years old. The child's dark curls were darker where the blood had thickened. Ray was trying to wrap the small, cold limbs in a measure of coarse gray cloth, but her hands would not answer her brain, nor let her do anything but hold the child against her bosom, rocking back and forth, whispering rhymes.

Katy's eyes were dry. That scared Becca worse than seeing Ray's more manifest grief. The stead teacher smiled a brittle smile and, in her classroom voice, said, "Becca, it's so very good to see you. Have you come to help? That's good; that's very good. You know I simply can't trust Del with any assignment. She's being no help to us at all, and we really must have all this seen to before noon meal. I don't have any notion of what to cook, though by rights it should be Selena's turn. You can't rely on Selena either. The men are even less help. So much wood to haul, so much wood, that's all they talk about. They insist we bring the children to them this morning, all in order, and there's only the two of us to see to them."

She waved her hand casually over the row of bodies. Her own youngest son lay among them. He was one who still had a face to recognize. She fished a bloodstained nightshirt out of the basket and flapped it smooth. "I'm as good a bleacher as any woman, but without more hands to lay to this…I just don't know. So much to do before noon meal," said Katy, shaking her head.

The older wives were seated in the seeing-room when Thalie brought Becca in. They occupied a row of stiff-backed chairs and wore their best dresses. Not a hair was out of place on their heads, not a face but as carefully scrubbed and composed as a bride's.

"Michal."

The eldest of Paul's wives gave no sign that she had heard Thalie call her name. She looked straight ahead, into a future that was measurable in hours.

"Michal, have you done with him?"

Still not shifting her eyes, Michal answered, "We've seen to him. We used his office for all. It was out of the way, as we were told to keep it. None who see him can charge us with shame, or shirking our last service to our husband."

Thalie tittered and swung her torch so that it swept within inches of Michal's stoic face. The old wife never blinked, never moved. Thalie brought the flame near a second time, slowly, until a careless twitch of her hand might lay fire to Michal's dark gown. Nothing.

"Face like a plow blade." Thalie laid her lips beside Michal's ear to whisper harshly, "Nothing marks it but the rock that breaks it, is that your way?"

Michal didn't look at Thalie. The younger woman was a breeze, a littlesinger's buzzing flight, a wisp of waking dream. To Becca and to Heaven alone, Michal said, "They have named her name in truth, a prophecy."

The blood went out of Thalie's face. She stiffened and

stepped away from the line of older women. Puzzlement sat on Becca's brow to see so strong a reaction to so slight a saying.

"Athaliah. Athaliah who slaughtered all the royal seed of David's house, and did herself die violently at the very horns of the holy altar."

Becca jerked her head at the female voice so suddenly at her side. Gram Phila cocked her head and winked like a mischief-bound child. "Well, that *is* her name, ain't it?" To Thalie she said, "You pay Michal no mind, dearie. Women, when they set their minds on higher things, there's no getting civil talk out of 'em. Don't make such a much out of your own name, Thalie, else your new husband might see it as you holding yourself better than you are. He's one for preferring proper women, is Adonijah of Make—of Wiserways."

The crone looked narrowly at the row of women younger than herself, older than full usefulness. "What will you have of me, Michal, Ophir, Delice, all? Anything I can do for you to ease the wait, or after?"

"God be with you, Phila, we shall soon have all we need."

Gram Phila shrugged. "God be with you also. If you change your mind, you can call my girl to fetch me." She turned from them to Thalie. "Got what you asked for all ready, and my girl's waiting on you out the back door. And see you put out that torch of yours before you go after it! I haven't lived this long to die in a burning house."

A fierce eagerness colored Thalie's words. "How soon will it take effect?"

Another shrug of age-twisted shoulders. "Three hours, four. You'll have your warning before it happens."

"Mind this one, then." She gave Becca a little shove in Gram Phila's direction as she rushed off. She only paused long enough to douse her torch in a bucket of water at the hearthside.

"What was all that?" Becca asked. The stead crone chuckled.

"Womanlore," she said, and gave the two men a meaningful look. The old woman's leer set them to fidgeting as if their skins had come a-crawl. They edged out of hearing range, leaving Gram Phila and Becca relative privacy.

"It's because she's still fruitful, isn't it?" Becca said before Gram Phila could speak. "Some potion you've made her to kill Pa's child in her womb."

"Hush now, such talk's wicked and wrong." The crone tried counterfeiting Hattie's starchy righteousness, but her withered lips betrayed her by a feline smile. "Thalie hasn't been feeling so well, Becca, and she's asked for that from me as will settle her stomach. Of course, there are some women as can't abide strong medicine, and if things should fall out ill for the babe, well…" She spread her hands. "Being Paul's get, what does it matter when the poor soul dies?"

"What does it matter…" Becca gazed at Michal and the rest, remembered Ray and the small sleeper she cradled close. Slowly, she gave her full attention to Gram Phila, and her words were thick with bitter resentment. "But you're still here, old woman."

"Not dead yet, not I," Gram Phila replied as blithely as if there had been no barb in Becca's saying. "Not for lack of trying, but my Martha's found a spirit I never dreamed she owned. Two of 'em tried to do for me last night. They're still up attic, the old fools, but not like to get much good of the lodgings for long." In a more subdued voice, the stead crone said, "I know the hurting of your heart, child. The first time pains the most, always. How many winnowings have I seen, do you think? Not just when alphs change, but when a harvest goes wrong or a great sickness comes to call. It's nigh the same story, then. I've been fighting for my life this night as well as I could do, same as all those poor babes lying cold today. You can't take my allotted time from me and give breath back to them."

"I wouldn't if I could," Becca said almost too low for hearing.

The old woman had a keen ear when it suited. "I know you wouldn't. Let's set your hurts aside. I'm famished for news, Becca. I've not dared come downstairs until this hour. Tell me: How many have gone from Bethlehem? How many mouths have closed to air and opened to angels' song so that the baby Jesus might live in plenty?"

"How many?" The words danced beauty all around their ugly core. Becca had been as well lessoned in Scripture as any willing girl of Wiserways. Gram Phila's meaning came to her by hints and degrees. She could have given back a similarly gauded-up answer to the old woman, but a thin cord of baby hair stiffened with blood tightened around her throat.

"No," she said, speaking plain. "I don't know how many infants Adonijah's murdered."

She regretted her boldness the moment it slipped from her lips. *Gram Phila lives today because she's learned survival to the bone. If she's too feared to call slaughter by its rightful name, there must be good cause. Plain speech might get me killed, dear Lord. And if they do kill me for this, what of Shifra?*

Esther M. Friesner

She thought of the baby in her hiding place, and the death-fear in her stomach doubled its chill.

But Wiserways had had enough of death. The killing time was done. Any child past toddlerhood who had escaped the Lord King's sword thus far was safe. Becca caught sight of a half-grown boy huddled between the widespread skirts of two elder wives, Delice and Metria. The steadman with Becca saw him too, and Adonijah's man; but neither one went up to drag the lad outside and deal with him. He was of an age when his death wasn't needful to the new alph. If boys and girls of his age did die, it was only in the first frenzy of stead changes, the explosion of old frustrations into wildest license. Sure as bone, Becca knew that all the changes in her life were limned with blood.

But we are a godly people. Hattie's teachings were an ironic echo in her daughter's mind. *Nothing we do but is as Scripture teaches. We cannot hope to know God's purpose in all things; that is arrogance. We obey, and are therefore blessed. What is man, that he would dare defy the Word of God?*

The surviving boy cowered and shook like a palsied old man. Becca tasted bile to see how terror had driven sanity from his eyes, leaving the beast behind. The child lived, but if he did not recover the full use of mind and body, that would be a temporary thing. Scripture would be found to justify the judgment that cleared unproductive mouths from a stead. The proper Scripture line was always found when needed, and twisted until it fit.

The Word of God. The thought no longer wrapped itself around Becca's shoulders like a warm, golden shawl, giving comfort and security. Now it brought a resonance of silent children whose only crime was being young enough to keep their mothers from serving their new master in all ways. If other children died too, that was just the way of things: The Lord's way, accepted without question by the godly.

We obey.

I am not a godly woman, then. Realization was not so fearful. Becca felt as if someone had brought her a great light in the shadows, but that was all. All of her mother's Scripture talk, all the hewing to lore and stead tradition like a dutiful daughter of Wiserways, all these fell away from Becca's soul like husks from an ear of barley. She stood alone with only the knowledge of her capabilities to back her, and she was not afraid.

Thalie was back. She nudged Becca roughly with her elbow. "He's waiting."

Becca slapped the woman's face hard. "He'll wait. I'm not a cow for you to prod along, Thalie. I'll go where I'm bidden, so you keep your hands off me."

"Proud talk, you little—" Thalie's own hand flashed for Becca's face.

Becca's fingers snapped shut on Thalie's wrist, holding the hand motionless a hair from her cheek. "Don't." Becca said it softly, with all the world of promised pain that such soft words could hold.

Speechless, Thalie indicated the doorway leading to the stairs. Becca strode from the seeing-room with her head high and a queenly dignity in her every step. Behind her, she heard Gram Phila's husky laugh.

Upstairs she went, with Thalie coming after as if she were Becca's handmaiden, the two men her hired guard. Unerringly, Becca found her pa's old door and turned the knob before any of the other three could prevent her.

Little Rusha sat sobbing in the great, rumpled bed, her small breasts bare, her jawline striped with bruises.

Adonijah lounged in a plump chair by the window, a glass of water in his hand. One of Paul's old nightrobes covered him. He had the air of a man born and raised to lord it from that very room. Everything there, including the girl in the bed, was his birthright.

"Becca!" Bland hospitality coming from his mouth jarred her nerves. "We missed you last night. You've always been so shy, so modest. My sire taught me that's a fine quality in a woman. He never mentioned how damned inconvenient it could be."

"*Becca!*" Little Rusha held out her arms as her sib's name ripped a sob from her heart. Becca didn't bide for any permission. She flew to the bed and hugged Rusha tight. Sweat and sex and a stronger smell clung to the sheets. As miserable as the lowest sinner, Rusha gulped out her confession into Becca's bosom: "I came into my times last night."

"Now *that* was convenient," said Adonijah. "It's always fine if the new alph can light upon some sign of God's immediate favor when he first comes to rule. I had hopes of you sharing the moment with me, Becca, but that infernal modesty of yours—" He clicked his tongue. "Fortunately, the Lord saw fit to reward his worthy servant."

He drained the water glass and held it out toward the bed. "I'm thirsty."

Rusha scrambled out of Becca's arms to bring a blue clay pitcher and refill the glass. Adonijah's pleasure in seeing the woman-child's tame obedience seemed to swell his skin. Rusha didn't even try to cover her nakedness before the eyes of the two other men. The elder closed his eyes; the younger goggled shamelessly while Rusha served her master, then crept miserably back to the shelter of the sheets. In the interim, unwilling, Becca bore witness to that small stain that marked Rusha's lost maidenhead.

Adonijah sipped his water and tilted his head back as if to dream. Becca found herself staring at his bared throat with irrational desires growing strong and stronger in her belly. *Dear Lord, if You could only make me a man for the time it takes to snap that accursed neck!* She was relieved when he spoke, bringing her back to reality.

Relieved, until she actually heard his words.

"—the bones are seen to. The older wives can turn their hands to that, instead of sitting around the place like lumps of potter's clay. Time enough to see to them later, after I've cheered up my wives."

The old steadman spoke: "Takes a week, sometimes two, before they come back into their times. It's customary to wait until they've made proper mourning, Adonijah."

The young alph was out of his chair and on the steadman before a body could blink. His right fist jerked the elder man's head violently to one side, his left rammed up into the man's gut, folding him down to meet a barefoot kick in the jaw. The steadman crashed backward into the old case that held Paul's few books. It teetered, looked like to fall on top of him, but only a few volumes pitched out onto the floor. Blood rolled from the older man's nose and mouth. He'd spit a tooth or two when he got back his senses.

Though his victim was far from hearing, Adonijah said, "I'll take advice from my own folk, and then only when I want it. And by God, the next time I hear any of you Wiserways relics call me by my Christian name, it'll be your death. I'll teach you to know your master."

Becca glided around the bed, came to the sill where Adonijah had set down his water glass. Adonijah's man gave a wordless cry, tried to come forward to stop her, but she was fast and spry enough to elude him. He and his master both had vanished, so far as she was concerned. She grabbed the glass and moved deliberately to reach the fallen steadman. Thalie tried to put herself between him and Becca. She got a dry curse and a stiff-armed shove that threw her into the bed beside Rusha.

Becca's hair was half in and half out of its normal plaits and hindered her seeing. She poked it back behind her ears as she bent to wash away the blood on the steadman's face with her own hands. She heard Adonijah laughing, saying something to his man in a voice too low to be heard. She ignored him. She felt a man's hand on her shoulder; she shook it off impatiently. The sour contempt, the hate, the impotent thirst for guilty blood, all these she pushed down into the darkest corner of her soul. If she let them surface now, she knew she'd do something so foolheaded that she'd have to die for it. She wasn't about to die, not with Shifra waiting helpless for her to come again. An old ghost of a Becca dead long ago rose up to be her salvation: *I want to be a herbwife and a helper, just like Miss Lynn. I want to heal.*

The ghost whispered, and the living girl turned all the killing passions of her heart to the work beneath her hands. She cleansed the steadman's mouth and nose of blood as well as she was able. She laid cool, wet hands on his brow.

He stirred; awareness came back into his eyes. She smiled at him, welcoming him back into the waking world.

His first voluntary expression was sheer horror. "Get away from me, damn you! You want me dead? Don't touch me!" He spat in her face and pulled himself to his feet before the glob of saliva had rolled halfway down Becca's cheek.

Hands hooked under Becca's arms, hauling her from the floor. This time she did not resist. Adonijah chuckled in her ear. "Temptation's a wicked thing, now isn't it? And those of Eve are always the worst, too. Women are sly and mask their snares, but God sees all. He punished them for their sins, right enough; sins as brought the hungering times. Well, a man's got only two ways out of temptation: flee it or master it, and a godly man flees no evil, however great." He turned to smile at the steadman and his own crony in turn. "Brothers, witness how a true man masters temptation. Come forward and be first to greet my chosen bride."

Becca stared straight ahead as Adonijah's man kissed her deferentially on one cheek. Automatically, she turned the other and felt the cool, wrinkled lips of the steadman rasp across the still-wet trail of his earlier censure.

"Tonight," said the bridegroom. "Rejoice in it."

Chapter Seventeen

Cold the wind, cold the sin,
Both to wrap my baby in.
Evil counsel, evil days,
Follow the ungodly's ways.
Clean my soul, loud my song,
Lord King make thy servant strong.

    The slaps turned to a wild, ineffective pummeling, but sharp sting or dull drubbing, it was all one pain. Becca pulled her head down between her shoulders and crept into a corner of the seeing-room so that her mother's blows all landed on her back. She could hear Hattie's gasping dry sobs and the muted thumpings when the older woman managed to land a few hits. These, and Becca's heartbeat, and Becca's carefully husbanded breath were the only sounds now to fill the big room. The other folk, men and women alike, had been ordered out by a smiling Adonijah.

"Let her mother reason with her," he said, shutting the door. "Hattie will best bring her around."

Hattie's try at "bringing her around" had begun by reasoning with her girl, but that didn't last long. There were no more arguments now, nor calm, sensible speech, nor cajolings, nor blatant, incredible threats. Becca had said *No* once too often, and Hattie had smacked the word from her mouth. Other slaps followed easily then, and no more words. Mother and daughter fell back to wage battle armed with stubbornness, desperation, and pain.

She must be crazy, Becca thought. Her hands were white as lily flowers against the blazing red of her throbbing cheeks. *Yes, she's run mad, mindless.* Over and over, Becca's brain repeated the assurance that insanity alone bore blame for what now passed between her and Hattie. She feared that if she lost belief in her mama's madness she would rise up and kill the woman.

"Where is she? Where's Shifra?" Hattie's voice raked over Becca's bent back like the thousand tiny teeth of a blacksmith's file. "Lord King smite you for an evil child, where's the baby?"

Lord King… The worm laughed, but Becca knew it for a thing less terrifying than true insanity. Satan's worm, Becca's self, all it wanted was answers. That wasn't madness; she knew it with all the certainty of a heart she'd once given to her faith. To obey without hesitation, to do a thing that ripped you open from heart to womb, to lift up your eyes blindly after wickedness and be its smiling handmaid just because it was the way things had always been done—no reason given more than that, no reason more asked—that was lunacy.

"Why do you want to know?" Becca mumbled, the words dribbling down into her chest. Her own voice sounded alien to her. Silent resistance had been her way ever since Adonijah's folk had taken off the older wives to the winnowing, leaving Hattie to deal with her.

"Why?" Hattie sounded astonished, as if she'd forgotten that her girl still had the power of speech. "Why? Because I've a right to know! I'm her mother as well as yours. I want my child."

"You want her body." The words came louder, easier. *If I'm evil, let me be full sunk in it. If it's wrong to defy those that sired and bore you, I'm already damned.* "You want to trade her skin for yours before Adonijah's feet." She lifted up her burning face and shouted, "You want her dead so he'll let you live! I saw your eyes when they took the others away, I smelled your terror. Well, I'm not afraid. I want her alive, even if I die for it! Who's that babe's true mother now?"

"Not afraid, no," Hattie echoed. "And why should you be, young and tender as you are? He'll keep you." No need to lay a name to that *he*. Adonijah had gone from the seeing-room, yet his presence overlay all Wiserways Stead like a winter fog. "You've a pocketful of coins to barter for your life. What do I have?"

Becca heard her mama's voice break. Though the worm inside chittered scorn at her weakness, she couldn't hold down a pang of compassion for the older woman. Gently, she said, "You're young yet, Mama. You've proved your fruitfulness. Any wise alph'd be glad—"

"—to keep a nursing woman?" Hattie shrilled. "To bide feeding her until she comes into her times again, maybe years later, when the babe's weaned?"

Becca knelt like a supplicant, begging a measure of sense from her mama's fear-crazed mind. "The babe doesn't have to die. If you leave off nursing, won't your milk stop too? Your times will come on you that much faster. Miss Lynn taught me, as she'd seen—"

"The Lord King's curse on Lynn and all her wicked teachings! Taking your head and filling it with vanity, making your eyes full of the gadding life she leads. The sword smite her barren! You'd never be this undutiful a child if not for her devilish preachings."

Becca set her lips together, reining in hot words in Miss Lynn's defense. If Ma wanted to blame someone else for what Becca had become, let her. Shifra's life was more important than any point won in petty argument.

"A woman comes into her times soon after her milk stops. That's how it is, Mama, and you know it. Shifra needn't die. No more did the rest."

"Evil." Hattie clapped her hands to her ears. "Evil words, devil's words to go against all Scripture-learning. I won't hear you! Lord King shield me from it."

"Lord King shield you from your own blindness, then!" Becca shouted. "From your own stupidity!"

Hattie sucked air between her teeth and her hands shriveled to fists. Her own face went scarlet. Becca saw her step forward, ready to hit her again.

"Enough." Becca stood up, her own hands rising to meet and break any new assault. She had taken enough. She was almost as tall as Hattie when she straightened, and Gram Phila's girl had taught her how to fight. Any love she'd held for her mama, any fondness that survived the woman's blind, stubborn hewing to Lord King's will and Scripture above simple good, had been shaken free from its last tenuous hold by the doings of the past half hour.

She didn't face Hattie as an equal. There could be no equality between beings from different worlds.

"If you hit me again," she said in the same soft voice she'd used with Thalie, "if you even try, I'll break you so that Adonijah wouldn't have you in his bed with the corpses of a thousand Shifras for your dowry."

Hattie's eyes were shallow saucers of horror. Slowly, her hands lowered; she stepped a pace back from Becca. A single word formed on her lips, uttered hushed enough to be nigh soundless: "Demon."

"Maybe. Maybe that's no bad thing for me to be, if my choice is that or to become another like you."

Hattie was backing away in earnest. Her finger shook as she leveled it at her child's heart. "You'll pay. As the Lord King loves me, you'll suffer for this. You think Adonijah will play your games? In your times, you've that to save you, but not for long. A day or two more and you'll be done; you can't hide the blood, and that'll be your death-sign, Lord King mark my words!" She shook her head as if despairing over her daughter's foolheaded doings. "He'd have wed you before witnesses, made you his first taken wife. Your place at Wiserways would have been supreme. You haven't the wit to see it. All he asked was to have the old business done with. Keeping shut-mouthed, you stand between him and what he desires— and for what? For an infant who'll die anyway! Wherever you've hidden her, it wants a living person to bring her back, feed her, tend her wants, and you'll be dead. He'll take you the way he took Rusha, and use you, and when your times are done he'll be rid of you!"

Becca felt her mouth going smaller and smaller, tightening around the coal of hate that had worked its searing way up her throat. "I don't kill so easy, Hattie."

Her mama's smile wasn't pleasant to see. "You'll kill easy enough. It's your dying that will be hard. I think I can go to my own death with a better heart, knowing what the one who murdered me will suffer. It'll be Adonijah for you while you're yet in your times, but afterwards…all the others."

She turned sharply from Becca and slammed the seeing-room door behind her.

Becca stood alone in the big room, steady on her feet. Inside, her veins jellied. There had been too much truth mixed with her mama's bile to leave her hope. A woman out of her times couldn't take a man and live—not live long, any road. To be torn open, like she was a sacrifice to woman's pride, a judgment on her for her wickedness—

—*split…and a long time dying.*

Daylight was fading fast from the windows. She walked to the eastern-facing side of the room and put her nose to the pane. Through the flecked and watery glass, she saw many trails of smoke mounting the sky. The winnowing must be done, Paul's old wives sent on their way. She crossed the room and gazed westward. Katy and Ray were walking down the path to the girls' dormitory, each bearing a basket of fresh, white sheets. Men were wrestling trestles and planks through the yard, heading for the cook-houses, readying the tables for supper. She recognized her sib Tom among them.

Tom: So big, so strong, and yet he'd done nothing to

stand between Adonijah and the past night and day of killing. Why hadn't he? The answer was so plain that it sent the worm on a roar of laughter.

Because that's the law, and the lore, and the Scripture-teaching, that a man newly come to power sweeps all the old one's life aside, and his life-leavings, and makes what's left behind his own. Let no one interfere! Let the chain of bones be unbroken. Worse will come, if once we shatter the old ways. Worse how? Only the wicked ask such questions, and they know nothing of the hungering times.

I know nothing of the hungering times, Becca thought. *Yet I fear them. They're a terror in my heart, my blackest dream's icy soul. But for all that, what do I truly know of the hungering times that isn't womanlore, or frighty tale, or fancy?*

She paced the width of the long room again. The eastern sky had faded to gray, the smoke trails smeared out of all distinct seeing. Becca strained eyes and mind to the east. When she was small, she recalled how she and her sibs used to stand tip-toe and swear that they could see the silver and blue towers of the city. After Eleazar left, Becca always claimed that she could see her brother himself, atop one of those impossibly high turrets of brightness, waving to her.

A wave of the hand can be plain greeting; likewise a beckoning, an invitation, a summons.

In the cities is knowledge, not lore, the worm said, all demure. *In the cities, they know.*

A fringe of crenelated battlements unrolled itself against the far side of the windowglass, a phantom seeing conjuring out of Becca's yearning mind. She no longer fancied she saw her brother's face—she was too old now for her fantasies to veer so wide of possibility—yet over the hope-kindled mirage of shining towers lay a transparent vision of her sire's face, and in her ears was the fading echo of the wistful, humble, all-reverent way he spoke of the distant city, the earthly Paradise.

Pain real as any slap shuddered Becca's heart. Her sire's face faded from the window with the daylight, and the ghostly city with it. She turned from the gathering dusk outside to the dim doorway midway down the seeing-room. Not open, like the passage to the upper floors, not barred and guarded like the door leading from this room out of the house itself. Anyone who cared to turn the knob could open it and enter. Eventually—tomorrow, perhaps—someone would have to. Until then, no one would. There was nothing good to see beyond that door.

Nothing good for most, but Becca was different. She left the windows, left all new remembrance of her mama—no, not her mama, not now; Hattie—and herself, and even Shifra's haunting presence. Another phantom beckoned her. She opened the door willingly and went into the room that held the dead.

He lay on the makeshift bier of planks set across his desk top. His body was sheeted over, a cold presence, imposing even before Becca could kindle the lamp. When the wick flared, it cast sharp shadows over his sunken cheeks and eyes. No one had bound up his jaw or even bothered to lay a drape of cloth over his face. His mouth hung open, ghastly, as if he gaped in sleep for a breath that would not come.

Becca stood beside her sire's corpse and laid a hand over his stilled heart. "Oh, Pa, why?" Her words were little slivers of pain. Her hands were so chill that she noted no difference between her flesh and his. "Why couldn't you be strong enough just that one time more? What happened? Why didn't you falter like that when it was Jamie's life in your hands? Why'd Adonijah slip through your fingers? You whipped him right at Harvest Home! What stopped you from killing him?" Tears leaked from her eyes, though the hot steel inside her commanded them to hold back. Her nose began to run with thin, salty mucus that she rubbed roughly away on the back of her hand.

A sob burst from her chest, followed by another and another. Nothing could hold them in. No matter that the worm protested loudly in her skull, rightly claiming that her father had walked the same ashen path to power that Adonijah now began. No matter if Becca knew he had been the one to winnow the old and the young, been the one whose word had added however many small, staring skulls to the tally within Prayerful Hill, given her Jamie back to patient death. All she could recall of him now were the sweet times, and the pride in his children that had made his voice go tender, and the love.

Through the hurting, her mind was still set and determined. *In the cities*… Suddenly, it all seemed so easy. Here under her hand, in this very desk, was a secret Pa had shown to her alone. In the lower drawer, under the false bottom, lay the brown metal box and its treasure. The gun and the bullets, a great power for protection, just like she'd read in the old stories; but that wasn't all. There was also paper in there, paper that must be as important as the gun itself for Pa to have kept them both locked away all these years. The gun was meant to bring Eleazar safe to the city if the coopfolk couldn't come back and claim him on their own, so could be the paper had to do with the same task. She'd see. What might have brought her brother to the city years ago would serve as well to bring her there now.

She would take the box, find a way out of the house unseen or die, fetch Shifra from hiding and flee with the babe. Together, they would go to the city. Once there, they'd find Eleazar. He wouldn't fail them. He'd stand up for them against Adonijah and never fear; coopfolk were stronger, smarter, more feared than stead or grange. Everything would be well once they joined Eleazar. That was Becca's plan.

How? whispered the worm. *How long, how far, how will you take a baby on a road you don't even know?*

Becca hushed it, her eyes now dry and shining with the same bright hope she'd once brought to Scripture tales of Ruth and Jael, Esther and Miriam. She chose not to hearken to the worm's nagging questions; the dream was all. If she lost hold of it now, of its bright splinter of hope, she knew she would slip into an abyss from which she would never escape again. Belief was too much a part of her blood and bone to cast aside entirely. She had to believe in something.

She would take what she needed from the secret place and go, but there wanted one thing done before that. She knelt beside the bier and clasped her hands, trying to pray. "Sweet Lord and Mary Mother, rest him now. Forgive him what he's done. Don't lay Susanna's death on him too hard, or the others. He didn't know any better than doing things the way they've always been done. He was a good man when he wasn't wearing the Lord King's yoke. If You're more than us, forgive him."

Words, scoffed the worm, but Becca's heart sent more than sound behind them.

She ended her prayer, and from where she knelt reached out to pull open the desk drawer.

"Oh, that's a pretty picture."

Adonijah stepped sideways into the room and closed the door fast. He pinched the cuff of his left sleeve with the thumb and forefinger of his right hand. The lamplight glittered on the joint-length, straight pin he pulled free, except where the tip of it was dulled by something darker than waxed metal. He held it up to bisect the iris of his eye.

"Your mama's been and gone. Time you talked, Becca. As you will, for me."

Chapter Eighteen

Jacob served Laban seven years for Rachel, whom he loved. But Laban tricked him and caused him to marry Leah, whom he loved not. Then Jacob served seven more years for Rachel, and he valued her above her sister because she was fair. So it was that Rachel came to despise her sister Leah, and said to her, "See! Willingly, Jacob has served seven years and seven more for me. Yea, even seven years and seven and seven more he would serve for my sake."

Leah chided her sister, saying, "It is not right to speak so of our lord." But Rachel would not hold her tongue, and so it happened that her words reached Jacob's ears. Then Jacob was full of sorrow.

Jacob took counsel of the Lord, saying, "My heart is toward Rachel, but she is unwomanly of speech. Because I find her fair, and value her above her sister Leah, who is plain, she has grown proud and does not fear me. Tell me how I may teach her a woman's proper way, and cure her of pride."

"Fear not," the Lord replied to Jacob. "Pride is not the virtuous woman's portion, but her fall. I will amend her."

Then Leah bore Jacob ten sons, but the Lord shut up the doors of Rachel's womb so that she was barren. Moreover, the Lord punished her thusly, in that, as much as Jacob's heart was toward Rachel, he would not know her until the time of her punishment had ended.

And Rachel saw that she was barren, and that her husband might not know her, and that her pride had led her into deep sin and sorrow. So Rachel was humbled and called out unto the Lord in her grief. And the Lord heard her voice, and opened the doors of her womb that her husband might know her. Rachel bore Jacob two sons, but lest she fall again into pride, the Lord in his mercy took Rachel at the birth of her second son. She is buried by Bethlehem, which is the house of unfailing bread.

Becca lowered her hands to her lap. When Adonijah's cursed eyes fixed themselves on her that way, she felt as if he had the power to peel away the layers of her skull and read thoughts from the surface of her living brain. The schoolroom books that spoke of guns were full of tales of men who knew how to use them. It was manlore, so it seemed, the mastery of guns—nature's own part of a man, alien and wrongful for a woman. It was power, too. That much was what she remembered.

He's not to have the gun, he mustn't find it. Her thoughts were desperate, interspliced with flashes of Adonijah guessing her purpose through a devil's insight, discovering the false bottomed drawer, claiming what it hid. *The city* man left it for Pa. Adonijah's not to have that too, after all else he's stolen. I won't let him. Becca's heart made a silent promise to the dead man stretched across the desk. It's to be our secret, Pa; ours. I'll pay what it takes to keep it.

"Where's Hattie, Adonijah?" She spoke to distract him from maybe wondering what she sought in that desk drawer. As well, she spoke to divert her own instant, unreasoning fear of the man. "Gone with the others you've murdered?"

"Hattie?" He mocked her. "Is that how Wiserways girls are taught to mouth respect for their mothers?" The straight pin between his fingers shook slightly when he laughed. "Call him by his Christian name too?" He jabbed the gummy pinpoint at the corpse and laughed again. "No, Becca. Your mama's still got years left in her: good working, breeding years. We'll have the stead crone see what she's got in her sack to scare the milk from Hattie's breasts and leave her ready for me. That granny-woman's brewing worked slick enough to empty Thalie's belly, but if her best's no use, I'll send for Lynn. She's got her ways, too."

Becca spoke low. "It's sin to trifle with a fruitful woman or a nursing mother."

Adonijah's flinty eyes twinkled. "Worse than sin, it's contrary to all law. But if Hattie's a nursing mother, where's her babe, eh? Care to tell me that, Bec'?"

Becca only stared at her folded hands.

"As for Thalie's belly," Adonijah went on, "why, that poor old granny-woman told me that the brew she gave her wasn't meant to do what it did. Accidents happen. It's a hard world. But if we hew to the Lord's word, we'll thrive."

"Where does lying fall, Adonijah? Is it sin, or broken law, or stepping outside the bounds of what's lore-taught? You lied to Hattie. You let her think you'd kill her if she didn't make me speak."

Adonijah hunkered down beside her. "I'll tell her different when we've done."

"You mean she doesn't know?" Becca couldn't keep the pain from lancing her breast at the thought of Hattie's unsalved agony of mind. *She loves her own life dearer than Shifra's, sweeter than that of the babe she bore, and still I can't help but pity...Oh, sweet Mary Mother, why'd you ever let something as careless-cruel as Adonijah come to birth?* "You can go tell her now, Adonijah. You won't get more from me than she did. You won't touch the child."

Now the pin danced before Becca's eyes like a coiled snake's head. The boldness withered up in her throat. She could see a few dry grains of white standing out from the smoke color of whatever it was stuck 'round the point.

"Oh, she'll know, she'll know," Adonijah drawled. "I'll tell Hattie by and by." He rolled the pin lazily between the balls of his fingers. "Don't reproach me for taking my time over it; there's time enough for all. I had to test her, didn't I? A fine woman, your mama, worthy of her bread. But my sire told me how she was always Paul's favorite wife. Could I take that to my bed, maybe turning my back on a death I never deserved, unless I knew she'd serve me wholeheart?" His free hand darted out to immobilize one of hers. "But now I know," the pin jabbed down too suddenly for her to jerk away, pierced her skin in the midst of his deceptively gentle speech, "that she's left nothing of herself in Paul's grave."

Becca hardly heard the last of what he said. Her small, offended scream smothered over his words. She fell back against the desk, clutching her wounded hand. Adonijah made a tender O of his coarse lips.

"Why, Lord King have mercy, did I hurt you, Becca?" He didn't bother hiding the falseness of his concern. He flicked the pin away into the darkness behind him. "Only a pinprick, though; nothing much. Here, give me your hurt and I'll kiss it well." He reached for her hand again.

She drew back. She tried to. There was a strange coldness radiating from the tiny spot on the back of her right hand where the pin had gone in. Her arms were slow to answer what she ordered them to do. When she tried to reach for the corner of the desk, to pull herself farther away from him, there was a small eternity lying between the frantic commands of her brain and the sluggishness crawling through her limbs.

Adonijah had no trouble at all taking her into his arms, cradling her with a false tenderness that left her stomach sour and burning. "Not so shy any more? No longer frighted of me, are you? If you were, you'd scramble away, but here you stay in the circle of my arms. I told your mama that I'd have a better way with you than she would. She didn't seem ready to credit that, but I told her I'd work a charm."

Becca's lips were turning to wood. She slurred when she spoke, asking him, "What'd you do t'me? Wha— charm?"

"Magic, sweet Becca." His hand caressed her hair, slid quickly down to undo the fastenings of her blouse in nimble order. "Not man's nor woman's to know, but only those the coopfolk favor. A charm past all value, a powdery white miracle in a coarseweave sack that came to Makepeace Stead when Harvest Home was done.

Stood me good luck, it did; not only now, for taming a wild girl to consent."

He cupped her breast, a touch she sensed only faintly across the dark chasm of numbness tearing open between her mind and body. A brief frown creased his brow—she realized that he *knew* how little she could feel—and his hand tightened around her breast until she gasped, unable to escape the knowledge.

He dragged her a little way from the desk and stretched her out on the bare wooden floor. Her arms and legs were miles away, her hands and feet as if they'd never been part of her. Only the keenest of sensations reached her. She could not tell the moment when he stripped her of her skirts, but she knew when he shoved her limp legs apart so hard that one knee slammed against the boards.

Sight and smell and hearing were all she had. They were enough to deny her the refuge of believing that this was all a nightmare. Her mouth was very dry. When he pressed his full weight on top of her and forced his tongue between her lips, she tasted a hot flood of bitter chicory and apples and bread.

She tried to strike him, to call up all the lessons she and Gram Phila's Martha had tussled through so many times. *Even when your enemy's bigger and has you down, there are ways.* There were, and she remembered every one she'd been taught, and knew she'd mastered them. Where were they now? Her arm came up in a lazy, graceful arc and Adonijah grinned as he plucked it from the air, his grip crushing her wrist hard enough for her to feel it.

"Are you a fighter too, Becca? Take after Paul?" He cupped her face roughly, coming up sharp under her jaw so that her teeth clacked together. By degrees he drove his fingernails into her cheek, watching with avid interest for the moment when she registered pain. "A little of that cooplore miracle of mine did to slow him down to where I could handle him, and it took still less to bridle you." He pressed his nails in deeper until she groaned. "'Watch out how you handle that stuff, Zach!' That's what I heard the coopfolk tell my sire. 'Spread it on your fields this spring and you'll have a richer harvest next fall. Keep track and tell us how much heavier the crops come in, so we can report back home. But have a care! The field's the only place it belongs. Get the littlest bit of it in your lungs or under your skin and you'll be nigh paralyzed, Lord King knows how long.' *Paralyzed*," he repeated, leering down at her. "Had to ask Lynn what that word meant." He pinched her nipple until she gave a ragged little cry. "But the coopfolk were wrong, Becca. Their miracle's let me reap my harvest now."

His hand between her legs was a clumsy, perfunctory presence. Suddenly, he seemed in a hurry, like a spoiled child given a plaything long coveted. She felt him enter her and there was no pain.

See, Mama, you were wrong. It doesn't have to hurt. A strange, mind-mad sliver of a smile curved her lips. She would take the horror that pinned her helpless, that thudded against her body and thrust blindly into her core, take it and turn it into cause for laughter. She would share the joke with Mama—not Hattie, but the mother Becca had once loved. Hattie lived, the other was dead, and so she sought her mama's ghost among the rafters, fleeing the belabored body on the floor, hovering safe above it to trade woman's secrets with a phantom.

Now, Mama, why'd you have to go scare us all about how hurtful it's got to be, first time? I don't feel a thing.

And her mama's spirit gave her a warm smile. *Why, child, then he must love you very much.*

That was even funnier than what Becca had said. She wished she had someone else to share the joke with her. She wondered if Jamie would find it so mirthful. She had to bite her lip to blood to keep from laughing aloud.

She made her eyes trace the paths through Adonijah's foxy hair, tried to weave together the pattern of his whole past day out of the scents now pouring from his body: *Woodsmoke…that means he was near the cookhouse, else the grove. But do they take the winnowed women the same route as the babies? The cauldron didn't look that big…Food, many kinds…He must've checked out the winter stores…* The litany of speculation unscrolled to keep Becca's self far and farther from the reality assaulting her. Her true self had no flesh or bones to be oppressed. Her true self lay as far beyond Adonijah's power to master as the moon.

He shuddered over her and gasped. A new smell insulted her senses. When he rolled off her, she continued to stare at the ceiling. She would try to build a labyrinth out of the woodgrain patterns on the big beams and escape to its center. He would never find her there.

Adonijah loomed across her sight, breaking down all the walls of her creation. She closed her eyes against him, but he yanked her to her feet and gave her one hard shake that made her look at him. Her knees were water.

"Not so bad as you feared, was it? Now, next time I'll want no more of your fussing. That's for virgins. You're sweet, but I've had sweeter. If there's anything you've been taught to make yourself more welcoming to a man, I'll want you to show it to me soon."

He let go of her arms. Dizzy, she thought how odd it was that her feet still held her upright. She tried to walk and staggered so badly that he had to grab hold of her before she fell.

"Whoa, take it easy! You'll be back to yourself in an hour's time, maybe less. I didn't use all that much on you. See, your full color's coming back already." She followed his glance down the front of her body. All he had left her was the rumple of her open blouse, her sagged knit stockings, and her shoes. She began to giggle, a jerky, brittle sound with no true human mirth behind it.

Adonijah stared at her and shook his head. "If that don't beat all."

She still laughed, laughed until she fell against him, clutching at his shirt. He set her standing straight again with as much care as if she were a wood-carved doll. Still she laughed, though the tears turned hot on her scratched and bruised cheeks and she realized she could feel them sliding down like littles balls of flame.

Her laughter wrought a change all its own, a magic greater than Adonijah's double-damned pin. Through lashes matted thick with tears, she saw his face melt from wonder to unease, from unease to edginess until he was gaping at her with true fear. Did he think she'd gone crazy? She knew the tales: Madness was sometimes a catching thing, like the weak lung. Here was a petty vengeance she could take, and she took it gladly, with both hands. She made herself laugh louder, until the gusts of sound bursting from her chest were like the roaring of a fire to end the world. She prayed from the deepest, darkest, blood-reddest marrow of her mangled heart that her insanity would become a blaze to devour them both. She laughed and prayed so hard that she thought she saw the fire itself, and Jamie's arms open for her on the other side of the flames.

E s t h e r   M.   F r i e s n e r

Nothing answered prayer but silence. Adonijah muttered something about sending for her later, and scuttled. She heard the door latch shut behind him and knew that her wild laughter wasn't loud enough, her madness fierce enough to overcome his blind, simple strengths. She threw her head back and let the tears trickle over her temples. Mucus tasted salty in her mouth, mixed with the metal tang of blood. More of the old wife-told tales came flooding into her mind. Pictures conjured by the chanted words trailed across the hot, red insides of her eyelids.

Now when the Lord saw how women had risen up in pride, naming themselves in His stead the decriers of life or death, He was greatly wroth.

Firelight dancing in the dormitory as Ray spun out the tale. Becca dreamed of all the proud women of long ago, arrayed in sparkling gowns to rival the rainbow. They paraded through the streets of cities a-glitter with golden spires and airy palaces. Even though she knew it was wrong to put a fair face to evil, Becca dreamed those women beautiful.

And even as it was with Rachel, because they would heed no counsel, He shut up the doors of their wombs so that which had been fruitful with each turning of the moon was now fruitful only by His grace at the turning of the year, and it was no longer for the women to say yea or nay. In their weakness they were humbled.

The shimmering gowns were gone, the beautiful faces crushed into tears and lamentations. Becca shuddered at the lesson of their fall, trembled at the words that always came after:

This was in the hungering times.

Specters rode the winds, toppled the airy towers,

breathed a creeping black rot over the golden spires. The way Ray told it—the way it was always told—was as if somehow the ravening ghost of those hollow ages were a monster brought to birth in the last moments of those unnatural women.

The men also did He punish mightily, for they had turned their eyes from His laws, so that they did not discriminate male from female, and abominations spread throughout the land. And it was the Lord's will to try them, that each might come again to his proper place, male and female. Therefore the Lord did seal up the womb of the land so that it did not bring forth, and He opened the gates of the seas so that they rose, and He loosened the chains of the lightnings—

Becca crumpled to her knees, clutching her middle as if she could wring Adonijah's seed from her body. The faces of the wicked, proud, sinful women who had brought the Lord's wrath down on all the generations to come circled her head like a glowing crown. She could feel a noose of tiny skulls pressing into her temples where the blood throbbed.

"O God," she moaned, clawing away the invisible band, working short, sharp nails mercilessly across her wrists, up the battered insides of her thighs. "O God!" The shriek was as poorly answered as the moan.

The echoes of it died. She harked to the stillness of the locked room, hugging herself to keep in the warm and to keep out the devils. Only sorrow wrapped her 'round.

"Shifra…" Whispered, the name was a warm breath that stole the sting from Becca's bitten lip. She blinked, awakening, tears now dry, crusting at the corners of her eyes. Bit by bit she came out of the chilled curl of despair. Like a babe standing upright, she braced herself on hands and knees then labored to her feet, leaning on the side of her pa's desk, leaning at last on his body.

Becca looked down at the corpse, cold and solemn, keeping no more manlore secrets. The bout with Adonijah played itself out in memory. She knew where to look, this time; knew she would find what she sought, knew there was no use in the knowledge but felt compelled to seek it anyhow. She lifted the sheet and touched the body.

There! Just below his left armpit, the tiny nub of metal. She pulled the straight pin from her sire's flesh and twirled it slowly in the dying lamplight, the way Adonijah had worshipped the second dosed pin before using it on her.

Manlore, womanlore, cooplore, stead—none of the boundaries mattered. None of the holy separations that had named and tamed Becca's life until this. Not now. Not to her. A man had lessoned her as to how easy it was to breach those boundaries. All it took was a pinch of cold white dust and the point of a pin.

In the shadows it took some scrabbling and patting over the floorboards, but she found the other pin too. Adonijah had thrown it aside as if it were a wisp of chaff. She smiled over this second trophy, rolling both pins together over the palm of her hand.

Sticky warmth crawled down her thighs, taking her unaware. Her touch came red. The red flowed brighter and freer than should be for a girl who'd just had her first knowledge of a man. She recalled the small stain Rusha's torn maidenhead had left on the bedsheets. A mark of blood, but a small mark; that was normal.

Not like this. She stared dumbly at her hand. *I'm still*

in my times; the blood-sign shouldn't touch me for days yet. It never came on me like this before. This isn't the way it's supposed to be for a natural woman.

For a natural woman. But for you… The whispering in her head she knew was her own voice.

It didn't take her long to wad together a generous portion of one of her skirts and tend to herself. The task was done quickly, an afterthought almost, and none of the deep-shamed daintiness about it that the wives had always preached. Less time than that for her to pull her clothes back on, to jam the two pins deep into her waistband. Then she was tearing out the secret drawer, flinging back the lid of the metal box, cramming the papers into her blouse, pouring the silvery gray bullets into her thirsty palm, hugging the gun to her breast. Her fingers pressed small webs of blood against the icy metal.

Chapter Nineteen

It's a lone road I'm walking,
Lord, see me home.
It's a hard road I'm walking,
All on my own.
It's a lone road I'm walking,
World without end.
Walk a hundred roads more
Just to find a friend.

When the men came to bring her to Adonijah's bed, Becca was ready. Her heart thudded against her breastbone like a fist. She made an effort to bridle her every movement.

I am Becca of Wiserways, she told herself. *I know a woman's proper place and all the ways to pleasure a man. I am going to serve my lawful master in thanks and humility, the way I've been brought up to do. I am. There is no taint of anything wild or unwomanly to me. I am Becca, Hattie's child, Paul's get, of Wiserways Stead.*

So she told herself, over and over, using words to form the bonds that must hold the crumbling shell of appearances together, words that must prevent her true self from bursting through too soon.

Through the mask of her face, she cast sly eyes from one to the other of her escorts. Did they suspect? Did it show? Could they guess what manner of creature they were bringing to the bed of their new master? Their faces were slack as empty gunnysacks, bored with a chore like fetching water or drawing firewood. One of them was an older male, Wiserways bred and maybe born, the other a youngling from Adonijah's invading pack. He caught a glimpse of her quick, studying glance and winked, mistaking it for what he wished to see in a woman's face.

Let him think what he likes. Becca let the corner of her lips tease him with a hinted smile. *Let him think anything at all. But if he tries to put some bone behind his wishings, I've got the power by me now to blast him clean to Hell.*

The gun was slung in a pocket she'd made by tucking up the front part of her underskirt and pinning it secure. A small, wolfish grin licked her mouth when she thought of which pins they were that had served her so neatly. Only two, but two were plenty strong enough to hold; strong with her sire's death, strong with her ravished maidenhead.

The weapon's swinging weight was a pendulum that sometimes bounced against one leg then the other as the men marched her up the stairs. Any bruises she got would be lost among the rest that Adonijah had already given her. They dappled her skin, angry marks darkening on breast and arm and hip. The place where she'd bitten her lip open was swelling, giving her mouth a ripe, pouting look. She thought of Del practicing such vixenish airs in a basin of water when she thought no one was watching, all to lure a man to her come Harvest Home.

I could lesson you some now, Del. I could show you how to come by the look that brings you a man. I learn fast—ask any who've lessoned me: Miss Lynn, Katy, Selena, Gram Phila's Martha. Yes, I learn fast, and I lesson faster, and there's that I'd teach you, Adonijah, that you won't soon forget.

After all the hard lessons of her life, learning the gun had come almost too easy. Aside from not knowing how much time she'd have alone in that room with the dead— the jump-stomach way she had to hunch over the piece, ready to thrust it beneath her skirts every time she dreamed she heard a sound at the locked door—it had been simple. The weight surprised her some, but the talebooks Katy loaned her made some mention of men managing such weapons two-handed as well as one. The trickiest part was making the bullets go in, and that all came right when her thumb found the little latch. The spinning chamber fell open like a welcome.

Bullets were round and the chamber holes were round and the pointier end had to point the way the bullet must go once launched—it would take an idiot to foul up something so obvious, so plain to any sighted person. She filled each hole just as slick as sticking seed-corn into the earth and clapped the chamber back so it stayed. The trigger, too, was an invitation, its shape just calling for a finger to crook 'round it and pull. In the stories they always *squeezed* the trigger when they shot, gentle. She'd remember that. It was going to be easy as pie.

Shifra... The weight of steel pulled at her skirt no heavier than her sister's name pulled at her heart. *Hold on, baby, I'm coming for you. You hold on, and Becca's going to bring you something better than that old raggy sop.* Her heartbeats measured out time; too much time. It had been too long since she'd tucked up the child the safest place she knew and prayed sweet Mary Mother to keep her safe from harm. Every pulse of Becca's blood stood alone, another slab to mark the paces time was taking, putting more and more distance between the babe and any chance of life.

Soon, Shifra. It's going to be soon. It must.

They stood before the bedroom door once more. The younger man knocked, grinned like a cat at Becca when Adonijah bellowed for them to bring her in. He was waiting for her by the window, wearing just his robe. The bed was new-made, the sheets crisp and white, all properly turned back over a quilt Becca recognized as the work of Thalie's hands.

She dropped her head as if it were a sickle-ready head of barley, heavy with seed. His chuckle of satisfaction rasped her skin, made her clench her legs tight together beneath her skirts when he strode by her to send his men about their other business. She folded her hands before her, pressing them down against the comforting shape of the gun.

"Come willingly, I see," he said, flicking the iron bolt into its hold high on the doorframe. "Changed your way of seeing it, then?"

She said nothing. With her eyes downcast, she could only hear the brush of his bare feet over the floorcloth, the creaking protest of old boards in a house he had conquered by deceit.

"Well?" His voice rose a little with irritation; the knowledge left her strangely warm. This was a game to play, a pleasure knowing she could still provoke him so, without saying a word. Then he was suddenly before her, her jaw vised between his fingers, old hurts blazing back from dull aches to searing life. "You'll answer me." She felt the hot pollution of his spittle on her chin. "Yes, you will, or it will be *this* again for you"—a splinter of gray metal hovered at the border of her sight—"and then I'll give you over to the rest of them."

Her gasp was not calculated nor her fear feigned. All that he had done to her in the little room below came back, torn from the cold safety of memory by that tiny pin. Her tongue was papery as she faltered, "No…please."

Then the shame of her own fear rose out of her belly in a spate of acid. What he had on hand to use against her was nothing, *nothing*! Her demurely folded hands darted back, jammed into the hidden pocket, clasped the smooth handle of the gun and jabbed it hard into Adonijah's belly.

She could have laughed out loud at how his face went all fishy white, bug-eyed with startlement. *Dear Lord, what's he think I've got under here?* Just so he'd know, just so he'd mind close when she gave him his long-coming lessoning, Becca said woman-soft and gentle, "I've a gun, Adonijah; that's what you feel. I haven't been wonder-touched to grow an Adam's mark, so clean your mind of miracle tales. This gun's miracle enough for me. You know what guns can do? You have that much learning at Makepeace Stead?"

"Where did you get—?" His voice was parched with terror. *He* knew about guns, that much was plain.

"Shut up." Again she jabbed it into him. He staggered

back and she jerked the weapon from concealment, let him feast whitening eyes on its sleekness and its silent message of power. "You listen."

"You can't shoot that, Becca." Oh, how the words shivered with sick laughter! He was trying to put a bold face between himself and his fright. "One shot would be loud enough to bring down the roof on you and me both, like Samson in the Philistines' temple. Those things bang so loud, it'd bring everyone on the stead running."

"I'll risk it. Will you? Your head would be split right open, Adonijah, your facebones smashed bloody right back through your brain." She told him that in the same way she'd always recited her lessons for Katy when she was dead sure of the answers. Her certainty left him no margin to doubt her, to save himself with hope. "They'd come running and they'd find you dead, crushed worse'n if any temple building fell in on you. Half your skull lifted off, and all your face torn away so raw they'd have to remember real hard what you ever looked like. You want that, Adonijah?" Coaxing sweet she spoke to him, raising the barrel so that she could aim her sight right down to the little niblet of metal perched on the end. "'Cause if that's what you want, I can give it to you any time."

Adonijah said nothing. His mouth opened once, but no words came out and he lost the will to close his lips again. He blinked and gulped, his hands making little flapping motions at his sides.

Trying to shoo me off, trying to blink himself awake from a nightmare. If Becca smiled any broader, her cheeks would split like overripe fruit. Her front teeth were dry from the deep gusts of air she sucked in through them, cold as the weapon in her hands.

Esther M. Friesner

Adonijah wasn't talking any more. He wasn't moving, or blinking, or taking breaths deep enough to move his ribs so she could see it. Stillness had settled over him like a soft blanket drifted down over a cradle, a witchery of her weaving.

"All right." Her own words were cotton-light. She didn't want to risk loud speech that might fray the spell. "Now, you'll just listen. Listen close and do as I say, and then I'm going to let you live." She saw doubt spark up in his eyes and it made her face ache with wanting to laugh. Instead, she just nodded. "I said that, Adonijah; you heard right. I'll swear it to you by the Lord's own Name, and by sweet Mary Mother, if you want; it's so. If you do what I tell you, it'll be so. I promise. I swear. I'm leaving Wiserways and I don't care who's alph here after I'm gone. I don't want another winnowing if it doesn't need to be. When I've got what I want off this place, you can have the rest."

His mouth wobbled, like he was struggling between wanting to ask her something and fearing what would befall him if asking wasn't allowed. Becca nodded curtly so he'd know she'd tolerate maybe one question.

"Where?" It sounded like a sifting down of sand in the watch-glass. "Where will you go?"

He could ask, but he couldn't force any more answers. Just knowing that was like a tonic to her heart, a strong heat in her that fast kindled to a clean white light. *He can't force me to anything any more!* It burned away all the pain he'd forced on her, lifted her spirit high as any littlesinger's soaring flight. Part of her joyed from soles to crown. Gratefulness brimmed up in her, all of it for the long-gone coop man who'd taken such a shine to Eleazar and left this gun with her pa. He'd given more than he knew, whoever he'd been. If there was any way to learn his name once she brought Shifra into the gates of the city, she'd offer him the Kiss and the Sign freeheart, in thankfulness of soul for this, her freedom.

But part of her still bled. Part was hurt deep, too deep to the bone for any fire of joy to ever fully burn it out. She forced the pain away, focusing all her being on the task ahead.

"The first place I want to go, Adonijah, you'll take me."

❧ ❧

Strange to feel the evening wind on this hillside and know it was for the last time. Strange to stand here listening when before all sounds from this place were a dread. She shifted her shoulders and leaned into the night, pricking her ears keen as could be. Cloth rasped and rustled too loud for her liking. The bundle on her back was poorly rolled—Adonijah's hands had trembled so!—but once she and Shifra were safe away she'd have leisure to make it right.

The moon was high already in a sky grown early dark. She wished it were nearer the full to aid her eyes. When last she'd come here, she'd been driven. Haste made her careless; she had to leave the babe and get back to the stead before anyone found her gone or marked the direction she'd come from. It wasn't a big hillside, but broad enough for her to forget precisely where she'd left the babe.

Adonijah knelt before her, facing upslope like she'd bid him. No sense in keeping him on his feet when he might be tempted to cut and run, figuring the poor moon would put off her aim. She wished there'd been a way to tie up his hands, but she couldn't figure the how of it, not without setting her precious gun aside. That she never would do. All the way out here, once they'd cleared the main stead buildings, she clutched close to him, the muzzle of the gun pressed into his back. Part of her made the excuse that she did it to make him suffer terror that much closer to the skin, but the deeper part of her knew the truth: She was just as feared of the gun's untried power as he was.

So much I don't know! And so much riding on my knowing it. She stared at the back of his head, imagining how simple it would be to lodge the muzzle of the gun right where the skull balanced atop the spine and give the trigger that book-learned squeeze.

And then? She didn't know—not how loud the shot would sound, nor how widespread the destruction it would wreak, nor whether she herself would survive the blast. There were tales of folk who mastered guns only to have the weapons turn against their masters, of that she was near gospel-sure. There were tales of other weapons too, some not named, that took out the ones that used them as well as the ones they were used against.

And if I do kill him, what's to come of Wiserways? She couldn't see the dormitories from the hillside, but she could imagine. The children who had survived the winnowing must have crept back home by this. They slept beside beds emptied of their less lucky sibs, listening to the lonesome thudding of their hearts until exhaustion dragged them down to slumber. Their minds still bled, but time would heal over the torn places, turn their lost sibs into angels warbling sweetly beneath the wings of Mary Mother's sky-blue cloak. The Lord King's will had been done, the dead taken because they were chosen special for this hard salvation. They would be the guardians of their surviving sibs, their deaths softened over, a field of blood become a garden of blessing. That had always been the way of things. Children who survived, healed; none survived who didn't find the way of turning sour pain into a lie candied over enough for reason to swallow it whole.

But if there came a second winnowing so soon on the heels of this? Come it would, outside the time set sacred to a stead's healing, if the new alph died before the term of truce was done.

No, she couldn't let her own fear demand so much of the sibs she left behind. Adonijah would have to live.

A muted cry yanked at Becca's ear. A muffled whimpering twitched her attention upslope sure as if it held her by a plaited bridle. "You don't move," she told Adonijah. "If I call you, you come." She saw his head bob in the moonlight, the only sign of agreement he dared to give. Setting her feet carefully on the winding path between the broken jars and the ravaged baskets, she picked out her way, following a baby's lonesome cry.

It was slow going. Sometimes she spied bone underfoot; sometimes worse. Not every stead that shared this slope was as scrupulous in tending to those infants they abandoned here, after they'd cried their last. Not every alph was as neighborly as Becca's pa had been, seeing that the dead were brought home again for proper burial. She tried not to look inside each open basket she passed, nor each clay ark. She tried, but flaglets of unwilling sight flashed themselves before her eyes: little bare toes curled inward like the legs of winterkilled spiders. A tiny brown hand, dry and rustly as a seed pod, clutched the scrap-end of a swaddling blanket. Small sockets gaped sightless in a feasted face where the tiny scurriers had reached the Lord King's chosen child before anyone could come to free its bones.

Only the knowledge that the scurriers were too cowardly to approach any babe still living had allowed Becca to leave Shifra here. The breathless time flooded back across Becca's eyes, waves of memory crashing over her with each pulse of her blood. Running from the stead, Shifra in her arms, hearing the start of Adonijah's sanctified slaughter at her heels…stealing a cloth from the cookhouse, wrapping the babe warm and tight, snatching up a sugar-sop to still her cries…the hillside's haven, and still always the backward looks of pure, plain terror as she climbed unseeing among old leavings of basket and bone… finding a basket yet filled with another little body, the breath gone from it, spilling it downslope so Shifra might be nestled warm for the day it would take Becca to make better preparations for their ultimate flight, for the scant day it would take her to come back and gather up her sister, and both of them be gone.

It had taken more than a day. Too many men sniffing around the stead grounds had whipped her fear into a frenzy to turn herself invisible, driven her to earth in the storeplace. It had taken too long. Shifra's cry was thin and weedy, a hopeless keening instead of a healthy babe's lordly demand. It pierced Becca's side with a sharp-honed guilt despite her mind's insistant clamor that all the evil delay had been no fault of hers.

The babe knew nothing of blame; only hunger. Becca began to run. She spurned several objects in her way, telling her heart they were only loose hillside stones. The baby's cry was stronger, urging Becca on. The borrowed basket cast a moonshadow like the tender swell of a fruitful woman's belly.

"Oh, my Lord."

Becca fell to her knees, set the gun down on the cold earth. Her hands clasped one another between her breasts, setting the hidden papers rustling. She had to hold fast to something or her every sanity would burst from her brain and leave her with the wind howling through her skull. Even the worm in her mind was stricken silent by a sight like this.

The basket was upended. Shifra was a big, healthy babe. Once she'd slept enough and sucked enough at her raggy sop, she'd grown angry at abandonment. She'd kicked. The basket was made for a smaller nestling. It didn't take a strapping child like Shifra much to rock it over, even swaddled as she was. That was about all she could do, though. Once tumbled out, she'd worked her swaddlings loose, but she couldn't cover ground.

What will a babe *not* take into its mouth when it's hungry? If there's nothing else to hand, even something as dry and nasty-tasting as what the scurriers had left behind will do to fool a clamorous belly.

—and in the first years of the hungering times, there were many abominations. Until the Lord filled the ears of His prophets with the lesson of the Lord King, there was great evil in the land, and the hunger grew therefore, because the people sinned mightily. Those that were to be the givers of life became the takers of their own gifts, and the living ate of the sins of the dead. That which might hunger most unnaturally did assuage hunger, and that which should have been the people's increase, that they might raise up hands to till the land untouched by the great barrenness, was instead its diminution.

E s t h e r   M .   F r i e s n e r

But the Lord raised up mighty men to lay the sword across the necks of those who practiced infamy; and holy men to teach the people the prophets' lesson of the Lord King; and righteous men to lead the people from their own damnation back into the light. Then the land began to turn again, by their sanctification thereof. Nevermore did any man, however famished, eat of any unclean thing for his soul's own sake. This was the way of the children of God.

But vermin had no souls, no way to know anything but hunger and the feeding of it. The scurriers who'd been feasting on dead flesh—well, their brains weren't any more particular than their bellies. A nibble at the living while the living lies entwined with the dead? It was bound to happen. Only a first nibble until the living kicked the scurrier away, but a first nibble from so many little mouths—

"Oh, Shifra!" Gently, Becca unwound her sister's pale fist from the grisly pacifier she'd taken up when the raggy sop rolled too far off for a baby to retrieve. The end of the small bone was still warm and wet from Shifra's soft mouth. The place where the scurriers had come and tried and learned they didn't care for living meat was also warm and wet. Becca tore strips from the dead child's swaddlings and bound up what was left of Shifra's foot. The babe whimpered in pain and nuzzled into Becca's bosom, seeking comfort.

Rustling murmurs cut across the grim silence with which Becca worked. Running footfalls behind her jerked her mind away from its hurried inventory of curative herbs stowed deep in the rolled pack she'd forced Adonijah to make for her. The moon spilled across the reaped plowland surrounding the hill, caught Adonijah's fleeing body skimming above the stubble like a dawnstruck ghost.

"*Adonijah!*" Her shout didn't stop him, hardly slowed him. He'd made his choice, snapped at the chance that maybe she wasn't as fully master of that gun as she pretended. If he ran, he'd have a chance. If he stayed, he had just her word that she'd let him go free after she took Shifra. He measured her promise by the worth of his own and ran.

Kneeling, she set the baby by, groped for the gun, raised it in both hands and sighted down the nubbin on the barrel. He wasn't far—moving fast, yes, but she'd allow for that. In all the stories, guns brought down their prey slick as whistling. The butt warmed in her cupped palms as she squeezed off the trigger.

The blast kicked the gun up and back hard, raged through her ears. The recoil threw her backward and sideways. Her shoulder dug into the dirt, scraped against fragments of shattered clay. For a moment she thought the shot had bolted out the back, blown the barrel clean open, taking her chest with it. Gulping down air, she turned her empty hands this way and that, but they were whole. She grabbed up the gun again and leaped to her feet, seeking Adonijah's dead body.

Only he wasn't dead. The shot had stopped him, but not by anything more than plain surprise. He stood in the middle of the field, a crouched black shape against the moonwashed gray. She could see his shoulders heave for seven breaths before he whirled and ran again.

"Adonijah, you stop! That was a warning!" The lie came cold, but not clever enough. He didn't heed, didn't believe in anything but his own damned luck and the speed of his running feet. "I mean it, Adonijah! Next time

I'm blasting you to bits!" Her grip on the gun butt was tighter now, her jawline taut. This time she'd hold her aim—it would be easier to do it standing than on one knee. This shot he'd die. Her finger trembled as it tightened around the trigger. She heard the whispered click as the hammer drew back, then the explosion that jarred her teeth together and tossed her arms skyward like windblown branches.

Adonijah was still up and running, a moving mockery of all her cherished newfound power. He ran for the distant stead buildings, ran to fetch his men. Already there must be lights kindling in the dormitories, folk a-stir, sentries roused, all asking one another what that hellish noise had been and where it had come from. If she chased after him, she'd as good as give herself and Shifra to their deaths. If she scooped up the babe and ran now, she'd never put enough distance between them and Wiserways before Adonijah sicced his men on their trail.

Echoes still hung on the cooling air, fading reverberations of the shots she had fired uselessly. They seemed to swell, growing unreasonably louder, filling her head with ringing. She stared at the weapon in her hands, the manlore weapon that would not answer to a woman. She twisted her wrists so that the barrel gazed at her with its hollow eye. She had failed; Shifra would not live. Could be there was one last wish she might beg of this Coop city toy.

The metal tube was hot on her tongue. It was awkward, holding the gun at that angle, but it wouldn't be for long. Becca wished her ears would stop ringing so. It made it harder to pray.

The blast that shattered the moonlit sky made her clank her teeth against the muzzle's acrid end. The gun dropped from her mouth to her thigh as she strained to see the impossible. Adonijah pulled up short, staggered. Becca watched him tumble to his knees as if it were a dream, a wishful gift from God in honor of the hour of her death. She licked an oily residue from her swollen lower lip as she watched Adonijah sprawl down in the mown grainfield.

"Missy, you're all right?"

She gasped at the slight impact of a hand falling on her shoulder. Instinctively, she lurched forward, out from under. The gun swung around, up, as if its empty eye could see for itself, find and kill this stranger who'd sprung upon her out of the night.

Sight came slowly through the white panic bandaging her eyes. Becca lowered the gun and praised Mary Mother who had kept her finger from closing too hard on the trigger, to her own damnation.

"Hey! Easy there, missy. I didn't mean to fright you. You can put that away." He nodded at the gun.

Of course she could; no choice about it. He was holding Shifra to his chest with one arm, holding a long-nosed black gun in his other hand. Bitter smoke clung to him. The baby sneezed.

"Give her back," Becca said. It hovered between entreaty and demand. She still held the gun, but he held more. She was lost in an alien land.

"I will." His broad, plain face didn't look likely to hide too much, but the stakes were past the point where Becca could play this game on trust. "What about that man, though?" He held fast to Shifra, waved his weapon downslope. "You want him dead? 'Cause if you do, I've done a piss-poor job of it for you."

Becca stared at him, head to foot, willing him to give back the babe. Shifra squirmed, but he held her expertly. The little one had a fistful of fringe from his jacket crammed into her avidly working mouth. His clothes and hair were nothing like a steadman's. For an impossible instant, Becca's head filled with stories of angels.

"*Do* you want him dead?"

Becca turned from the question and the stranger. Downslope, across the fields, there must be great stirrings all over Wiserways by now. The children would be awake, the older, cannier ones already scurrying off to hidey-holes. What must come, would come. There were too many lore-lessonings, too many years of Wiserways breeding to stand between Becca's desire to save them all and her need, even now, to try to save Shifra.

"Will you keep her safe for me?" Her voice was a stone.

He looked astonished at the question. "Why, sure. That's why I showed myself. I couldn't let a woman go—"

"I'll be fast."

She rushed down the hillside, skirts held high, her gun knotted up in the fabric. She was panting by the time she reached Adonijah where he lay among the shaven stalks. He had rolled himself onto his back, his eyes on the moon. Blood blackened his trousers at the hip. Becca counted the quicksilver drops of sweat on his face as she crouched beside him.

"Adonijah." He turned from her voice. "*Adonijah.*" She laid one hand over his heart, with the other brought the gun to nuzzle under his chin. "You shouldn't have run."

Flakes of dry laughter shuddered from his mouth. The

working of his jaw jiggled the gun barrel. "Guess not. Now what, Becca? Kill me and name yourself alph of Wiserways?" Another shower of bright, razored particles of sound from high in his chest. "There'd be a turning for this old world to take! It'd have to mean we've finally come into the last days. But then you're guilty of breaking the truce time. Can't have one alph come in after another, no space to breathe between, no time for new babes to be born, too many other children dead."

"Too many," Becca agreed. She put her gun by, tucked it well away from his possible grasp. He was downed, hurting, but she knew better than to trust Adonijah. "I'm not the one come to change the law. I don't want you dead by my hand. Take the truce time you've earned, Adonijah; enjoy it. No man will dare come against you while it lasts, will he? That's law. And after…however long you rule Wiserways is the Lord's will."

She drew out the two straight pins from the waistband of her skirt and let him see them. "His will be done," she said. Then she used them, short and sharp, so they were the last things Adonijah ever saw.

Chapter Twenty

*I am a brother to my brothers, a strong hand to
their friends, an arrow in the darkness to their foes,
and dead before dishonored in their eyes.*

He moved with a silent grace she had never before
seen in any man, not even Jamie. His eyes could pierce
the dark as if carrying their own inner light. At first she
was badly feared, seeing him lope over rough, unfamiliar
ground so swiftly, Shifra in his arms. Becca's breath was
a lump in her throat hard enough to chew on as she
scrambled after him, stumbling.

He wouldn't give Shifra back to her. Not even when
they were over the crest of the hill and away into a
splintery stand of old apple trees, branches clawing like
a hungry hag's fingers. Here he stopped, casting around

for something, holding firm to the baby while he searched.

They could yet hear Adonijah's shrieks and groans, thin as watered-down barley pap at this distance. The air was still among the perished trees, no breeze to bring Becca the full sounds of that one's pain. She strained her ears to sift every last grain of Adonijah's agony from the night. It was a sweet hearing.

"Ah! Here it be, right where I left it." The man swapped Shifra from one shoulder to the other, then stooped to dip his gun-toting hand through a broad leather carrying strap. A boxy red container, too big to be a canteen, slapped him on the hip as he straightened.

Becca caught the scent she'd only smelled when pa had let her have a go at riding the big reap-and-sow. The whole barn where the precious vehicle was kept stabled always reeked just like that. Now that she recalled it, she'd seen her male sibs loading a lot of similar big containers into the back of one of the Wiserways wagons while they prepared to leave Harvest Home. The containers vanished under a coarse tarp, but the smell carried well on the crisp autumn air.

"You stole that!" she cried, pointing at the ponderously swinging can, and wished she'd bit her tongue off raw as soon as the words came out. Who was she to lay accusations on him when he held every advantage? Oh, it was a bad thing for a woman to slip her bridle even once; she never more could wriggle it back on to keep her sufficient safe of tongue among the men.

To her surprise, the man looked shamed instead of angered. There was moon enough and plenty for her to see how he cringed. "'Tisn't all that much in here, missy.

Just one scant cannikin full. We'll use it to trade. The trade goes around and comes around; that's what Mal told me. I've seen that to be true. By the time it comes 'round to your stead again, we might bring back something your folks need more than this little measure. Who's to say?" His voice went shaky, uncertain. "Missy…you won't hold me wicked for this?"

Becca found no humor in the man's cruel funning. *She* hold *him* wicked? As if that would matter! She had a gun but so did he, and he knew how to use it. And he held Shifra. Every edge was his; what need did he have to speak to her so meek and tender?

Unless he's scented something. The trail end smell of a woman coming out of her times, the blood-sign of it on her. There's some men who don't hold to the niceties, who think it's proper to claim their rights to a taking woman even when she's as good as done with taking.

And rogues don't care for distinguishments at all.

The worm-whispered thought made her giddy. The sick feeling lining her belly was stronger than what she normally felt when her times drew to a close. The rag she'd bandaged between her legs felt heavy, a comfortless bulk. All Hattie's housewifely lessonings bristled up prim in her mind, bidding her find a place to tidy herself better. Hollow, skull-spoke laughter harried such finicky notions far, far away.

The man was still staring at Becca, but not as a man looks at a taking woman. There was no lusting in his eyes that she could see. More and more peculiar, this one. She stood outside her own body and heard herself mouth some short, harmless words of reassurance that washed the hesitation from his face.

"Thank you, miss," he said, even sounding appreciative. With no more to say to her, he turned and started east through the starveling trees.

"Wait! Where are you going?" She lunged for the arm that cradled Shifra. The baby was whimpering. Soon she would scream, either from the pain of her ruined foot, or hunger, or wet, or cold. Becca clawed at the fringes of the man's soft leather sleeve. "Give her back to me."

His wide, brown face was placid as the heart of a well. "I can bear her better than you over the land we've got to cover tonight, missy. Swiftly does it, if we're followed. I can fight, but God knows how many steadmen gonna come after once that one manages to raise the 'larm. I want my brothers 'side me if there's that many to stand down." He hitched the baby a little higher against his chest and smiled into the small, pinched face. "'Sides, I think someone's gonna be hungering soon. There's what to feed her where we'll go." His mouth and eyes went abruptly tight and lightless. "What to treat her hurts with too, before it's too much later."

He slewed his eyes from Shifra to Becca, and in them was a cold, severe judgment the like of which Becca always dreamed the Lord Himself would turn on her quivering soul come Doomsday. Every word-bearing breath in her throat shriveled up to dry husks under that look. This strangerman knew who'd left the child alone on that ghastly hillside. By whatever cursed knack he owned, he knew. It was her turn to stammer explanations and excusals.

"Please, mister, the baby—I didn't have a true choice. I was the one left her on the hill, but I *had* to. Nowhere else I'd know for sure she'd keep safe. Shifra's my sister, my full sister, not just a sib. Our pa was killed, as was alph over Wiserways Stead—killed by treachery, by that one back there." She motioned behind her, vaguely sweeping in the field where she'd left Adonijah lie. "After Pa was killed there came the winnowing—"

"Don't talk to me about such." He sliced the air with the long nose of his gun, cutting off all further talk. "We've heard tell enough of stead doings where I come from. God help you, the tales are true."

He looked at her so pitying then that Becca felt resentment boil up her insides. It was just the same expression that always watered down the steadwives' faces when they spoke of the hungering times, and the people so bone ignorant they wouldn't heed the Lord King's prophets when they came, and they turned with all their dwindling families from the new law and perished for it.

Ignorance, killing ignorance alone summoned up so much pity in another human's face. And did he *dare* to look at her that way?

"Mister, I don't know who you are or where you're from, but if I was you I'd check these *tales* you've heard against how things rightfully are."

The strangerman only shook his head. "My name is Gilber Livvy. Where I'm from, we've had folk enough come through to tell us the truth of stead ways." The way he said it, *stead* became an obscenity on his lips. "I'm a priest's son. I can't listen to such foul doings without taint, and God knows where I'll find to cleanse myself proper this side of the city."

City! The word snapped Becca's head back sharp as any blow. Questions crept up under her tongue, but before she could force them out the man bent his gaze over the fretting babe. "She's all that matters now," he said, so loving it made Becca's own heart yearn worse than ever toward the child. This time there was no staying him as he marched away into the night.

They were not followed. If they were, Becca heard nothing of it. She kept her mind on the path, her eyes on Gilber's broad back. The apple trees were soon passed, the ground turned briefly level, then plunged into upgrown pineywoods. Becca had no notion where they were or which stead lay nearest. The sky might give her some little measure of direction, but once under cover of the prickly branches she couldn't see the stars.

Shifra began to raise a wail. Gilber murmured sweet baby talk to her, but to no use. The child was past responding to such meatless bribes. She set up a shrill, rhythmic cry that was as much rage as need. Becca heard Gilber curse many things—luck and the steadfolk and stupidity and waste and even her—but never once the baby.

It was then she caught sight of the fire's glow.

❧ ❦

"A baby?" The man nearest the campfire looked like he didn't know whether to laugh or swear. Flames and shadows turned his scarred face into a grotesque mask. Becca kept her hands folded and her eyes downturned, though her heart had emptied itself of prayer. Whatever this man chose to do, it was all up for her and Shifra. She heard his chuckle crackling drier than good firewood, and the question: "What's got into your head, Gilber, bringing these two?"

Esther M. Friesner

Gilber didn't seem to hear him at first. He'd greeted the older man readily enough—Mal was his name—but then it was like speech would cost him too dear. The first thing he'd done when they broke into the circle of firelight was scoop a handful of something gray and mucky out of one pot warming by the flames, slop it into another, pour canteen water over it and spoon the runny mess into Shifra's mouth. The baby devoured it greedily and was content. None of the twelve men there said a word or raised a hand to stop him.

Now Shifra was lying on her back near the fire, making soft sounds like sweetwater lapping stone. Gilber had her wrappings undone, his lips white as he stared at her ruined foot. Mal leaned near as he could without actually getting up; he made sympathetic sounds.

"There's some of Ryan's salve left yet, if you think it'd help. Clean cloth plenty, in Yaysu's kit."

Gilber nodded, accepting the offer. "I'll want water too, fresher than what's in my canteen. Save the salve."

"What, more of your mountain powders?" Mal laughed so freeheart Becca could see the stumps of broken teeth that partways lined his jaw. Those few teeth he still kept whole—a surprising number—were clean white as the moon. "Go on, get 'em and help yourself to the water you need from the camp jug. Corp found us a goodly spring while you were off recruiting these two able bodies. Go on, I said. I'll mind the—whatsit? Stitcher or stabber?" He jerked his thumb at the baby.

A half smile lifted one corner of Gilber's mouth. "I thought that part of lore was much the same everywhere. But if you need me to tell you while you've got eyes—"

Mal snorted. As Gilber went off after the things he

wanted, the older man edged closer to Shifra and gingerly pinched a corner of the cloth still lying across her hips.

"She's a girl!" Becca's sharp words acted like a rap across the man's knuckles. He dropped the cloth brisk. Becca fell to her knees beside her sister and rearranged the baby's poor covering so that none of the men gathered there could see her shame.

"No harm meant," Mal said. "Sorry." His soft words took her startled, one more shock that tore raw everything she'd ever heard tell of the rogue bands. "I'd've asked it out plain, only we ain't had two words out of you since Gilber came bringing you and she."

"Thought you was maybe a dummy," a lank boy put in. He looked too much like Becca's sib Tom, only Tom pulled fine and thin as stretched honeycomb.

The man beside the boy gave him a healthy shove that knocked him down and came near to pitching him into the fire. "Dumb thing to say to her when you can hear she *ain't*. All holy, Sarj, we got to teach you visiting manners all over again?"

The boy Sarj just picked himself off the ground, muttering. Somewhere in those tangled words might've been an apology.

Gilber returned with a small wooden bowl, its sides water-slick in the firelight. He squatted down beside Shifra and tugged a little rolled-up brown cone out of his belt. It crackled between his fingers as he unfolded the tuck-in flap keeping it sealed. Carefully, he knocked a sprinkle of powder out of it into the bowl. It was too dark for Becca to see what color the powder was—no need for her to learn such a fact, truth to tell—but she leaned nearer anyway. The dark and evil questioning presence in her heart—her worm, her whispering shadow of Satan, her stripped-plain self—pushed her toward Gilber as surely as if it had two taloned paws to lay on her shoulders.

"What's that?" she asked.

For awhile he paid her question no mind, his whole being focused on the powder, the bowl, the babe. The tip of his tongue stuck out some at the corner of his mouth. She'd seen Jamie do so, times a dream called his attention more urgently than she could.

Jamie's gone walking far, the worm whispered. *Wonder if Pa's caught up with him yet, that long road?*

She squeezed her eyes shut, forcing away the loved spirits that haunted her heart, forcing herself to concentrate on Gilber. She was near enough to smell how he was different from the other men—not clean-washed or labor-sweated like her grown male sibs and the other steadmen, nor sour and rank like his comrades Mal and Sarj and the rest—but a green scent to him, wild green. The pineywood around them seemed to have stolen in under Gilber Livvy's skin until it was the fresh, sweetly pungent breath of the trees themselves that blew from his body. As he worked over the powder and the bowl, that scent scoured all others from Becca's head, folded over her like the wind's wing when it blew from the ice mountains, left her dazed.

Lore says a man can tell a taking woman by her smell alone, Becca thought, dazzled. *That what this is? Some new monstrosity spawned out here in the wilderness? A man that can be in his times, and taking?*

Her pulse throbbed in her throat so that she realized he'd finally answered her question and had posed one back.

"I'm sorry, what—?"

"I asked if there was maybe some stead words you folk liked to say over a hurt to make it heal faster, missy."

"Words…"

"You know, witching."

"Dear Lord." Becca rested a hand at the springing of her throat, pushed past horror by Gilber's words. So innocent he said them, too. *Like it's common knowledge, wherever he's from, that steadfolk are such…such…*

"Where's your head, Gilber?" The boy Sarj dropped to his haunches between him and her, unasked, and gave Gilber a light thump on the arm. The bowl of mucked water jiggled but didn't spill. "Your folk *did* live halfway up the backside of beyant, no lie! Thinking the *steadfolk* do witcheries? Haw! That's a crime that'll buy you your death if they so much as smell the *word* 'witch' on your lips." He showed Becca a mouthful of teeth in worse shape than Mal's. "You gotta let most of what Gilber says fly over you, miz. He wasn't stead-bred like some of us, and Lord Ki—God knows, not reared to the marches either."

"Are you stead-raised, then?" The question left Becca's mouth before Hattie's specter could rear up and condemn such unmaidenly forwardness.

"Me? Sure am. Me and Corp and Lu—him with the pocky face 'crost the fire. Could be there's others in this scuadra were stead-bred, but they've served long enough to lose the stink of it and have a name again."

Becca shook her head. "I don't understand."

"Well, beggin' your pardon, miz, but it's not your place to understand."

Sarj said it easy and smiling, a man stating facts only a fool would dispute. He meant no malice. The worm howled with glee and Hattie's shade wailed in despair as Becca shot back, "Why not? Your head likely doesn't hold

half of what I've *understood* 'til yet. You know any herblore? You know how to read? To write? To help a woman
birth? It's my place to understand all I can, by trying. You
don't have the brains to *explain* something to me, say so;
don't go laying blame on my *understanding*."

"Whoa!" From his place by the fire Mal laughed and
slapped both legs. "Poison tongue, Sarj! Gonna give it
some edge, she is, and come looking to cut off your balls
tonight. I'd give up my turn, I was you."

"Yeah, Sarj," pock-faced Lu gibed. "Trade it to me for
an extra cut of saltmeat, keep *your* meat from shriveling
up when she gets hold of it." The other men chimed in,
all chaffing Sarj unmercifully, all advising him to leave
Becca be, later.

Later.

Becca drew herself up small. The word was a hatchet-
head of ice buried between her breasts. No pretending
she'd misheard. She tucked her head down low to her
chest and hugged her knees tight, willing that word and
all its kin to melt away, starkly knowing they must stay.

Lore hadn't lied. The men's soft speech and kindliness
had sopped her for a time, but the truth was still waiting
when the sop was sucked dry. The reckoning for falling
in with a rogue band would surely come to her as it must
to any other hapless woman. Not so sudden or violent as
the tales told, but still come it would, as it must, and be
full paid.

—a long time dying.

Even with the blood-sign on her, so she knew the
doors of her womb stayed open and there was maybe a
chance she'd live through it, it was still a nightmare
waiting patiently to have her. What if it fell out with her
after the way of most taking women who accepted a man's

seed? If she turned fruitful from this, what manner of monster would she bear, child of so many sires? A host of small shudders shook her and she dug her head yet deeper into the sheltering dark.

She only lifted her eyes once, to steal a look at Shifra. Sarj had retreated to the other side of the fire. Gilber had finished treating the baby's foot and was cradling her close to his fringy coat again, smiling as pleased and proud as any newmade mother when the child gave him a bubbly smile. Becca might as well have vanished into the earth for all the mind he paid her while he held the babe.

A life for a life, Becca thought. *Mine for yours, Shifra. Oh Mary Mother, give my sweet babe the holding of Gilber Livvy's heart! Then, if I die, at least he'll stand by her for me. Lord grant it be so.*

The Lord's help's for those that help themselves, the worm whispered in her ear, and sent a seeing of all the lessonings that Pa's wives gave the maidens before Harvest Home. *There's ways to send a man's heart down whatever path you choose. If you're still living when it's his turn with you, make certain you send his after Shifra.*

If I live, I will. Lord send me strength for it, and courage, and the will to—

She was still lost in her prayers when Mal tapped her on the shoulder and said, "Corp says he's made the place soft for you, miz. Come along with me now. It's time."

Chapter Twenty-One

*In the old times, in the lost land, we went up to
the mountain and found wisdom.*

Becca hadn't counted them as they came to her, one
by one, always each with the put-on face of a man who
stumbles over something unexpected in his path. She
didn't tally them up because, if she took them that way,
one by one, she could pretend more easily that one was
all there was. One by one, and for each one she uttered a
new prayer of thanksgiving to Mary Mother that he
respected the blood-sign on a woman, and asked only that
she serve him with the Kiss or the Sign. One by one, but

every one that reached for her in the dark was not the one she waited for. Clothed or clean-stripped, not a one wore the fringy coat, not a one had that wild green smell to his flesh, not a one was built square-shouldered and strong like Gilber Livvy.

Strong for Shifra, she thought. *Strong to bring us through.*

When Lu came to her, he brought a little coal of fire with him. The small blaze he kindled beside her pallet of downed pine boughs made the markings on his face look like they'd been gouged there. Becca just looked at him steady and cool. If he searched her eyes for a welcome, he wouldn't find it; but he'd find no refusal either.

"I just wanted to see—" He motioned at the fire, burning safe enough in its own shining bowl. "When you first came, I thought you were maybe pretty, but in the dark, all the confusion, I couldn't tell. And then by the fire you were too far for me to make out…I hoped…I wanted to be certain…"

She realized that he was apologizing for the fire he'd brought and she wondered why.

She said the prescribed words, hoping he'd just come to her and let her do what had to be done and get it over with. Only he kept on staring at her, like he'd eat her up with his eyes. A famished look like that cut too close to old bones not to leave her all a-shiver. There were worse stories than women taken out of their times, dying split. Sometimes, often, back in the hungering times, a lone woman was used for more urgent needs than a man's seed.

There was a reason they were called the hungering times.

The silence thickened between them. She tried to act like it was nothing—and that's what silence was, after all; wasn't it? But the worm in her was a mocker, telling her to her face that she was wrong. This silence had a weight to it, a storm-hung quiet, a brooding hush like some tales told once hovered over the wide green waters that pulled away noiseless from the land only to rush back in with a roar like demons and smash flat the towers of pride.

Finally, it was her woman's weakness made her break the iron silence. "Where you're from…were they different words the women spoke?" Maybe he hadn't understood her dutiful invitation.

Lu turned crimson. He squatted across the firebowl from her, knees up. Her questions only made him tuck his legs in nearer until, in the leaping little shadows, he looked like the crackly brown shell of a winter-sleeping littlesinger. If he didn't have a misery-face the like of which folks couldn't forget, she'd never have thought him the same fellow who'd teased Sarj so sharp before, offering to take two turns with her. Now it looked like he'd be lucky to take one.

The longer he bided, the longer it would keep Gilber Livvy away, and Becca had a business to do with Gilber Livvy. She tried to stir up Lu again. "Your old stead, did it lie mountain-wise or coop-wise from Hallow?" She named Weegee's place instead of her own, hoping that the little man's fame for "seeings" might make Hallow Stead a good landmark to draw out Lu. Weegee was the only far-famed thing she knew.

Lu shook his head, refusing to be drawn out. "All that's past," he said. "Lost to the vow. Now I'm this scuadra's man—not born to the marches, but getting near to be almost as good as that. Earning back my name." The way he said it was like a sword to cut off all further asking after his past, cut it off dead and still. "You sure are pretty," he added, seemingly for no reason at all.

Becca didn't know how to take those words. Instead, she shifted herself on the piney boughs and motioned for him to come nearer. She didn't know—she never would know—which stead he'd come from or why he'd left or how young he was. All she could tell was the fear clinging to his skin like oil, ready to take flame and burn him alive. A film of fear over a core of some unspoken shame, she could taste it, fat on her tongue. They were always real good about lessoning shame into a stead-bred child. Sometimes they drove it in so deep it wove its own darkness around. A child could get lost easier, find fear stronger in the dark. It was the lost stead-child she coaxed into her arms.

He came to her by degrees, his body trying to say how brave he was, his eyes giving it the lie. Her gestures welcomed him to lie beside her on the pallet. Soft, so as not to fright him, she began to recite an infant-tale:

"When women walked with sin, and had the misruling of themselves, and could be taking a man any time they liked or turn his seed away on a whim, the Lord saw it and was sad. He turned to sweet Mary Mother and He said, 'Where are the children?' And Mary Mother wept, because the women walled away the seed, or let it fall on parchy ground, because they turned from the cradle and kept it empty. They were always running after the bright toys of the Devil, kicking away the cradles like they were snares.

"Then the Lord King Herod saw the sorrow of the Lord and said to Mary Mother, 'See how ungrateful they are, these daughters of Eva. What they might have freely, they tear away and destroy. What they should not desire, they run after in their pride. Because of their selfishness the cradles are empty, but the wrath of my sword will fill the cradles again with their blood.'

"But Mary Mother said, 'No, for these are the daughters of two wombs, my daughters as well as Eva's. Lord King, you are not my Lord, whose wrath filled the world's womb with water, yet spared Noah and his wives to people it again. I say that your unsparing sword shall not fill the cradles with blood. There is too much blood, but this shall change.'"

Becca felt Lu's breath grow softer and more even, like a young one settling in for sleep. She touched his hair, thick with dust, but not so badly matted as she'd thought. It held tiny stirrings that made her fingertips quiver. She prayed she'd have the chance to cleanse herself thoroughly after this, ward off any hap that she'd catch a plague of small creepies from him and the other men. That was for later, though. For now she had to bear with his presence if she ever hoped to see Gilber before sunup. She spoke on, her voice lulling out the old story:

"Then Mary Mother wept and numbered her tears, and the number of them was the number of the hungering years. And in those years there came changes, even as Mary Mother had said.

"For the Lord King rode over the land and his sword destroyed, but only so far as the Lord allowed. And the Lord Himself rode before him, angels in His train, and every angel set his seal upon the womb of every woman and whispered in her ear, 'This is the womb of Eva which your evil has made barren. Because you scorned the cradle, you shall yearn to see it filled. Now you hunger for bread, but soon you will hunger for more.' And the blood ceased, and the gates of the womb shrank small with the fear of the Lord King's sword, and it was so."

Lu shuddered in her arms. Maybe the words had been different, but this was one tale Becca knew he'd been told in his growing. What decent stead ever allowed a child to be brought up without it? It taught them to know the goodness of God, Who might have wiped away all life for the sake of woman's wanton pride, but Who showed mercy instead. It showed them why the hungering times were something to be borne, the passage through fire that tempers the steel. Most of all, it was a lessoning on proper womanly gratitude, and the payment for the old debt of sin.

It wasn't charity to keep the sinner from paying out what she owed.

She didn't have to finish the infant-tale. He knew her meaning and his obligation. She felt his hand slip inside her blouse, blundering, using the alien touch of her small breasts to excite himself. She waited until she felt the first faint swelling against her, then reached for him to give him the Sign of Gratitude and hand him into Paradise. Some few of the others had let her know—by sign or by plain speaking—that they'd sooner have the Kiss of Thanks, but she reasoned it would be too much for one already so skittery to have her do that for him.

Think you'll remember you've got teeth sometime they want that? The worm shrieked with obscene laughter. *Just be glad the smell of a taking woman's gone from you or you'd be doing more than this for all of them. It's a rare thing for a rogue band to mind the sight of blood.*

She banished the laughing demon from her mind and focused on her task.

It was quickly done. When she heard his groan of pleasure she knew that he'd discovered God's reward to man for helping guide proud woman back to her rightful place. She wished there were no light so she didn't have to see him. His pocky face shone with such joy that she knew he was brimful with gratefulness that wasn't a man's portion at all.

Go away, she willed at him. *You don't owe me anything but your going. The woman's debt is mine to pay; we're quit. Mary Mother willing, I won't have to pay it out double. Go.* She felt very tired.

He lingered beside her in spite of all her will. It made her stomach turn to see how soft and melty his eyes had become. "I can bring you some water—"

"No, thank you."

"A bowl to wash in? I could fetch one from our mess."

She tried to use his thankfulness to hurry him along. "I'd as soon not until you've all been and—" Becca left the rest unsaid on purpose. He would know, unless he were wit-wanting. Somehow she doubted Mal would keep any man with him that couldn't be brought up to the way of this—what did they call it?—*scuadra?* Learning new ways took brains.

"'Til you're done with us? Oh, if that's all, you can rest easy. I'm the last." Now very much the man—her gift— Lu stretched himself out on her crackly pallet and folded his hands beneath his head. "That's how the lots fell out." His eyes picked out stars through the spindly upper branches. "Ain't that dusting pretty?" He pointed to a smear of white light against the black. "Mary's Milk we called that on my old stead."

Becca clenched her fists impatiently. She didn't give a handful of husks to hear about his stead now. She only wanted to know why he acted like Gilber Livvy had vanished. The stickiness gummed between her fingers, made her madder. Trying to wipe it off on the boughs just glued brittle dead pine needles to her palms.

She took a breath and let it out slow, so the idea that had just come to her wouldn't go slipping away into thin air. *He's just forgotten Gilber. I'll help him recall.* "I think I would like that water," she said. "No need for you to trouble yourself running back and forth with it, though. You could have Gilber Livvy fetch it when he comes."

Lu's eyes got big, as if they had to swell that wide to take in all her craziness. "You 'spect Gilber Livvy's gonna come to you, miz? For this?"

"No?" There was just one cause Becca could think of to put fact behind Lu's words and it didn't bear saying aloud: *Abomination!* If that was so and Mal still tolerated Gilber's share of breath, then scuadra ways were different than stead ways truly.

It didn't take much for Lu to pick that thought out of her head though; not when it was writ so large on her face. He made a sound part snort, part laugh, then got to his feet. "Nah, not for that reason. Think Mal'd let one like them taint his scuadra? When he had me join, he made sure to nose out the reason I ran off from—from where I come. Sent Yaysu in among my folk, sly, but all Yaysu come back with was—" He darted his eyes at her, realized what he'd been about to give away and bit it back fast. "Nah, he found me clean. I'd'a been one like that— carrying death, refusing life—he'd've killed me right there. Same with Gilber Livvy. Mal just got the man's own word to go on for that—no one's gonna hike all the way back to where Livvy comes from to check if he's a clean man—but Gilber Livvy carries his own proof with him, so to speak."

Her face all screwed up with confusion made him pat her on the cheek. Her gift had made him up into a man, let him make her down into a child with pretty ways. "I'll send him with that water for you, sweetheart. Then, maybe if you've got the wit, you'll find a way to see for yourself. And if you do, I've got a genuine trade chip come all the way from Bee City I'll give you for working that trick!" He chucked her chin roughly and strode back to the campfire singing an old praise-song of the Lord King with the words twisted into lumps of filth.

Alone again, Becca was thankful he hadn't taken the firebowl with him. The night was thinning out toward morn. She was cold, and caught between uncertainties. Would Mal himself come to fetch her back, acting as if she'd spent all this time by herself among the trees freewill? Or was she supposed to pack herself up and join the men without being sent for? Lu's fire was dying down. She fed it some dry twigs and watched them pop and sizzle while she tried to decide whether to move or stay.

Then she heard a swift, even stride and saw a second light come bobbing through the brush. Gilber Livvy came, a bowl of water carefully carried in one hand, a second firebowl in the other.

He hunkered down beside her, put the firebowl next to its mate, and made the water into an offering. "I've a cloth for your hands, missy." His eyes were so dark she imagined she could see a tiny trail of stars mirrored there.

"Thanks. I'll use it after."

"After?"

"It's your turn, isn't it?" She moved over some on the branches, a clear asking, brazen enough even for her sib

Lenora. Inside, her throat was bathed in acid from shame. More flowed up out of her belly with every second that he remained where he was, as he was. When he didn't make a move toward her, she spoke the words and waited longer: nothing. Not even the breath of womanfear she'd sensed blowing over Lu.

"Missy," he said after a time when Becca thought her skin would itch itself off for waiting. "Missy, this isn't for me, these doings." He thrust the bowl of water at her. "Lu was the last who'll use you that way tonight. You can make yourself clean and come sleep. The baby's sleeping now. We've got to move on early with the light." When she stayed still, he took her hands one at a time and tenderly washed the stiff-dried seed and the dead brown needles away. His strong hands had a fearful gentleness to them as he bent his head over her palm and stroked her fingers dry.

"What are you?" The words crept naked from her mouth. "Are you a man?"

He raised his head and pulled back a few sleek black locks of hair. There was that in his look that made her cringe down small and white inside, as if he had God's power to fly in at her eyes and search out her soul and weigh it in the balance over hellfire.

"I say I'm a man," he told her. "If I don't share this scuadra's whore it don't make me any less of one."

"How *dare* you call me that!" Her hand flew before she could stop it, cracked across his face.

The worm crowed. *Again! Hit him again!*

The red of the firebowls fountained up and filled her vision with rage. Too late, helpless, the ghost of Becca that was Hattie's sensible child saw the knives at his belt.

Again, I tell you! What can you lose now? They've all had a turn with you that wanted one, the worm hissed. *Who'll care if he kills you? Yes, hit him again! Again! Rack up the tally! He can only kill you once for all of these.*

Goaded, Becca whipped her hand back for another blow. He was quicker. The gentleness was gone as he gripped her wrist. She thrashed to pull free; he countered, using his arms this time to bind her against him. *So, a true man after all.* She could almost see the worm smirking as she felt a familiar stirring against her thigh.

Then he was saying, "I'm sorry. I had no reason to call you that. I know your ways are different from ours. I'm shamed." He let her go and pulled away. "You had every right to strike me."

She sat watching while he folded up the damp cloth and used what water was left to make a cool compress for his reddened cheek. Her words came out scarce above a whisper: "Whores do for pay what good women give for gratitude's sake; they live blasphemy." She had never seen a whore, never known one, but there were tales to hear tell. The men of Wiserways swapped them, their eyes a-shine with longing. Her saying came out sounding like a feeble excuse, a lie even to ears raised to call it truth.

"I know." His eyes still asked her pardon but his lips were smiling friendly at her. "That's part of your beliefs, isn't it? Before I left home, my father warned me to open my mind and lock up my temper. Things would be different among your folk, he said, though he couldn't tell me exactly how, not entirely. Course we had some old travelers' tales, but those were so way old that—He just hoped I'd learn before I got someone mad enough to kill me." He put the cloth aside and touched his cheek gingerly. "Whew! You'd had a rock to hand, you just might've proved my father right." His smile winked out. "I hope that babe's got some of your strength in her, missy."

The old cold that nested in the heart of Prayerful Hill lapped its way up her spine. "Why do you say so? You told me she's sleeping."

He got up and helped her to stand, brushing pine needles from her tousled hair. "Just come with me."

She followed him back to the campfire, carrying the cloth and the waterbowl while he used the dying firebowls to light their way. All the men were sleeping except for Sarj who stood watch and Lu who must have been on post farther off among the trees. Gilber led the way around their bodies stealthily in just the wordless way to tell a woman that she'd be wise to respect their rest.

Shifra was bundled in a heaped-up blanket surrounded by a small nest of boughs Gilber had gathered. He placed one firebowl at her head, one at her feet in a way that made Becca's flesh creep. They knelt on either side of the sleeping child.

Like all those old picture-book pretties of the kings who came to see Mary Mother's newborn Babe, Becca thought. *Only this kneeling's blighted some way. Lord, I'm afraid!* The baby's face looked corpse-pale by the feeble light, the slight movement of her dreaming breath hardly enough to break the illusion.

Then: "Look here," said Gilber Livvy, and he pulled away a dogear's worth of blanket from Shifra's feet.

Becca throttled the cry that leaped up from her belly, clapped spew-staying fingers across her mouth. All the sour burning in her throat before was nothing next to this. The baby's bitten foot was puffed up and discolored. The flesh around all the little bite-marks looked almost black by the firelight.

"This is more than any of the powders I brought from the mountains can heal," Gilber said, just saying what he knew, without malice.

"The city," Becca said quickly, her hand on his arm. Her feet itched to match the beating of her heart. *Haste! Haste!* The cry inside her skull was shrill and insistant. "I've got to be on my way now, soon, as soon as there's light to see a path. I must get her to the city, find our brother. He'll get a healing for her! Nothing that can't be healed in the city." Her fingers tightened, digging into Gilber's arms until she felt bone, trying to force her own panic under his skin.

He never flinched or changed that sad, stone-cut expression. "No time for that," he said. "I don't know what city you mean—not even sure I know how many there are once you make the coast road—but the maps I've come by all jibe with what little city-lore this scuadra's got: It's far yet, any road, to what we're after. She wouldn't survive."

Becca let go his arm. She let go more than that once she saw that there was no measure of meanness or deceit in what he said; just truth as he saw it, was all. Truth keen enough to cut out her living heart and lay it at Shifra's ruined feet. She crumpled down until her forehead pressed itself into her knees and she raked the air into her lungs in long, razored gasps because she didn't dare wake the encampment with a woman's tears.

Chapter Twenty-Two

*"Which is easier?" asked the Tempter. "Knowing
what's yours or knowing what's right?"*

"Missy." The word was a summons, loud and clear, for
all he spoke it in the softest whisper. "Missy, get up.
Follow; it's past time."

Becca rubbed sleep from her eyes and the smears of
grime that had stuck to the pathways of her tears. It was
hard to know she'd waked; she had no recollection of the
moment she'd exhausted herself with noiseless weeping
and tumbled into dreamless sleep. The campsite was
silent, her place beside Shifra solitary and secluded. *A
woman's place,* the worm hissed. *So they can make believe
you're not even there...until you're needful to them.* And
that was so. Mal and his scuadra—named and nameless

alike—just somehow managed it so that the females were part of their encampment yet not a part of their true lives at all.

See where their loyal hearts lie! If an enemy attacked, the men were well placed to spring to each other's defense, then maybe see about her and the babe.

So it was clear ground around her, and shadows, and the forest wall at her back. The sentry—the lank boy Sarj—held his post tight, like he feared to wander far or try showing some independent action by prowling beyond the campsite's cleared perimeter.

Stupid. Becca's waking thought was groggy, but sure. *So if someone comes up on us out of the woods, it'd be all up for*—

"Missy, *now!*" the husky call from the woodland shadows insisted, and a sliver of sight gave her Gilber Livvy's face, more smeared with moss and dirt than her own.

Then she saw what he held, what squirmed and struggled in his crooked left arm. A cry rose in her, and holding down that outraged howl of loss was nigh more than she could manage and still leap up, plunge after him into the trees.

Shifra's raggedy wrap flickered before her, a flag to tempt and provoke and lead still farther on. The woods swallowed them whole, all three. Some corner of Becca's mind still clutched tight by Hattie's ghost urged her to scream, to shout, to rouse all Mal's men and sic them on Gilber Livvy's trail. But Hattie's ghost brought too many memories of death and betrayal for Becca to heed it now with anything but hate. She kept her silence and her speed, hotfoot alone after the childstealer.

He moved through the woods like wind, like dusk. A hard stone glowed hot in Becca's chest as she knew that Gilber Livvy was woodsborn same as she was stead, that the smells and the shadows were tight-wove to him, flesh and soul, blood and bone. Any time he liked, he could sidestep her, maybe even melt into a tree, and take the babe with him easy as thought. There was always just enough of him to glimpse so she could follow, but she knew there didn't have to be, that the glimpse was his gift to give or take back again, and that frighted her worse than anything.

That was when she ceased to think of him and her as quarry and hunter. Like it or no, he was leader, she follower, just as he'd commanded. Searing and bitter gall rode up her throat. The cursed unwomanly worm in her shrieked red rage. He'd stolen more than her sister from her, that weird, woodsborn creature: He'd stolen her every right to question him, to choose, to do anything but hark and obey. He might as well have been a man of the steads, alph over her, and she might as well have never left Wiserways. The notion whipped up her insides to helpless wrath.

By the time he slowed that easy, ground-eating lope, they were far from the camp and Becca had most of the wind gone from her. She never dreamed there were so many trees left standing in all the earth, yet in this place Gilber Livvy'd chosen to wait for her, nothing but trees embraced the light. She rested her hand against shaggy bark and glared hate at his heart where he stood, pack on his back, gun on his shoulder, baby in his arms.

Silvery false light seeped in among the trees, leading dustmotes in a dance. In another world, it was coming on for dawn. Wiserways would be full waked, the men already to the fields, the women bustling to their chores, the children still left maybe going mouselike to fetch water or run after doing small tasks the women named. Or were there any children left at all? Had there been a new terror, this one of Becca's own summoning?

What she'd done to Adonijah—*Gladly! Gladly* done! caroled the worm—would be sufficient to provoke one of that evil man's followers to wrest the new alph's power away, lore's truce or no. A blind alph was no alph, and even if the lore said there was to be a time of safety after a changeover, what of it? Adonijah wasn't the only man sly enough to bend and break lore to his liking. Lore said he might live, but he could as easily be dead, a new alph in his place, and the children…No alph ever took his stead from another without some blood to mark the event eternal in memory. He needed the blood to make him real.

Becca heard the wordless cry, the husky snarl of anguish and guilt rasp itself from her throat almost without knowing it was her own. Too much was risked already for the babe this wildman held. Too much lost, and Shifra's life itself in the balance now, for her to stand for this. "Give her back, Gilber Livvy," she said straight out. "Set her down now, or I'll kill you."

With what? the worm taunted, and lodged a brutal memory of how that man had used his gun to bring down Adonijah when Becca herself could not.

And if it had been just a matter of sense, she'd have heeded the worm, but sense was all burned away. There was just the anger left her, and that a blaze to scour the world clean of manlore, womanlore, all. "Give her to me, or you're dead."

"Now, missy, you don't see—"

"Give her!" Becca shouted, and the woodland rang.

"You damned fool, you want to draw them on us, why don't you just set fire to the brush?" Gilber Livvy shouted back. He held out Shifra in her tatty blanket, his face all a-twist the way most men got when the littlest ones had fouled themselves. "Here, take her. You haven't even got rocks for brains, you dumb stead cow. Take her and you and go back to Mal, if that's what you like. But she'll be dead in less than one shabbit's coming."

Becca's eyes and mouth were cracks in drought-parched earth. She crossed the space between her and Gilber Livvy briskly, nigh snatching Shifra from him as if the child were a head of grain to be reaped. A nubbin of damp cloth in the baby's mouth fell away. Shifra let loose a wail and kicked, but the hurt foot struck Becca's hip. The babe tore the roof from the forest with her shrieks of agony.

All Becca's hard wrath flowed out of her, flooded off by the sickness in her belly when she looked at Shifra's foot by the growing light of day. The wound was ugly to begin, made uglier now by swelling all around it. Brown pus oozed up from puffy flesh too clogged and clotted over for its true color to be seen. Becca stared and stared, afraid to touch it. It looked like the smallest prod would burst it like a bubble of pond water, and the stench of rot was strong.

"She'll die." This went past the sorrow of last night's seeing. There wasn't even the hope of prayer left in Becca's voice. All she'd done, all she'd suffered for Shifra's sake, for the sake of her pa's last getting, it was all for nothing. Her plans were cut off, dry now and lifeless as the crackly pages of the old stead books with their pretty lies. Only one truth filled the world: "She'll die."

"You want that?" Gilber Livvy was at her right elbow, the green smell of him nearly strong enough to beat back the waves of corruption wrapping the babe snugger than her blanket. "You want her dead, or you want to listen to me?" His words sailed past her, the horror holding her ears and eyes. He joggled her arm; he'd *make* her hear.

"I took that child with me 'cause I figured it was the best way to make you get up and come with me—no explaining 'til later; 'til now, that is. I'd've wasted time giving you reasons, we'd still be back in Mal's camp and maybe no chance left to get away."

"Get away…" She repeated the words as if they held a power. "To where?"

"To somewhere they've got the means to help this child, that's where!" Gilber Livvy made a short, impatient sound. He'd called her a dumb stead cow in his anger, and Becca blushed to realize that, the way she was acting now, she was just proving his words were true.

She forced herself to shake off the nausea and give poor Shifra what comfort she could. Shifting the babe to her shoulder, she took a steadying breath and said, "Well, thanks. I'm sorry I was so—Just waking like that, seeing a man holding her, after what happened—"

Gilber Livvy's brown hand stroked the baby's back. "I know," he said. "Guess I could've found a subtler way to let you know what I had planned, but—All right, we're both of us fools. Now let's forget it and save our strength for this one." He offered his arms for the child, and after only a little pause, Becca gave him her sister's keeping. Shifra didn't care for the young man's soft-eyed smile and yowled worse.

"Get a fresh tit from my pack," Gilber Livvy directed, turning his back to Becca so she could reach. "Wet it down good from my water-gourd." Soon the cloth sop was stuffed into Shifra's mouth, the child happily sucking on it, pain forgotten.

"Merciful Mary," Becca breathed, all a-wonder at the sharp shift in the baby's mood. "The pain can't be too bad if a sugar-tit distracts her that easy."

"Wish it were so." Gilber lost his smile. "I dosed the tit with something good for blunting pain is all. And pain or no, she's got to be helped soon." His look pierced Becca's eyes. "Can you read maps, missy?"

Becca nibbled her lower lip. "Some."

"Never saw one in your life, did you," he stated.

"I did so!" The papers in Pa's old box rustled louder in her memory than in her pocket.

"Fine," he said in a way that let her know he'd play out the game. "There's an outer pouch to my pack, a tube inside, and in that tube there's some maps rolled up clean. They're old—steads may have changed since they were made—but if I show you where we are, can you tell me what's the closest settlement we can reach, and if they'd be friendly?"

Becca nodded. "Except Wiserways," she said. "We can't go back there."

"Lots of places we can't go back to, missy," he replied, catching up a little of his old smile. "But lots more waiting for us to see."

The maps were new, and they were old; fresh copies of charts first made Lord knew how many years ago. Becca didn't recognize the names of some of the steads picked out on the parchment. There were also regions where steads now ruled that were only dubbed territories of clan, tribe, family, pack, band. Terse words of caution warned the traveler off from certain areas, and here and there were witchy-seeming scrawls with the look of letters, but no letters Becca had ever learned.

"This mean something?" she asked Gilber Livvy, jabbing at a line of the finely drawn scribblings. They were both of them heel-sitting with their backs against close-grown saplings, the map between them, Shifra drowsing across the man's updrawn knees.

He leaned forward as much as the babe would allow and squinted at the writing. "*B'ruk atah 'doshem*— Oh, that's just a blessing the scribe put down for the traveler's sake. Goes on to ask that we be led in safety." He grinned. "Can't say I don't welcome that wish."

Becca screwed up her face and got nearer the lines. She knew her letters better than most—hadn't her own pa said the cityfolk would've been glad to have her?— but these characters must be witched somehow if Gilber Livvy could cipher them so plain and she couldn't. Those strange sounds he'd made before he told her what was writ on the map, maybe those were the spell you had to say for the letters to turn clear.

"*Brook ataaah doshem*—" she began. Nothing. The letters laughed at her, and Gilber Livvy with them.

"Ha! Not bad, missy, for a woman. But scrollspeech never was for your folk, not even the men. Don't fret over it, it's got no meaning you need to know. Look, here's where I figure us to be." He pointed at a spot on the map that lay too far for Becca's liking from the coastline with its starry string of cities. "And here's the nearest stead that I know's still standing. Mal's scuadra just misses having it inside their patrol, but I think some of the men hailed from there: Sarj and Lu, at least. They talked about it over the fire. It's maybe two days' march from here, but the second day's all across open country. I wouldn't risk it if you know something dangerous about the folk there."

Becca stared stubbornly at the mysterious letters, ignoring Gilber Livvy's patient waiting for her reply. "*Brooka tado shem…*" She *would* know what they meant! Yes, even if she had to spend all day muttering them over her tongue, she'd know. Then Shifra pushed the tit from her mouth and made a whuffly sound of pain not fully muted by drugs and dreams, and Becca forgot everything but the moment's desperate need.

"That stead, I'm not sure—Did the men say anything about it? Some detail? A story?"

"Not much." Gilber shrugged and let go his end of the map when Shifra's groping hand closed around his thumb and brought it to her mouth. "When a man joins a scuadra—a steadman, I mean—he comes because he's got nowhere else to go. Maybe he's done something, maybe there's something he refused to do, but whatever brings him to the scuadra short of abomination, that's his to bury. He's given a new way to be called—like Sarj or Corp—and only after he's run with the scuadra long enough, done something fine enough to make the leader and the men proud to call him a full brother, only then he gets a new birth and a name."

"But you didn't," Becca said, looking at him level.

"I didn't come to the scuadra to join up," he answered. "They were going my way, the way to the coast and the cities. Mal told me that the scuadras are there, always have been there since the bad times, to keep peace and ward travelers from harm. There's lots he's not sure of, but he knows that much."

"They *protect* travelers?" It was a lie big enough to rock Becca's brain to the core. "That baldfaced—! Then who was it caught any woman fool enough to leave her stead and killed her by—by—" It wouldn't bear saying. "Who turned their guns against the steads and stole our food, our babies, 'til we learned to mount guards of our own? What are the rogue bands, then—night-frights? 'Ward travellers from harm,' *ha*!" She finished with an explosion of sarcasm.

"I just know what I know of Mal's men," Gilber Livvy said slowly. "And I know that for as long as I was with them, he kept them to the rules that say their job's to keep the traveler's way open and do a bit of trading on the side, outside of the harvest fest seasons and the Coop caravans." He tilted his head back so his tousled dark hair rubbed against the equally shaggy brown treebark. "I also know that Mal's not the only leader, and his men ain't the only scuadra in this land. What the others do, how they keep to the rules or break 'em, that's where your scare-tales come from. But Mal's a good man."

"If he's so good, why'd we have to steal away from his camp like thieves?" Becca challenged.

Gilber's eyes held hers with only simple truth. "Because you're a woman."

Becca's face went hot, her stomach knotted. "So they'd've kept me their slave? And Shifra, too?"

"Oh, never that, missy." Gilber shook his head emphatically. "That wouldn't be right. They'd see you safe to anywhere you wanted to go eventually. Only things have got so bad for the scuadras that I hear there's some down to three men. Mal said so, 'time I asked. He told me how there's a place only the scuadra leaders go once every two, three years to count off and compare how it's going in their territories. Last time two of the leaders never came—their patrol lands were left open until the council ordered new leaders named from other units and given the commands. And there was some leaders told how they were on the marches with just themselves and two, three other men at most."

"So they need men, not women," Becca said.

"They need women," Gilber replied. "Women to give them new men." Numb, she heard him go on to say, "A woman alone, traveling, running away, she'd never make it anywhere alive. A life for a life, the scroll says. It's only fair. The scuadra gives you the saving of your life, you give them a life to raise to the marches. Oh, it's not bad for the woman, Mal said. She's cared for royal, and no need to—to do for the other men once it's sure she's carrying a child. And when her birthtime's near, there's at least one stead in every scuadra's patrol that'll put her up and see her through it. If it's a son, she's free to be on her way. If it's a girl, she's only got to give it one more try before they release her of the bond. It's only fair," he repeated, like he was trying to make himself believe it too.

"Scuadra's so desperate for sons, I could show them where they'd find enough and to spare," Becca said grimly. A dark hill of bones humped itself up in her mind's eye. "I could give them a harvest of sons."

Gilber squeezed his eyes shut, his dark skin suddenly pale. "I know—" He swallowed something hard and keen-edged. "I know what you mean, missy. I wish to God I didn't know. The places like that I passed when I first came from the mountain…" Breath jerked from his chest, half a groan, half a sigh. "But some scuadras won't go near such places. Holy ground, they call it. Stead business. And they're not stead."

She knew it was no use arguing the point. Gilber's useless sorrow for the lost babes matched her own equally useless anger, but what good would either do? There'd been too many years passed over the doings of stead and scuadra and city for any hope of change. *But this is how it's always been!* the worm mocked. *And always, always will be, too! And the Lord Himself couldn't voice the "No!" loud enough to blast these brain-blind creatures out of the rut of always-was-always-will, oh no!*

Becca's spirit turned from all thought of the scaudras' doings as if that were a magic powerful enough to wipe them and their cold mercies from the face of the earth. "Satan take them, then. I still need to know anything they might've let fall about this stead." Her finger poked the map nigh fierce enough to punch on through.

"Well…" Gilber Livvy considered. "They did tell one tale, when Yaysu was teasing Sarj for being so puny. Yaysu, he said he wondered they'd let something as meager as Sarj live, and Sarj came back with how on his stead being small ain't any shame. He said there was one man there no higher than a nine-year child. That was when Lu knocked him down and told him to shut up with such stories. But I never picked Sarj to have the brains to talespin at all."

"He never spun that tale," Becca said. "He was just

telling too much truth for Lu's liking. Oh, Gilber, if this map's right and we're near, let's find that stead."

"Friendly, is it?"

"Better than friendly." Becca's face was bright with joy beneath the grime. "It's home to a friend."

Chapter Twenty-Three

There was a steadman and he had no wife,
And the land wanted plowing and the land begged life.
There was a steadman and he had no child,
And the land wanted sowing and the land was wild.
There was a steadman and he found a babe.
Where did he fetch it? From out the grave.
There was a steadman and he raised that child,
And the wise didn't question and the tamed land smiled.

The silent girl who shared Weegee's house always looked ready to dart off even when she was standing still. Now she offered Becca a freshly folded pad of clean cloth, but behind the simple, helpful gesture were wiry limbs poised for flight and pale marigold eyes that danced from one possible escape route to another. Careful not to spook her, Becca took the cloth and spoke thanks, though the truth was her nerves were skinned almost raw by the silent one's quirks and cranks.

"I don't need it more now," she said. "I'm clean again. But if you don't mind, I'll pack it away for when we take up our journey. Mary Mother grant we get no hurts, but it's wise to be ready for them."

The girl bared her teeth in what should have been a smile. With that one, Becca wasn't too sure. She didn't know much of wild beasts—only what her readings gave her—but some old, hidden chord of deep recall resonated inside her when she looked at Weegee's strange, mute companion.

The two young women faced each other in the one main room of Weegee's dwelling. From the pantry came the thin, fretful wails of the baby. The silent one didn't react to the shrill sounds at all, no more than she did to any other noise.

When first Becca and Gilber had come stumbling out of the night and burst unasked over Weegee's threshold, after a long, belly-low dash across the reaped fields, the clatter of their feet onto the floorboards raised the little man from his hearthside seat but never roused the girl at all. She'd slept on, curled in her place by the fire like a dog. She only grew aware of their invasion when Weegee laid a hand to her shoulder and shook her. She'd surged up then, all right. Becca still saw the glint of the blade that flew from its sheath at her ankle to deadly readiness in her grasp. Odd sounds, low and primitive, rumbled in her throat as she faced them. Then Weegee made swift, definite hand-signs where she had to see them, and the knife sank back into its sheath, reluctantly. Her goldy eyes lost the flare of fury and hooded themselves as she bobbed her head in welcome. Becca didn't feel any welcome, though.

Watching her now, hearing Shifra's cries at the same time, Becca felt a bitter pang of loneliness. "I can't even go to her," she told the silent one. "Weegee said not to, not until he's sure the wound's healing right. He's feared that too much handling—But a babe needs touch almost more than milk, isn't that so?"

The other girl just stared at Becca with the same old, cold suspicion, as if her life depended on eternal vigilance. Her stringy yellow hair hung tousled over half her face, another barrier between them.

"I wish you could talk," Becca went on. She knew she wasted words, but Gilber and Weegee had gone off two days since—no need to tell the women why or where— and Becca had to talk to someone or break clean open with pain. "I wish you could know how much—how much I envy you. Maybe you wouldn't hold me so far off, then."

The silent one cocked her head, a dreadfully close parody of someone listening keenly, eager to hear whatever the speaker might say next. Becca supposed it was a trick Weegee had taught her, so that he could palate the illusion of having a true partner out here, in the farthest corner of Hallow Stead.

Shifra wailed louder. It wasn't just the pain of recovery now. Becca recognized the hunger note. She gestured toward the pantry, rocked an invisible infant in her empty arms, then pointed at the damp-stained front of the silent girl's cotton shift in a way that left no possibility of question. "She's hungry," she added, even knowing that words were lost.

The girl looked down, back up to meet Becca's eyes, showed her teeth in that bone-scraping way again, bobbed her head happily, and went off after the babe. She came back from the pantry with Shifra swaddled in clean blankets and seated herself in Weegee's rocking chair by the hearth. Her duty to the child gave her the right to claim the chair—the only halfway comfortable seat in the house—and in her odd, unspeaking way she was still able to let Becca know that this privilege gave her the right to lord it over her uninvited guest. The rope-lashed rocker joints moaned and groaned as she jerked open the laced neck of her shift and shimmied out of it slick as a snake shedding old skin. Her breasts were small and pale-tipped, but they did the job if Shifra's contented guzzling was any gauge.

Grief crept up Becca's skin as she watched the silent girl nurse the baby. No memory hurt her half so dear as the ache of emptiness now filling her arms. *She isn't even my babe*, Becca thought. *It shouldn't hurt so. But it does.* A perverse part of her prayed that Adonijah's damned seed had rooted in her so that she might bear a babe of her own that no one could usurp. *Getting's not birthing nor raising*, she reflected. *Even was it his child, I'd find ways to make it only mine.* But the bleeding that had so recently left her told another tale. His seed had come to her too late into her times. She knew how deep the emptiness in her ran.

And there's still the Coop to reach, she thought. *A breeding woman can't travel. It'll be months yet 'til I'm in*

my times again, and by then we might've made the city, found
Eleazar. Sad eyes sought the suckling infant, the
complacent wetnurse oblivious to all but her private joy.
If they'd only let me hold her some, it wouldn't be this bad.
But once we're all on the road to the city—

At the thought, Becca's glance fell automatically to
the babe's well-swaddled feet. *No,* she thought. *No more.*
Where once two small, strong feet had pushed and kicked
against the blankets, there was only one.

Memory opened its cold, waxy petals.

The horror of that first night at Weegee's would never
leave her. Hearthlight and lamplight softened what the
little man found when he and Gilber Livvy unwrapped
Shifra's foot, but the damage was so far gone that there
could be no softening their verdict.

"I can do it," Gilber said. "My father taught me the
way, back up the mountains. I'd've done it sooner, if I'd
had the tools"—a glance at Becca—"and with your leave,
missy, It has to be done. But I'll want the things for it to
be clean, or it's for nothing. Can you help us?"

Weegee nodded and signed to the girl. She piled more
wood on the fire, then shuffled out to fetch a big pot full
of water. Hallow Springs was famed for the coldness and
purity of its source—there were even songs of past war
for ownership of the leaping waters—but no one could
argue that, once boiled, this water would be the cleanest
any healer might desire. Still, it wasn't clean enough for
Gilber Livvy.

"You got any spirits, sir?" he asked.

"Only the dead, and none of them's been 'round to
have a chat with me lately." Weegee chuckled in the way
folks do when the work at hand grows too grim to be
borne without something snapping inside a soul. "No,

boy, I know what you're after. Out back by the chimney piece, I've got a shed standing. You'll find a jug of the raw in there."

Gilber found more besides. Becca took one look at the sawblade's ravening teeth and fled. She clung to the outside wall of the house and edged around until she was on the side that sheltered her from sight of Hallow Stead. From there she saw one small, gnarly tree. Its leaves were gone, its trunk and crumpled branches black, so that even if some wandering eye from the stead happened to spy her crouched presence beside it, she'd seem like no more than another outgrowth of the pitiful, warped bole.

Cold earth-smell filled her nostrils as she made herself part of the tree. Hunched down into a ball, she stuffed her fingers in her ears, waiting. Her own breath sounded loud in her head. *Coward!* the worm shrieked. *Shame! Come all this way for your sister's sake, then run off when there's something you might be doing in there to help her.*

Go away! she shouted back into the dark places of her self. *Be silent! I've done all I can and more. I can't bear to watch, I can't. Better I'm out here, where I don't need to see or know what he's doing to her, than in there with him depending on me when I might…I might…*

Run? the worm taunted. *Faint? You, take on the weak ways you despise in other women? Here's the girl who wanted wholeheart to be a healer like Miss Lynn! But healing's not just sweet words to fruitful wives and refreshments in the seeing-room after. Here's the fighter who thought she could face any foe with what she learned from Gram Phila's Martha! But fighting's more than floor tussles with a skinny bit of bone and meanness like that one.*

Leave me alone! The plea was a sob in her mind, but the worm was ruthless as the Lord King himself.

Esther M. Friesner

*Never alone, while you live. Never alone while you hold
the knowledge that all your courage can do is maim a man
already helpless. But when there's true heart needed, when
that babe feels the bite of the sawteeth through her flesh and
into bone, and the searing fire that comes after to seal the
wound—*

"No! No! Shifra, oh my sweet Shifra!" Becca thrust
herself to her feet and stood clear of the tree, eyes half
mad, hair flying loose. She flung herself with outstretched
arms at Weegee's house, calling her sister's name.

A small shape like a stump reared out of the night and
seized her wrists. "Back, Becca," Weegee said with that
calm, gentle strength of his. "Your man and my girl don't
need more help from us than this." He let go of her and
shoved a pair of polished redwood blocks into her hands.
She gawped at them like a wit-want.

Weegee held up the battered fiddle so she could see it
too, despite the dark. He ducked his head in the direction
of the stead. His own house, the harvest of the steadfolks'
awe of his seeing-spells, stood on a little hillock
overlooking fields and buildings below. The same
reverence his sibs felt for him was dyed with enough fear
and hate to make the little man's separation an insult as
well as a tribute, stead and other at the same time.

"They leave me to my own devices, mostly, them down
there," Weegee said. "That don't mean they wouldn't
come running if they heard a 'larm. Your man's given her
the strongest drugged sop he could brew without sending
her into a last sleeping, but she'll still feel—Well, not
too much, I hope. Not too much, Lord have mercy." He
tucked the fiddle under his bearded chin. "Down there,
they've heard my music many a night, me and the girl.
She can't hear, but she can feel it when she pounds them

blocks together, the louder the better. No one questions when we rouse all Hallow of a midnight with our caterwauls." He drew the bow experimentally over the strings and seemed satisfied with the answering note. "We give 'em what they're used to hearing, loud enough, and they won't never hear any noise your sister might make when—"

"We won't hear her either," Becca said. She stooped to kiss the little man. "I don't think I could've stood that. Mary Mother bless you, Weegee."

"She should've done it before this," was his mysterious reply. Before Becca could question him, he shouted off a count of three and dove into the music. She took up the beat on her blocks and soon all the hillside and the vale beyond was filled with the mad, wild song. Lights came on in Hallow. One or two men strode out of their dormitories to shake their fists and shout things unheard at the music-makers up on Weegee's hill, but they knew the little man didn't answer to the same laws as they, and soon they went back in to broken rest.

Becca and Weegee didn't stop or even pause until the silent girl came out to tug at his sleeve. Back in the house, Becca found Gilber seated by the fire with his face in his hands and basins of bloody water on table, chest and floor. A puckery smell hung on the air, and the scent of badly burned meat. Gilber had laid aside his fringed jacket and the shirt beneath. They lay neatly folded atop the table that was still draped with a brightly stained sheet. Watery red streaks trickled down his bare forearms, blotted in the curling black hair of his bare chest, and when he lifted his head to meet her eyes she saw his face was splotched with blood too.

"Becca…" There was misery in his gaze, but not death. It was the first time she'd heard him speak her name.

"Where is she?" she asked.

"In the pantry. We fixed up a box for her in there." His eyes showed her the half-open door. "Sleeping natural, now. Weegee even let her have his own pillow. Becca, I'm sorry, I—"

"She'll live, won't she?" The words were bitten off short and tough, like jerked meat.

"She'll live," he admitted.

"Then why be sorry? You saved my sister's life, Gilber Livvy." She went to kneel beside him where he sat and laid her hands on his knees. The fire felt hot and good on her side after the chill night air. "You must be the priest's son you call yourself, to have that much holy healing in your hands," she said, and kissed them, knuckle and palm.

For answer, he just hid his face again. "How long?" he groaned, shaking his head. "How long will she live if we ever cross paths with other folk? And when we reach the city and they see she's maimed, what good will I have done her? Your people kill babes for less than this."

He was right; she knew it, and it was her heart's breaking. Too tired for tears, the cold crept out of her marrow in spite of the fire, eating up everything but despair so that she shuddered in the dark. Warm arms fell over her and around her, the clean smell of deep woodland tainted with the tingly scent of blood and sweat's rank perfume. She circled his neck with her own arms and felt him shake out the sobs inside him. No comfort left in her, still she managed to offer him words and soothings for his sorrow.

In a dim, quiet corner of her mind the thought came:

She's not even his child, a stranger, no kin at all. Why does he weep? And an answering thought came, swollen with wonder: *I never knew there was a man could love so much.*

Somewhere faraway and near a door creaked. "Well, she's sleeping comfy, sure enough," came Weegee's chipper voice. He shook them both by the shoulder, as if to wake sleepers. "Hey, there! Never saw a trimmer job of healing done, so why the crying? My music wasn't half *that* bad."

"Oh, Weegee, what's the use?" Becca's cheek was wet with Gilber's onflowing tears. "Crippled up like she is, there's no place for her in this world. She's as good as dead!"

Weegee tugged at the end of one brown mustache and looked ready to utter another of his jollyings, when the change came over him. His eyes lost focus, seeking out a sight invisible to anyone but him. His voice softened to a vague, lilting hum. "As good as dead, you say? No. Nothing's as good as dead, nor dies forever. You should hold that knowledge in you with all your other secrets. Hold them *there.*" Becca gasped as the little man thrust a stiff hand at her belly. It hovered an inch shy of contact, then turned palm upward to float like a leaf on a rising stream.

Weegee watched his own hand rise as if it were part of another creature. Owl eyes never blinked. Becca felt Gilber tense against her with astonishment. She wondered what he'd do when this seeing ended and the little man collapsed in a thrash of masterless limbs. Practical even now, she gave the hearthside kindling bucket a glance to see if it held a stick suitable to press between the little man's jaws when the seizure hit after.

"Your job's not to talk of death, sweet Becca," Weegee

said in that distant voice. "Life's yours, and the choice of life over death, and the sword to teach them as claim they serve life when what they truly serve are lies. That babe's but the first of your saving, Becca. She'll live, live here with me in close safekeeping. What's one more mouth under this roof? I am the crooked man who gathers in the marred and maimed and misbegotten. In times to come, they'll speak of Weegee's harvest, Shifra's reaping. What she's tasted, Becca, that won't be mouthful enough for your sister when she's grown."

"Tasted…" Becca lost her breath. Weegee's seeing flung her back to the nighted hillside, made her look down again to see the grim thing that Shifra had grasped and mouthed in her hunger. Everything was bones before Becca's frozen eyes, bones of the living feasting on bones of the dead.

"Grown…oh, well-grown she'll be! And what she'll bear within her to rival you—" Laughter rattled poor little Weegee's head-heavy frame. The spasms worsened, ended as Becca had seen them end before, a thousand years ago at Harvest Home.

The little man's attack had one good effect: It snapped Gilber Livvy out of his mourning and into action. He did what he could to help Weegee ride out the seizure without doing himself any harm, throwing orders at Becca to fetch this and that as needful. Throughout it all, seeing and seizure alike, the silent girl sat by herself in a corner playing with a skein of coarse yarn, smiling her sharp-toothed smile.

After, when Weegee was better, they settled up the details. "We'll care for Shifra well. She'd have to stay with us any road," he told them. "You've a sight more traveling to do yet, I'll wager," he added, canny. "Hallow wasn't your goal."

Becca rested her right hand on the bulge in her tucked-up skirts where she still carried Pa's gun and all the old papers. "We're for the coast and the Coop city. Adonijah's got a true reckoning coming to him," she said. "If he still lives—"

"Oh, that he does." Weegee didn't look pleased to say so. "We got the news fast. I don't know what possessed you to do like that to him, girl, but word says he's still alph of Wiserways."

"Mary be praised for that." Becca spat out the blessing. "Not for his sake, but for the winnowing the children are spared."

"Amen."

"And for the sake of what the Coop city folk will do to him when I tell them how he stole their gifts, how he used them to take my pa's stead and his life by trickery!"

It all burst from her lips hot with well-banked hatred. She didn't take many words to let Gilber and Weegee know what had set her and Shifra on the coastbound road. "City justice outrules stead law. Without them and what they know, we'd still be scratching the earth with pointy sticks. No caravans from them, and our big machines'd just stand there idle in the fields, parched for fuel. Without the machines, we'd never grow half enough to feed the folk we do. Coop's always taken care of stead, and they'll take care of this matter too," Becca maintained.

"Justice…" Weegee rubbed his bearded chin. "So you'll seek your brother there, for a start?"

"Eleazar, yes."

"You'd best take the sugarbeet field road from here, then. It hits treed country soonest. And I'd steer clear of other steads from here out. A devil-woman's the nicest thing I've heard you called, and that's just by the females!"

"That figures," Becca said with a bitter little smile, thinking of Hattie.

They were all three of them seated on stools around the table. Weegee reached across to pat Becca's clasped hands. "Don't you worry about Shifra, sweetheart. I've lived long, but not so long that luck's stopped surprising me. You see that one there?" He indicated the silent girl who remained contented in her corner. "She's even got the wherewithal to feed your little sister right. Don't you, honey?"

There was no way she could hear the hail, but Weegee backed it up by stomping hard on the floorboards so the vibrations reached her. She looked up and he signed to her. She grinned and pulled down the top of her shift, scooped out a scrawny breast and squeezed it until blue-white milk ran. She had no more shame than Eve. Gilber Livvy hid his eyes from the sight.

"Weegee, where's her babe?" Becca whispered, even though she could as well have shouted the question. The silent girl was again absorbed in her yarn.

"Dead." The little man's voice quavered. His eyes rested on the silent girl, shining with too much feeling. "She wasn't born the way she is. She was the sweetest, the brightest, the prettiest thing I ever saw running across the fields. Many times I'd sit up here by my lonesome and watch her play, counting the years 'til she'd be grown and gone. I used to tell myself tales then, old tales of how the beautiful princess came to wed the ugly old troll and her love turned him straight and handsome. Old tales, old dreams…" He closed his eyes, his mouth full of thorns. "Then a sickness came and laid her low, a burning in her that almost ate her away. When it had its fill, she was skinny, scraggle-haired, and deafer than clay."

He looked down at his own hands, their soft skin too pink for a natural man. "Times are I wish they'd never spared my life just for my seeings. Lord knows what other powers I've got, and no more do I. Who's to say that I didn't pray too strong for something this evil? I wanted her for mine from the first, and after that sickness marred her—" A sigh ruffled his mustache. "They'd've winnowed her right there where she lay fighting back to life. Once they knew how it was with her, she lost all value. So I stepped in, said I could use a helpmate. Jed laughed, thought it was a good joke, gave her over to me."

The womanish hands clenched. "No power without payment. No prayer answered for free."

"Her baby…yours…" Gilber couldn't find the words for awhile.

"The Lord giveth," said Weegee, gazing once more at the girl in the corner. "The Lord King taketh away. Sometimes He don't even wait 'til they're laid in the cradle. Sometimes His sword pierces the womb. The healer didn't come 'til after the birth. I was outside to meet her. Time we came in, she was lying there quiet, the babe dead blue at the foot of the bed." Weegee's fists pounded the table until the plump pink flesh bristled with splinters, purpled with the trapped, burst blood.

The petals closed in on themselves, a cold, cut flower of memory fading away with the sunset, an iron prison of the past.

Esther M. Friesner

Shifra was still sucking hard on the silent girl's breast. Becca fetched a crooked-leg stool and drew it up so close the girl had to notice her.

"You can talk, can't you." Becca sounded like she'd made up her mind about the answer already; there was no need to make it a true question. "You were all grown when the fever came, so you could speak then. Why don't you now?"

The girl just stared at Becca over Shifra's head and leered. Her eyes were fixed on Becca's face with an unnatural intensity.

"Why don't you speak?" Becca repeated. "If you couldn't make a sound at all, I'd think that fever stole your voice, but I've heard you grunt and hoot and snarl like half Noah's ark. You've chose silence. Why?"

She got nothing back but that same unwavering stare, that wolfish grin.

Becca pushed herself back so that the little stool nearly tilted over, "What's the use? Maybe you can talk, but no way you can know what I'm asking. Mary Mother grant Weegee doesn't hold himself too man-mighty to spare an hour for Shifra while she's here. If you don't talk to a babe, how's she to learn common speech? Guess I'll make sure when Weegee comes back—"

"What d'you want me to tell her?" The voice was hoarse, nasal, the edges worn off the words. Somehow, hearing it like that, Becca wasn't at all surprised; just curious.

"You heard me?"

Again those teeth, that smile that was no smile, and a shake of the limp blond hair. "I hear nothing." Then, voiceless, she shaped her lips with exaggerated precision around the words, *But I see.*

Becca was confused, unable to read silence even when it came so carefully framed. "I know the shape of words," the girl explained. "On your lips."

"Weegee teach you?"

The girl's laugh was part bray, part shriek. "He teached me to be his *dog*! He give me his bed only when I can let him stick his thing in me. *Little* man, they call him!" The walls shook with her terrible amusement.

Becca was beginning to wish she'd never pressed the girl. "You'd be dead now, but for him," she said, though the worm inside was using its iron tongue to strike wicked little sparks. *How* proud *Hattie'd be to hear you! How right you are to defend the man against this ungrateful woman! That's my girl, my well-bred child of Wiserways!*

"I be dead anyhow, someday." The girl cast the thought aside like chaff. "When *they* say." She lifted her chin at the window that looked down on Hallow. "They choose my life, they choose my death, they choose it's all right the little man takes me, fucks me"—the word brought color flashing to Becca's face—"sticks his babe inside me." She bent her head over Shifra, and with a gaze of tenderness worthy of Mary Mother she purred, "But *I* choose his babe dies."

"You...killed it?" Becca could feel her heart trip over its old, placid beat. The girl didn't respond. Becca forced her to look up again and made her read the question from her lips. "You killed Weegee's babe?"

"You care? I won't kill this one. It's not his."

"Name of Heaven, *why?*"

The girl used one finger to gently break Shifra's suction on her left breast and switched the baby to nurse at the right before answering. "I told you. This time, I choose. Not him. Not them. When it came out of me, I choked it with the cord. So what? One more voice for me to hear. You know, night times from the hill."

Becca couldn't tell whether she was more aghast by the girl's plain-faced admission of cold murder or by the question she knew she'd have to ask, the ungiven answer she trembled to hear. "What voices? What hill?"

Honest puzzlement creased the girl's sharp features. "You don't know? The hill where they put the baby bones. Their voices. That I do hear."

"So do I." *My name…That vigil night long gone, I heard them crying, and they cried for me.*

The girl laughed in Becca's face. "Crazy! Like me. Okay, good. You won't tell about how I killed that baby, and I'll take good care of yours. That's fair. Anyway, you say I told you, they'll say you're crazy. Everyone knows I can't talk," she finished, smug.

It was the last Becca got out of her. Gilber and Weegee came back half a day later, a few hours before sunset. The little man had been scrounging them journeyfare and gear in bits and pieces from the stead stores, and any gossip that might help them pick their way more safely to the coast. Woodsborn Gilber had scouted out the start of the best path for them to take from Hallow to the sea.

"He showed me his maps and I showed him which Coop's the one that's tradebound to Wiserways, Becca," Weegee said. "You could make it in under two months' hard march."

"With luck, yes," Gilber put in.

"Luck? Want me to lend you a gourdful of mine to steer by?" Weegee winked at her, but Becca didn't like thinking of the sharp-fanged smile Weegee's "luck" wore, or the sharp-edged blade it carried, or the sharp-honed hate it cherished in its heart for all the breed of men who'd taken away every choice but the last one.

She would have left that place at once, gladly. Now more than ever she felt the imperative to reach the city, find Eleazar, make him rally the all-powerful coopfolk to follow her back to Wiserways and purge the stead of all its evil. The need to trust Shifra to the silent girl's care left her teetering over a chasm of dread. No question of taking the babe with her to the city, but what would become of her if left here?

Where else can she go? her dark self inquired slyly. *Even after Wiserways is cleansed, where in all this world can the cripple go?*

There's a place, Becca stormed back at herself stubbornly. *There must be! I just have to have time to think of it.*

I already have, said the worm, too sweetly, and let Becca see. And the black specter of Prayerful Hill haunted all her dreams until she and Gilber Livvy left Hallow far behind.

Chapter Twenty-Four

The way I hear it, the Lord told Abraham to
sacrifice his son Isaac—two sons he had, mind,
though the older one was black as midnight in a cow's
belly—and it must've been hard times then. But if a
man's got one son left him, that's fine, no matter
what color he has to be. Better that than both sons
starve if he hasn't got what to feed the two of 'em.
Sure, that makes sense. But Abraham, you know,
he wasn't a Christian man, and he said no. Stiff-
necked, that's what, thinks he knows all the answers
like they all do, them people. And the Lord—well, I
guess the Lord knew He'd have to let it go by this
time, because if He smote Abraham there wouldn't
be David, eventual, and after David no Son of Man
to be born from David's house. Or if he was, he'd

*be a black man, too, and that—well, that wouldn't
be holy. And there had to be a Son of Man, 'cause
it was prophesied. So the Lord sends them all a big,
fat sheep to eat instead. That's Scripture. You could
look it up.*

"It won't kill you," Gilber teased, holding out the leaf.

Becca sat back on her heels, regarding the jagged edges
askance. It didn't look like anything she'd ever eaten
before, back home. "What is it?" she asked, cautious.

"You think I'd poison you?" Gilber laughed. "All this
time alone with me on the road, never a hard word or an
insult to her privacy, and she still don't trust me!" he told
the trees.

Truth was, Becca didn't trust him. Casting her mind
back, she had a hard time dragging up a memory of when
there'd been a person or a notion she could trust. Things
she'd used to know as firm ground underfoot had shattered
like so much glass, leaving her walking barefoot over
clear, knifing shards that let her look down into Hell.

The city, she thought. *That's where I'll know what's so,
what's not. The coopfolk, they'll make it all right again, and
then—*

Then what? The thought shot off like a tunnel into
night. She lacked the heart to follow it to its end. Better
to turn all her thoughts to now, and to whatever piece of
trash it was that Gilber Livvy was trying to force into
her mouth.

"I just want to know what you call that." She folded
her arms in a pig-stubborn knot. "I'm tasting nothing 'til
you tell."

"You think just knowing the name of a thing makes it all right?"

"It makes it familiar, and that's enough for me."

Gilber made a great business of rolling his eyes. His teeth tore away a big hunk of the sawblade leaf and he chewed it with relish. "Lion's tooth," he said. "Dandelion greens never poisoned any man I ever knew. Back home, my mother sent us out to gather her bushels. Tasty, too, but if you want to keep gnawing at dry bread 'til the coast—"

Becca snatched the half-eaten leaf and stuffed it in her mouth. She thought she'd be tasting the throat-choking crumbs of Weegee's hard brown bread until Judgment Day. Anything to take away that taste! And anything to wipe that joshing, superior look off Gilber Livvy's face.

Anything but the bitterness that pulled her cheeks in and made her mouth overflow with water. More bitter than sin, the taste of the lion's tooth. She held her lips tight closed, her cheeks pooching out with the partways chewed mass of greenery. Gilber was biting his lip to keep from laughing. She wanted to spit it out on his boots, except the tricksy twinkle in his eye told her plain that he was counting on her doing just that.

She'd be damned to Hell before she'd give that half-man the satisfaction! One more chew and she forced the whole nasty mess into her belly.

"That's how!" Gilber patted her knee in congratulation. "Not so bad, eh? Course the leaves do taste better boiled, this time of year. Now I recall, my mother never did serve 'em up salad-raw except in spring."

Becca wiped her still-watering mouth with the back of her hand. "I'm gonna kill you, Gilber Livvy."

"Been practicing your aim with that gun, then?"

"You know I haven't."

That provoking grin of his went away sudden as a startled littlesinger. "Maybe you should," he said.

"How?" she wanted to know. "I only got so many bullets for it. Once they're gone, how can I get any more 'til we reach the city?"

"If you think they'll just hand over a box of bullets to you there…" The rest of what he said was lost in an unintelligible muttering.

Becca felt the balled-up place in her skirts where the gun now rested. "I guess I should give it to you," she said, trying not to sound as reluctant as she felt. "At least you know how to shoot so you bring something down."

"I'm already carrying one of my own, and that's enough for any man to manage. You keep it." He couldn't know how much his words cheered her. "Even if you can't use it good enough, now you know how it kicks. You could probably do better than most with it if you're defending yourself at close range."

"You think I could do that?"

"Why not? Not like you'll run yelping from the noise of a gun going off." A hint of the lost smile picked up one corner of his mouth. "I wish my mother could meet you. You've got spirit enough for her to train up for a keen fighter."

"Your *mother* trains fighters?" Becca was certain that any minute now Gilber Livvy would tell her that, where he came from, the men birthed babes. And she'd believe it, too. Whatever he was, he wasn't a natural man. These many days on the road and he still hadn't turned to her for Kiss or Sign. Either it had something to do with him being a priest's son, like he said, or there was something frightful wrong with him. She hoped that wasn't so.

"Everyone learns how to defend himself where I come from," he said. "We don't all do it with guns—precious few we got, and ammo—but once we set ourselves to living that way, none of your folk found us to be such easy pickings any more."

Becca thought she understood. "The land wars are mostly done with hereabouts. I'm sorry to know they still fight them out where you come from."

"Nobody wants our land," Gilber said. "Nobody but us cares to live off those mountains." He looked back the way they'd come. Just beyond the fringe of trees the sun was nearing the western horizon. "Guns or not, there's lots you should be learning, Becca. My mother teaches the children of the tribe so that each can live on alone if need be. If something was to happen to me, what'd you do?"

"Nothing's gonna happen to you." Becca spoke it with her old mulishness, but the fear slipped under the words and made them quake.

"What's wrong? You afraid to learn woodslore?"

Becca bristled. "I'm not afraid to learn anything!"

"Good." Gilber reached into the leather pouch at his side and spread out a handful of odd-looking vegetable orts where she could see. "You told me you studied healing, so I bet there's plenty you already know 'bout medical herbs. Trouble is, what's good for the body's outside ain't always good for the inside."

"I know about brewing tonics, too," Becca told him proudly. "Teas, tisanes…"

"You try making a meal off herb teas, you'll have a

belly full of wind." He didn't say it meanly. "Look at these here." He pointed at the leaves and stems, roots and leathery scraps of fungus. "I've been harvesting these today. Just samples, but I know where there's more of each kind, free for the eating. The way we're going, steering away from the steads, Weegee's supplies won't take us to the coast by a long measure. I know how to live off findings like these, but I'd feel better if you did, too. I'm not planning for anything to happen to me—my city business is too important to too many of my tribe back home—but just in case, just on the off chance—"

"Nothing's gonna happen to you, Gilber," Becca said again, turning it into a spell to ward off evil. "But if it'll make you feel better, lesson me."

"It'll do me more good than that, to tell you truly," he admitted. "The lands we've got to cross starting tomorrow are leaner than twine. If both of us know what's good to eat and what's not, we could glean enough from this stand to see us through to next shabbit, hold most of what Weegee gave us as emergency reserves."

When he mentioned tomorrow's march, Becca felt a chill. Gilber misunderstood her shivers as true-felt cold. He took up a long stick and prodded the small fire he'd made for their campsite. It was the last such comfort they could risk for awhile, and they both knew it. The next day's march would take them into open country, the waste places where the ravaging that had heralded the hungering times had done its worst work. The earth had given up its soul there, Gilber said. Crops wouldn't thrive in that earth, nor most of the wild growths. The land wasn't naked any more—too many years had passed for that—but what grew on the savaged soil was like lichen on a corpse.

Esther M. Friesner

A fire out in the waste places during their first few days' march would be a beacon to any steadfolk whose eyes happened to wander in that direction. After what Becca had done to Adonijah, it wouldn't pay to chance any situation that would bring her back into the power of an alph. *Devil-woman* the other females might call her where the men could hear, but who could tell what worship they gave her in their secret hearts? No alph was secure under his own roof while the telling of her deed rustled its way through the reaped fields, passed from woman to woman by the hearthsides. She had taken a choice when manlore decreed she had no right to choose, and Weegee's mad, coldheart girl had showed Becca just how far some females were willing to go to take back their choice-right, however small. She had stood up to her stead's new alph and told him *No* and put two thin, sharp, steely teeth behind that saying. She had done what many females only dreamed of doing as they labored at their tasks and bore their babes and saw those same babes taken from them at an alph's will. She had become legend.

But if you caught hold of a legend and showed the others the color its blood ran, how loud its bones could snap—

Becca gave her whole mind gladly to Gilber's lessoning. It beat thinking of what still lay between her and the city and justice.

"Well, I know what this is, any road," Becca said, picking up a button mushroom. "Katy always brought some in for our stews."

"Katy ever show you how to tell the kinds apart?" Gilber inquired.

"Oh, sure. Some are white, and some are brown, and

some are soft enough for eating raw, and some want cooking first, and some—"

"—can kill you," Gilber said, putting an end to Becca's airy recitation. "Do you know to tell the death-marks? The white gills, the little cup that grows down near the bottom of the stem, the rings growing out above?" He used his big skinning knife to whip a sharp point onto one of the fire-stoking sticks and began to draw pictures in the dirt while he spoke on. Soon Becca's head was a whirl of tips and cautions: fungi that grew on tree-bark, tough but safe to eat; stems that stained yellow or red when bruised or cut that warned the gleaner off to less fatal fare; mushrooms whose caps grew inverted into tiny cups and could be a feast or a funeral if you didn't know the telltales distinguishing one sort from the other.

"Puffball's good to eat," Gilber told her, "and hard to mistake. They're ground-growers, big and roundish and white. Some of 'em grow bigger than your head. They're fine eating, and you can even use them packed into a wound to stop the bleeding."

Becca shook her head slowly. "Too much to remember."

"And that's just the fungusses," he said. "Listen, with them it's best to stick to a kind or two you know's safe eating and pass up the rest. Not even cooking takes the poison out of the bad ones. I'll let you study the ones I brought back with me, so you'll have something to go on. And with other plants, I'll teach you how to test for wholesomeness. But you've got to go slow, and that's hard when there's an empty belly."

"You just show me what's what," Becca said, "and leave me the ruling of my own belly."

Esther M. Friesner

She'd had better teachers, but none she paid as much heed to as Gilber Livvy. As he taught her the ways to gauge the safety of wild things, he let slip more and more about how he'd come to learn this lore himself. Reaping the wild, that was how his tribe lived, mostly, and how they'd managed since the hungering times.

"They drove us off the land that was left. Some said we'd had a hand in the poisoning of it. So we took to the places no one wanted, but sometimes they followed us even there. Time was there were some of your high, holy-minded steadfolk thought that they could win back the land to fruitfulness with blood—ours. There was some stead used to send its young men out to prove themselves by going up to the mountains and stealing away our children for the sacrifice. 'Going to Moriah,' they called it, for the place where Father Abraham was turned away forever from spilling human blood to the Lord."

"I know that tale," Becca said, hearing the terrified wailings of other babes come creeping into the place in her mind that held the phantoms of Prayerful Hill. They weren't stead babies, but death marked no differences. Sand choked her throat. "They'll burn for their blasphemy, the folk of that stead."

"They did worse than burn, when we caught them," Gilber replied.

"You were there?" The frost that had fallen over Gilber Livvy's eyes gave Becca pause. The way he spoke of that ungodly stead made her think of Pa's face when he read of the Patriarchs' doings, the hard judgments in a hard age. Every word, every act of this man pulled him farther and farther from the humans Becca knew until all he needed was wings or a tail to be full alien in her eyes. "You went out with your folk to…to stop them?"

"That was long ago," he answered. "Long before even my father was born, or his father's father. No one knows how long, exact, but nearer to when the waters were at their height and the hunger—" He spat four times into the soil, cleansing his mouth of naming those accursed times.

"Anyhow, we're taught to think as if we were there in spirit, marching down out of the mountains, strong enough at last. We did what needed doing, so no other stead would ever think that we'd be easy meat. I guess it worked. You can still see the place on my maps where we marked that stead's old site, *Gihinnom*. Nothing's there now, but we've got to remember. I don't know what they called it, the folk that used to live there. Doesn't matter much, now they're all gone, and no other of your people damnfool enough to try taking up a living where those bastards used to be." He was a man stating fact, not swaying his own deeds to meet another's judgment of right and wrong. "They killed our babies until we said *no more*. My folk don't care to wait for your god to get 'round to punishing sinners."

He looked westward, where the mountains stood and where the sun was slowly sloping down to set. "Look at the time." He seemed relieved to change the subject. "Not much light left, and shabbit coming on. Tell you what, Becca, you take what you learned and go a ways into these trees, see what you can find. I've some preparations to make, but then I'll check over what you find and see how well you've learned gleaning the wilds." He tossed her a square of carefully hemmed cloth from his pack and bid her to use it for a gathering basket.

Becca did as she was told, her mind too taken up with all the things Gilber had taught her about free-growing forage to bother asking him what he meant by this shabbit-thing he'd mentioned times before this. Always it left her puzzled, but always some other business had come up to keep her from asking its meaning. Whatever it was, it wasn't as important as the task ahead. She was bound and determined to show her friend that she'd snapped up all his lessonings well. She resolved to bring back a cloth full of good eating, with not a morsel among them he could pick out as poison.

It wasn't all that hard. This year the weather after Harvest Home had turned colder than anyone remembered. Becca recalled hearing the women talking over how the chill seemed to get deeper into the land with each passing year. They even asked Gram Phila to confirm their own limited observations, and the stead crone launched into a rambling tale of how in her girlhood there wasn't even any season you could honestly call cold.

Let the seasons turn as they would, chill weather yielded a bumper crop of wild berries. Even Becca knew these must be good to eat by signs of littlesinger feasting at the bushes. To these she added some tree-growing fungi and more of those lion's teeth she found growing where the trees thinned. There were nuts, too—the funny-looking acorns with their tiny caps, fallen from the same tree from which she'd gleaned the fungi. Gilber had said they were good eating, only not raw. She grew so sure of her gleaner's eye that she even risked adding some ground-growing mushrooms that she checked with care for death-sign before adding them to her trove.

The sun was nearly gone by the time she headed back to camp. She'd marked her way—another lesson Gilber had given her—and didn't even need the telltale of woodsmoke and firelight to see her home.

Then she heard the voices.

A tree cast up its friendly bulk to give her cover as she strained to hear who'd come into their camp unasked. There were just four of them, but four faces she'd never wanted to see again: Lu and Sarj, Corp and Mal, all of them carrying long guns. Gilber's own weapon lay farther from the fire than Becca remembered, propped up against a tree with her friend's big knife and three smaller blades she'd never seen before this. A length of rope ran around the base of the tree in a carelessly knotted loop that served no visible purpose. The scuadra leader was running a hand through his own prickly hair and telling Gilber very softly how they were going to kill him.

Gilber knelt in their midst and heard the older man out with a face too placid to conceal a reasoning mind. All Mal's talk was of betrayal, and bond-breaking, and thievery. For each there was a punishment the scuadra's justice assigned, none pretty. Fire and knives had uses on human flesh Becca'd never dreamed, and Mal spoke of how the soft tissues of the eye held more potential for obscene, lingering destruction than a feeling man could hear out without begging mercy.

But Gilber never flinched. The dusk had come on into the scanty woodland, kept at bay by the beggarly flicker of their fire and the golden, steady glow of two stubby white candles laid out before him in blue clay cups.

"I said I'd repay," he told Mal in calm, measured tones. His brown cheeks were flushed. A third blue-glazed cup rested between the candles, and beside that a small drinking skin that was as much news to Becca as the three little knives by the roped off tree. "Both for my passage, as far as I went with you, and for hers."

"And the babe's?" skinny Sarj blurted.

"Who cares about the babe? That stinkfoot pup's dead by now. Talk when you're told." Mal slapped the boy's face as if the act were an afterthought. "You don't mark me at all, Gilber Livvy," he said with a sigh. "You served my scuadra well enough while you shared our march to pay for yourself and a full gaggle of females. But it's not for me to change scuadra rule. The full complement sets the passage pay-rate, and they liked that little girl so fine they—Hell, they had so damned much to say 'bout her going, that's why I'm here with this crew to fetch her again, even if it is outside our assigned marches."

"I thought you were the leader, Mal," Gilber said. "Not errand runner for your men."

The scar-lines on Mal's face went some whiter. "I lead, but my men know they've something to say before they follow. When a female comes to us for shielding, we've the right to try bringing new blood into our ranks through her. A proper grateful woman sees it as right. That girl you stole off'd be hurt to the bone if we didn't let her show us her thankfulness for all we've done for her."

Gilber still wore that smooth, serene smile. "Ever run across an *im*proper woman?"

Corp let out a bellow and bashed Gilber's cheek with the butt of his gun. The woodsbred man splayed sideways in the dirt, landing on the little drinking skin. The stopper burst out; dark, pungent fluid squirted into the fire with a great sizzle and flare. Mal pivoted and drove his fist into Corp's gut. "You fucking steadworm!" he shouted while the man doubled over, choking. "You wait for an order or I'll give you something sharper than that in your belly!"

Gilber pushed himself up slowly and spat a broken tooth. There was a lot of blood in his mouth and more flowing from the split open wound Corp's rifle butt had gouged him on the cheek. "I spoke without thinking, Mal," he managed to say, though his lips were already thickening and the blood made him spit again. "I'll ask your pardon for it."

Mal scowled. "I don't remember you being this womanish, Gilber Livvy. When you first joined with us and Yaysu caught a look at you pants down and said what he said, you laid him out skinned for the stewpot. Corp broke order; you know I'd never raise a hand to stop you if you went for him yourself, yet there you lie. I know you've got more strength than that in you, and more gumption. This smells funny. What're you up to?"

"Nothing," Gilber replied. "I swear by Almighty God and His bride."

"That vow from *you*? Hunh! Live long enough, hear it all. But play sly with me and you won't hear much more."

Gilber sat up and reached out to reseal his gutted drinking skin. He shook it and looked rueful at the scanty amount of liquid it still held. "If you want a fight out of me, come by tomorrow. This is peacetime. You can kill me if that's God's will, or you can take whatever goods I've got as payback for the two girls' going, but you won't make me break shabbit. I'm a priest's son."

"You're meat," Mal said without passion. "We don't need your say-so to find the girl, you know. I was reading trail since before your mother fucked every beard in your godless tribe."

Gilber tensed so that Becca could almost see the muscles in him coiling for a spring at Mal's throat. With a great effort, he turned the potential for a killing, dying leap into the shudder of exhaled breath.

Mal went on: "We'll find her on our own, and it don't look like you'll be doing much to stop us taking back what's ours."

Becca knelt behind her tree and scuttled back, away from the campsite, into the full dark of the grove. The bullets she poured into her hand rattled too loudly for her liking, but she worked with a cold, swift skill that surprised herself. This second time the loading of her gun went somewhat slicker. "It kicks," she muttered. "Remember it kicks *up*. And get close to them or it won't be any use; *close*, curse them."

She heard Mal ordering Sarj to try his luck reading her trail. The skinny boy made more racket passing among the trees than four Beccas. He carried a knot of burning wood to light his way, his eyes fixed on the ground.

"Steadworm," Becca pronounced with scorn for her ears alone, and knew that whatever she was now, being *stead* no longer touched any part of her. She held her gun with two hands and slipped back campwards.

Oh, how the worm crowed to see Corp jump when a woods shadow sprouted the silvery barrel of a gun that jabbed between the man's ribs! Her one-handed grip on the butt was sure enough, at pointblank, for her to use her other hand to nab his shaggy hair and jerk his head back. *First you have to get his attention.* The tail end of an old joke she'd overheard Pa telling his cronies at Harvest Home tweaked her mind, though damned if she knew what all the laughter was about.

Then Corp quavered, "Oh, Mal…" and she had to choke down her own uproaring laughter as his rifle fell into the dirt.

"Let us be," she told them. "Go your ways."

Mal turned. If he'd ever beheld a spectacle like this before in all his years as scuadra leader, he never let on. "I can't do that, miz," he said. "The other men are back in camp, waiting for me to fetch you."

"Let them wait. Tell them you couldn't find us."

"Miz, that'd be a lie." Mal regarded her with sober disapproval. "I can't betray my brothers."

"Then tell them any side of the truth you like, but get out! I can do for this man and you, too." *Pray God I can*, she thought. *He's close enough…Up! Remember to allow for it kicking up.* "And him"—she tossed her head at pock-faced Lu—"and the fool you sent after me."

"I don't doubt so." Mal rubbed his chin. "Lord have mercy, I *have* seen all there is to see, now. What kind of creature are you? Not a woman."

"Not anything that cares what you call me," Becca shot back. "I know what I am, and that'll do for me."

"That so." Mal considered matters, then concluded, "I don't guess I'd be doing my men any favor, bringing a whelp of your blood into the scuadra. We'd never be able to tell was it male or female, that's sure. That's not worth losing a man for, even a nothing steadworm like Corp. Dumb pinwick, letting a woman sneak up on you that way." Mal said it free of anger, but Corp cringed. "Fine, we'll go. You must be clear crazy, and Gilber Livvy's crazier still to want truck with a misbirth like you. Though who knows where his like draws the line on what they fuck anyhow."

The scuadra leader whistled shrilly between his teeth.

Becca heard the crunching, pounding sound of Sarj galloping back obediently at his master's summons. The boy broke into the firelight panting. It took a beat or two before he saw how things stood, and then his eyes looked ready to pop from their sockets.

"Wha—?" he gasped.

"Shut up," Mal said. "Use your eyes to some good. You too, Lu. Know her face. She's out of our territory now, but if you ever see her in our march again, don't stand on law: Do her how you want, any way you want, how often. She don't want to be treated like a proper woman, we'll oblige."

"I'll remember that," Becca responded, using all she had to keep the words even. "And I'll remember your faces, too. Now get them out of my sight. I'll let this man of yours go free soon as you're a hundred count gone. And don't you come back!"

"For what?" Mal wanted to know. "For *you?*" Laughing, he led his men off, back the westward way they'd come.

Becca was true to her word, praying all the while that Mal would be true to his. She counted out a hundred, then told Corp he could go. He stooped for his fallen rifle, but she planted her foot on the barrel and made him acquainted with the bitter-smelling nose of her handgun. "That stays," she said. He hovered so long she could count the beads of sweat on his forehead before he finally made up his mind she was earnest and sprinted away after his comrades.

Becca sank down in a puddle of skirts beside Corp's rifle. She let her gun fall into her lap and pulled back her damp hair hard, relishing the relief of a cool evening breeze. "Holy Mary, I can't believe that's done."

"You were something, Becca," Gilber said, face a melting shine of admiration. "Just…something glorious."

"*I* was something?" She was too tightly wound to know what to do with the leftover surgings of pent strength within her. Lashing out was easiest. "And what in the Lord's own name were *you*? Mary's mercy, Mal was right: What's got into your skin to let you sit there and take the half of what they said to you?"

With a rueful smile, Gilber asked, "Don't suppose it had anything to do with how there was four of 'em?"

Becca clapped her hands to her knees. "Don't give me that story! Four, fine, you'd be an idiot to fight them, but not even a man's *word* to kick back in their teeth? And you heard Mal: He'd never have stepped in if you'd taken Corp down. I want some truth."

"Do you." He didn't ask it.

"Yes, I do! Four of them, you say, and three of that four so bad at woodslore that I bet even *I* could've heard them coming."

Gilber chuckled. "That Sarj does make a racket. He'd best improve his skills soon, or Mal's going to—"

"*Gilber Livvy!*"

It stopped being funny for him. "All right, Becca. You're no fool. You know I could hear 'em coming. Any other day, I'd've taken my blades and my rifle with me into the shadows and met them halfway. Mal's the only one would've given me trouble, and I think I'd still be his match. But not this day. It's shabbit. I'd kindled light, poured out the wine, made them blessed. See there?" He motioned at the tree where rifle and knives stood waiting. "Inside that circle means outside of my life for this one day of peace. If I touched them, it'd be the losing of me, everything I was born to. Like I said, I'm a priest's son, and shabbit peace, she's my bride."

"What kind of priest talks so—?"

"A priest of Israel."

"Oh, my Lord." Becca's spine froze, her eyes fixed on a creature beyond lore, all awful legend. "You're a Jew."

Chapter Twenty-Five

Blessed is the Lord, the God of Israel, who has made me a shield of life.

That first shabbit Becca spent with Gilber Livvy was like sitting in a prickle bush. After she got over the initial horror of what he was, she kept an eye peeled for him trying any of the ungodly tricks his folk were known for. It didn't signify that they'd been traveling in company for nigh over two weeks: This shabbit-thing of his was holy time, and lore taught that Jews had the power to pass for real folk except when their holy times came on them.

What counted for holy with them, that is.

It gave her the twinge. First, he almost let their fire go out, even though he was nearest the pile of brushwood. Only when she saw he had no intention of perking up the blaze did she take over that task. Next, he had a full-blown fit when her trailing skirt brushed too close to his fubsy candles and she said they were a danger so she'd blow them out.

"You try watching your step instead," he told her, teeth grinding together. "Leave the lights in peace." Shabbit was supposed to keep him from every business but peace, yet his face had some remarkably eloquent expressions to let her know that there'd be her skin to pay tomorrow if she didn't mind him today. She was too frighted already to object.

She tried reclaiming the comradely air that had been between them before this by showing him her gleanings and asking him to teach her more. He told her lessoning was work, and work wasn't something his shabbit-bride would have this day. "She wants me to herself," he grinned.

"She can have you," Becca grumbled.

There was no question of a cooked meal that night, either. Becca might not know Gilber's new bride on a first-name basis, but shabbit said cooking was labor and Gilber ruled out her labor as well as his own. He picked over the scant portions of her woodland harvest that could be eaten raw and divided them, adding a couple of hunks of the dust-dry stead bread. There was water to drink, though not much. Becca had used most of it for the cleansing of Gilber's battered face, and he refused to go in search of more.

"Tomorrow at sundown," he promised. "Can't go across

the waste without water. I've got some spare skins in my kit, and there's watersign to the northeast."

"We're to lose a whole day?" Becca shrilled.

"It's shabbit," he replied, and that answered that.

Gilber's bride might bring him peace, but she brought Becca sheerest misery. Though Gilber wrapped himself up in his blankets and slept soundly, she couldn't close an eye for fear the fire would go out or the strange shabbit creature would come up with a new command for Gilber to run berserk and call it holy. Next day came in a silvery dawn, touching the trees with beauty, but Becca crawled out to meet it draggled and fierce.

A night without sleep peeled her down to no other feeling but bone meanness. In the early hours of cold dew she'd watched his untroubled sleep, and envy turned her fear to simmering anger. She was just waiting for him to say one word out of place to her and she'd lift that brown head of his clean off his shoulders.

Gilber refused to oblige. He woke, stretched, tucked away his gear, and began chanting more of those outlandish sounds. On and on he went; it was the longest Becca'd heard him run the flow of that gibberish. He pulled a finger-wide strip of white cloth trimmed with knotted blue threads out of his pack and hung it from his neck at one point. Doing that provoked him to louder caterwauls, and no thought to folk who were dangerously weary and more than ready for breakfast.

Breakfast: There wasn't any. The leftover gleanings were only acorns and some fungi too tough to eat raw. The acorns had to be prepared a certain way before you could eat them, but such instruction was sure to come under the heading of lessoning, and that was forbidden. Becca delved into Gilber's pack without a by-your-leave, silently daring him to bar her audacity. He rocked back and forth, singing in a way so no human could fathom the words, and paid her no mind.

It's like he really did have a new bride in his arms, Becca marveled, observing the look of quiet joy that spread wider and wider over Gilber's broad face the longer he sang and chanted. *He's gone away with her and left me behind.* The thought left her feeling small. The piece of stale bread she pulled from the pack tasted ashier than before, and she lost heart for further pryings.

Eventually, Gilber ceased his carryings-on and went into the woods, with no word to spare for Becca. Misgiving seized her. For all she knew, the witchy chants he'd been prattling were a Jew-spell to lure the shabbit into solid womanly form. He'd go and find his bride, and when he did he'd forget all about Becca.

She stole after him because she was too flustered with lack of sleep and hunger to recall one simple cause for a man taking himself off solitary that way. She didn't know how good she was at letting go of all her common sense until she heard the thin, pattering sound on treebark and nearly stumbled into him as he was finishing up his business.

"Oh, *Lord!*" She slapped her own mouth closed two words too late. She just couldn't look away from what was so plain to see. And so very, very different from the wood-carved lessoning aids the women used to coach the maidens back at Wiserways.

"You!" Gilber gasped and whirled from her, hands flying to do up his breeches. For a time it looked as if Becca had found the magic key to lock away all Gilber's shabbitlore and open his mouth to the rippingest, fieriest, most air-charring speech ever uttered by man. Then he took a real deep breath, let it out, did another the same, and said, "When the sun goes down, Becca."

She drooped her head, boiling with shame. He stalked past her like she was stone. Soon she heard him take up his old tune beside the smoking embers of the fire.

The day spun out its hours. Near noon he stopped long enough to mete out portions of their stores for a light meal. This time there was a skinny slice off a brownish, greasy, unidentifiable slab for each of them. "'Traveler's bar,' Weegee called it," Gilber explained. "He couldn't spare us much, so we'll save what we can, but it *is* shabbit. Hallow's famed for this stuff; a little bit'll carry you a long way down your road. The city merchants take in trade as much as his folk care to produce."

Becca dutifully rolled her first bite around in her mouth without making up her mind about the stuff. "It must be good then, I guess." She couldn't get too much sincerity into that saying. It tasted awful. Maybe coopfolk didn't know everything after all. "Did Weegee make this lot himself?"

"Making traveler's bar isn't man's work. He just helped get us some while I was gone."

"Gone?" This was news.

"You know. Those two, maybe it was three days we left you and Shifra in Weegee's house with that queer, quiet girl. I'm sorry for it, Becca, but I had to get off somewhere I could greet my bride without fear someone would find me. Weegee said that while I was away might be the best time for him to raid the stead stores for us."

"So that's where—" More and more things about Gilber Livvy started sliding into place.

He went back to his chanting and didn't leave off until the sun dipped low. In the first increeping shadows, he took off the fringed strip of cloth and tucked it away. Dusk darkened, and he rummaged down to the very bottom of his pack for a little wooden box. It was lined with finest suede leather, the kind that seduced the eyes with promises of how soft it would feel to the touch. Three layered trays nested within. From the bottom one he took out a tiny, glimmery egg of pierced silver and shook it. Dry stuff rattled inside. Gilber pressed it to his nose and inhaled deeply, contentedly, then offered it to Becca. She sniffed it with caution, as if expecting an infant viper to dart out of one of the holes. All she got was a breath of fading spice.

A candle like a woman's plait also lay cradled in that bottom tray. Gilber lit it, tilted his face skywards, and sang a new song beyond Becca's power to grasp. When he was done, he snuffed the light; silver egg and braided candle went back into the the bottom tray. On top of them went a compartment a third full of those plain, squat candles. Last of all, he fitted the three blue cups into their molded niches in the uppermost tray and latched the box.

"Well, she's gone," he said to Becca, leaning back on his heels.

"Who is?"

"The bride, of course!" He shook his head over her thickness, the way Katy'd done when one of the children failed to get a long-taught lesson. His rifle and knives were retrieved from the tree, the blades stowed at belt and in boot, the gun placed within easy reach, the loop of rope coiled tight and bundled into the pack. The wooden box followed. Very seriously, he added, "I hope you're a quicker study than that. By next shabbit, the kindling of the lights'll be your worry."

"Mine? Oh, no." She put up her hands to push the notion far from her. "That's none of my concern. I'm a Christian woman."

"I know." Gilber sounded glum. "That'll make the lessoning all the harder." He took flint and steel from his belt and made them a new fire to chase the night. By the dancing flames, Becca saw him say, straightfaced, "It's not unheard of. Father Abraham took Hagar the Egyptian when Sarah couldn't bear. Joseph himself took an Egyptian woman, too. You're not Egyptian, but I don't guess that matters. It's the thought that counts. It won't be so much of a come-down, and there's no need for my mother to hear—"

"What are you talking about?" Becca demanded.

"Our spousals," he answered, as if her query came as a surprise to him. "We're to be wed."

"*Are you crazy?*" Visions of Gilber's unnatural manhood wouldn't leave Becca be. The thought of what he was suggesting, and all the meanings it carried along with it, set her nerves shrieking. "Me, marry you?"

"I don't like it much either, but there's no help for it." Gilber went on about the business of getting a sparing meal together while he spoke. "You steadfolk get raised on Scripture, so you ought to know. You uncovered my nakedness, Becca. That's one deed both your folk and mine teach is a sin. Isn't that so?"

She had to admit it. If not called upon to render Kiss or Sign, a woman must respect a man's most secret parts; to do otherwise was yearning after whorish doings. Gilber spoke the truth of things. When she nodded agreement with him, her head felt heavy enough to snap right off her neck.

"I thought as much," Gilber said, satisfied to be in the

right. "You're in trouble deep enough without adding to your lot by living with that sin, so I'm willing to make the sacrifice, for your sake."

"Your nakedness...Oh, Lord."

"You said that before." Gilber passed her a portion of bread and some dried apples. A chunk of bricky cheese came out of its wrappings to be sliced and shared, too.

"But how can we? I mean, don't your folk have some rite to make a marriage? Us, we go to Grange, but I can't go near any such settlement." For the first time, that knowledge was a comfort.

Gilber shrugged. "All my people have to do is have the man say *haray at mikoodeshtli bita*. How does it go, again? *Bitabat*, I think, *zokid—zokid—*Well, I do recall the gist of the words, and I don't need to say 'em exactly, nor in scrollspeech for it to count."

"Oh, I think you really do have to say them exactly, Gilber," Becca said hastily. "It might get your god mad, else."

"What do you know about my god?" he returned. "What do you know about my people, for that matter?"

"I've heard—" She stopped. She owed Gilber Livvy too much to tell him all she'd heard about Jews back home on Wiserways. "Not much," she finished lamely.

"I'll bet." He ate his dinner all gone before noticing her untouched share. "You'd better eat, Becca. I mean to marry you this night, and I wouldn't want to have you come into my tribe on an empty stomach. It ruins the meat. Go on; the cheese is pretty tasty."

She ignored the cheese, even when he took her portion and ate it himself. "Ruins...the...meat?" Her hands drifted toward her gun.

Gilber was quicker. He had her hands fast between his

and pressed them to his heart. "Oh, Becca, sweet Becca, I swear I'll make you a good husband!" His eyes rolled and the words came lush with too much feeling. "Every breath I take, I'll say your name. When I lay you down, I'll be gentle. Arise, arise my love and come away, for the winter is gone, the rain is past, the flowers appear on the earth"—one hand let go just long enough to grab the gun from her lap and fling it away—"and I promise I'll bury everything I don't eat!"

The full-throat scream that started deep in Becca's gut was nothing but a whimper when it came out.

"Why, sweetheart, what's wrong?" Gilber chucked her under the chin. "You look so shocked. I swear, don't these steadfolk teach you *anything* about us Jews? I thought it was common knowledge that when we wed a Christian, we always eat 'em up the very next day."

"Just...raw?" Becca peeped.

"Raw?" Gilber was insulted. "That wouldn't be civilized." It would have been as convincing a saying as all that went before if he hadn't lost the last of it to a snicker that became a chuckle that ripped out of his control into freeheart laughter.

Unbridled hilarity shook him like a dishrag, sent him rolling on the ground next to Becca. He drummed his heels dangerously close to the fire, whooping to bring down the stars.

If Becca's expression could put on fur, Gilber Livvy would've had his liver and lights yanked out of him by a bear the size of Verity Grange. Her eyes couldn't hurt him, but they were handy for spotting a likely bunch of leftover brushwood by the fire.

"Oh, oh, *oh!*" Gilber gasped for breath between the gusts of laughter. He had to hold his ribs to keep them whole. "If you could've seen the look on your face! *'Raw?'* she asks! Heaven's pity, you swallowed it whole! You thought *I* was gonna swallow *you* whole, too, I bet. Oh, just let me live long enough to tell this one to the tribe and I'll—OW!"

"You *bastard!*" Becca brought the switch down across Gilber's shoulders again. "You miserable, gut-stuffing, stink-breath meal for a half-starved scurrier!" She took another swing at him, but he rolled aside rapidly and sprang to his feet, still laughing. Taunting her with his eyes, he leaped easily just out of range of her wide, swashing blows. "Stand still, you cursed coward!" she screeched.

"For what?" he riposted, side-stepping her accompanying swipe gracefully. "I learn from past mistakes, I do. That *hurt*, little wifey. I don't guess I'll be eating you all up after all." Another swing of the switch, another teasing evasion. "Your meat's probably just as tough as your pretty white hide."

Becca lost all ability to namecall. Her whole rage plunged down into her belly and came streaming out in one ear-blasting, tendon-straining, inarticulate roar as she charged Gilber Livvy for the kill.

He gave a little hop out of her path, then stuck out one foot and stomped it down on her skirts as she careened by. The cloth went taut and Becca went tumbling over in a squawking tangle, twigs scattering. Gilber threw himself down next to her, pinning her arms with his own, holding down her vicously thrashing legs with his body. "Now what other crackpanned stories can I make you believe about us?" he asked.

"You...you..." Becca bucked and twisted, too riled to call on all the fighting tricks she'd learned from Gram

Phila's Martha. Her seething bubbled itself out by degrees. Anger was a grand way to cover the uncomfortable sensation of knowing you'd been a fool, but it wasn't the sort of anger that could last. When she stopped struggling, he let her sit up right away. "I'm sorry," she said low, chin down and hair obscuring her face.

He managed to hear her. "That's all right. I don't blame you for what you were taught—mistaught—but I will hold you to account for any stupid ideas you make up about me on your own."

She pushed most of the blond curtain out of her face and looked at him sidelong through the wisps. "So I don't have to be your wife?"

"Or my dinner. Ah-ah-ah!" He held up a finger to stay the fist he saw her making. "No more joking about that, I promise."

"Gilber…" What she had to ask was hard. "I'm sorry I uncovered your—I'm sorry I intruded. Does it—? When you were cut, did it—? Is it—? Are you in pain from it still?"

"Pain, me? From—?" He caught her meaning and had a hard time holding to his recent promise. "Becca, that was done to me when I was barely one shabbit in this world. It don't hurt at all now, and it don't make me less of a man."

"Is that why you didn't come to me the way the others did?" This was no easy asking either, but she longed to know.

Gilber nodded. "I suspected how you'd act if you saw. There was enough troubling your mind, what with all you'd come through and the baby sick and all. And the other men. I couldn't vision putting you through more that night." Past laughter might have never been. "Not even as much as I would've liked to—"

She put her arms around his neck and laid her cheek to his. There was a rough, blue-black stubble that raked her skin. He'd scraped his whiskers off last before the shabbit, but she didn't mind the roughness. That sweet, piercing scent of green woodland was strongest at his nape. She let her fingers trace the cords of muscle that ran from behind his ears, down his neck, following the trail inside the opening of his shirt across the collarbone.

"Becca…" There was longing in that whisper, and pain.

"Hush." She unlaced his leather tunic and helped him pull it off. Her hands slipped up underneath the coarse cloth shirt to stroke his chest, the balls of her work-worn fingers making ever closing circles around his nipples. When they went hard, he moaned and siezed her.

"Behold," he gasped. "Behold, you are consecrated to me according to the laws of Moses and Israel." To her they were just words, but to him they were a sign that he could respond to her burning touch with touchings of his own. He released her from her clothing like a man unveiling the statue of his goddess. When she tried to serve him as was a proper grateful woman's duty, he held her off. Always before she had been the giver or the taken-from. Now his every caress was itself a gift offered up to her shyly, reverently, without any certainty that she would accept it.

All the words, the proper words she had been so thoroughly lessoned to say, deserted her. His mouth tasted of warm bread. Her hands hovered over the still freshly split skin of his cheek, fearful to give him pain, aching to hold his mouth to hers forever. His hands wandered elsewhere, cupping her breasts with care, his thumbs tracing over the rosy peaks until all Adonijah's harsh assault melted from memory before the rising heat he conjured from her soul. When his hands strayed lower still, she balked.

"I won't hurt you," he breathed into the richness of her hair. "By all I hold true and holy, I swear I'll only please you, my sweet love."

She let him have his way, and gasped with surprise that quickly turned to wonder at the magic his hands wrought. Flint and steel, sparks that caught inside her and smoldered, a wink of fire that crackled up from her core and spread, racing eagerly from belly to blood to brain until her whole world rocked with joy so that she couldn't keep silent, no, not without her self flying apart into a million stars. She thought her cry would shake folks from their beds at steads a mile and more away, but she couldn't help it.

After, she could hardly find her voice at all.

"What—?" The word felt like no more than a shape her lips formed. She rested her hand on his chest and lifted her eyes to him for answers. "What—?"

"Ssshhh. It's all right. It's righter than you know." He kissed her again, and then his kisses followed the same path his hands had marked before. This time her fears were far more quickly stifled as she gave herself up willingly to him. Fresh shudderings shook her, left her trembling and spent in his arms.

"Let me go." She tried to push away from him. Even in the warm haze robing her, the voice of duty, propriety, what was owed, a woman's debt of gratitude, all these would not let her rest. "I have to—"

He pulled her back down gently. "You have to sleep," he said, and she obeyed.

There was new loving with the dawn. His kindling touch woke her, and only latterly did she become aware that he had pulled the blankets around them both into a coccoon that itched her naked skin. Pretty soon, though, she forgot all small discomforts as he proved to her that last night's doings weren't dream or miracle.

"I wish…I wish I was in my times," she murmured.

"Why?"

"Because, for the first time, I don't think I'd be dreading it." She sighed. "I know we can't, though. Mostly there's a babe for that, and we've a long way to travel yet."

"A babe…" His voice grew dreamy. "A healthy little one. Wouldn't that be the way for me to come home again, with a healthy baby in my arms."

Becca frowned, not sure she liked what she was hearing. "What do you mean?"

"Just talking about what'll be after."

"After what?"

"Why, after we've reached the city, I mean, and I get what I'm going there for." He shifted so that she could nestle closer, but in the light of these strange new sayings from Gilber she stayed stiff, attentive. "We need their help," he said. "My tribe, most of the others. None of the elders will admit it—they say the only thing they can be sure of getting from your folk is death—but here's one thing we can't face on our own any more. It's touched the children."

Little bones haunted Becca's eyes. "They're sick? Badly sick?"

"Born sick, some; some are born dead, and the living

often—" The words choked him. "The living often would be better off if they'd never survived, may I be forgiven."

"Why?" His anguish drew her deeper into his arms, desiring only to ease him. "What's wrong with them? I know herblore. I could go back to the mountains with you and help. You wouldn't have to waste any more time reaching the city."

"And your own need to reach the coast, sweet Becca?" he asked mildly.

"That can wait." She got the old, headstrong look back. "Shifra's safe enough, and how long could the trip possibly take? If there's babies hurting—"

His embrace tightened until she lost some breath. "You're a wonder. Ready to risk yourself all the way back to the mountains when every stead between here and there is alerted against you, but for the sake of the children—I wish your heart were enough to heal them. If it were herblore alone could do it, I'd still be home. It's gone past that, Becca; we need the citylore."

It was a hard tale he told her of how his tribe had fled into the mountains like the others, ages since, each keeping to a portion of the ungenerous land and keeping to itself. Given time, and the starveling living to be gotten in the mountains, the tribes drifted farther from each other, some even falling out of ken altogether.

As for those that remained...

"There aren't many of us, Becca," Gilber said. "There never were, and the distances are too great for us to have much meeting between our tribes. So the families keep to themselves, don't know hardly anybody out-kin. I've been studying the scrolls, asking myself if we've broken some law that tells us to go out and join with the others more, not leave them to their own portions of the wilderness. I can't find it, and I can't find a word to justify why so many of our babes are born lacking, sometimes in body, sometimes mind. My own cousin's almost of an age to join the congregation, but he never will. Can't talk more than a few words, and the rest are grunts and snufflings."

"How old's that?" Becca asked.

"Almost thirteen. And lately there's more and more like him being born to us. They know things in the cities. I hear they know enough so that all their children are born alive and whole and shining. Maybe they'll find the pity to share out just that scrap of knowledge with me, so I can take it home. If they do, my cousin will be the last."

"This cousin, he's thirteen and lackwit? When did it show?"

"Show? Why, from the time ordinary babies leave the cradle, I hear. Poor Yeshua."

"But if that's so, then when your folk first knew how he was, why didn't they—?"

"Kill him?" Gilber snapped. "Like yours?" That stung her, and he saw it. "Sorry, love. You're not to blame for ways you were taught. We don't take lives that don't threaten our own."

"But doesn't he eat?"

"Yeshua, eat?" Gilber guffawed. "Like a forest fire. No good at tending to his hunger himself, either; he just sits there in front of his mother's tent and bangs two rocks together when he's peckish until someone gives him to eat."

"No work from him, and you feed him; no mind, and your people let him live…" Becca mulled this over long and long. "Gilber, if your folk let every babe of theirs live, no matter if each one's as useless as your cousin, you'll starve off the mountainside!"

"So we would've long ago," he agreed, "if we bred like you. We know what our land will support, year to year, and we choose when a wedded couple can try conceiving a child according to that. If it's born dead, they're free to try again; if it's one like Yeshua…" He shrugged. "They don't live that long, as a rule, and they're sweet-tempered souls. They're life. We've chosen life."

Becca thought about the men and striplings back at Wiserways and tried to figure them waiting for some sort of tribal approval before they took a woman in her times. No matter how she turned it, it wouldn't work, and she said so.

"I think I liked it better when you had us pegged for cannibals," Gilber responded when she told him her thoughts. "Beats the clay out being called a saint! A man and a woman together do what they've always done, and when she's in her times there's ways to enjoy all the sweetness without chancing a birth."

"What ways?" Becca perked her ears. Here was something.

But Gilber told her never to mind. "From what I know of steadfolk, you'd call me a worse monster than before if I explained."

"Well, I know you're not a natural man already," Becca teased.

"And how do you come to that?"

"A natural man would let a woman show him some thanks, as is proper!"

Gilber stretched his lean, strong limbs and arched his

back luxuriously. "Far be it from me to stand in the way of propriety."

"Good," said Becca, and tended to her business until neither one of them needed to recall any worry but bringing each other joy.

Chapter Twenty-Six

Little girl, little girl, tell me where you're going.
Out to dance by the pale moonlight.
Little girl, little girl, do you have a lover?
No sir, no sir, it wouldn't be right.
Little girl, little girl, shall I show you magic?
Do as you like, sir; this country's free.
Little girl, little girl, I'll make you a woman.
Bless you and thank you, and dance with me!

Part of Becca's heart wanted the wastelands to go on forever, the part that clung to Gilber so jealously that the thought of sharing him with any of the world again was torment. Part of her heart that still cleaved to sense wished the barren places were crossed and done with and had never been.

Gilber called it sacred ground. Becca couldn't see what was so sacred about land parched of all usefulness. Everywhere she looked, the earth was a woeful parody of the green fields of Wiserways. All that Becca knew of bounty was tied to memories of the stead. Sometimes she had found old pictures in Katy's books of farmlands that made Wiserways' yield seem paltry and hardscrabble, but next to the crisped and impoverished wastelands Wiserways was Eden. Even the sun overhead seemed niggardly with its light in these godforsaken regions, and the chill northern wind guttered out to puffs of cold across the plain.

There were ruins in the waste, spindly remnants that Gilber said had once been settlements. Each time they neared one, Becca thought that maybe it would be like a preparation for what she'd find in the Coop city. She dreaded coming there cold, with no idea of what awaited her or how she'd find Eleazar, or even if they'd let her in at all. Some hint of what a city was like, that was all she wanted. She didn't get it from the lonely ruins of the wasteland.

"Stripped above, stripped below," she muttered as they trekked past yet another of the relics. They gave them all wide berth. Lore taught that those sorry sites had nothing left to give, and from what Becca could tell at this distance, lore taught true. "Someone came and gnawed that place clean."

"Lots of someones," Gilber said, not looking back. That was how he'd treated all the lost places they'd passed, averting his eyes. Becca didn't need telling that the Scripture tale of Lot's wife burned brightest in his mind out here among more shattered cities of the plain than any man of Sodom ever visioned. "I hear that when the hunger came"—he spat repeatedly at his own mention of it—"the great settlements and the small first thought they could survive on what they had. But there were fires, I hear, and fighting to seize more than any one man's fair share of the stores still left. Folks pillaged anything to survive; what they couldn't use themselves to eat, they coveted as trade goods to buy them food. It was like ants picking a bone. We were animals, worse than animals."

"I know." The abominations of that time were kept painted fresh in all good stead children's minds, the illuminating brush dipped in the memory of human blood.

"Most of them went back to the land eventually, I hear," Gilber said. "When the settlements couldn't support them any more, when they'd sucked out the last crumb of food, the last drop of fuel, the last scrap of anything usable, they ran away."

"Isn't there anything left?" Becca asked a little wistfully. She paused to shield her eyes and gaze at the crumpled remnants of towers on the northern horizon.

"Nothing."

"Hard to believe. Maybe if our road takes us nearer to the next one, we could try—"

"I wouldn't." Gilber's mind was made up. "The folk who didn't flee the cities for their lives stayed and lived off the ruins how they could. Some say they bred down small—those that still could breed—and their eyes turned red as coals, and their hands shriveled up into claws, and their ears grew big with always listening, listening, listening for the sound of footsteps after them. Their teeth grew long and sharp for tearing flesh and gnawing out burrows beneath the ruins, and if any strangers dared to pass the night in their territory, they'd swarm all over him in a black cloud and devour him alive."

Esther M. Friesner

"You forgot the part about tails," Becca said dryly.

"What?"

"The part where they all grew long, naked, pink tails. Or don't you think I know what a rat looks like? The women set me to killing enough of them when I was small."

Gilber winked at her. "Should've known better, trying to scare you with kiddie stories. I'm just looking for an excuse to get you to snuggle nearer to me tonight."

"Like you ever needed an excuse!" They walked on.

The waste was wide and, for the most part, desolate. There were about three major roads that crossed it in this region, trade routes used seasonally by some of the Coop city caravans. Broad, well-marked, fairly level and beaten smooth by years of use, the roads strictly avoided the skeletons of the old settlements. Occasionally, when Becca and Gilber crested any slight elevation in the terrain, they could see one of those roads, a yellow scar across the dead brown and gray. For themselves, they steered a middle course between trade route and ruins, only stealing down to meet the road where there was a water source noted on Becca's map. They would be weeks crossing the waste; they couldn't carry enough water, and toward the end they knew they might find themselves short of food.

"We should take the main road to the coast; it's swifter going, and we'll have supplies to spare when we get there," Becca pleaded when Gilber first decreed their manner of travel. "So what if we run into other travelers? Even if they know I'm wanted, the coopfolk won't care what I've done."

"Coopfolk and steadfolk help each other," he replied. "If not, why bother going to the city for your justice? And why assume the coopfolk wouldn't be as ready to help their chosen stead get justice too?"

"Turn me over to them at Wiserways?" Becca was appalled. "They wouldn't! Not for defending myself, not for standing up to a liar and a cheat who stole my pa's place. He broke the law, not me!"

"But he's still alive," Gilber said evenly. "His hand might've been the one to send word to the other steads about you. What guarantee do you have that he told the truth? How do you know the crimes he accused you of, except at a guess? If ordinary coopfolk catch you, his lies might've poisoned their minds so deep that they'll just march you back home for judgment, and you can holler that you want to see your brother until the end of days."

She saw his point, much as she wished it weren't so likely. They went on, avoiding the roads when they could, avoiding the ruins always. By night they wrapped themselves in the same blankets and clung close for warmth. Even if Gilber hadn't been feared that a fire would attract notice from far away, there was nothing growing on the wasteland that would burn.

Yet Becca dreamed of life in the desert. The worm slept in her, had slept so since Gilber had come to her in love. There was nothing for it to hate, to snap at, no target for its bitter venom. And once that hard, cynical voice of herself was stilled, it was amazing how many other voices of the wilderness she could hear. When they camped one night less than a quarter-day's march from a well, she heard the chirrings and the rustlings in the low, rugged growths of the plain. The moon was nearing full, and it silvered over the lost land until it looked almost beautiful.

Becca rolled away from Gilber and laid her cheek to

the earth. Was it singing? Even here, where the destruction of ages gone had done so much to tear out the heart and soul of the land, was there still a hope of someday coaxing it back to full life? Her own name ran beneath the soil like a hidden stream, rushing on, bubbling with promises, bidding her follow, hinting of seeds that slept until someone might learn the secret spell to wake them to fruitfulness.

It was a pretty fancy, spying out the earth's old song, but there were other sounds as well that were no illusion. In the silence, the littlesingers' chorus sounded loud, and the patter of tiny feet beneath the thatchy ground cover made Becca's sleep turn guarded. Small did not mean harmless, not in a place where a sleeping traveler might be easy nibbling to something close kin to Gilber's storybook rat-people. Any bites she or he got could turn foul, even if they were little wounds to start. Again Shifra's puffed-up foot loomed before her eyes. She couldn't chance it. And yet, though awareness of the small rustlers stole some of her rest, in her heart she blessed the stubbornness that let life triumph even here, where only death seemed to reign.

It was worse when they camped in sight of the ruins. Nothing sang in that soil, and all that bustled through the shadows were Becca's nightmares.

"There might be some living beings near the wells," Gilber admitted, "but there's nothing near the settlements to lure anything alive. Used to be beasts haunted the place—true beasts, Becca, I'm not telling fool stories now. Either they starved for lack of prey or else they died when humans hunted them."

"Hard to imagine a place so lifeless," Becca said, looking at the far moonshadows of the jag-toothed ruins.

"Eaten, all," Gilber said. "Down to the smallest thing that hands could catch, eaten. When the desperation gets so great that all that counts is *now*, you won't find many folks with control enough to leave some poor creature alive to breed more for tomorrow. Then tomorrow comes."

That was why, when the hushed sound of something crackling over the wasteland growth touched Becca's ears one night and no well was near, she knew they were in danger.

"Gilber, wake up." She grabbed the arm he'd thrown over her and squeezed hard, her voice muted, urgent.

"Go back to sleep, Becca," he muttered. "You're dreaming. There's nothing for leagues around—" Then the rock came down on the side of his skull.

Becca screamed and pulled herself upright. Backlit by the moon, the skinny form looming over her was human, but faceless. Becca clutched the blankets to her, feeling Gilber's limp body roll away, knowing the stickiness matting the whip-stitched hem between her fingers was his blood. Her gun lay wrapped in her dayclothes, an arm's length from where they slept. Gilber's rifle was already in the hands of this unknown attacker. He didn't handle it with Gilber's long-taught expertise, but he seemed enough at home with it to pick her off without a thought if she made any lunge for her own gun. Fool's heroics would be a leap to meet her death. Becca could only sit, and shiver, and force her inmost heart to hold off asking whether Gilber was dead.

The rifle barrel leveled off between her breasts. "Stand up."

She knew the voice, though reason tried to deny it. "C—Corp?"

"Don't call me that no more! That's that scuadra shit; I'm through with it. I've got my own name back, and I didn't need that old cocksucker Mal to give it to me, either! Now you get to your feet, woman; sharp, when a man tells you!"

Trembling, Becca obeyed. This was a different man from the shy, fearful thing she'd had to coax into her bed to receive the Sign. All his tenderness, his soft-eyed, womanish gratitude for her attentions were gone, as if the barren land had gobbled it up, drinking his soul down after. How long had he been on their trail? In her mind's eye, she saw him crawling after them on his belly, taking what cover he could by flattening himself to the soil, holing up in the lee of the low hills. If there'd be light, she wagered she'd see that he'd rubbed his clothes with dirt enough to avoid detection at a distance. It helped that she and Gilber weren't expecting pursuit, fools that they'd been. It helped better that Gilber refused to look back whenever they passed one of the ruins. He'd paid high as Lot's wife for the niceties of his precious Scripture-learning.

The night air was cool against her bare skin, but another chill ran deeper into her flesh. In that crystalline cold, Gram Phila's Martha was a frosty phantom, dodging and ducking, pirouetting and rolling through the steps of all the fighting moves she and Becca had shared.

But I can't! her thoughts wailed.

But you will. The worm stirred sluggishly and hissed in her ear, *And it will be sweet to do. Only let him put down the gun...*

She knew truth when it faced her. Yes, it would be sweet to use what she knew on this man. Ordering things so that she could give him twice the surprise he'd given

Gilber—(*No, don't think of Gilber that way now!*)—well, that might take some doing. First he had to believe she feared him more than she truly did. Feigning that was easy. The anxiety gnawing at her for Gilber's sake, the bleak not-knowing if he still lived, these channeled themselves up from the pit of her stomach and made every word she uttered a shivery mew.

"What do you—what do you want? Why—?"

"Shut up! I'll give you something to shout, soon enough. I was thrown out of the scuadra because of you, bitch. Any other sin but that and he'd've overlooked it, Mal said: Letting a woman best me. Stinking bugger. I'll give him those words back to eat, show him who paid most in the long run." He gestured with the rifle to a strip of ground that lay between the campsite and the ruins. "Over there. Lie down."

Becca made as if to take a blanket with her, but the rifle barrel jerked up and smacked her jaw hard enough to make her teeth clack. "Awww, thinking to keep us snug? Real nice. Leave it."

She had no more choices. If she bolted, he would shoot her down. Even if he were as poor a shot as she, and she escaped, where would she go? Gilber might yet breathe, but not any more if she left Corp free to finish him. After making sure of Gilber's death, he was strong enough to carry away everything in the camp. Naked and alone, no maps to guide her, she wouldn't survive to reach either border of the waste. And if she made the trade road? There was word out from the steads to take her, like Gilber'd said.

No choices.

She walked the way he'd commanded until a new command told her to stop. "Far enough. This'll do. Get down." She felt the harsh growths of the barrens scrape and scratch her bare buttocks and shoulders and the backs of her legs. Her hair was all a-tangle in the turf. She lay like one awaiting burial, ankles and knees pressed tight, but she left her arms straight at her sides. What was the use of modesty here and now? A sour joke. Overhead, the stars laughed at her.

Corp echoed the tinny sound. She noticed he had a laugh like the most thin-nerved of her younger sibs, a nervous maiden giggle kin to madness. "That's good," he said, nodding approval as he stood splay-legged above her. The crooked bones of an ancient settlement poked out the silhouette of shadowy horns behind his head, and two tumbled walls formed the peaks of his black wings. He flung Gilber's rifle far, far from him, farther than she could hope to scramble even if he hadn't flashed out that big-bladed hunting knife and set it to her throat in the same move that dropped him hard atop her body. In the time it took her to think of lashing up at his crotch with her feet, it was too late. His weight on her stomach pushed the breath from her, and the steel bit cold, smelling still of leather sheathing.

He was breathing hard. "Now I'll tell you how it'll be, bitch," he said. He leaned forward, squatting on her like a nightmare. His feet pinned her hands to her sides. "I'm going to kill you one way or another, that's given. In your times, are you?" She rolled her eyes and shook her head as much as she could without daring the kiss of the knife. "No? That's too bad. Because I'm going to have you anyhow, like an alph takes his wives. And if you're tight, I'll tear you open, and when you bleed you'd better pray you bleed enough to die before I'm done, because there's one last thing I'm going to do for you before I go."

When his free hand grabbed her there, she winced so sharply she nearly did his throat-cutting work for him. "You won't be needing this when I'm done," he told her, teeth hideous in a leer keen as the skinning-knife in his hand. "Mal wanted it so bad, I think I'll take it back and give it to him. Throw it right in his face, yeah! Then let him say a woman bested me!"

"You do that," she said, daring a whisper, "and he'll kill you."

"The hell he will. You heard him. You're not a woman any more, after what you did. It's only real women a man's born to protect. You're a freak! Your sire should've left you out to die soon as you were born. It's late in the day, but I'll see to it for him." He shifted himself, but the knife moved less than an inch along her neck; he was nimble. Now he overlay her, and she heard the sound of his free hand tearing open trouser lacings. "Start praying that you bleed," he whispered, and thrust himself in.

Her cry was pain, but not the tearing pain she'd thought to feel. Surprise, mostly, and coupled with a grunt of equal shock from him. "You lying cunt, you said you weren't in your ti—!"

She seized his shock the same way she seized the wrist that held the knife to her throat and bit down, hard. He screamed, his fingers flying open automatically. The knife fell against her neck, just the flat of the blade, and slid away. She felt it slip to the earth beside her. Her mouth was coppery with his blood, her teeth aching from where they'd hit bone, but her mind was clear. Gram Phila's Martha loomed up behind the gasping, whimpering man, her eyes blazing more brightly than the stars, shouting out the one lesson above all others a woman had to learn if she meant to fight at all: Fight any way you can, but fight to win!

Becca grabbed the knife and jabbed up, into the little niche of flesh just above the collarbone. The blade met gristle, but even one-hand she had the strength to push it home. It went in about a third of the blade's length before it lodged firm. Corp made a horrible gurgling, choking sound and slumped over her. His blood flowed over the hilt of the knife still clenched tight in her hand, staining her breasts scarlet.

Now Becca shoved and wriggled her way out from under him, using feet and hands to push the dead man from her. In her hurry, she dislodged the skinning knife. Blood flowed free from his torn throat, flooded her hand when she stooped to retrieve the blade. She stared at her dripping fingers and, for no rational cause at all, she began to weep.

"What you cryin' for, stupid? Didn't you want him dead?"

Becca's head jerked up at the words, the piping voice that uttered them.

In the lee of the ruins, the child stood leaning on a broke-handled hoe, watching her calmly out of old, empty eyes.

Chapter Twenty-Seven

Jacob went his way and met the angels of God.

"She don't know how old she is," the boy said, "so you can stop askin' her."

Becca looked up from her latest patient, a mop-headed little girl with tawny hair. The child had only a superficial scrape—natural enough, given where and how she lived—but she'd come to the "strange heal-lady" anyhow, as much for a little kindness as for the cleaning of her hurt.

"I was just making talk," Becca told him.

"What for?"

"She's shy; it'll set her at ease. You mind?"

The boy shrugged. It was of no importance to him. Precious little was, as Becca had already learned in the two days they'd spent here. He shifted his skinny hams on the cement outcropping and continued to scan the plains for movement, life, anything that might require him to attack or filch or flee. He took his responsibilities seriously, no one knew that better than Becca. What he asked in return was to be let alone. She could understand that very well. Being left alone was what suited her more than anything, these days.

"There, honey, that's all," she told the little girl. She patted the light brown curls and stood to stretch all the sit-down kinks from her neck and back. The child watched her, owl-eyed, then scooted off into one of the thousand nooks and crannies of the ruin.

Becca's heart ached after her. This place was a honeycomb of small spaces, cells closed off from the light. Children shouldn't have to live like this, going to earth for shelter like the little things of the waste. Yet what were they but larger kin to those small rustlers in the starveling soil? No one knew they were alive save Becca, and no one cared.

"Any more coming?" Becca called up to the boy on watch.

"Dunno," he replied, never taking his eyes from the dangerous *out there*. "I guess they'd be here if they was gonna come at all." He had a grown-up man's way of making Becca's every question sound small and stupid. "You wanna go tend your man, go 'head. Virgie'll get you when it's eating time."

"Who's Virgie?"

"The one I'll send t' fetch you, course." He gave a half-swallowed laugh at the woman's dumb questions and spat with the wind.

Becca rinsed her hands one last time in the basin of

water balanced on the block beside her. Her cleanly nature shuddered at how she'd been forced to use and re-use the same basinful to wash off between patients, but when she'd treated her first and asked the boy for fresh, he'd told he straight out that there wasn't any to spare. True or not, she was too deep in his debt to disbelieve him. She'd resigned herself to making do, figuring that children living out here had stood up to worse things and survived.

Worse things, oh yes.

She dried her hands on her skirt because every available scrap of cloth had gone for bandages. The box of herbs was Gilber's, its stock carefully eyed, arranged, and closed away safe before she headed into the deep ruins where he lay waiting.

She could come and go as she liked—the boy had made that clear from the start. He was all of twelve years old, but here he was king of tumbled stone, shattered glass, dry fountain. All of the other children Becca had seen so far were smaller than he and likely younger. She had counted nine or ten—they moved so quickly and were of such uniform raggedyness that an exact count was hard to get. How many were boys, how many girls was guesswork, except when they sat still long enough for her to tend them. Even then, it was hard to tell. They wore what clothes there were with no distinction between what suited male or female. So long as they covered their shame, they were content. As far as Becca was concerned, none of them had names for her to call them by yet, not even their young lord, except the mysterious Virgie. Down to the smallest they gave away nothing but silence.

This whole place seemed to burgeon with silence. Though no one dwelled for leagues around—no one to hear little ones' laughter and bring trouble on their heads—still the children kept quiet as the dead. Becca could almost feel the tug of the silence on her, a bottomless hole lurking somewhere deep inside the ruins that sucked the spark from anything alive. If there'd been other shelter, she never would've let the boy help her bear Gilber so far into that unwholesome place.

The entrance to the deep ruins scared her. Too many thoughts of Prayerful Hill's hungry maw flitted out of the dark, gliding on silent wings through her soul. It was like going to view Gilber in his tomb. She paused, laying her hand against pink stone smooth as glass, and called back to the boy, "Could someone take me to him?"

Ancient eyes never left their shepherding of the horizon. "I had Tee mark you the way. There's a slicky to show you where the trailwire starts. Lay your hand on and follow."

"What's a 'slicky'?"

Another laugh that was more like choking. "You don't know nothing, do you? *Woman.*" In his mouth, it was a worse insult than all the foulness Corp had spewed.

He didn't offer her any more help than that. In his eyes, he owed her less than nothing. Until Gilber was fit again, Becca couldn't say a word. She was the stranger here, with no idea of what had moved this alien child to show himself to her after she'd killed Corp, to offer her help with Gilber, to find shelter and food for them both. For that matter, she had no way of knowing if a whim mightn't make this uncanny boy suddenly do to Gilber what she'd done to Corp.

Or to you, come to that, said the worm.

She went into the dark. It wasn't so bad once she

passed the portal. The roof of this place hadn't held
entire—what could, untouched, unmaintained, after all
these ages?—and so there were small drifts and spears of
natural light ahead to help her. She found the "slicky":
A bright red piece of some alien material like nothing
her fingers ever knew, shiny like it'd been polished metal,
flexible as cloth, slippery to the touch. The scrap was no
bigger than her thumb but distinctive enough to be an
unmistakable marker for the start of the path that would
lead her back to Gilber's burrow.

It was attached to what the boy had called
"trailwire"— not anything so precious as real wire, but a
strand of many remnants of cloth and string and the
tough stalks of unnamed things that grew in the
wasteland, all braided, tied, and somehow stuck together
to make one long, continuous cord. It wasn't good for
anything but this, to be a guide in the labyrinth. Becca
had seen trailwires here before, likely for the benefit of
the smallest children who might otherwise wander lost
inside.

She followed the trailwire without touching it, relying
on what tag ends of light could guide her eyes. They had
carried Gilber far into the bowels of the ruin, whether
for his own sake or at the boy-king's pleasure she couldn't
tell.

They had carried Corp elsewhere.

Memory came easy in the dark; too easy. Becca hadn't
slept for remembering how they'd come at her out of the
night, swarming around their leader like meeker cousins
to the rat-folk of Gilber's scare-tale. Little hands had
pawed the dead, turning the bleeding body over and over,
rolling it like a log until six of them got a grip on Corp's

clothes and hauled him away. The rest scattered, leaving Becca and the boy with his hoe to shoulder Gilber along after. He didn't give her time to throw on a piece of clothing, just laid hold of Gilber with one hand and hauled. She'd had to hasten to his aid naked as she was or risk seeing Gilber die from such rough handling.

Shards cut Becca's bare feet that first time she'd dared the ruins, but her mind was elsewhere. The way in was a blur of blackness, small shapes darting through the dark, whispers of burning light like vagrant stars to let her see her way, tiny torches borne in the hands of children.

The boy directed her to a certain chamber. Cupped in a rusted metal holder, a twist of cloth burned in a lump of foul-smelling fat. There was something like a low table, only made of thin strips of metal and panels of glass, some broken, most miraculously whole. The true miracle, to Becca's eyes, was what else she found awaiting her in there on the tabletop: the contents of the camp, down to the last portable item. Gilber's rifle stood propped in a corner next to the one they'd taken from Corp, her own revolver lay waiting for inspection atop her perfectly folded clothes. Only the big skinning-knife was missing.

The boy only gave her a stiff, funless grin when she questioned him with a look. "We don't take from them who're hurting. But if you try to hurt us, you'll see."

It was a peculiar warning, and one Becca had no wish to test. The floor beside the glass table had been swept clear of debris, one of the blankets folded in half the long way for ground cover, the others neatly stacked nearby. With the boy's help, she laid out Gilber there, wrapping him warm. She dressed herself with speed, then saw to tending him. He was breathing shallowly, quickly, the wound on his head still bleeding. She rummaged through his pack until she found the herb box, a knife, a spare shirt she could cut up for dressings. The boy observed all her procedings with distant interest, but when she asked for water he sprang swiftly from the room and came back with a handleless pailful.

The water was filthy; Becca couldn't use it. "Oh, you want *soup* water!" the boy exclaimed, making it sound like she'd been the one at fault. He lugged off the pail and came back soon after carrying a pot of boiling water that still steamed. This time she saw that he carried Corp's knife at his belt. It seemed he'd watched the doings between her and Corp long enough to gauge that it wasn't her blade; taking from the dead was no theft.

She cleansed Gilber's hurt and bandaged it. He was breathing more naturally when she was done. She had found some bulbs of garlic in his healer's box and juiced them, to keep the wound clean the way she'd learned. The pungent fumes clung to her hands, so she washed them off in the cooling water and tossed the pressed bulbs in too before the boy carried it away.

He came back later to bid her come eat. Gilber slept peacefully, so she went lightheart. The boy conducted her through knife-straight corridors, each more or less obstructed with fallen rubble, until they reached a kind of great courtyard where the domed ceiling was nigh wholly intact. Here, in the heart of the ruins, a lone girl of about ten minded a simmering cauldron.

Becca wrinkled up her nose at the reek of the fire. "What do you find to stoke it with out here?" she asked the boy. "There's no trees."

"Shit," he answered. "Mix our shit with some of what

grows on the flat and it burns good enough. Someone'll bring you a pot for yours and your man's, you do it in there, piss where you like." He produced a black metal bowl—not made to be a bowl when it was new, but turned to this use now. When the boy shoved it into her hands, Becca studied and studied it but couldn't figure out what it had once been. There was a patched-over place at the bottom and a twinkling crumb of glass still clung to the rim. She plucked that away.

"Go on," the boy said. "Take enough for your man, too, if he'll eat."

Becca approached the young cook hesitantly. The bubbling pot threw off a savory smell almost strong enough to cover the stench of the dung fire beneath. Pot and ladle looked as if they at least had been born to their current function. Stead goods? Trade goods stolen from some passing caravan? Becca couldn't tell.

But she could tell right enough what simmered in the pot. No one had ever taught this young cook to cut up her meat small for the stewing. Pictures in the old books never prepared her for how those inner parts of a man would look when swimming in broth. Liver and lights bobbed and tumbled lazily around in the froth. The tang of garlic from her old wash-water, likely dumped in the stew with as little ceremony as Corp's innards, was bracing enough to help her rule her heaving belly. The girl looked up at her quizzically, ladle poised, wondering what was wrong.

Becca backed off. Behind her, she heard the boy chuckling. "You're missing a treat," he said as he took back the bowl. "We haven't had a meal this good in—"

"Are you eldest?" Becca demanded, bile in her throat.

"I'm alph; that's better."

"Then why—why are you letting this happen? To them, to the children, this—abomination?"

Again the shrug, the dead eyes meeting hers. "We're hungry. On my stead we don't put the kids out to starve."

"Your stead? Where's your stead?"

"Here, dummy. Where'd you think?" His hands spread to encompass the ruins. Small forms detached themselves from the darkness by ones and twos. They crept up to the cook's place, holding out salvaged bowls of many shapes, many hues. As soon as each was filled, the children dashed back to haven.

"Don't call me dummy," Becca said, seething. Her anger meant as little to him as the moon.

"Call you what I like. An alph gets respect on his own stead; his word's law. You owe me that."

"How do you figure that?"

"Because I let you live." He said it as if it was the plainest truth in the world. "When that man was fucking you, I could've snuck up behind, killed the pair of you with my hoe. Could've killed your man, too, if I wanted. He'd'a been easy pickings."

"Why didn't you, then?" Becca snapped. "No place to smoke that much meat?"

The boy showed his teeth, uttered a clattering laugh. "Hey, I like you. You do got spark. Smoke the meat… hmmm…" He scratched his mare's nest of black hair thoughtfully.

"Listen, they mustn't eat that." Becca laid a hand on his arm and did her best to coax some realization of sin into the boy. "Gilber and I, we've got some supplies. We can share, and when we reach the city we'll send someone back here to help you."

"The city…" He rolled the words around on his tongue like they were sweets. "You can't get into the city. Inside, they got food enough to last them forever, places where there's nothing but good things to eat, plenty to wear, magic gardens where you don't gotta break the stones outta the soil to put in seed. Hell, not even soil—their crops grow on air."

His mouth hardened up. Twelve years old, maybe, and already there were deep lines cutting gullys down the corners of his lips. "No children there. Best place in all the world, and they want to keep it that way. They don't want us, they won't help us. It's only grown folk they aid, the city people. Only grown folk from the steads got anything the city folk want to have; kids got nothing, only mouths to feed. They'd come here, all right; come and make us tell where we come from, name the old steads. They'd take us back, then, 'cause we was bad and we run away instead of letting them kill us when our old alphs—"

Becca tried to touch him with comfort; he pulled back from her hand like a spooked cat. "Child—"

"Don't call me that, woman! I *ain't* a child! I'm alph here. I feed my folk and I keep the females from harm like I'm s'posed, and when they're old enough to be fruitful women I'll have wives and babies, and when it's my time to step down I'll just go away into the waste and the one who comes after me is *never* gonna kill my babies, *never* make 'em run, never, never, *never*!" He was gulping for air, shaking in every limb. There was a grievous weight of weeping in him; he'd die before he'd shed a tear of it.

"Honey, honey, all right, be still, don't fret, please!" Becca still tried to take the boy into her arms the way she'd soothe one of her younger sibs, but it was like groping after wind, raking your hands through water. He jerked his scrawny body out of reach.

"You mind what you call me, woman!" he shouted. The echoes under the dome threw his shattered voice down a dozen corridors. "You mind what's your proper place, else I'll lesson you good!"

His panicky shrieks were like iron nails pounded into her ears. All his threats were air; she could break him in two with a few of the fighting tricks Gram Phila's Martha'd taught her. He'd done nothing at all to stop her from fetching along her gun or one of the rifles and putting him down like the wild dogs she'd read of. For all she knew, he'd welcome the peace of death.

He was a child crying alone in the dark of Prayerful Hill, and his back was bent with carrying the bones of so many others.

"I ask your pardon." Becca bowed her head. "Forgive me, please. You're alph here; my sin for forgetting my place. You've given us help and shelter, and it'd be evil payment if we didn't respect your wishes. Mary Mother be my witness, I won't say a word to a soul about you when we reach the city."

The boy gentled little by little, though it took time before the wildfire fear in his eyes died out entire. "Okay," he said, throat working. "That's fine. Now, you don't want to share our supper, you can go."

He whistled up one of the smaller children to guide her back to Gilber's chamber. It looked like a girl, but not for certain. The only sure thing about the child was the shirt it wore: bloodied over, blackening, the collar gashed, a part of Corp's last gift to babes he never knew he'd sustain so well. Mal would've been proud.

The tale of Becca's grim memories reached an ending

Esther M. Friesner

just as the trailwire brought her back to Gilber's room. He was sitting up, checking over his rifle. He beamed when he saw her.

"How's our little angels?" he asked. Ever since she'd told him what had happened out on the plain—once he'd come back to himself sufficiently for talk, of course—that was how he'd spoken of the children.

She managed a weak smile. *Angels*... "Well enough. Lord be thanked, not much ails them."

"One of them came by while you were looking after the rest. She left us a pail of fresh water hauled all the way from the nearest well."

Becca clicked her tongue. "That's a far ways for a child to haul water."

"Oh, this one was pretty well grown, almost of an age with our host. Not too much meat on her bones, but strong, wiry, black as Sheba's queen. She'd be a beauty if she could eat regular." He never noticed how Becca shrank when he spoke of such things. "They haven't been here that long, none of 'em."

"How do you know?"

"Virgie told me."

"So that's Virgie..."

"Yep. She and the most of 'em hail from Sacrament Stead. Their father was the leader there until about three months ago. Virgie said he'd been ailing awhile. Everyone on stead could see the change coming, and knew what to expect."

"The winnowing."

Gilber looked at her sharply. "I can't call it that, Becca. Babies slaughtered, and your folk talking of it like it was no more than casting off the chaff from the grain."

"It's just a word."

"When you can talk of horrors too easy, it's too easy afterwards to do worse atrocities."

Becca knew he was right, even if she didn't know how to say so. She came to kneel beside him and examine his wound. "How's the head?" She got some more garlic bulbs from the herb box and pounded out the juice on a piece of broken tile before undoing his dressing.

"All ri—OW! Careful, love—all right. I was lucky."

"I'll say so. Hit you with that rock a little closer to the eye and you'd be— Don't squirm! I'm not getting my hands in a stink just to have you wriggle away from what you need done."

"Yes, missy," Gilber said with just the right note of contrite obedience guaranteed to vex her. For reward he got the garlic juice applied with a heavy hand. His stubbornness was her match. Rather than give her the satisfaction of crying her mercy, he talked his way over any temptation to yip or yowl at her rough nursing.

"I've been—aaahh—thinking, Becca…"

"News to me," she grunted, dabbing on more of the juice. "What about?"

"These children. They can't live like this, not for long. The growing season's done, and it's getting colder than it's been in *yeeee!*—years. Virgie said that the caravans from the coast don't really start running regular again 'til spring; they're too far ow—ow—*out* in the wilds to steal from the steads."

Becca paused. "That what she told you they've been living on? Things they stole?"

"She said the boy who saved you—Mark's his name—he came here before they did, from another stead; he won't say which one. When his father was killed, he ran here with three of his sisters. She says he used to run away from home regular, come here all the time. When he saw how his father wasn't going to survive the next challenge, he started taking things from the stead stores and hiding them in these ruins. It was a march of several days each way, but he was smart enough to bring some seeds and some solid tools."

Becca shriveled up inside, remembering how Mark had spoken of using one of those tools, talked of putting the hoe blade to cold-blooded murder as easily as if he spoke of splitting stony ground instead of human skulls. She made herself go on dressing Gilber's hurt. "Seeds, hmm?" she managed to remark. "Out here where nothing'll grow?"

"There's places in this maze where the floor's cracked away and you can dig up deep earth that isn't as tainted as the barrens outside. Lots of big tiled spaces here with knee-high fences around them, too. I don't know what they were ever for, but Virgie says there's little nubs of metal sticking out of their centers with holes pierced like the nozzle of a watering can. They stand under places where the roof fell, so the sun gets in. He and his sisters filled them with soil that'd bear something and farmed them."

"How long they been here for seeds to grow and bear?"

"His stead had cold flats, Becca, to get the jump on planting time. When he figured his father's time was close, he made four packs full of seedlings, all wrapped up well. I guess they're what's bearing for the children until the other plantings are ready. Good thing they had all that here, Virgie and her kin showing up the way they did."

"They bring anything?" Becca asked, retying the bandage.

Gilber was free at last to shake his head. "Not much. When the killing started on her old stead, Virgie was old enough to stay on safely, but she couldn't bear that, knowing nobody'd raise a hand to save a few of the little ones. She gathered all she could to her and lit out with them. She'd managed to grab some water gourds and provisions, but nowhere near plenty. She didn't have any idea how much they'd need or where they were going or—"

"I did too." A tall, lissome black girl stepped into the room and sat down gracefully, tailor-fashion, at the edge of Gilber's blanket. "Mark says it's time to eat," she told Becca. "He says not to be scared, it's just mush tonight."

Gilber raised an eyebrow. "What've you got to be scared of, Becc—?"

"You feel well enough to come with me, Gilber?" Becca said fast enough to divert him from the question.

"I guess so," he replied, starting to get to his feet. "The sooner we can be on our way, the better. It's about ten days' march to the coast, I think, and there's bound to be some yielding land between here and there, or how do the cityfolk survive? I thought we could leave the children some of our supplies in pay—I oughta be able to forage us something on the road. Just until we can bring someone back here, it'll help see them through."

"You're not gonna tell the city folk about us?" Virgie tensed.

"Of course not." Becca didn't give Gilber time to argue. Her expression left no room for nonsense as she told him firmly, "I promised Mark I wouldn't."

But you never made any such promise, Gilber, she thought at him. *Please go along with this, just for now! Virgie mustn't run back to Mark, bearing tales. Lord knows what he'd do.*

Esther M. Friesner

Gilber looked perplexed, but said, "All right, love; if you promised." He turned kindly eyes to Virgie. "You shouldn't be afraid of the cityfolk, you know. Becca here's got a brother among 'em."

"That so?" Virgie regarded Becca with decided suspicion.

"Gospel true." Becca traced a tiny cross at the base of her neck where the blood throbbed. "That's why I'm on the road, to see him. I don't know what scare-tales Mark's fed you all about the city, but I know different. If they didn't have enough to live on and more, why would they invite some outsider like my brother to join them? Why open their doors at all?"

"Might be your brother's special."

"Special stops when you're hungry. I say even if they don't have bounty, at least they can scare up food and clothing and shelter for this handful of little ones."

Virgie drew herself up. "We got enough right here."

Becca leaned forward and the girl did not recoil when she took her hand. "Enough to eat, Virgie?" she asked very, very gently.

Virgie burst into tears and fled into a labyrinth. Gilber gaped. "What'd you say to her?"

"You heard me."

"I know I did, but I can't believe—Why'd a simple, kindly question set her off like that?" When Becca didn't answer immediately he added, "Or is that part of another promise you made not to tell?"

Becca ignored the jab. For the last five minutes she'd had a dangerous feeling at the root of her belly, and she knew she'd better see to matters. She stood up, the herb box tucked under one arm. "Think you can find us a trail from here to where they're having supper, now our guide's flown?" she asked.

"I didn't come all this way from home with any guide, love," Gilber responded cheerfully. He stood up and slipped his arm around her waist.

She twisted away. "Wait for me. I'll be right back. You know…"

"Oh. Oh, sure. I know."

But you don't know, Gilber Livvy, the worm hissed as Becca crouched beside the open herb box. *All you think of is natural calls to make a woman need some privacy. How would you react if you knew the truth? Mal and Corp and all the rest who called you freakish, they spoke true, Becca of Wiserways!*

"No," Becca breathed. She unfurled a length of cloth from the box's bandage compartment and refolded it to exact measure quickly, heedfully. "No, that's not so. I'm not— I—I'm ailing, is all. Running like this, poor Shifra left behind, the scuadra, eating strange food, Corp and how he—how he hurt me. No wonder that I—"

The worm would never be denied; not at Wiserways, not here. *A natural woman comes into her times once, twice a year, and other days no man can take her that way without there being blood and pain and dying, more than not. But you! Corp took you with no trouble, didn't he? No hurt, no tearing, no payment for the sins of too proud women, generations past! Not what either one of you expected, was it? And that was why he let his death come leaping out at him that way.*

"Oh, Lord." The bandage wouldn't fold up right under fingers gone suddenly clumsy. She could feel the need for it growing greater by the moment. A deep breath steadied her enough to finish. The exchange was done swiftly, as it must, until the bandage she held in her hands was the old one. She stared and stared as if she could ever hope to see the answer she sought written in the marks of her own blood. "Oh, Mary Mother, what's it mean, what I've become?"

"What, Becca?" Gilber's voice made her whirl—no easy thing done crouching so. "Sweetheart, what's wrong?" He came closer, hands outstretched, hands she didn't dare to take now. She dropped the stained cloth, wishing for it to fall into the fires of Hell.

But he'd seen. He knelt to peer at it more closely, though the way he held himself was like an invisible wall had reared itself up between them to keep her and her shame at bay. He met her gaze, and for a marvel still spoke her tenderly. "I thought…I thought you said this'd come on you not so long ago, before. I thought women weren't—couldn't— not so soon as this, and that a man could tell when—"

"Hardly a month since I—" She crumpled into a quake of dry sobs. "My judgment on me," she groaned. "It's the Lord's punishment for my unnatural—"

"Yes." He made as if to lift her chin, but his fingers paused an inch from contact. Still, the gesture made her look up to see the wonder, the adoration, and the love in his eyes. "There's nothing natural to a miracle."

Chapter Twenty-Eight

There is a city, shining bright,
Fair Jerusalem, my love.
Shines by day and glows by night,
Jerusalem of gold.
Who sins is there made new,
Fair Jerusalem, my love.
Thither let me fare with you,
Jerusalem of gold.

The next night, Becca stirred from sleep to find Gilber gone from her side. She groped for her clothes, threw them on any old way in the dark, and fumbled for the tinderbox that lay to his side of the bedding. The children who dwelled in this place had eyes grown used to darkness, and there were times that Gilber's nightsight was nigh unnatural, but Becca still needed to strike a light to see by. She and Gilber had been allotted one of the rag-wick lamps, and she used it even though she felt a little twinge every time she looked at the lump of fat it used for fuel. No matter what Virgie told her of scavenging raids on Mark's old stead, Becca held to her dark doubts.

Lamp in hand, she started from the room, only to stop short before she'd gone ten paces outside. It was Gilber's voice that checked her steps, his and another's. Laying one hand to the trailwire, she blew out the lamplight and made her way onward as secretly as she might, harking to a clew of words.

When she came near enough to make out what was being said, it was Mark's voice that first reached her. "…tomorrow. You and her both." He sounded decided.

"All right." Gilber spoke more slowly, with just a touch of hesitation. "If that's how you want it."

"That's how. Didn't I say so to start with? Then you come arguing, jabbering, talking to me like I wasn't nothing!"

Gilber released a long breath into the dark. "I never meant it to sound so. I know what we owe you, son, and—"

"I'm not your son!" The shout must have roused the other children, but not a one stirred in the shadows. Either they had their sleeping quarters far from here, in some distant cranny of the ruin, or else they trembled under orders from their alph to bide where they were this night, no matter what they might hear. "Not your son, not no one's! I'm my own man, alph here, and don't you forget!"

Gilber began to make shushy sounds, thought better of it, held his peace awhile until Mark calmed. Only then he said, "My fault. I misspoke; you've got my word I didn't do it on purpose."

"Your word…" That scorn could melt stone.

"Yes." Gilber wasn't rising to the bait, though Becca herself felt ready to slap some manners into the boy's head.

"Well, now you listen to my word: You and her, you're off my stead by tomorrow. That's what I came to tell you and that's what I mean."

"I heard you, so—sir." Gilber wasn't one to misspeak himself twice. "And I said we'd abide by your wishes. All I'm asking is that you open your wishes to some change. It's not for our sake I'm asking—though I'll still be telling you truth when I say I could do with a few days' more rest. It's for the other children. We can help them—help you. I'm strong; I can break up more earth for your plantings, and I know how to make things you can use. The life I lived back home was nigh as hard as this; with what I know, I could make it easier for all of you. And as for Becca, I don't have to tell you what a fine healer she—"

"What do you mean, 'the other children'?" Mark growled low. "You've got me numbered in with them, don't you? Don't you? Just another boy-child, that what you think of me? With a stead free for the taking? Is that what's in your head?"

"Look, I never wanted—"

Mark didn't heed a word Gilber said or tried to say. "Out! Out or I'll make it hot for you! Maybe you're bigger than me, older, but this is my place, my stead, and no one's taking it from me. No one!" There was a scuffle of retreating footsteps. By the time Becca took another pace toward the sound, she bumped right into Gilber heading back along the trailwire to their room.

Esther M. Friesner

"Becca?"

"Yes, Gilber; I heard."

"No need to tell you what you already know, then." He sounded sheepish. "Better start packing our things, love. We leave come morning."

When morning came, they were ready to depart. Becca had objected, tried to persuade Gilber that Mark was in fact just a boy—albeit so uncanny a child he made her skin crawl. She used his own argument, that his hurt needed more time to heal proper. He'd have none of it.

"I know you mean me well, Becca, but we're bound to go. Biding here we're extra mouths, and we can't give much back until the growing season comes around again. Besides"—his mouth twisted into a sad smile—"we're guests, and our host's told us we've lost our welcome."

"That mannerless little—"

"Mannerless as may be, love, but I don't want to learn what sort of teeth he puts behind that bad breeding."

Recalling the cold way Mark spoke of Corp—and of her and Gilber too—as meat for the smoking, Becca swallowed all further protests. That boy wasn't one she'd want to have lurking for her in the dark, and darkness was all that dwelled between the walls of the ruin he called stead.

The children came out a little ways into the sunlight to see them off. Not a word of farewell was spoken to the travelers, not even when Becca patted the littlest ones on the head and gave them sisterly kisses. They didn't bolt at her touch, but it was like pressing her lips to a raggy doll's cheek. When Gilber stopped about forty paces from the ruin and turned to wave, they had all vanished from sight. Becca thought she saw a single small figure go scampering back beneath the overhanging entrance to the ruin. It moved too fast for her to tell, but she was mostly certain it was Mark, making sure they kept going.

When the ruin was well out of sight, Gilber said, "The city's some ten days' march from here, if my map says true and the land favors us. And why wouldn't it? God speeds us, for your sake."

The old tenderness was gone from his voice, a new feeling couched among the words he spoke. Like a tiger in tall grass it was beautiful but beyond any human's full knowing. It set Becca's hair crossways, the way he looked at her now. Still loving, yes, but too much more than the simple way he'd loved her before. What he knew of her secret had changed him—she wasn't sure how, not exactly—and it left her feeling like Gilber Livvy was dead and an alien spirit had come to make its nest in his bosom.

Stranger in his skin or not, she needed him beside her. If there were unspoken things lying between them, they could stay unspoken until the Coop city came into sight.

They had made camp two days' march from Mark's stead when Virgie joined them. The black girl came ambling along through the wasteland carefree as if she were just out gathering sweetmist posies for her ma. Queenly tall, she carried two big gourds at her hips and a rolled-up blanket lashed to her back with strips of cloth. She seated herself beside Becca and undid her makeshift pack. A half-dozen wizened roots, too twisted to own to a name, tumbled from the tattered blanket.

"That's all Mark'd let me take with me," she explained by way of greeting.

"That'll be plenty to take you right back to his stead, then," Becca countered.

"I'm not going back." Virgie was good-humored in the face of Becca's sternness and Gilber's confusion. "Isn't much way you can make me, is there? I'm heading for the city, same as you. I thought 'bout what you said." She looked Becca square in the eye. "You're right. I'm old enough to bear the sin for what those poor babes've been doing to survive, what's been passing their lips. I take it on my head, but there's only so much sin I can carry. If your brother's a city man now, like he says"—she nodded at Gilber—"then when they pass you through the gates, they'll have to let me in too, child or no. Once I'm inside, there's plenty I'll find to fetch back for my kin; I'm strong. All the things Mark and the other boys bring home from his old stead, they'll be nothing next to what I can scavenge up in the city!"

"Little girl, you got any idea how far a stroll it is from your place to the city?" Gilber asked, eyes twinkling over Virgie's boldness.

"Don't matter." The girl's lower lip stuck out, stubborn. "I covered two days' worth of it on my own already, didn't I? I'm not afraid of a march. It's what's needful, so it's what I'll do."

"Mark knows why you've left?" Becca asked. The boy was no man, but he was alph in his own eyes, and every steadborn female quickly learned how most alphs dealt with rebels. If he thought Virgie had crossed him and he couldn't take out his rage on her, there were too many hostages of her own blood she'd left behind in his hands.

Virgie understood Becca's true question well enough. "My sibs are safe. I asked his leave before I came. He said if I was so eager to be gone, then go, lessen the tally of hungry mouths for him. He's counting on me to watch these cityfolk careful, not let 'em know nor guess nothing about us or our stead. Mary my witness, I'd sooner have my tongue torn out than bring home any more harm to my kin."

"It's still a wonder he let you go, just like—"

"Not such a wonder: No matter what he says, Mark knows we can't go on forever as we are."

"Praise Mary Mother for that," Becca murmured.

"Well? Can I come with you?"

Before Becca could say yes or no, Gilber leaned forward and hefted one of the dwarfish roots. "How can we say no," he asked with a smile, "when you're ready to share such delicacies?"

All the old lessons of the Lord's hidden plan came back to Becca on that trek over the barrens. Sometimes He foresaw needs before a body ever suspected they were needful, foresaw and provided against them. Virgie's unexpected presence was a true godsend. She became an extra pair of hands, much needed. There was something peculiar about Gilber now: Even though he still lacked his full strength and knew Becca's capabilities on the march, he fought a strange battle to keep her from laying hand to any task at all. Between his own labors and those he now snatched from her, he was a wrung rag. If not for Virgie, he might well have worn himself to death. That would have been a sorry end for more than just himself. The road had turned hard; the survival of one was the survival of all.

Neither Gilber's map nor Becca's prepared them for the obstacles in their way. The nearer to the coast, the thicker grew the ancient ruins. Though they cleared the waste proper in three days' time, the scrubland beyond didn't yield the wild harvest Gilber had anticipated. Scraggly trees grew in clumps here and there; no true forest. They lost precious time scavenging for additional food, more when Gilber had to stop to keep the customs of his shabbit. Flood gullies cut the land away from the trade roads—dry now, but a hard descent and climb over scarp and scree. Too, Gilber tired more readily than before; even so, he carried his pack and Becca's own load besides.

"What's that man's complaint?" Virgie whispered one night when they'd camped inside a two-walled wreck of a building. There were many others like it nearby, the walls mostly all down but enough of the foundations showing for a body to tell they'd been laid out in orderly rows once upon a long-lost time. Gilber had gone off to scrounge the fixings for a fire, if he could. "He's ailing, but he won't let you pull your weight. He keeps staring at you with big ol' moon-eyes, but he won't touch you or—Mary my witness, I swear I think I even saw him balk at taking something from your hand. What is he, crazy?"

Or is it you? the unspoken question came through loud and clear.

"I wish I knew," Becca replied. She got to her feet and headed for the shadows. "Excuse me, there's something I've got to do." Although she didn't yet feel the need to steal away and change her bandage, she took it as an excuse to absent herself before Virgie pressed the issue. The girl was bright and inquisitive, but there was a sharp, hot current of fiercest love for her sibs running beneath her surface. She wasn't with Becca and Gilber as an equal companion so much as they all traveled in a state of tense truce.

Becca could understand that. Sometimes at night, in

the half-dreaming time that enfolded her just before she fell asleep, her thoughts would drift back to Wiserways; Wiserways as it had been before Adonijah brought it his dooming. Shifra slept in the big cradle—Shifra sweet and pink and whole, her lips untouched by any food but Hattie's warm milk. Becca's heart ached over that seeing and her arms reached out for a child no longer there. They closed on air, and Shifra's face became the face of Weegee's girl. She laughed without making a sound as the infant nursed at her small breasts, but when she forced the babe's mouth from her nipple Shifra's lips shone with droplets of red.

Becca couldn't count the times she'd thrown herself upright, away from the unholy vision, choking back her scream.

"Maybe I should talk to Virgie," Becca said to herself. Out here in the midst of so many hauntings, she didn't like to be far from the sound of a human voice, even if it had to be her own. "We should trust each other; we're driven by the same rod. Poor child, I know I could help her, and she—"

Don't let her know about you, the worm cautioned. *Let her think you've stolen away only to relieve yourself, like you were still a natural woman. Gilber called it miracle, what's come over you, but the oldtime saints who worked such wonders were often burned to death for the doing of those self-same acts. He is a Jew, outcast; what can he know of the way real people regard such freaks of nature? Don't let Virgie know. It will be a greater weapon in her hands than any gun.*

Becca took herself far from the campsite before she saw to her business. Undiscovered, she returned only to find Gilber earnestly telling Virgie, "Wonderful! No other woman in all my tribe's history ever showed such signs more than a sixmonth apart. In the commentaries they write about the true scroll, there's lines and lines about how we're to treat a woman in her monthly impurity—*monthly*, Virgie! That's how it was, before the evil days. You see now why I treat her so? She's not like other women. She's a sign from *h'shem* just like Noah's bright skybow, a sign we've been forgiven. The forty years' wandering's done, the land of milk and honey's ours again."

Virgie was staring at him askance, her long legs folded up beneath her like she was getting ready to dash. "Gilber Livvy, what are you telling that little girl?" Becca demanded. "Can't you see you're frighting her half out of her wits?"

"She was just asking why I've treated you like a doll on the march," he replied. "Is it so frightening to hear that the end of the evil times have come?"

"He says you don't come into your times like my mam does," Virgie said so that it sounded like an accusation. "He said you do it every moon!"

"I've only had the shame of it twice since I met him," Becca conceded. There was no sense in pretending, in trying to hide the plain, ugly fact that set her apart more finally than any unwomanly deed of her own doing. No use trying to take refuge in a lie, to set her protest against Gilber's testimony: Virgie would sooner take a man's word for truth than that of a woman barely a few years older than herself. "It might not ever happen again, except the way it's supposed to."

"Oh, sweetheart, you talk like it's something wicked!" Gilber exclaimed. He reached for her hand, but jerked his own back as if in realization.

"There, you see?" Becca pointed. "You talk like it's so

grand, what's happened to me—call it a miracle—but you won't touch me or anything I've touched!"

"Well, how can I?" Gilber responded. "Didn't you just hear me say there's writings about how to treat a woman in her impurity? Before I knew, I couldn't be held accountable, but now I've got no excuse. I'm a priest's son; I don't dare touch you or what you touch until you're clean again."

"Some fine miracle," Becca muttered so that only she could hear. "Would you call it impurity if it touched manlore? I don't think so."

"On my old stead, we had one girl did that," Virgie said. "My sister, Huldah. Come into her times first when she's thirteen, and all the old wives took her off somewhere. My mam was nursing Tabitha—she's dead now—and she told me that's what they do with every girl, the first time: take her off to see when she's over her times, wait up 'til six moons' passing to know if she's normal or a judgment on us. I guess she was a judgment, 'cause the wives all come back alone. I heard one of 'em tell my mam, 'Back into her times a month later, lickerish as Jezebel, ready to take on any man.' Mam was crying." Virgie's face fell at the recollection. "She asked that old wife, 'What difference does that make? I hear it used to be like that for all of us, before the hungering times. Why can't we just let them live?'"

"They *killed* her?" Gilber was appalled.

"For that, always," Becca said.

She thought of her own sib Margaret, Ray's girl. Sweet Margaret who always had the time to pick up little Becca and tell the child fine tales out of the old books to dry her tears or still her prattling. Doomed Margaret who hadn't passed her Sixmonth vigil clean. One day Becca tugged at Hattie's skirts and asked after her adored older sib. For reply she got a slap and hard words, most of them too far beyond her infant understanding. Only a few clung to her memory: *Curse-touched…not be let live…gone.*

"On stead we're taught that an untimely woman is touched of the devil," she told Gilber.

"That's what they *say*," Virgie sneered, "but I know different. That old wife who came to tell my mam her daughter was dead, she told the truth. Too old by half to live another year without being winnowed out, what'd she have to lose? 'We can't let 'em live 'cause if we did, you know what'd be?' she said. 'Wouldn't take long before every man for miles around learned there was a woman who could take him on any time at all—and not just the Kiss or the Sign! These men, as is they think more with what's between their legs than what's between their ears. One sniff of a woman who's taking all the time and she'd be piping just the tune they want to hear! And how long before she's the only piper? What'd become of us then, eh? Why shield and shelter us when we're just good for twice a year? And maybe it'd happen so the female babes she'd bear would take after their unnatural mama. So you dry up your tears, woman!' she said. 'You dry 'em up and you give thanks your daughter's dead, else you and all your other girl-babies'd be the same.'"

"I heard stories," Gilber mused. "Back home the boys spin tales of hidden cities where just one woman rules. She's like that, always free and able to take on any man she pleases, any time, with no harm coming to her. And just for that, they do her worship. But if that's true and she bore daughters after her kind, wouldn't there be so many more women like that in this world?"

"That's just a story," Becca said. "We had such making

the rounds at Wiserways of the queen cities. But what Virgie's saying isn't any tale; it's true."

"What Gilber says 'bout you, is that true, too?" Virgie wanted to know. Becca had no choice but to admit it.

"This makes us equal, Virgie, secret for secret. I don't know what they do in the city if a woman's not—if she's different. I don't know, and I'm afraid. I guess this guarantees I won't talk out of turn about Mark's stead and the children without your say-so. No more will Gilber." Becca gave him a hard look.

"I swear it." He confirmed his words with a rapidfire gibber of that weird scrollspeech of his, but Becca supposed it was as binding as an ordinary person calling the Lord and the Lord King and Mary Mother to witness. "Not a word about you, love, if this is how your people act against one of *h'shem's* own miracles."

"Whose?" Virgie asked, and had a hard time following most of what Gilber told her of his god after that. Becca didn't even bother trying to understand.

Ten days' promised march stretched into fifteen, then twenty. They found water in a lake where late-season bracken fringed the shore with brown lace.

"This is fine," Gilber said, beaming, as they stood at the waterside. "Now you can make yourself clean according to the laws."

"Laws?" Becca brows came together. "I'm minded to wash out what needs washing, but we never needed laws for that."

"You'll have to cleanse yourself as well," Gilber told her. "And for that, my people do have laws, strict and taught to the letter. I'll give you them so you can be clean again."

"I'm sick up to here with your fool's talk of cleanliness. The blood-sign's been off me for days! What's cleaner than that, I'd like to know?"

"Law says that until you cleanse yourself after the proper manner, it's the same as if the impurity was still on you."

"Seems to me your folk and mine could do with a measure less of law and lore," Becca grumbled. "You'll tell me when I'm clean enough so your god'll approve, I s'pose?"

His mouth twisted up to one side, tangling with a smile he didn't want to wear. "No need to put a sassy face on it, angel."

"What'll you do about it?" Becca retorted, enjoying herself some for a change. "Duck me in the lake? I'd like to see you try! Can't lay hands on me while I'm in my im-pu-ri-ties." She stuck out her tongue at him.

"I can," Virgie said, and with a thrust of her hands as economical as her words she gave Becca a shove that ended in a splash. She and Gilber came near to killing themselves with laughter while Becca flailed and floundered and spluttered in the water.

Becca stumbled to her feet and waded toward them, hollering, "Virgie, when I get out of here I'm gonna—!"

The black girl danced away from the shore, flying on joy, indifferent to anyone's threat. "First you complain he won't let you do for yourself or him, then you fight 'gainst doing the one thing that'll set it all right," she shouted at Becca, cheer-faced. "I was just helping you make up your mind!"

Gilber was waiting to give Becca some help back onto dry land. She glared at him from behind a waterlogged curtain of hair and snarled, "One laugh out of you, Gilber Livvy, and you'll get a taste of the same."

"Not even in my dreams," Gilber said, nailing on a straight face as he clasped her hand securely. "I'm not sure whether you'd satisfy *strict* law with that cleansing, but I guess it'll do."

While Becca got herself dried off and wrapped in a blanket, Virgie came back to wash out all her soiled linens for her without being asked. "Pay for laughter," she explained while she worked. "Feels good to laugh."

Becca's soaked clothes and the rest of the laundry took time to dry. Gilber built a sorry fire from what he could find around the lakeshore—not much by any measure—and cooked up an even sorrier dinner. Virgie looked at the mess of limp stuff that was her portion and said, "Too bad there's no fish in there." She nodded toward the lake.

"Thanks to you," Becca teased. "Fling me in there like that, I scared 'em all away."

Gilber only shook his head. "That's not the way of it at all, Virgie. Even if there was fish, I couldn't eat 'em after Becca used those waters for her cleansing. When the blood was on her, it made her impure; when she freed herself of it, the taint passed to the water and all it holds."

Virgie frowned. "What? Now you mean to tell me that those fish are gonna bleed every moon?"

Gilber laughed aloud. "Let me explain, honey," he said, and that was what he did his best to do.

Virgie heard out all his explanations with lively curiosity. When they took up their road again, she didn't leave her questions back by the lakeside. Gilber was as willing to teach as she was to be lessoned. She got to be so familiar with the shabbit doings that Becca once caught the girl singing one of Gilber's scrollspeech songs under her breath by the campfire.

"Maybe you ought to wait until she's grown and marry her," Becca joked. "She'll take to your Jew-ways; I won't."

Gilber didn't choose to see the funning in her words. "I'll only take one mortal bride, Becca, one love. I've got faith enough to wait for you to see that my…my ways are good. You'll come around."

He spoke so firmly, so certain of the future, that Becca decided not to waste time and energy arguing with him. If he thought time was the great convincer, so did she. She could wait as long as he for the truth to show itself.

They went on. Smashed stone and concrete were underfoot more often than soil, and the travelers made their nightly stops in the haven of great, broken bridges that hung over them like black tidal waves frozen in place forever. The land was hillier than in the waste, and there were places where the earth had crimped up to partways cover old signs of settlement. Not every evidence of human life had been wiped clean by pillage. Wind and weather and the passing of the years did more than enough damage to gnaw away at the pathetic remains of hearth and refuge. One dawn Becca woke to find Virgie cradling a babydoll with rigid limbs, shiny eyes, and a body made out of something like leather, only harder and a queer pink color under all the filth. Earth still nestled in the hollow body that was broke open like a blown eggshell.

"I found it over there," the girl said, gesturing vaguely to where the land heaved up in a mound. "It's a place a lot like Mark's stead, only smaller inside."

"Is that all you found?"

The girl bunched up her shoulders. "Most else I found was just trash. D'you want to come see?" Becca said no, and gave thanks when Virgie tired of the doll in three days' time and left it behind her.

One night they made camp in the very shadow of one of the bridges. Becca had never seen such a place for rubbish and refuse, none of it worth the scavenging. A fine rain was coming down, a cold, blowing mist that flared her nostrils with an alien scent, pleasant but unknown. Becca sat wakeful by the fireside, sifting and sifting the air, trying to read the riddle of that smell. Virgie and Gilber lay asleep beside the small blaze, both wrapped snug as littlesingers in their blankets. Gilber slept more, these times. Becca thought it was the nursing of his wound that tired him so.

At least he's consented to let me keep watch, she thought, staring into the flames, then into the dark.

The hours waxed and the mist blew away entire, taking its briny scent with it, letting the stars peep out. Becca felt lone. It was a wonder to her how she could feel so, with Gilber and Virgie so close to hand. She had come to feel a kin-fondness for the girl. She wasn't used to being without sibs. She took Virgie to her heart in their place, to salve that wanting ache. She stared at Virgie's sleeping face, wishing her awake, needing the sound of her voice. A twig on the fire crackled and broke into a shower of sparks, tiny red stars dancing. Becca looked up at the true stars in their heaven and sighed.

They tell that every star's the soul of a good man gone to rest, a voice whispered in Becca's head. *That's what they taught me, anyhow. But when I had the audacity to ask where the souls of good women are...* Bitter laughter shattered the night.

Esther M. Friesner

She sat across the fire from Becca, her knees drawn up almost to her chin, her arms wrapped around her legs just so, the spirit and image of Becca's own pose. Hunched over like that, there was no seeing the slashes on breasts and thighs, all the marks of blood, but Becca still knew her: She was the girl who'd come to her on her vigil night, the visitation whose words—written down in a book so long-hidden, spoken over softly in Becca's mind—had come to be tumbled and plaited with the whisperings of the worm and the misgivings, the protests, the howlings of Becca's own soul.

Where do we rest? the girl asked again. *Not in Prayerful Hill with the innocents. Not in the sky-reaches with our men, blazing so glorious, so cold. Where can our souls find refuge, Becca, when every lesson we're taught from the cradle up says that all the evil times are laid to our charge?*

"Maybe…we've no souls to rest at all," Becca whispered.

Think like that and you serve them, the ones who'd make us less than who we are, the girl said, her words cold and blazing as the stars. She rose from the fireside. The marks that bit so much blood from her flesh were plain to see, every crimson trail sparkling with tiny worms of fire. *And if you do, then why this search? Why come so far? Why the fight in you? If you're meat and mud, why take the road of pain? Follow your mother's path instead, and know peace. Accept! Submit!*

"No," Becca said softly. And then, louder, stronger: "*No.* Lord witness, I don't know where this soul will rest when all's done, but that's no matter. What's needful is what's *now.* For Shifra, for Virgie, for Gilber's tribe and for those poor lost babes Mark's leading so sinful wrong— they're what wants saving." She was on her feet, staring into the ghost-girl's cloudy eyes. "They're who I serve, none else."

How do you serve them, Becca? the ghost-girl asked. *By swearing not to speak of them when you reach the city? By letting silence keep them?*

"I promised Virgie—"

—the impossible. How can you help the children if you won't speak of them? If you won't speak for them?

"I—I can't. If I do, Virgie will tell about me, my secret, and then—"

You talk of saving the world, the ghost murmured. *But all you want to save's your own skin.*

Becca bent her face to her hands. It was true. The worm was a torment, but never a lie. "What will I do?" she moaned under her breath. "Oh sweet Mary Mother, what in the name of all heaven can I do?"

And the girl of stars and blood and voices folded herself over Becca like the presence of an angel's wings. *You'll do what you've hungered to do and what you've been denied: You'll choose, Becca. You'll choose.*

Becca lifted her face, feeling the cool breath of night on her cheeks. "Choose…"

She faced her ghost. "It's so hard—" she began.

The girl nodded slowly, a single star winking through her brow. *It was never easy,* she said. *But it was always better than having no choice at all.*

Then: *Come,* she said.

She walked away into the dying night, out of the shadow of the bridge. Becca followed after. Beyond the firelight, the girl herself glowed, a beacon to light the way. She led Becca to the top of an earth mound where the wind blew chill and sere grasses rustled. The star on her brow still shone bright, and where her breasts had bled, Becca saw roses. The girl turned her face to the east and pointed into the darkness, her hand white and slim, showing transparent flesh over the bones.

Becca looked the way the ghost-girl pointed. At first she saw only night and stars, the darker outlines of other mounds in the distance. Then she saw that not all the lights twinkling afar belonged to heaven. They seemed to rise out of the dark and come slowly nearer, mounting the air. Her breath grew soft with wonder when she saw that these were the lights of palaces and gates, towers and avenues leading straight and shining. They swirled around each other in a dance of silent music, a ring moving toward her with untellable grace. The city she'd sought had come forth to welcome her in. She stretched out her hands to the circle of light as if to claim her crown.

"Becca…?" Virgie's sleep-muffled voice called to her. There was a little shake of fright to it. Distracted, she turned from the ghost-girl and the city, went scrambling down the side of the mound, back to the campfire.

The fire was almost out, burned down to embers. Virgie sat huddled up beside it, thin limbs shaking. Becca flew to her and threw her arms around the girl. "Don't fret, honey, I'm here."

"I had a bad dream, Becca," Virgie said, clinging to Becca's neck like any child. "I was back in Mark's stead, and there was hard times on us, and so Mark he said"— her very skin quivered—"he said we'd eat what we had to. We drew straws and the lot fell to my little sib, Nomi, and then Mark took that big knife he got and he—he—" She dug her face into Becca's shoulder and sobbed.

"Hush, hush now, ssshhhh." Without thinking over what she did, Becca began to rock back and forth with

Virgie in her arms as if the girl, near woman-grown, was still only a babe. "That won't be, I swear to you. I won't stand for it to be so." She tightened her hold on the girl. "I pledge my soul that before I plead one word of my own cause with the cityfolk, I'm going to fetch their help for the children."

"You—?" Virgie stared, then began to struggle and shout. "No! No! You promised!"

The ruckus roused Gilber. He rolled over and sat up slowly, rubbing his eyes. "What is it, Becca? What's wrong?"

"She's gonna get 'em killed!" Virgie shrieked. "She's gonna break her given word, tell the cityfolk where we're hiding!" The girl kicked herself out of Becca's arms, sprang to her feet, leveled a finger like the Lord's own charge to His prophets. "You even try and tell on us, I'll tell 'em all about you! You and how you ain't no natural woman, how you bleed every moon, how—"

"Then that's your choice, Virgie," Becca said without raising her voice. "You make it just as I've made mine." She stood, turned her face to the east, and started walking.

Gilber clambered to his feet, came lurching after her. "Where are you going?" he cried, catching hold of her arm.

"To do what's needful," she answered level. "Needful before any plea of yours or mine. You were right with what you told Mark that night, Gilber: We should've stayed on. No matter how loud he yowled for us to get gone, we should've faced him down. But we found excuses to let us back off—telling ourselves we feared what he'd do, saying it was his stead, saying we owed him courtesy for what he'd given us—excuses to let us leave for the city because leaving's what we wanted to do any road! We've been blind to everything but our own wants, Gilber; we've let our fears turn us from where our first duty lies."

"Our first—? You mean those poor little souls Mark rules? Becca, that's not the right direction you're— Oh, tell me you're funning! Come all this way and now you say we're turning back?"

"I never said that. I said we've got to serve their needs before our own. Men want, women want, but it's the children who can't speak their wants that suffer. You know that same as I do, Gilber Livvy—you know it too, Virgie, like it or not!—you know that if we've any hope at all of saving them, the city holds the key."

"They'll kill us," Virgie groaned. "They'll send us back to our old steads and that's the same as killing us! There's nothing for us in the city but death!" She curled herself up into a ball of tears.

Kindly, firmly, Becca stooped beside her, raised her up, held her still however much she struggled in her grip and made her look her in the eye. "Listen to me, Virgie: Gilber says I carry a miracle." She spoke with a conviction she didn't know she had. "A miracle that's a hope for change; for life. How can I carry hope and leave your little ones to hunger? How can I bring them their deaths when I'd sooner embrace my own?"

Virgie stared into Becca's eyes. A change came over her, a realization. She stopped her tears, her twistings. "What've you seen?" She searched Becca's face closely. "Mary my witness, you've had a seeing, and I want to know what it is!"

Becca let go her hold on the girl. "Come with me," she said in all serenity. "Come and see it for yourself."

She laid her hand on Virgie's shoulder, beckoning for Gilber to join them. One arm around each, she led them from the dying campfire, across the hard earth, up the slope of the mound. Dawn was coming, a bright greeting. As they climbed the crest, Becca urged them on, her face aglow, until at last she broke from them in a run, her arms wide, embracing the light.

"There it is!" she called into the eastern sky. "See there! All the beauty and all the hope of the world!" Dawnlight washed her eyes.

She felt them come up behind her, heard them catch their breath in awe as they took their first distant sight of the waking city and the great water that lay beyond. It lay much farther off than the city of her past night's vision, but none the less marvelous to see. They could not help but share her exaltation. She heard Gilber mutter a scrollspeech prayer, heard Virgie gasp, then laugh for joy.

Pink and gold and shining, the city waited. "How can it hold anything but life?" Becca cried out, enraptured. She started toward it, singing the old pilgrim's song of triumph, leading those she loved by the hand.

end

Esther M. Friesner

Esther Friesner was educated at Vassar College, and went on to Yale University, where within five years she was awarded an M.A. and Ph.D. in Spanish. She taught Spanish at Yale for a number of years before going on to become a full-time author of fantasy and science fiction. She has published twenty-two novels so far.

Ms. Friesner won the Romantic Times award for Best New Fantasy Writer in 1986 and the Skylark Award in 1994. Her short story "All Vows" took second place in the Asimov's SF Magazine Readers' Poll for 1993 and was a finalist for the Nebula in 1994. Her Star Trek: Deep Space Nine novel, *Warchild*, made the *USA TODAY* Bestseller list.

She lives in Connecticut with her husband, two children, two rambunctious cats, and a fluctuating population of hamsters.

Coming in October 1996
from White Wolf
Publishing

THE
SWORD
OF
MARY

by Esther M. Friesner

The sequel to
The Psalms of Herod

*Look for it at your nearest
Bookseller or Distributor.*